VALENTINE'S WITH THE SINGLE DAD

SINGLE DADS OF SEATTLE, BOOK 7

WHITLEY COX

Copyright © 2019 by Whitley Cox

All rights reserved.

No part of this book may be reproduced in any form or by any electronic or mechanical means, including information storage and retrieval systems, without written permission from the author, except for the use of brief quotations in a book review

ISBN: 978-1-989081-27-3

For Ana Clemente
An amazing new friend.

1

SHE WAS BACK.

Same time.

Same table.

Same drink order.

Same little pink notebook and pen.

Only today, her hair was different. Normally, she kept her short, chin-length, dark brown bob straight with a soft swoosh over her forehead, but today she'd gone and let it get all wavy and had secured the swoosh with a little silver clip on the side of her head.

It helped him see her eyes better.

He really liked her eyes.

Bright gray with soft flecks of white around the iris. He'd never seen anybody with eyes like that before. And the way the corners crinkled when she smiled or took a sip of her wine made the apples of her cheeks lift and go extra round.

He had no idea what her name was because she kept to herself, but for the past three weeks, the woman had been coming into his bar every Tuesday and Thursday night. She would sit in the same spot every night. Order the same thing every night. And there she would stay from eight fifteen until ten fifteen. She would drink nothing but wine or water, and over the course of those two hours, she would entertain—though it looked more like interview—a different man every half hour or so. Some men made it to nearly the one-hour mark, while others were sent on their way before their drinks turned warm.

They would chat. She would smile but ultimately let him do the majority of the talking. Then they would shake hands and the man would be on his way—never to return again, or so it seemed.

Was she doing her own variation of speed dating?

Was she interviewing them for jobs?

Was she a pimp—or a madam—and vetting potential gigolos?

All the guys who had sat down with her so far were not trolls. In fact, they were all pretty decent-looking, so maybe she was interviewing them for an all-male burlesque show.

Either way, the woman who sat at the table by the window intrigued the crap out of Mason. He thought about her all the time. She was like a song or tune stuck in his head. He just couldn't shake her—and he didn't want to.

He looked forward to Tuesday and Thursday nights. He'd actually switched his shifts around with the general manager so that he always worked Tuesday and Thursday nights. This mystery woman had put a spell on him, and he just needed to know more.

What was her name?

Where did she work?

What was she doing every Tuesday and Thursday night, sitting in his bar with a different man every thirty minutes?

Normally, he would have had no problem walking up to the woman, offering her his hand and asking what she was up to. He was, after all, the owner of Prime Sports Bar and

Grill and a very friendly, outgoing person, but for some reason, he got the impression that she wanted to be left alone. She had a slight sense of almost embarrassment in her face as she met each man, shook his hand and sat down with him. As if she didn't really want to be there but was doing so because she had to. It only made the mystery behind her all the more alluring, all the more exciting.

She was also crazy-cute, and for the first time in a very long time, he felt butterflies in his stomach at the thought of approaching her for more than just her drink order.

He glanced at his watch. It was closing in on ten o'clock. She would be leaving soon.

Pulling the lever on the tap for the San Camanez Lager, he filled up a pint for an order that had just come in. He'd gotten so good at filling up a draft that he didn't really have to pay attention or watch what he was doing. He simply counted in his head, tilted the glass just right, and ninety-nine percent of the time, he was dead on when he dropped his gaze again and pulled the pint glass free.

Tonight was in that ninety-nine percent.

He plopped the beer stein down onto the bar so the waitress could come and grab it along with the rest of the drinks ordered. His eyes remained glued to the back of the head of the man who was currently entertaining—or should he say failing to entertain—Mason's mystery woman.

Then the guy stood up.

Mason glanced at his watch again. Oh, this dude was obviously a dud. He didn't even make the full thirty minutes.

The dud grabbed his coat off the back of his chair and slipped his arms into the sleeves before nodding at Mason's mystery woman and then making haste to leave the bar, leaving *her* sitting there all alone, a bored, disappointed look on her face.

Was she going to get up and leave now?

She never stayed past ten fifteen, and it was now ten o'clock. Surely, she didn't have another "date" lined up.

He hoped she didn't.

He checked in with his mother to see how his four-month-old daughter Willow was doing. She'd had a bit of a cold last week and was still a touch congested but seemed to be sleeping better and in brighter spirits. His mother claimed that all was well with Willow and that she'd fallen asleep on Mason's father's chest, and even though Willow could sleep in her bassinet, Mason's dad hadn't bothered to move her.

"They're only little for such a short time," his mother had said. "Let us indulge in her babyness for as long as we can."

Mason simply rolled his eyes. Who was he to get upset when he did the same thing? Whenever Willow fell asleep on his chest, the world stopped and he simply took in the moment. His mother was right; they were only little for such a short time. Before he knew it, she would be crawling and then walking and then out with her friends, with no time for dear old dad.

His heart ached at the thought of his little Willow old enough to go to parties and spend time with boys. Was it too late to have a tracking device implanted behind her ear?

Slowly, as the minutes ticked by, the bar began to empty, but his mystery woman remained. All the servers left, and the kitchen closed in ten minutes. Lingering were just a couple of women in their mid-forties chatting away near the back of the pub and Mason's mystery woman.

She was staring at her notebook, but he could tell by the way she tapped her pen on the paper and chewed on her bottom lip that she wasn't really paying attention to whatever she'd written. She was lost in thought.

He needed to let her know it was last call. They closed at eleven on Tuesdays.

He dried his hand on a towel and stepped out from

behind the bar. Tossing his shoulders back and cracking his neck side to side, he approached her table. "Hey, there. It's last call. Would you like another pinot?" He stopped directly in front of her and waited for her to lift her head. Her eyes slowly climbed his body. He resisted the urge to grin, even though he secretly got a big thrill when her gray eyes widened as they fell to the front of his pants.

She swallowed hard when her gaze finally landed on his face. She blinked. "Yes, please," she said softly, her eyes drifting back down to her notepad.

"Are you meeting anybody else tonight?" He couldn't stop himself. The curiosity was like an itch he just needed to scratch.

Slowly, she shook her head but didn't lift her eyes back up to him. "No, I'm not."

Swallowing, he shifted on his heels. "Can I ask what you've been up to all these weeks? You're here twice a week for two hours meeting with several different men an evening." He scratched the back of his neck. "The waitresses are starting to talk."

That wasn't a lie. The servers were beginning to question what this woman's angle was, but Mason doubted their curiosity was as strong as his. Otherwise, they could have asked her.

Once again, her gaze climbed him. "I'm trying to hire a date," she said, her cheeks turning a beautiful shade of pink. "I'm hiring a date for a wedding."

His brows shot up his forehead and he took a small step back. That hadn't been the answer he'd been expecting at all. Why in the world did this gorgeous creature need to pay somebody to date her? He could only imagine that any red-blooded man in his right mind would jump at the chance to take her out her for free.

He needed to know more. He needed to know the full story.

"You hungry?" he asked.

She squinted at him but then nodded. He could just see the cogs spinning in her brain as she tried to figure out what he was up to.

He wasn't even sure what he was up to yet. All he knew was that he wasn't ready to watch her walk out the door, and now that he'd started talking to her, he needed to continue. He needed to get to know her.

"Gonna see if Barry in the back can make me a plate of nachos before the kitchen closes. Wanna share? On the house if you tell me the full story of why you feel the need to *pay* for a date."

She was very cautious. The way she stewed on his words and took a serious pause before replying had him wondering if he'd come on too strong and she was suddenly going to grab her purse and dash out, never to return.

But that wasn't the case.

Thankfully.

She gathered her coat and purse from the back of her chair and then finally that little pink notebook and pen. "I'll join you at the bar," she said, standing up to her full height, which was a hell of a lot shorter than him. He hadn't realized just how short she was. He'd always approached her when she was sitting down.

Nodding and resisting the urge to fist pump in the air, he grabbed her empty wineglass off the table, as well as the half-finished beer of her last potential date for hire, and headed back behind the bar.

He quickly poured her a glass of the pinot she'd been drinking every night for the past few weeks, then slid the glass across the shiny wooden bar. "All right, Ms. ... "

"Lowenna Chambers," she said, accepting the glass and immediately taking a sip.

Lowenna Chambers.

He rolled her name around on his tongue for a moment. He liked it. It suited her. It held a sense of sophistication he'd picked up the first night she'd come in.

"And your name?" she asked, her head tilted to the side, waiting.

He paused what he was doing and thrust his hand forward. "Mason Whitfield. Pleased to meet you, Ms. Chambers."

Her smile warmed his chest from the center outward as she took his hand and shook it with a strength he felt all the way down to his balls. "Pleased to meet you too, Mr. Whitfield."

With a grin, he began to punch in their nacho order on the computer screen in front of him. "All right, Ms. Chambers, do you like jalapeños on your nachos?"

Her smile was small and almost coy, but she nodded. "I do."

"What about olives?"

She nodded again, her grin spreading across her face. "The more the better."

His smile also grew. "My kind of woman. Me too." He hit the *extra olives* button a few times to emphasize their obsession. "And guac?"

"Is it nachos without?"

Oh, he liked her. She'd been a bit timid at first when he approached her, but now she seemed to be a bit more comfortable with him, more relaxed.

"Absolutely not," he agreed. "I'll order us an extra-large guac." He hit the button to send it off to the kitchen, then went to work putting the stack of dirty glasses through the cleaner. "Okay, nachos are on their way. Now let's talk about this date-for-hire thing. Why in the world do *you* need to pay for a date?"

She took another sip of her wine before answering. "The long and the short of it is, my sister is marrying my ex-husband, and I need a date to their wedding who will upstage them and their pompous, ostentatious, pretentious affair in every which way. I need a show-stopper. I need an underwear model with an Ivy League education, a six-figure salary, who dances like Fred Astaire."

Whoa!

She lifted one shoulder. "You know ... a unicorn."

Mason had two glasses in each hand, one of them slippery, and he nearly dropped it. "Um, can't you just ask the guy to say he's all those things?" Wouldn't that be easier than hunting for the holy grail and paying the man to be her date? Surely there was a man out there who fit the bill for at least a few of those things, and they could fudge the rest.

She shook her head. "I don't want to lie. Lies always have a way of coming back to bite us in the ass. And if for whatever reason he forgets who it is he's supposed to be, that'll ruin everything."

Fair enough.

"So you're vetting dates in my bar then?" He resumed putting the glasses on the rotating cleaner.

"Seemed like a safe place to do it, out in public, and you seem like a man who would jump to my defense if the guy I was interviewing got belligerent."

Oh, most definitely.

"So you picked my bar because I'm a free bodyguard?" He cocked an eyebrow but couldn't stop the smile that crooked his lips.

"I'm spending an awful lot of money on wine each week. I wouldn't call it free," she countered.

Fair enough.

"So, I get that it's a sore spot that your sister is marrying your ex-husband, but why not just boycott the wedding entirely? Why even put yourself through all of this and go in the first place?"

She exhaled out a deep breath. "Five years ago, I was diagnosed with uterine cancer. I had to have almost a full hysterectomy, because once they got in there, they found out the cancer had spread to one of my ovaries. They removed my uterus, the bad ovary and my cervix. My husband, Brody, was a first-year law associate at the time. His benefits were good but not great. They covered a fair bit, but things still became tight, and we struggled financially. My treatments and surgery were not cheap, and the insurance company did everything they could do to deny us coverage."

Something began to tingle at the base of his neck, but he couldn't put his finger on it just yet. "Motherfuckers," he grumbled, shaking his head.

"Agreed," she said with near tangible venom in her tone. "Anyway, Brody and my sister, Doneen started sleeping together shortly after my surgery, once I started chemo. I was too sick to even think about being intimate and was also in recovery after major surgery."

"You're fucking kidding me?" This time he actually did drop a glass, the sound of it smashing to the tile floor startling both of them. His mouth opened in surprise.

She shook her head, completely unaffected by the shattered glass. "Nope. They don't know that I know, but I do. Brody filed for divorce once it was declared I was cancer-free. He stated that although he still loved me, he was no longer *in love* with me. He also wanted to be a father and have children the *traditional* way. He just wasn't sure I was the woman for him anymore. Three months after he filed for divorce, he and Doneen made their relationship public."

Mason was busy sweeping up the glass, his knuckles

white around the dustpan handle as he swept the shards into a pile. Rage pumped hot through him at the thought of this Brody douche and Lowenna's sister sneaking behind her back, all while she was fighting for her life.

He dumped the glass into the trash bin, then turned to face her in utter astonishment. "And you're going to their wedding?"

She nodded, her smile stiff. "Oh, there's more."

What else could there possibly be?

"I own a chocolate shop, and my parents, who are paying for the wedding, asked me to do the guest favors. They want boxes of chocolates at each place setting. I was reluctant at first, but eventually agreed. Once my sister got wind of my generosity, she then piled on a big, gaudy chocolate feature for the dessert table—for free, of course. I've been told that this can be my wedding gift to them."

"Isn't it going to be like thousands of dollars worth of chocolate?" he asked.

"Yep. Sure is. But here's the real kicker ... it wasn't until I agreed to do all the chocolate stuff for them that Doneen asked me to be her maid of honor. I nearly had a coronary I was so surprised."

"Are you the maid of honor, too?"

She shook her head. "No. I was forced to decline her very *gracious* offer." She rolled her eyes and smirked. "I said I couldn't do her bridal shower, bachelorette party and all the chocolates for the wedding. I made her choose, and she said the chocolates were more important."

"Is your sister a psychopath?" he asked, completely serious in his question.

Her lip twitched. "More like socially unaware, completely self-absorbed and a vapid narcissist. I'm not sure she has any empathy either." She paused for a moment, then shrugged. "Maybe she is a psychopath. I have heard more of them walk among us than we realize. Not all of them are machete-wielding lunatics."

Oh, he knew that well. He'd met a fair few psychopaths in his day. Most of them high-powered CEOs that had zero qualms destroying lives, businesses and entire communities if it lined their pockets with more cold, hard cash.

The bell in the kitchen dinged, and he stepped around the corner to the food window to grab their nachos.

Lowenna's eyes turned hungry as he plopped the big tray down on the bar in front of her, the top a delicious, steaming blend of cheddar cheese and black olives. His mouth watered.

"So you run a chocolate shop?" he asked, handing her a plate and a few napkins. "Not that new chocolate place around the corner?"

"Wicked Sister Chocolates? Yep, that's me." Her grin was just that—*wicked*. "Bit of an ironic name, which is why I picked it. Doneen told me, when I was in the middle of my chemo treatment, losing my hair and no more than a hundred pounds, that I was making everything all about me. She told me that I brought cancer into our family and that I was all our parents ever talked about. That they forgot her birthday because they were at the hospital with me after I had a bad reaction to the chemo. She said I was wickedly selfish and milking my illness, that women got uterine cancer all the time and lived through it. That I was clearly making it out to be worse than it really was."

"What the ever-loving fuck?" he blurted out, a chip loaded with guac and salsa falling from his hand onto his shoe. "What. The. Fuck?"

All Lowenna did was her lift her eyebrows. "Yep. That's dear ol' sis for you. Nicest big sister I ever could have asked for."

"And you're going to her wedding?"

"Yes. I am. Albeit reluctantly."

"Why go at all?"

"My parents—particularly my mother—has perfected the art of the guilt trip. She thinks that me going to the wedding will serve as the olive branch needed to begin mending the fence between my sister and I." She rolled her eyes and scoffed. "A bit of a pipe dream if you ask me, but sure, I'll bite."

"But the woman is a fucking psychopath who started sleeping with your husband while you were still married to him and battling cancer. Do you even *want* to mend that fence?" He shook his head. He just couldn't wrap his brain around why Lowenna hadn't cut her sister out of her life with a broadsword.

And then impaled her with that sword.

If that had been Mason, he would no longer have a sibling. He would sever all ties and live his life as an only child.

Thank God his sister, Nova, had the biggest heart in the world and was one of his best friends. It just sucked that she and her husband had moved to Australia last year for her husband's job. He missed her madly.

"I'm going because I need to show them that I've moved on. That I'm better than I've ever been now that I'm cancer *and* Brody free. And besides the fake boyfriend, the rest is true. I am doing awesome. Business is booming. My life is really good right now. But I just feel like a show-stopper of a date, one infinitely hotter than my ex, will help boost my confidence. Something that I've been lacking since, you know ... my husband left me for my sister and all." She shoved a chip heaped with guac into her mouth, chewed, swallowed and continued. "I have already booked dance lessons if he looks like Channing Tatum but doesn't dance like him. If he doesn't own a suit, I will rent him one. I will pay for his haircut. I will foot the bill for everything so long as he pretends to be madly in love with me and wins over every person at that party."

"But you said you want him to look like an underwear model and have a six-figure job, so he can probably afford all of that himself?"

She shrugged, then dipped a chip into the salsa. "Perhaps. I just need him to be more successful than my ex-husband and more handsome."

"When's the wedding?" he asked.

"My birthday," she said with a snort.

He cocked his head and hit her with a probing gaze. "Which is?"

She drained her wineglass and then snorted again. "Valentine's Day."

2

SHE'D BEEN nervous at first, accepting Mason's offer to share a plate of nachos. But now that she was sitting at the bar enjoying the olives, cheese and Mason's muscular tattooed arms bunching and flexing as he worked, all her nerves were gone, replaced only with a sense of calm and gratitude. This whole ordeal trying to find a date to Doneen and Brody's wedding was turning out to be an absolute nightmare.

She'd also been working like a dog for the past six months, getting her business off the ground and training her staff. Then the Christmas season hit, with New Year's Eve following on its heels, and now Valentine's Day was only five weeks away. So many holidays where everyone celebrated with chocolate. It was good for business but bad for her blood pressure.

In the end she wound up turning customers away, particularly those who wanted to place big chocolate orders for Christmas and New Year's parties. She just didn't have the time, space or manpower to do it all. They were slammed.

Maybe next year she could hire more staff or rent a bigger

space, but for now, she had to make do with the facility she had, even if it meant losing business in the process.

She watched Mason's muscular forearm stretch, the veins beneath his tattoos bulging as he slipped the martini and margarita glasses up into their holders above the bar. He was a handsome man for sure. Dark hair, dark, short-trimmed beard and mustache, dark blue eyes, thick brows. A lady-killer for sure.

And tall.

Boy, was he tall.

And not lanky tall either, no. The man had some breadth to him, and by the looks of things, it was all muscle beneath his black Prime Sports Bar and Grill T-shirt. Despite him being a bartender, danger and intrigue seemed to ooze from him, along with a fresh and manly scent she couldn't quite place but found intoxicating.

Tall, dark and dangerous.

Yum.

She licked her lips, tasting the salt from the nacho chips.

"More wine?" he asked, lifting his eyebrow at her.

She shook her head reluctantly and made a dismissive face. "No, I shouldn't."

"On the house. After a story like that, I can't charge you. Hell, I should be paying you." He grabbed the bottle of pinot off the back counter and waggled it in front of her. "You sure?"

She rolled her eyes and nodded. "I'm not driving, so why not?"

"You live nearby then?" he asked, pouring what was left of the bottle into her glass.

"Yeah, about a fifteen-minute walk or so. Not too far. Makes commuting to work pretty easy."

"I bet." He plopped the wine bottle into the blue recycling bin behind him, then returned to their well-eaten plate of nachos. "So, what are you going to do if you don't find Mr. Perfect for your date?"

She lifted both shoulders and shook her head at the same time she picked off a cheese-covered jalapeno slice from the plate and popped it into her mouth. "No clue."

"What about me?"

She wrinkled her nose in confusion. "What about you?"

"As your date?" He placed a pint glass beneath the spout for draft beer and pulled the lever. "I mean, I'm not trying to be conceited or anything, but I've turned a few heads in my day. Unless your ex-husband is a giant, I'm probably taller than him. I am six-foot-five. I have a six-figure job."

Lowenna nearly choked on her jalapeño. "As a bartender?"

His blue eyes narrowed on her.

Oh, crap, had she offended him? She hadn't meant to, it was just that she had never met a bartender who made a banker's salary. He'd also caught her entirely off guard with his offer to be her date.

"I own the place. Didn't you know that?" he said, his tone not quite harsh but still with a slight edge to it.

Shit, she had offended him. Oh, no.

She shook her head and reached for her wine. "No. I ... I thought you ... "

"Were just a lowly bartender who busted his ass for tips? No, not quite."

She lowered her eyes. "I'm sorry. I didn't mean to judge. I just ... "

"Lowenna, relax. It's okay."

She lifted her gaze once again to his face. His smile was warm, wide and so damn sexy.

Thank God.

"So you own the bar then?" she asked, her cheeks hot and

her chest even hotter in embarrassment from her judgmental blunder.

He nodded. "Yep. And before I bought this place, I worked for a Fortune 500 company as an investment banker. Boon Investments."

Her eyebrows nearly flew off her forehead.

Every day on her way to work she walked past the skyscraper where Boon Investments made up the top six floors. They were a big company. Big and successful.

"But my conscience got the better of me, and I left that about five years ago," he went on. "Took off traveling to find a bigger and better meaning in life than money."

She swallowed. "And what did you find?"

He reached into his back pocket and pulled out his phone, showing her the wallpaper, which was of the most adorable baby she'd ever seen, in a pink and purple polka-dot sleeper. "Her," he said matter-of-factly. "Her name is Willow, and she means everything to me."

"You adopted her?"

He shook his head, pulled his phone away and stared at the photo for a couple of seconds. His blue eyes softened, and a smile coasted across his lips before he stowed his phone back in his pocket.

"Nope. She's mine." He scrunched up his nose for a moment. "Not that she still wouldn't be mine if I adopted her, but Willow is my blood, is what I mean. Two of my best friends from college are married. They're lesbians and don't want children of their own. But Katya offered me an egg, and Delia offered me her womb. They're Willow's aunts and love her implicitly. But she's mine. I'm the only one on her birth certificate. I'm the only parent that she knows. I wanted a child. I wanted a greater purpose in my life than the endless money-grubbing loop I was in. I wanted a family, someone to care about besides myself. I wanted a legacy and to look forward to getting up in the morning and spending my day with someone that I love and that loves me. I also wasn't getting any younger and hadn't found the right woman, so I went it alone."

Holy shit.

She didn't think there were men out there like Mason. Single dads, yes. But a single dad by choice? She'd never met such a unicorn.

"She's adorable," she said, still in awe of the man in front of her. "And I love the name Willow. Willow Whitfield, it's great."

"Willow *Olivia* Whitfield. Her initials spell out the word *WOW*. Apparently, it's good luck for your initials to spell something." He scratched the back of his neck. "At least that's what my mom says. I'm Mason Otto Whitfield."

"*MOW*," she said, grinning.

He nodded. "And my sister is Nova Emily Whitfield. She didn't take her husband's name either because it would stop her from being ... "

Her smile grew to the point where her cheeks hurt. "*NEW*."

"Exactly. His last name is Atkinson, and that just doesn't fly. NEA doesn't mean squat."

Lowenna giggled, instantly cringing from how girlie and flirty she sounded.

Gah, that was not her at all.

Mason didn't seem to mind it though and simply smiled, continuing on with his explanation. "So when Willow came along, I had to keep the trend going."

She giggled again, but this time she didn't care. He made her smile. He made her laugh, and she liked how it felt to be around him. "I like it," she finally said. "What would you have chosen if Willow had been a boy?"

"Wyatt Otto Whitfield. My children will always *wow* me."

His smile made heat pool in her belly and dirty thoughts instantly flood her mind.

Was it wrong that she immediately checked to see if her initials spelled anything?

Lowenna Amélie Chambers. *LAC.* Nope. Nothing. At least not in English.

Then she checked her former married name. Lowenna Amélie Hawthorne. *LAH.* Nope.

Now, what if she married Mason and became Lowenna Amélie Whitfield? *LAW.* Yep. That worked.

Hmm.

Then out of sheer curiosity, she checked her sister's name. Her maiden name initials didn't spell anything, but once she married Brody she would be ...

She tossed her head back and began to laugh.

"What's so funny?" Mason asked, his voice a touch shaky, as though he was unsure if he was allowed to laugh with her or not.

Her eyes opened and she wiped the tears from beneath them, she'd been laughing so hard. Oh, boy, did she ever need that laugh. Taking a much-needed sip of her wine, she smiled against the rim. "Sorry, I just checked to see what my sister's initials would spell, and right now with her maiden name, they spell nothing, but once she marries my ex-husband, she will be Doneen Ursula Hawthorne." She snickered and waited for Mason to spell it out too.

His face split into a grin just as big as hers. "Your sister will be *DUH.*"

She snorted, most unladylike in the back of her throat, smiled like an idiot and nodded before breaking out into yet another fit of laughter.

It was a stupid thing to laugh about. Foolish, really. But she had to take the little victories where she could find them.

And knowing that her sister was going to be *DUH* for the rest of her life made Lowenna just a touch happier.

"So what do you say?" Mason's voice cut through her laughter.

She reached for her wine and took another big sip, allowing her breathing to settle before she replied, otherwise she'd surely get the hiccups.

"Say to what?" she finally asked, setting her wineglass back down and reaching for a nacho chip.

"To me being your date?" he replied. "You never did answer me. We got a bit off topic."

She blinked, then slowly, her eyes drifted down his body. His very toned, tanned and tall body. Oh boy, he was a triple threat. A triple T and all with that aura of danger surrounding him. She'd never dated a man like that, but always wanted to.

Could she take Mason to the wedding and steal the show? Would he steal the show? He would certainly stop traffic. And he was tall. And he had a good job. And he was a devoted father to boot.

"Can you dance?" she blurted out before she could stop herself.

Something unidentifiable flashed behind his dark blue eyes, but he quickly snuffed it out and took a sip of his beer, shaking his head at the same time. He wiped the back of his wrist across his mouth. "Not really. No more than club grinding, not that I've done that shit in years. But I have some friends who are professional dancers, so they could probably swing us some lessons."

"I've already booked lessons with Benson School of Dance."

"Oh, that's where my friends work."

That smile of his was going to be the end of her for sure. It was definitely going to make women—and a few men—at the wedding swoon. Her nipples pebbled beneath her baby-blue sweater. "You know Violet?"

He nodded and reached for a nacho chip. "Yep. I've known Vi since we were kids. Her brother, Mitch, was my best friend in high school. And now Mitch and Vi's man, Adam, and I all play poker together on Saturday nights. Single dads club. Mitch and Adam's ex-wife are together now too."

Lowenna's head suddenly hurt. What did she just hear?

"Mitch is with his sister's boyfriend's ex-wife? Did I hear that right?" she asked, squinting at him as if that would somehow help her make sense of what she'd just heard.

The chuckle that rumbled in his chest said she wasn't the first person to look at him like he'd just sprouted another head. "Yep. Not all divorces have to end badly. Sometimes couples can separate and remain friends. They all even go on family holidays together. Mitch has Jayda, Adam and Paige share Mira, and now Adam and Violet are expecting. One big, confusing, happy family."

She pressed her lips together into a thin line in thought. "As long as they're happy, I guess. Can't say I'll be booking adjoining tropical bungalows with *Duh* and *Duh-mmer* anytime soon. More like never."

All he did was nod and stuff more chips and guac into his mouth.

"And you'd be able to commit to dance lessons twice a week for an hour until the wedding? What about Willow?"

He shrugged. "She's four months old. She can either come with me and sit in her car seat, or I can wear her in the Ergo if she gets fussy. My mom is also available to take her. Mom is Violet's receptionist at the dance school."

"Wow, you're just *all* connected up, aren't you?"

He shrugged a broad shoulder. "One big, happy, confusing family. Wouldn't have it any other way. We have each other's backs. The same for all The Single Dads of Seattle."

Family. Right.

She hadn't considered her family a happy one since, oh, God, maybe high school? Even then, Doneen had always treated her like crap. She had always been a mean older sister.

Lowenna never knew why. Never knew what she'd done to make her sister hate her so. For years she had idolized Doneen, followed her around and copied everything she did. And Doneen hated every minute of it. Hated having to share anything with Lowenna, whether it be her time, space, toys or parents.

Lowenna swallowed down the emotional lump in her throat that always seemed to get clogged there when she thought of the terrible relationship she had with her sister. She knew Doneen didn't really like her, but she hoped deep down Doneen loved her. At least she used to hope. Now she wasn't so sure. Not after Doneen committed the ultimate betrayal—sleeping with Lowenna's husband.

Mason cleared his throat. "You okay?"

Nodding, she finished her wine and blinked back the sting of tears before they spilled over. "Yep. Just, uh ... just thinking." She lifted her gaze to his. "You're going to be okay being away from Willow for the wedding?"

"I'm away from her now, and she's doing just fine. She's the first grandchild, and my dad is retired, and my mom works part-time. They're very available and eager to take her. I've told them several times I have no problem hiring her a nanny, but my mother threatened to never have me over for pot roast again if I did that. So they're the people who look after her when she's not with me."

"They sound like amazing parents and grandparents."

"The best." He took a sip of his beer. "So, do I make the

cut? Am I your date? Or do you have a shortlist and you're going to call us all back for second auditions?"

"You're funny. No, no shortlist. I'm afraid not a one of them made the cut."

He whistled. "Yikes!"

"Do you have a suit?" she asked, not sure why she felt the need to stall but for some reason doing it anyway.

He nodded. "I have like twelve or more. You can come over one night in a few weeks, go through my closet and pick out which one you want me to wear. I go to Elliot Bay Barbers, so no need to book me a hair appointment. I can take care of that. Anything else?" His blue eyes held an eagerness she couldn't quite place.

And the fact that he'd invited her over to his house had not slipped past her either.

Not. At. All.

Was he doing this because he felt sorry for her? She hadn't told any of the other men she'd interviewed about her cancer. She hadn't told them much at all, really. She simply wanted to get to know them and see if they were worth inviting back for the next round of interviews.

Unfortunately, she hadn't met a one that she considered decent enough to invite back for a second interview. And time was running out.

"This would be a business deal," she said slowly. "I need it to be a business transaction. I am paying you to be my date— my escort—to a wedding. But I need the full boyfriend experience. Affection, hugging, kissing, dancing. You need to act like it pains you to be away from me for even a second. You can't keep your hands off me. Pretend you're madly in love with me. Convince me that you are, convince everyone at the party that you are, and I will pay you two thousand dollars at the end of the night."

She reached for her wine, her heart thumping wildly in her chest, then sat back in her seat and gauged his reaction.

She thought for sure his mouth would drop open and his eyes would go wide, but they didn't. He simply stood there, beer in hand, lips together, eyes focused intensely on her face.

So intensely, in fact, that she began to squirm in her seat from the heat of his stare and the way it made her insides liquefy.

She broke the eye contact and stared down into her empty wineglass. "It's a lot to ask, I know," she finally said, unable to handle the deafening silence any longer. "But it's what I need. It's what I require. Hence why I've been doing so many interviews. I just haven't found a guy who measures up, who I think has the acting chops needed to pull one over on nearly three hundred people."

"I don't need the money," he said, his voice just a touch above a whisper.

She shook her head emphatically. "Nope. This is a business transaction. I'm not a charity case." Anger began to worm its way up her spine. "If this is a pity thing because of the cancer, then I'm going to get up and leave right now. I won't be anybody's pay-it-forward, feel-good act of kindness."

Especially since she'd been that person before and had never been able to track down her generous, anonymous benefactor. As much as she appreciated the donation, she hated that it had been done most likely out of pity.

His pupils grew, and his blue irises darkened. If she'd been standing rather than sitting, she probably would have taken a couple of steps back, but she couldn't, so she didn't. The look he was giving her now was downright dangerous. Terrifying. But in the absolute most exquisite and exciting kind of way.

"I could never pity you," he said quietly. "Nothing but pure admiration is what you deserve."

Her pulse thundered in her ears, and her breathing stuttered. "But can you act?" Why was she challenging him? Why was she still stalling?

Because you like the way he looks at you when you make him wait, when you don't give him exactly what he wants.

Before she could blink, he was around the bar and beside her.

She swallowed the sudden lump in her throat and glanced up at him. Determination and something akin to the look a male lion gets when in rut flashed behind his eyes. Then his hand shot out from his side and looped around her waist. He tugged her hard against his chest and dipped her low over his arm.

"How's this for convincing?" Then he crashed his mouth to hers with a force that, had he not been holding her tight in all his manly muscles, would have knocked her clear off her feet. His tongue pried her lips apart and wedged its way into her mouth. Long, deep sweeps, followed quickly by little nibbles and erotic sucks. Oh, boy, did the man know how to kiss.

Unable to stop herself, she wrapped her arms around his back and held on as he deepened the kiss even more by shoving his fingers into her hair and tilting her head back. He was a man who took control, who demanded control and wasn't used to being questioned. She got that about him right away.

A moan fled from the depths of her throat. He caught it, and she felt him smile against her mouth. She couldn't roll her eyes because they were closed, but she mentally rolled them.

He knew he had her over a barrel. He was her date now; there was no doubt about that.

Not ready to break the kiss, she whimpered just slightly when he pulled away, immediately berating herself for being so easily manipulated.

"You're not my *pay-it-forward, feel-good* deed," he said, his mouth no more than an inch above hers. He tasted like beer and nachos. Normally, it wasn't a taste she wouldn't have enjoyed on the tongue of another, but on Mason, she would most gladly have gone back for seconds. "You're not a charity case, and I'll take that money. Put it into Willow's college fund."

She swallowed again and released his back at the same time he released her hair and his hand from around her waist. "Okay."

He stepped away and wiped his hand over his face, his cheeks a ruddy color beneath the sexy scruff. "I'll give you the full boyfriend experience, Lowenna, I promise. Not a person at that wedding will believe that I am not madly in love with you."

The wine in her bloodstream mixed with the passion from his kiss made her brain get all fuzzy. She wanted to reach out, grab him and kiss him again. But instead, she made fists with each hand until her nails dug painful half-moons into her palms. "You're hired," she finally said, unsure what else to say.

His grin as he made his way back around the bar made her panties suddenly get incredibly damp. "Good. And heck, my acting skills will be so Oscar-worthy, you might even believe it yourself."

With her wineglass empty, she had nothing to quench her suddenly parched palate. But he was already anticipating her needs, and his half-full pint glass was subtly pushed in front of her.

She took a sip. Then another sip. Then drained it, her eyes going wide over the rim of the heavy glass as the realization of what she'd just gotten herself into finally began to sink in. She was going to a wedding with the sexiest man she'd ever met, and he planned to kiss her like that in front of all her friends and family and convince the world he was madly in love with her. Convince her that he was madly in love with her.

Oh, yeah, this wasn't going to end in a catastrophe or heartache at all.

3

MASON HIT the fob for his Volvo SUV and locked it. Not that he needed to, because the neighborhood was the upper echelon of Seattle elite and incredibly safe, but it was habit. With his six-pack in one hand, he held the collar of his coat closed with the other and hightailed it toward Liam's front door.

It was an icy wind that had blown in from the north, and the smell of more snow hung crisp in the air. They'd had a lot of snow that winter, more than in past years, and clumps of it still lingered on street corners and at the ends of driveways.

Footsteps behind him had him slowing his pace.

"Hey!" Scott's feet skidded to a halt on the gravel. His breath sent heated puffs of air up from his mouth into the ether. His cheeks were a bright red and his eyes slightly teary.

"Did you run here?" Mason asked, knowing the answer but asking it anyway.

Scott shook his head and ran the back of his wrist beneath his slightly crooked nose. "Naw, caught an Uber, but the guy wasn't sure he could turn around in Liam's driveway so he asked if he could drop me off on the road. Can I grab a ride home with you?"

Mason nodded. "Sure."

Scott heaved open the front door to his brother's large Lake Washington home and let Mason go ahead of him. "Thanks."

They stomped their feet once inside the foyer but didn't bother to remove their shoes. Liam had recently redone his floors, having ripped out all the old wood and replaced it with fancy concrete. It wasn't Mason's style, but it was still nice.

"You any closer to getting a date with that mystery woman at the bar?" Scott asked as they made their way deeper into Liam's house toward the kitchen. Male voices rumbled and murmured in the direction of the dining room, letting them know that they weren't the first to arrive.

Mason grinned over at his friend. "Sure am."

Scott nodded and smiled. "Nice. What's her name?"

"Lowenna."

Whenever he got the chance over the past few days, he'd roll her name around on his tongue. He'd never heard it before, but he absolutely loved it. And it suited her to a T. Happiness, joy, bliss and cheer. At least that's what Google said her name meant when he searched it later that night after their nacho date.

It wasn't a date.

He had to keep reminding himself of that.

He was her boyfriend for hire.

Ugh.

How awful to feel the need to hire a man to pretend to be your boyfriend. He understood why she was doing it. And he fully supported her, but she shouldn't have been put in that position in the first place. Her sister and her ex-husband were class-A assholes, and Lowenna would be better off just cutting them out of her life completely.

"Cool name," Scott said, interrupting Mason's thoughts. "So you guys going out?"

More of the single dads meandered their way into the kitchen. Mason pulled one beer bottle from the pack and stowed the rest in Liam's enormous fridge. He popped the cap and took a sip before answering. "Kind of. She's, uh ... she's hired me to be her boyfriend at her sister's Valentine's Day wedding. Which, incidentally, is also my date's birthday."

"She what?" Scott's eyebrows flew up to his hairline, and his brown eyes widened in surprise. "As in a like a gigolo? Do you have to put out?"

Mason squeezed his eyes shut. He'd regretted offering to be her date the moment it came out of his mouth. That was not how he wanted his and Lowenna's relationship to begin. Not as a business arrangement where he was forced to *pretend* to be her boyfriend rather than actually be her boyfriend. And the fact that she insisted upon paying him made him feel all the dirtier.

They would, after all, have to take dance lessons together twice a week for the next month. Maybe they could take that time as an opportunity to get to know each other. As long as he didn't injure her with his clumsy two left feet, that is.

"Dude?"

Mason opened his eyes to find all of the Single Dads of Seattle standing in Liam's kitchen staring at him as if he was on the verge of having a stroke.

"You okay?" Liam asked.

Mason shook his whole body, then took another sip of his beer. "Yeah, it's just ... this whole thing is so fucked up."

Liam clapped his hands once. "Well, let's all start playing cards and you can fill us in. I'm feeling lucky tonight, boys. I'm in the mood to fleece you all."

Various groans echoed throughout their ten-man group as they all made their way through the kitchen to the dining room, where Liam's card table was already set up.

Atlas sat down behind the card deck and began to shuffle.

"So, spill," Liam said, his ice clinking in his glass of scotch as he brought it to his lips. "Tell us how you've gone from being part of a Fortune 500 company to a bar owner to Deuce Bigalow, Male Gigolo." He tossed his dark blond head back and laughed. "Oh man."

More groans echoed around the table.

"You're not nearly as funny as you think you are," Atlas said blandly, dealing out the cards.

"Why are you her boyfriend for hire?" Mitch asked, his tan from his Christmas spent in Hawaii making his green eyes practically glow beneath the lights overhead.

Mason exhaled, scooped up his cards and fanned them out in his hand. "Because Lowenna's sister is marrying Lowenna's ex-husband. He left her for her sister after she had a hysterectomy and went through chemo and radiation for cancer. Though Lowenna is convinced the two were sleeping together prior to her being cancer-free." He let that hang in the air for a moment, reading the reactions of each of his poker buddies.

They didn't disappoint.

One by one, shocked expressions formed around the table.

"Motherfuckers," Zak muttered.

Mason nodded. "Yep. Her ex-husband said he wanted to have a family the *traditional* way, and she couldn't give that to him, so he divorced her. Went public with her sister a few months later."

"And she's going to their fucking wedding?" Emmett asked, his amber eyes flashing with an anger that Mason had felt in every single bone of his body when Lowenna first told him her story. "Why?"

Mason nodded again before he shrugged. "Yeah, I have no fucking clue. Family loyalty? She's also that new chocolatier in town, so she's crazy busy."

"Wicked Sister?" several of the men asked in unison.

"Mhmm."

"Fuck, dude, she's hot," Scott added. "And her chocolate ... holy shit. That's how you deal with a sex dry spell. You go and buy a dozen of her habanero truffles, you sit in your car, listen to Enya and you gorge yourself."

All the men turned to look at Scott with slightly disturbed expressions on their faces.

Mason had to admit, that was not how he would deal with a sex dry spell or how he wanted to know his friend dealt with his.

"Whatever floats your boat, I guess," Mitch said slowly, making a cringy face.

Scott simply shrugged it off and shoveled a handful of potato chips into his mouth.

"So she hired you to be her date *why?*" Mark asked, placing a neat little pile of poker chips into the center of the card table.

"She wants arm candy to the Nth degree. She wants me to convince everybody at that party that I am madly in love with her and she is so much better off without this Brody douche."

Liam, Zak, Atlas, Mitch, Mark and Emmett all stilled simultaneously. Freaked-out glances shot around and across the card table.

"Did you say *Brody?*" Liam asked slowly, enunciating the man's name.

Mason took a pull on his beer and swallowed before answering, "Yeah, why?"

"Is the sister, the woman he's marrying, named Doneen?" Atlas asked, terror in his gray eyes.

Now they were all starting to freak him out. What the fuck was going on?

"Yeah." Mason nodded again. "What the fuck is going on, guys?"

"He works for our firm," Liam said slowly. "Can't fucking stand him. But he's invited everybody to the wedding."

"Aurora's been invited too," Zak said. "I'm her date."

"And I'm the photographer," Mitch said. "Hate them both, but they booked the ultimate deluxe package, and I can't say *no* to ten grand. Tori is going to be my second photographer, as she's got a good eye and has been apprenticing with me when she has time."

Mark, Tori's less-than-better half, simply nodded. "She says they're enormous tools."

"Pretentious as fuck. Super-demanding," Mitch confirmed. "And Paige is catering it. Comes home most nights and nearly kills a bottle of wine, they're stressing her out so much. The bride calls practically every day to make some kind of a change or request. Again, if it wasn't for the hefty price tag, and the fact that these two chumps are essentially paying for our new master bathroom, we'd have both told them to fuck off a long time ago."

"Zara's doing the flowers," Emmett chimed in. "She's a third-generation florist, and not much rattles her or pisses her off, but this bride you guys are talking about has made her want to pull her hair out. Impossible demands for a winter wedding. She wants tulips brought in from Holland. Plumeria brought in from Hawaii."

"So a bunch of you guys are going to be at the wedding, then?" Mason asked, relieved that he would know people there, have some allies.

Liam, Atlas, Zak and Mitch all nodded.

Mason tipped back his beer and guzzled. "Well, that's a relief." He turned to Adam. "Lowenna's apparently booked us for dance lessons with Vi."

Adam lifted his chin. "I think I remember Vi mentioning that. You want me there too?"

"Yeah." Mason needed to show Lowenna what a real family looked like, what real support and friendship looked like. Perhaps he could convince her that she didn't even need to go to the wedding and they could skip it altogether. Go grab dinner and a movie on Valentine's Day instead.

And fuck, it was her birthday too. She definitely didn't deserve to be faking it at her sister's wedding on her birthday. He still didn't understand why Liam and Atlas were going to the wedding if they hated the guy.

"Is she doing chocolate for the wedding?" Scott asked, his eyes gleaming. Mason worried the guy might also start to drool.

Mason nodded. "Yeah. They want her to do some big, ostentatious chocolate feature piece for the center of the dessert table, as well as all the guest favors. Like she has time for that during Valentine's season. And they want her to do it for free as their wedding gift."

"Fuck that shit."

"Motherfuckers."

"Tell them to go fuck themselves."

"Brody is such a twat."

Sentiments akin to Mason's bounced around the table.

"So why are you two going if you hate the guy so much?" he asked, focusing on Liam and Atlas.

Liam raised his bet, then took a sip of his drink. "Because we found out Paige is catering and that it's an open bar." He exchanged looks with Atlas. "Gonna drink that motherfucker straight into the poorhouse, right?"

All Atlas did was raise his dark blond eyebrows.

"So do we finally get to meet the elusive Richelle, then?" Zak asked, tipping his beer back and guzzling down half of it. "About time. You two have been together for a while now."

Liam made a noise in his throat. "No, she's not my date. And we're not *together*. It's a sexual arrangement and nothing more." He placed his hand over top of Atlas's hand, earning a glare from the tall, quiet, gray-eyed man. "Atlas has agreed to be my plus one. I'm a little worried he may expect me to put out on the first date though." He batted his lashes. "I'm not that kind of date. I need to be wooed and courted before I give up the goods. I'd also like a corsage. White roses, please."

Atlas pulled his hand free from Liam's. "You're a tool."

"A tool who you can't live without," Liam countered.

Atlas simply rolled his eyes. "Only reason I'm going with this fucker is because his nanny agreed to watch Aria and Cecily for me too. My nanny booked the night off weeks ago."

"How's that going, by the way?" Mason asked. Poor Atlas. The guy lost his wife just over a year ago, leaving him to raise their young daughter alone. He'd also recently gained custody of his cousin's infant daughter. Not to mention the man was also a senior partner at Liam's law firm.

And here Mason thought his life trying to juggle the bar and Willow was a struggle.

Atlas shrugged. "Taking it one day at a time."

Liam's face went from teasing to serious, and he rested his hand on Atlas's shoulder this time. "That's all you can do. Cecily is really fortunate to have you."

Atlas grunted. "We gonna play poker or what?"

Grunts and grumbles around the table had them all tossing poker chips into the center, taking long swigs of their drinks or scratching crotches beneath the table. Manly shit.

Mason fought the urge to roll his eyes.

Even though, yes, they all played poker, drank and occasionally—when doctors Mark and Emmett weren't around—smoked cigars, Saturday night at Liam's was more than that. So much more.

This was their safe space to gripe and commiserate, lend support and offer advice. This was their dad group, their extended family, their village. And even though Mason had a great village for Willow with his parents and Katya and Delia as Willow's aunts, it was nice to know he had more people out there who had his back as well. Particularly men who understood what it was like to raise a child alone—whether by choice or not. And enough of the guys had daughters too that Mason was already overrun with hand-me-down clothes for Willow until she was at least five, not to mention sage advice.

He was so thankful that Mitch had welcomed him into the fold shortly after Willow was born. He knew becoming a single father was going to be tough, but he had no idea how isolating it could be.

His heart went out to other single dads—other single *parents*—who didn't have a village or any kind of family or community support. How did they do it? How did they get anything done? How did they manage to work all day and then come home and then put in another solid eight hours or more?

Mason had a housekeeper. He had his parents. He had the single dads. He had a village, and without that village, he knew he'd be lost.

"You should introduce Lowenna to the women," Mark suggested, standing up and heading over to Liam's leather-top bar in the corner. "Aurora will be at the wedding. Tori too. That way she has at least a couple of friendly faces in her corner."

That wasn't a half bad idea.

Might give him more of an excuse to get to know her as

well. Spend some time with Lowenna outside of dance lessons.

"Tori's started planning Vi's baby shower. Plans to have it at The Rage Room," Mark went on. "Man, Luna must be just raking in the dough. Seems like every time we pass the place, it's packed to the rafters with people taking baseball bats and crowbars to printers and toasters."

Aaron, who had remained quiet until now, snorted. "I've got one more on the punch card and then the next one is free."

Emmett's interest piqued. "Hey, me too."

Mason scrubbed his hand down his short-cropped beard. "It's going to be hard to be civil to these motherfuckers at their own wedding. Knowing what they've done to her, to his own wife ... to her own *sister*. And all when she was battling cancer."

Eyebrows lifted and heads nodded.

"Tell me about it, man," Liam said. "Brody has only been with the firm for a few years, so we've only known him to be with Doneen, but they're both a couple of real snobs. Knew that from the moment I met the guy. Fancy car, fancy watch, fancy clothes. Nose in the air, stick up his ass. And the way he treats the associates, fuck, we're always on him to be nicer. He thinks they're his slaves. He made Aurora run out and grab his fucking dry cleaning."

Zak sat up straighter. "He what?"

Liam nodded. "Don't worry, Dina put a stop to that right quick."

"You bet she fucking did," Aaron said tightly. Dina was his sister and had passed away at the end of the summer. Aaron was now raising Dina's infant daughter as his own.

"Yeah, your sister even implemented a new hiring protocol after we realized what a total ass-wipe Brody is. We call the person back for a second interview and bring in one of the legal assistants, paralegals or receptionists. It's important that the new potential hire treats the support staff like they would treat any other colleague. If support staff are not shown respect by the potential new hire, then they're not hired. We can't have the glue that keeps our firm running smoothly feeling like they're not valued," Atlas said. Mason wasn't sure he'd ever heard the man string that many words together at once. "It's working out well."

"Brody is a typical yuppie," Liam went on. "He wants you to think he's loaded. Though I sign his fucking paychecks, so unless she's independently wealthy in her own right, they spend more than they make."

"This wedding is proof of that," Mitch added. "My services alone are costing them ten grand. Paige's catering is another ten, as she's also doing the cake, and there are going to be like two hundred guests or something ridiculous like that."

A bunch of the guys let out low whistles and averted their eyes.

"Fuck, I'm pretty sure my wedding to Cidrah cost us twenty-five hundred bucks total," Liam said, shaking his head. "We just weren't into the pomp and circumstance. A few friends, family and a barbecue in the backyard. That's all you really need. A fancy wedding doesn't necessarily guarantee a happy marriage."

"Not always does a cheapo one either, bro," Scott retorted. "You're proof of that."

Liam's face was that of resignation. "Touché, my good man."

"I don't think the bride and groom are paying for this thing, though," Mason cut in. "Not from what Lowenna has said. The bride's parents are selling their organs on the black market to pay for their daughter's outrageous demands."

"Jesus Christ," Aaron murmured. "Need to instill in

Sophie *now* that a big wedding is not a necessity. Add in inflation, and if she doesn't get married for another twenty-eight or so years, I'll be in the poorhouse simply from throwing a goddamn party."

"Dude, she's like six months old or whatever," Scott replied, giving Aaron a baffled expression.

"No, I agree," Mason said, nodding. "I'll start whispering that same shit to Willow tonight. Can't hurt. I'm not broke, but I'd rather have something left over for retirement, and not spend my life's savings on a one-day party."

All the guys chuckled and agreed as they tipped up beer and shoveled in potato chips.

"Just smile, wish them all the best, crush the shit out of Brody's limp-ass handshake and then suck face with Lowenna on the dance floor all night," Zak offered. "I'll be there too, so we can party it up. Get our ladies out on the dance floor, spin them around." His grin was playful. "Should we choreograph a dance number? Talk to Vi?"

Every single one of them around the table said *no* at the exact same time.

Zak's smile faded. "You all suck."

"Wait a minute." Adam tapped his chin, then reached into his pocket and grabbed his phone. He hit dial and put it to his ear. A moment later they all heard a woman's voice say *hello*. "Hey, babe. Quick question, what are the names of the couple who you are choreographing a big dance number for them for their wedding?"

No fucking way.

Really?

With bated breath, they all waited.

Adam's face confirmed it. "Thanks, babe. See you in a bit. Love you." He hung up his phone and stowed it once again in his pocket. "Yep. It's the future Mr. and Mrs. Pretentious themselves."

"You've got to be fucking kidding me." Scott shook his head, then finished his beer before he stood up to head to the kitchen for another.

Adam nodded. "Yep. Just the two of them, not the whole bridal party. But they've been working with Vi for weeks now to perfect their first dance. It's a mash-up with various songs, both fast and slow, lots of hip-hop. She says they're terrible dancers." He turned to face Mason. "So you've got it in the bag if you can manage to keep from stepping on your date's feet."

Well, that might be a problem right there.

There was a reason he never hit the club scene anymore, and it wasn't just because he was on the upper end of his thirties and finding gray whiskers in his beard ... and other places. It was because he didn't know how to dance to save his life.

Mason cracked his neck side to side, glanced one more time at the cards in his hand and tossed them to the table. "I fold," he said with a grunt, standing up and heading to the kitchen to grab another beer.

"It'll be fine," Liam called to him from the table. "We'll all just get shit-faced and dance. Once you're drunk enough, you don't care if you're a terrible dancer or not."

"*You* don't care if you're a terrible dancer or not," Scott corrected. "But some of us do."

Mason returned with his beer and sat back down at the table. All the men's eyes followed him.

"There's something more you're not telling us, isn't there?" Mitch said, tossing his cards into the center of the table as well. "What's wrong?"

Mason's fingers fidgeted on his beer bottle, his eyes glued to the kraken on the label. When he finally lifted his gaze, all the men were staring at him, waiting.

"Well?" Liam probed. "Don't tell us you've already

proposed to this woman or something stupid like that? I tell you this is getting a bit ridiculous with you guys and your obsession with finding love—"

"Shut it," Atlas said, or more like growled. "Let the man speak. We're in no mood to listen to your anti-love rhetoric for the millionth time. We get it. You, one of the Dixon Dickheads are a born-again bachelor." He stifled a yawn. "But we're tired of constantly hearing about it."

Liam grunted. Scott shuffled awkwardly in his chair, obviously put out that he was being lumped in with his brother as a *Dixon Dickhead.*

Most of the guys around the table snickered or guffawed. Some of them had the decency to hide their grins in their drink glasses or their beer bottles.

Mason shook his head. "No, nothing like that. It's just, I agreed to taking dance lessons, and I will, but I'm an absolutely terrible dancer. When you mentioned stepping on feet, I had this flashback to my sophomore year of college. I'm pretty sure I broke a couple of girls' toes on the dance floor of the nightclub. I'm a big guy, and I was born with two left feet."

Looks of pity stared back at him.

Fuck, he hated pity.

No wonder Lowenna had jumped down his throat when she thought the only reason he was offering to be her date was because he felt bad for her. That could not have been further from the truth.

Adam slapped him on the back. "Vi and I will sort you two out. She's a pro, and I've never danced better since being with her. We'll have you floating on air in no time."

Mason groaned. If only it were as easy as saying it out loud.

"Otherwise, we'll get you right plastered and you won't care if you look like a fool," Liam added, holding his drink up in a salute.

Mason groaned again. Yeah, he'd look like a fool all right, and he'd probably step on everyone's feet, break a few toes, and lose the girl in the process too.

4

LOWENNA TUCKED herself tighter beneath the eaves of the strip mall as she made her way along all the storefronts toward the dance studio. Benson School of Dance was just a few yards away, so she didn't feel the need to deploy her umbrella, even though it was lightly raining.

With nerves in her limbs, she walked briskly to the front door and heaved it open, causing it to chime above her head.

"Come on in," a woman's voice called out from the studio. She'd only met Violet Benson once, but she could tell that was her voice.

"Shoes on or off?" Lowenna asked.

"Off for now," Violet replied. "Socks too."

Nodding, Lowenna shed her coat and sat down on one of the numerous benches. She unzipped her black leather knee-high boots, then removed her socks, stowing them beneath the bench.

"Ready?" Her head was down so she didn't see him approach, and the sound of his deep voice made her nearly jump out of her own skin.

She lifted her head to find Mason cradling a baby in a

hippo-covered sleeper against his chest. Her one remaining ovary was threatening to explode.

"Is this Willow?" she asked, standing up and resisting the urge to extend her arms out and take the baby.

His smile was small but serene as he planted a kiss to the top of the baby's head. "Yes." He turned slightly so she could see her little face. "Willow, this is Lowenna. She's paying daddy to be her date."

Lowenna rolled her eyes and swatted him on the arm. "Thanks for that."

He was all grins. "Vi really wanted to see her, so I came by a bit early. She just had a bottle and is almost out. Vi has a bassinet in her office I can put Willow down in, so once she's out, we can start the dance lessons." He bounced the sleepy-eyed little baby in his arms, patting her bottom and humming a tune Lowenna didn't recognize. He looked so comfortable in his role as dad, so in his happy place.

She nibbled on her bottom lip and tentatively reached a hand out to rest on Willow's back. It was warm, and she could feel every breath.

"You wanna hold her quick?" he asked, his dark blue eyes squinting just slightly, causing the corners to crinkle. An amused smirk lifted one corner of his very talented lips—a talent she could attest to. "She's almost out, and now that we're on a schedule, she's pretty easygoing. Those first few months were a bit hairy."

She bit down harder on her lip. "Can I?"

He nodded, shifting Willow out of his arms and slowly passing her over to Lowenna. She cradled the baby against her chest just as Mason had and felt Willow snuggle right into the crook of her neck.

Every ounce of apprehension and nervousness that Lowenna had when she'd first walked into the dance studio evaporated. She shut her eyes and leaned her cheek against the top of Willow's head.

"She has that effect on everyone," he said with a chuckle. "She's like a drug."

Lowenna didn't bother opening her eyes, but she nodded and pressed her nose against Willow's downy soft hair, inhaling her sweet baby scent. "She really is," she murmured.

"Ah, there you two are." Her bump preceded the rest of her as Violet came around the corner. Their dance instructor had informed Lowenna that she was due the first week of March with her first baby, so that explained the bassinet Mason had mentioned. Violet was probably getting ready for when her own baby would join her at work.

A pang in the hollow where her uterus had once been had Lowenna hugging Willow tighter against her. Would she ever get to hold a baby of her very own this way? Cancer had stripped her of so much, and as much as she was thankful to still have her life, she still mourned all that she'd lost. All that she would never know.

"She's out," Mason whispered, craning his neck around Lowenna to check in on his daughter. "You've got the magic touch. Want to help me put her down?"

"Bassinet's in the back office," Violet said, pointing down the hallway. "I have the baby monitor all set up, so we'll be able to hear her and see her if she wakes up. You may want to close the door though, as the music can be quite loud."

Mason nodded, and his hand fell to the small of Lowenna's back. The heat of his palm was searing, even through the cotton layers of her shirt and cardigan. Or perhaps that was just the raging inferno inside her at the memory of his kiss one long week ago.

Had it really been a week since she'd seen him?

It felt like so much longer.

With a gentle but strong amount of pressure, he led her

down the short corridor toward Violet's back office. "Willow can sleep just about anywhere," he whispered. "But she seems to really like you. Zonked right out."

"Well, as long as she didn't start screaming when you put her in my arms," she whispered back, taking his cue and turning right into a small, dark office.

Were babies like dogs? Were they excellent judges of character? If Willow had started screaming in her arms, would Mason have rescinded on their arrangement? God, she hoped not. She'd gone and removed her ad from Craigslist. And thank God for that. The amount of creepers that she'd had to weed through each night to get at a few decent ones she responded to had been exhausting. Some of them even replied to the ad with dick pics. As if that was what would sway her?

"Right here," Mason said, stepping around behind her and standing on the side of a small but what looked to be state-of-the-art bassinet. "Just lay her down on her back."

"She won't wake up?"

He shrugged. "She might, but I'll probably be able to get her back down if she does."

Lowenna took in a deep breath, cradled Willow's tiny baby head in her palm, then leaned over into the bassinet. When she felt the bed beneath her hand, she gently pulled it out from under the baby's head.

"It's okay."

She could tell he was trying not to laugh from how slow and hesitant she was acting.

"You got this," he went on. "Easy does it."

Lowenna released her other hand from under Willow's butt, then slowly pulled it out of the bassinet. She stood back up, took a step back and threw her hands in the air, releasing the breath from her lungs in a deep *whoosh*.

Mason grinned that devilish smile that made her core

instantly tighten. "Great job," he mouthed before glancing back down at his daughter.

She nodded, then headed out into the lit hallway. "I'll meet you in the studio," she mouthed back.

His eyes flicked to hers and he murmured a "Mhmm," before his gaze fell once again to his sleeping daughter.

As much as Lowenna wanted to stay in that room and watch Willow sleep, she also had to get out of there. Her heart physically ached the longer she held that baby. She hadn't held a baby in a really long time, and it was because she knew what it would do to her. She knew how it would pull at the strings of her heart until they were so tight they nearly snapped and she would be reminded of all the things she might never have.

And that's exactly what holding Willow did.

Yet, despite that, Willow also brought Lowenna a sense of peace and joy she hadn't expected, and it softened the blow of her pain just a touch. It was a strange feeling to say the least. An ache and a calm all at once. Strange and confusing.

She entered the brightly lit dance studio to find the glowing Violet in a pair of black tights and a dark gray tank top standing in front of a very handsome man with light brown hair, both of them smiling. His hands were on her belly.

Lowenna took a deep breath, swallowed past the lump in her throat and tossed on the biggest smile she could muster. "Ready to dance?" she asked, clenching her molars together before her chin could tremble.

Both Violet and the man swiveled their heads in her direction. He dropped his hands from her belly immediately and took a step back, his face changing instantly to an expression Lowenna knew all too well.

Pity.

He knew.

Mason must have told him.

Her smile faltered a touch, but she forced the corners of her mouth up until they damn near reached her ears. "Teach me your moves, oh guru of the tutu." God, now she was trying *too* hard. She cringed inwardly.

Violet's green eyes sparkled, and she smiled. "Absolutely." Her eyes flicked up from Lowenna's face to behind her. Lowenna could see in the room full of mirrors that Mason had joined them. "Shoes off, Mase," Violet said.

"That way you don't crush your partner's toes," the other man said, winking at Lowenna. He approached her with his hand outstretched. "Adam Eastwood, Violet's partner and a friend of Mason's."

She took his hand. "Lowenna Chambers. Nice to meet you. Thank you for agreeing to hold private dance lessons for us so late in the evening."

His shake was strong. "Not a problem at all." He released her hand and took a step back, his gaze less that of pity now and more of determination. "We're going to get you two dancing like Fred and Ginger in no time. Mop the floor with those motherfuckers."

Mason was busy removing his shoes and socks in the corner.

"It's not a competition, dear," Violet said blandly. She faced Lowenna. "Though, unless both you *and* Mason have two left feet and are as uncoordinated as drunk toddlers, you'll be better dancers than your sister and her fiancé in no time. They're both terrible ... particularly him though. I don't want to use the word *hopeless*, but I'm getting to that point."

Lowenna's mouth twitched as she fought back a smile. "Yeah, Brody was never a good dancer, and my sister tried in grade school, but she just couldn't figure it out. The dance instructor suggested she try an instrument instead."

Adam and Mason both snorted.

"That's like telling somebody they have a face for radio," Adam said with a chuckle, wandering over to the big stereo system in the corner of the room. "Shall we start?"

"Yes, let's," Violet said, covering her mouth with her hand to hide her yawn.

Lowenna removed her cardigan and tucked it to the side of the room. That's when she noticed that her palms practically dripped with sweat. Was it because she hadn't been able to stop thinking about her kiss last week with Mason? Or that they would soon be pressed body to body and holding hands? And now those hands were sweaty as hell.

Great!

She made to wipe them on her pants, but his big, hard, warm body right next to her made her lose her train of thought. He offered her his hand, and she took it.

He wasn't smiling.

Why?

"I lied," he whispered as they made their way into the middle of the dance floor. "I can't just *not* dance. I'm actually pretty awful at it. But I promise to try my hardest for you, okay?"

Unease drifted behind his eyes as he stared at her, waiting for her response.

That's when she realized his palms were sweaty too.

"That's all I can ask," she said, placing her hand on his shoulder at the same time he wrapped his other hand around her waist. "Besides, how much worse than my sister and Brody can we be?"

"Ouch!" Lowenna winced.

Mason sucked in a breath and took a step back. "Sorry." Fuck, he was messing all of this up. How many times had he stepped on her toes now? He'd lost count. Thank God they were in bare feet, that was all he could say. If he'd been in his shoes, the poor woman would probably have a couple of broken toes by now, or at the very least her feet would be black and blue.

"It's okay," she murmured over the music.

Violet and Adam had decided to teach them the box step first, because apparently it was simple. Not quite.

Their dance instructors were beside them looking like a couple of professionals, in sync with each other and smiling ear to ear. They looked a bit goofy though, standing so far away from each other but still holding hands, what with Violet's baby bump between them taking up real estate.

"Let's switch partners for a bit," Violet announced, pulling away from Adam. "It might be easier if we have some one-on-one support." She made her way toward Mason and waited for him and Lowenna to disengage.

His heart sank just a touch when Lowenna pulled her hand from his and turned to Adam, whose smile was big and friendly.

Violet took Lowenna's place, stepping away from Mason just a bit to accommodate the baby. "You look sad," she said with a chuckle. "Am I not the woman you'd like to be holding hands with right now?" She took the lead, which was weird and awkward for Mason at first, but eventually he got the hang of allowing the woman to lead as she set them off across the room.

Truth be told, Mason had always had a tiny bit of a crush on his best friend's little sister. Violet was certainly a beauty and sweet as could be. But Mitch probably would have killed Mason if he'd made a play for Violet back in high school. And now, Vi was happy with Adam, expecting a baby, and Mason had his sights set on the chocolatier currently smiling and floating around the room with Adam.

"I can see that I'm not." Violet's comment interrupted his thoughts.

He brought his gaze back down to her face. "Sorry, Vi." He shook his head. "Maybe I need to go check on Willow."

Violet rolled her green eyes, amusement tilting the corner of her mouth up. "She's fine. The baby monitor is on the side over there, and we'd see little red lines shooting up the side if there was any noise in the room. She's fast asleep."

He shoved his tongue into his cheek and nodded once.

"Eyes on me," Vi ordered. "If you intend to impress your lady friend, you need to focus more on your dancing. I'm not saying you're terrible, but you're not great either."

Mason moved his gaze once again from Lowenna and Adam back down to Violet's face. "Thanks for the vote of confidence."

She laughed, just as her bump knocked his belly. "You'll get there. Unlike my other clients, I wouldn't describe you two as hopeless, just *not in sync* ... yet. But we have time. This is only the first lesson. You're back here Thursday."

Mason's hands were sweaty, and he was struggling to keep himself focused on Violet and not let his gaze wander around the room following Adam and Lowenna, who, by the way, seemed to be dancing beautifully.

So it was just him.

He was the dud on the dance floor.

"Look down," Violet ordered. "Watch our feet."

Mason did as he was told.

"Right. Good. One, two, three, four. One, two, three, four. Smooth movements. Don't overthink it. Let your body move with the music, move with my body. Keep your steps tight and light. As if the floor is made of eggshells." She nodded. "There you go. That's better."

Mason did what he was told as best he could.

"Ouch!"

"Fuck!"

He'd stepped on her foot.

"It's okay."

They paused, regrouped and once again took off into the steps.

"You got it. Good job," Vi encouraged.

She really was the best teacher. So patient, so positive.

She was going to make one hell of an amazing mother.

Mason groaned. "Thanks. I'm really sorry about your foot. I'm sure Lowenna's feet are going to be covered in bruises by the time we're done."

Violet giggled. "I think she's a pretty tough cookie." She glanced away from Mason. "Looks like Adam's not the person she's interested in dancing with either."

Mason's head snapped around so fast, he was sure he'd feel that in the morning. Lowenna's gray eyes were on him as Adam twirled her around the room. They were pinned to him, focused and intense.

What did that mean?

Violet cleared her throat. "Shall we switch back?"

Mason released Violet as if she'd suddenly told him she had a contagious disease, which only earned him another laugh from his pregnant dance partner.

"I can see you agree," she said blithely, rubbing her belly as she wandered away from Mason and back to Adam. "Okay, guys, watch us for a moment. Watch our feet." She took Adam's hand, and the two of them effortlessly took off around the dance floor.

"They're incredible," Lowenna breathed next to him.

The woman smelled amazing. Like chocolate and spice. A heady and intoxicating combination. He resisted the urge to wrap his arm around her waist and pull her into his side.

They weren't together, and he wasn't even her *pretend* boyfriend yet.

When did she want him to start pretending? Won't her family and the wedding guests be suspicious if she suddenly shows up to the wedding with a boyfriend they haven't met or heard anything about?

Should he start pretending now?

"Have they been dancing together long?" she asked, turning to face him and breaking him from the never-ending carousel of confusing thoughts spinning through his brain.

He shook his head, not bothering to watch Violet and Adam but instead giving the woman in front of him his undivided attention. "No, not very long actually. Only since last spring."

Her unique gray eyes flared open. "You'd think they've been dancing together for years the way they move so seamlessly." Her throat bobbed on a swallow, and she turned her head back to watch their instructors float around the room. "I'd love to get to that point with a person, where it's no longer work, where your bodies just come together and do what they do best."

Do what they do best.

Was that an innuendo?

Normally, Mason was good at reading a woman's cues. He knew whether they were interested in him in a matter of minutes. The flush of their cheeks, the batting of their lashes, the flare of the nostrils, hair tucked behind the ear in a flirty way. And he'd certainly been on the receiving end of a fair few fuck-me eyes, particularly working at the bar. But he couldn't get a read on Lowenna. Was she interested in him as more than just a date for hire, or was it all in his head?

Fuck, not even in high school or junior high had a woman confused him or frazzled him this much.

Nor has a woman beguiled you this much either.

"Come on, you two," Violet encouraged, she and Adam dancing right past them. "Start dancing again."

Mason slyly slid his sweaty palms over his pants before reaching for her hand. "Shall we?"

Her smile could have lit up a thousand cities. She placed her hand in his and stepped into his space, bringing her spicy, chocolaty scent with her. "We shall."

Mason began to lead them around the room, taking extra care not to step on her bright red painted toes. Even her feet were hot, and he'd never been a big foot guy. But if he were, Lowenna's would be in the spank bank for sure.

She cleared her throat, which caused him to lift his head up from where he'd been staring down between their bodies, focused on their feet and his not stepping on hers.

"You okay?" she asked, concern in her eyes and a half smile curving up on her lips.

He nodded and grunted, tugging her just a touch closer to him. He didn't miss the flare of her nostrils when her breasts knocked his chest. Was that a sign?

"Just don't want to step on your feet," he said, trying to keep the step counts in his head while talking.

She smiled again, and her hand on his shoulder squeezed. "I have faith we'll figure this out. It's only day one, right?" Hope glimmered back at him in her silver-gray orbs.

Only day one.

"We've got five weeks and nine more dance lessons before the wedding. That's loads of time to sort out your two left feet." Her giggle made his cock jump, and he subtly inched his pelvis away from her in case she felt it. Or in case his cock had some harebrained idea to suddenly join the dance party.

"Five weeks," he muttered. "Nine more dance lessons."

"Ouch."

Fuck.

Their steps faltered and their dancing stopped when he stepped on her toe.

"Sorry," he murmured, wincing at the pained expression on her face.

"It's okay."

Letting out an exhale and cursing his awkwardness, he led them off, back into the dance steps, counting the steps once again in his head.

He had a month, give or take, to prove to Lowenna that he could be more than just a date for hire. More than just arm candy to one-up her sister and prove to her ex-husband she didn't need him.

He had a month to woo her.

He had a month to make her his date for Valentine's for real, with zero strings attached, zero contract, and zero money exchanging hands.

Hell, he had a month to get her to fall in love with him, because over the past few weeks watching her interview those men, Mason had damn near fallen in love with her, and black and blue toes or not, no way was he letting her go.

5

THEY WERE two weeks into their *arrangement.* Two weeks into dance lessons. Two weeks into Mason stepping on Lowenna's toes and then apologizing profusely. Two weeks of Mason bringing Willow to dance lessons and letting Lowenna hold her. And each and every time she got to take that baby in her arms, it made it harder to let her go.

It was a rainy and blustery Thursday afternoon and Lowenna was busy doing up an order for the Windward Pacific Hotel Seattle. They commissioned her to make decadent mixed berries and mascarpone ganache bonbons with cocoa butter colors for their luxury suites. It was a huge boon to get such an account, and she was determined to get the order out on time and wow the pants off the hotel manager.

Who knew, maybe the hotel would then commission her to do chocolates for all their rooms. And then their gift shop and maybe even their kitchen. A contract like that, and she might be able to afford a bigger shop space and more staff. Right now, it was just her, Tricia, Pablo, Xi and David. But besides Lowenna, the others only worked part-time. She was already feeling the need for more employees, particularly with the high demand around Valentine's Day, but she wasn't even a year into running the shop. She couldn't extend herself any more than she already was.

"You need more sheet trays?" asked Tricia, her trusty second-in-command, wandering out from the storage room, her arms loaded with various supplies.

Lowenna used the back of her wrist to wipe a strand of hair from out of her eyes. "Yes, please. I think maybe two or three more will do it." She was almost done with the hotel's order, and then she had to get working on more chocolates for their display case. By the time she opened the doors to the shop at nine o'clock that morning, there was already a line down the block.

Who knew her chai ganache bonbons with caramel filling would be such a big hit? They'd sold out that one chocolate flavor before nine fifteen and then proceeded to sell out of another four varieties before ten o'clock. Another fan favorite was apparently the lemon ganache in a cocoa pod mold. Tricia had done an incredible job with the airbrushing on them, and their bright yellow and green coloring was truly eye-catching.

But it was their London Fog petite gateaus that were bringing in the social media influencers and the bloggers. They could not keep those decadent confections in stock. One guy had come and bought twenty-five that morning, all to the moans and protestations of a long line behind him.

The *bing-bong* of the front door chimed just as she was pulling off her latex gloves. Tricia would take the filled molds to the cooler while Lowenna handled the customers. She always loved meeting new people who she could sell more of her chocolate to.

Tucking that annoying lock of hair behind her ear, she turned the corner out into the shop only to come face to face with two faces she was growing very happy to see. He was busy stomping his wet boots and shaking the drops from his jacket while she seemed snug as a bug, with big, gorgeous blue eyes.

"Well, hello there." She grinned, making her way out from behind the counter to stand directly in front of Mason, who was wearing a very heavily bundled-up Willow in the baby carrier. Lowenna ran the back of her finger over Willow's rosy cheeks. The baby blinked and smiled a gummy grin.

Her heart constricted at the same time the hollow in her belly ached.

"How's your day going?" Mason asked, bouncing Willow and mindlessly patting her butt.

"Had a line halfway down the block this morning, so it's going pretty well. Somebody with some influence must have tried one of my chai and caramel ganache bonbons because those puppies sold out within minutes."

His brows rose. "And in this weather, wow! Gonna have to let me sample one of those one day."

All smiles because she was discussing chocolate and getting to ogle a baby—and that baby's handsome father— she bounced on her toes. "I might have a fresh batch hidden somewhere. Let me go check."

Why was Mason visiting her shop?

In the past two weeks, they'd only gotten together on their dance lesson nights. She'd stopped going to the Prime Sports Bar and Grill—which she missed—and he hadn't once popped into her shop. Not that she expected him to, but ...

Not letting her mind get too caught up in the mystery of her sexy dynamite date for hire, she ducked into the cooler, where a humming Tricia was busy reorganizing the racks of chocolate molds. "That new batch of chai caramels ready yet?"

Tricia nodded. "Should be." With latex-glove-covered hands, she reached up on her tiptoes and grabbed a sheet tray loaded with plastic chocolate molds. "Customer?"

Lowenna grabbed one mold that held a dozen chocolates and shook her head. "Not quite." Then she left the cooler, unable to stop herself from bringing the mold up to her nose to give it a big whiff. Mmm. The chai caramel ones were some of her favorites too.

"Fresh from the cooler," she sang, turning the corner once more, not surprised that her breath caught at the sight of Mason murmuring to Willow and then kissing her forehead.

Was there anything sexier than a man acting all sweet and fatherly with a baby?

Nope.

She could honestly say there wasn't.

Mason lifted his gaze to hers, pinning those dark blue eyes on her in a way that made everything girly inside her tingle. "Can't wait." His smile held just a touch of mischief, and before she could stop herself, her tongue darted out and slid across her bottom lip, her pulse kicking up a beat as Mason's eyes followed. She wanted to taste one of her chocolates on his smile. He would only enhance the flavor, if not make it downright irresistible. Downright deadly.

With her finger beneath the mold, she carefully popped a couple of the chocolates free, holding the whole mold out for him to pick one. His arm extended forward and big, long, capable fingers reached out, and picked one up. He put it to his lips, smiling before he took a bite.

That's when she realized she was holding her breath.

Just as he took a bite, sinking straight, white teeth into her heavenly creation, she released the oxygen from her lungs and willed her heart to stop beating so wildly.

Was he doing that to her on purpose? Eating her chocolate like it was ... *something* else? With his tongue, he caught the caramel that oozed out, and she sucked in a sharp breath.

"Mmm," he hummed. "This is amazing. No wonder you had customers lined up around the block." He popped the rest of the chocolate into his mouth, licking his lips before chewing and swallowing.

She'd been wondering how the man could get any more irresistible, coming in all wet and bright-eyed with a baby strapped to his chest, and he'd somehow managed to go and do it by eating one of her chocolates and loving it.

"You want another one?" she asked, hoping for an encore.

His eyes and nostrils flared, and he nodded. "Yes, please." He took another chocolate, and he glanced at it between his fingers, his gaze filled with intense craving. "How do you get them so shiny? They look like little half-marbles. Not only tasty but also beautiful."

She'd love it if a man could describe her in such a way. Not only tasty but also beautiful.

Now she was jealous of her chocolate. Oh, dear.

Collecting her wandering thoughts before they headed into a territory that was too dangerous for them to ever get out of, she blinked a couple of times, then took a deep, calming breath—not that it did much good. "You brush the mold with food-grade alcohol first. Gives them a really nice sheen when you pop them out."

He smiled and nodded in appreciation, this time popping the entire thing into his mouth. "I didn't come here for freebies," he said between chews. "Just so you know. Willow and I came here with the best of intentions—and also because she wanted to say hi. Asks about you all the time. Misses you like crazy when you're not around." His smile made Lowenna's panties instantly grow damp, and the gasp behind them told her that Tricia had emerged from the cooler and found Mason just as handsome as Lowenna did.

Was Mason using Willow as a cover-up for himself? Did he miss her?

She certainly missed him.

"She does, does she?" She rested her hand on Willow's back. "Have you been asking about me, sweet pea? Well, I miss you too." She leaned in and pecked Willow on the side of the head.

"We also came here to extend an invitation your way," Mason continued, his eyebrows lifting when she offered him another chocolate. He took one and tossed it into his mouth before speaking. "Violet's baby shower is this weekend, and Tori, her friend and a buddy of mine's girlfriend, asked me to pass along the information to you, see if you'd like to go."

Over the past few weeks, she did feel as though she and Violet had reached a new level of friendship in their relationship. She didn't feel like they were simply dance teacher and pupil anymore. She really was one of the nicest and sweetest people Lowenna had ever met, and she hoped the two could remain friends when their dance lessons were over.

"Why are you trying to get me to become friends with your friends' significant others?" she asked, cocking one eyebrow before she grabbed one of her own chocolates and tossed it into her mouth.

He lifted his shoulder. "Go, don't go. It doesn't matter to me. But I think that you could find some really great friendships with these women. And a few of them will be at the wedding, so it might be nice to see some friendly faces."

She slowed down her chewing and narrowed her brows. "Who's going to be there?"

"Tori, for one. She's helping Mitch with photography. Aurora for another. She works with your douche of an ex-husband—hates him—but she's going anyway. And then Paige is catering it and doing the cake, and I think Emmett said that Zara is your sister's florist, though I'm not sure she will be at the wedding, but who knows. And I don't know if Iz will be at the wedding, but she'll definitely be at the baby shower, and she's an absolute sweetheart. I think the two of you would really hit it off."

"And these are all the significant others of your friends?"

Did that mean he thought of her as *his* significant other?

He nodded, seemingly oblivious to where her mind had gone. "Yep. We're The Single Dads of Seattle, though over half are no longer single, but whatever." An idea of sorts seemed to have sprung into his head, and his eyes lit up. "Hey, you gals could start your own club. I think you're all entrepreneurs. You could start The Entrepreneurs Club for Women."

"Or Bitches in Business," Tricia offered from behind them.

Mason held up his hands in innocence. "I didn't suggest that one."

Lowenna chuckled softly. "All entrepreneurs, huh?"

He nodded. "Yeah, and the baby shower is being held at The Rage Room. Have you heard of it?"

Heard of it? She had only two more visits until she got her tenth visit free.

After her sister made her ludicrous request for the wedding, Lowenna found herself overcome with a white-hot, bubbling fury she had no way of expelling. Until a flyer for The Rage Room was slipped into her shop mail slot. She didn't just walk there, she ran. Luna the owner barely had the door unlocked before Lowenna was shoving cold, hard cash at the woman and asking for a baseball bat.

She'd gone three times that first week. And it had helped a lot.

There was something so utterly satisfying in the destruction of things. Taking a baseball bat to an old photocopier or a printer. Using a tire iron on a row of vases.

She'd even shown up with something of her own to demolish.

The *save the date* for Doneen and Brody's wedding. Luna was kind enough to put it in a hideous mosaic picture frame for her. Then Lowenna took the golf club and smashed that frame and hacked up their save the date until there was nothing left but shards of glass and tile and two stupid smiling faces with no eyes.

Oh, boy, had that been satisfying.

"I take it you've been once or twice," Mason asked, the twinkle in his eyes saying he'd just read her thoughts.

She shrugged and averted her gaze. "Once or twice."

He snorted. "Anyway, it's this Saturday at seven o'clock. Violet says she'd really like you there, but you two can talk more tonight at dance."

Right!

Tonight!

She was seeing him again tonight.

"My parents are taking Willow tonight, so she won't be at practice. That's another reason why we stopped in, so you could see her, as she'll be standing you up due to a date with the grandparents."

Her heart did a little somersault. He was such a thoughtful man. She really would have been disappointed to miss out on seeing Willow tonight. How did he already know her so well?

"Want me to pick you up?" he asked, his hand sneaking out, his mouth in a playful smirk as he snagged one more chocolate from the mold.

Another laugh bubbled up from deep in her chest. "Sure, that'd be nice. I'll be working late here tonight, so you can just come get me here."

His smile faded. "Will you have had dinner?" The look he was giving her was almost angry but not quite. She couldn't quite put her finger on it, nor could she put her finger on how it made her feel.

She shook her head. "Probably not. I'll just eat when I get home."

He shook his head. "No. I'll bring food. Thai good?"

Um. Yeah.

She knew nearly right from the start that he was a man who didn't like to be told what to do or given any answer besides *yes*. The authority in his tone and the way his words came out with a bite—it was a demand and not a question.

She liked this alpha side of him.

What the hell?

She liked that he was taking charge and, in taking charge, he was taking care of her.

"I love Thai food," she whispered, leaning in, her voice having just up and vanished.

He smiled once again, causing her to nearly drop the rest of the chocolates in her palm. "All right then. I'll be by at six thirty to pick you up. We'll scarf some food and then go dance it off. Spicy or mild?"

She licked her lips, unable to peel her gaze from his eyes. "Spicy. The hotter the better."

His mouth, oh, that mouth, spread into an even bigger, even sexier smile. "My kind of woman."

Deep breaths. Deep, deep breaths.

He glanced behind him, breaking their eye contact and giving her a moment to collect herself and tell her heartbeat to calm the hell down.

"We better get a move on. Looks like there's a bit of a break in the rain, and I think Willow might be hungry." He pressed his lips to the top of Willow's head, which was covered by a warm-looking knit cap. "What do you think, my little peanut, should we get going?"

Willow simply blinked, then yawned, and then—was that an eye roll from a four-month-old?

Mason snickered. "Sass already. Wow, am I in for a ride with this one. Good thing you're cute."

She tamped down the disappointment in her gut at the news of his departure and instead lifted the chocolate mold higher. "One more for the road?"

That smile was going to be the end of her.

"I'll never say no to *your* chocolate."

Was that an innuendo?

He grabbed one more and popped it into his mouth, his arm reaching out again and landing on her elbow, giving it a squeeze she felt all the way down to her toes. "We'll see you tonight."

Lowenna bit her lip and nodded. "Tonight."

"And I promise not to step on your toes ... " His face scrunched up. "As much."

She started to laugh, fully aware of his hand still gripping her elbow.

When she dropped her head again and opened her eyes, he was staring at her.

She couldn't place his expression, but nevertheless it unnerved her.

Did she have chocolate on her face? Spinach from her breakfast omelet in her teeth? Surely, Tricia would have mentioned spinach.

"What?" she finally asked, unable to handle the intensity held in his blue eyes.

He shook his head, shaking free the extreme expression as well. "Nothing, it's just ... you have a great laugh. I want to hear more of it as these weeks go by. All I want to see on Valentine's Day is your gorgeous smile and be able to hear that laugh from across the room."

Heat raced through her veins at the poignancy of his words.

She did have a great laugh. He wasn't the first person to tell her that.

But over the last few years, she'd found very little to laugh —or smile—about.

Until Mason, that is.

The man made her smile more than she had in a long time. She couldn't remember the last time she'd smiled or laughed this much. Maybe when she and Brody were dating, but even then, he'd never been as funny or sweet as Mason. He'd never gone out of his way to make her laugh the way Mason seemed to, particularly when they were dancing—or at least *trying* to dance. Brody had always taken life too seriously, taken his status in society too seriously. He'd been a social climber since the day they met. Maybe that was why he and her sister connected so well. Doneen was all about how the rest of the world saw her, what the rest of the world's opinion of her was. Even though deep down, Doneen was a terrible person, on the outside she looked like the model daughter, model fiancée, model sister. But when the doors were closed, she was an apple rotten to the core.

However, Lowenna knew she was a good person, a good sister, a good daughter, a good neighbor, a good boss, and a good friend. She knew all of that simply by the outpouring of support and love she'd received during one of the hardest times in her life. She'd nearly died, nearly let cancer take her, and the rallying by those closest to her had overwhelmed her, brought her to tears on more than one occasion and shown her just how much she meant to people.

Her sister had not been one of those people. Doneen had never shown up on Lowenna's doorstep in support. Only ridicule. Telling Lowenna how she had brought cancer into their family, made it all about her, stole the attention away from Doneen's birthday and her college graduation. That their parents never came to Seattle from Olympia to see Doneen anymore; it was to help out Lowenna after a round of chemo.

Doneen had called her selfish, wicked and an attention-seeking brat. And yet, all over Doneen's social media were posts about her support for Lowenna and how devastating it was for her to watch her baby sister go through something so wretched.

A shiny red apple, ripe for the picking on the outside, only when you took a bite, she was nothing but bitter and filled with worms and rot.

Even though they lived in the same city, the two were not close. They never had been. Since they were children, Doneen had always treated Lowenna as an inconvenience, as an intruder. She took sibling rivalry to the Nth degree.

When Doneen was old enough to stay home and babysit Lowenna, she used to lock her younger sister beneath the mattress of Doneen's daybed, sit on it and not let Lowenna up until their parents got home. Then she'd threaten to beat Lowenna up if she ever told their parents what she did to her.

Lowenna put up with a lot from Doneen as they grew up because she believed that eventually, maybe her sister would change. That they could one day be friends, allies, instead of the enemies or the rivals Doneen saw them as. And then Doneen stole Lowenna's husband, and that pipe dream exploded like a pipe bomb.

There would never be love between them now. Not ever.

"Lo?"

His hand was still on her elbow, and he gave it a gentle squeeze and tug, shaking her from her thoughts and plots of vengeance.

She blinked up at him and smiled. "Yeah?"

"You okay? You went a little spacey there for a sec."

Concern filled his rugged features in the way of narrowed brows and a pensive frown. "You need to sit down?"

She shook her head again and let her smile grow. "Nope. Just had an idea about a new kind of chocolate is all. I tend to space out when new concoctions pop into my head."

She didn't like lying to him, but she also didn't want to darken the mood with tales from her tortured childhood. He already knew her sister was a monster, that was enough.

His frown faded away, replaced with another panty-soaking smile. "Ah, well, in that case, get back to work. I can't wait to try whatever it was that made you zone out like that." He released her elbow, and she immediately missed his touch, wishing he'd put his hand back and then wrap it around her waist. "I'll see you tonight."

She nodded and swallowed. "Tonight. Right. I look forward to it."

"Me too." Then he was gone. With his baby strapped to his chest and the wind at his back, the sexiest man she'd ever met headed off into the Seattle drizzle.

"You seeing him or something?" Tricia asked.

Lowenna pulled her recipe book out from the pocket of her dark green apron and tossed it onto the stainless-steel table. "Uh ... something."

"Well, if he has a brother or a cousin or something, let me know, because that man is *fine* with a capital *F*."

"He certainly is," she said absentmindedly, thumbing through her recipe book. "Want to grab the food-grade alcohol and polish those molds for me?" she asked, pointing to the tray of round chocolate molds. She was going to mix up a batch of her dark chocolate habanero truffles—another customer favorite.

"Will do," Tricia said with a nod. "What new chocolate were you thinking about just a moment ago? You know I always love to hear your new ideas and what inspired them."

Lowenna rolled her eyes and smiled a lopsided grin at her co-worker. "No freaking clue, but now I've got to come up with something."

Tricia clucked her tongue. "I could watch that man eat chocolate and wear a baby all day long."

Lowenna's exasperated breath lifted the rogue strand of hair that fell over her forehead. Her shoulders slumped, and her mind raced.

I could watch him eat my chocolate while wearing a baby all day long every day for the rest of my life.

6

MASON TURNED off his SUV and opened the door. He knew she'd seen him. His headlights were tough to miss, but he could already tell, simply by the way she moved inside the shop, that something was wrong.

Leaving the takeout on the passenger seat, he locked his vehicle and briskly headed toward the front door of the shop. It would be locked, no doubt, but he tried the door anyway, and to his surprise, it swung open.

"Ready to go?" he asked, the slam of cupboards and her irritated panting and huffing the only sounds in the now quiet and dark chocolate shop.

Her eyes flicked up to his from where she'd been scribbling something in a notebook, and her angry gaze sliced his face. "Just gimme me a minute."

Not bothering to obey the "employees only" sign, he wandered behind the counter until he was standing right next to her. Heat and fury radiated off her petite frame in waves that would have sunk a luxury yacht. Her fingers clenched the ballpoint pen so tightly, her knuckles were white, and the way she raked the pen across the paper, it was only a matter of minutes until she gouged a hole right through.

Without really thinking, he reached out and grabbed the pen, prying it from her death grip and setting it down on the stainless-steel table. A quick glance at the notebook said she was sketching something, but he couldn't quite tell what. He brought her fingers into his and began to massage her knuckles, watching as the circulation returned and they went from white to pink once again. Her eyes had remained fixed on the notebook, but she seemed to mentally shake herself and slowly lifted her head to focus on him.

"Care to share?" he whispered, now massaging her palms with the pads of his thumbs.

When her shoulders slumped and her bottom lip wobbled, it was all he could do not to pull her into his arms and hug her as tight as he could. But when that lone tear finally bubbled over and slipped down her cheek, he could no longer stop himself, and she was in his arms, his nose in her sweet cocoa-scented hair, her cheek against his chest, her body trembling with each devastating sob.

They stood there for a moment as he absorbed her hurt, absorbed her pain and whatever had caused her emotions to become so strong they had damn near destroyed her. Once he could tell she had finally relaxed, her breathing slower, her shoulders no longer iron-tight, he pulled her free from his embrace and held her biceps. "What happened?"

Pink, tear-stained cheeks burned bright, and tired, watery gray eyes stared up at him. But she didn't say anything. Instead, she simply reached into the back pocket of her jeans and pulled out her phone. Her thumb flew across the screen, then she turned it around so he could read. It was a text message.

Change of plans. Instead of just our profiles kissing, can we have our hands clasped as well and a big heart arcing over up, like framing our kissing heads? Also, Brody wants to know if you can do chocolate-covered strawberries tuxedo style for the dessert table. We're thinking like maybe three hundred, enough for at least one per person, but with a few extras. Our caterer said she can do them, but that it'll cost extra and we're already paying like ten grand for the food so ... thanks!!!

Just to make sure he wasn't missing anything, and because he needed to keep his own emotions in check, he re-read it a couple more times before nodding and sliding his gaze back to her.

Her face was like stone, but her cheeks still held the color of fury, and the tremble of her lips said she was not far off from losing it once again. So angry all she could do was cry.

He'd been there.

It was a deep well to crawl out of.

"Tell her *no*," he finally said, his own breath coming out shakily. "You're already doing so much for that wedding. A wedding that shouldn't even be." He grabbed her notebook and held it up. "Is this a sketch of what she wants?"

Lowenna nodded. "Yeah. I don't even know if I can do what she's asking. It's tedious, and that heart frame could crack so easily in transportation, unless I assembled it there. But I don't really want to be assembling things on the wedding day."

Understandable.

"This is her fourth text message in the last two weeks. And every message involves a change or an addition. Something else for free."

"Don't do the strawberries," he said plainly. "Tell her *no*. Tell her you won't have time to get everything done. That she needs to make a choice, just like she made a choice about you being her maid of honor."

The memory of that hurt flashed behind her eyes. He could tell that wound hadn't yet healed over, and he could understand why. Lowenna's sister sounded like a complete bitch. Bridezilla didn't even begin to describe her.

She lifted her phone up once again to search for something with her thumb. Then she turned it to face him. "This one came in about an hour before that last one."

Hey! We're asking people ahead of time to say a little something at the wedding. That way you have time to prepare a speech and don't drink too much beforehand. We don't want any slurred toasts—how tacky. So could you please write up a speech about Brody and me and send it a week before the wedding so I can approve it and make any necessary changes? Thanks!

Mason's lips parted, but his fingers on her biceps tightened. "She wants to pre-approve your speech?"

Lowenna nodded. "She wants me to write one, first of all. Then send it to her for approval before I'm supposed to get up in front of all the guests like I am completely okay with my sister marrying my ex-husband and toast them into the next chapter of their lives with a big, fat smile on my face."

"What are you going to do?"

She blinked a few times before she glanced his way. "I'll come up with something. I always do." She shook herself free of his grasp and grabbed her notebook. "I'll come up with something for the chocolate centerpiece too. It's what I do, and I'll get the strawberries done. We have a machine that does a bunch at once, so it's not like we're doing three hundred strawberries one at a time."

He rubbed her back, the tension between her shoulders tight enough he feared she might spontaneously snap. "You sure you're okay?"

She nodded, closed the book and smiled an even faker smile at him. "Yep. Just needed to get that out. Her text messages always make me see red at first, then I calm down. Or I cry. Or I go to The Rage Room and Luna lets me channel my anger there."

"Love The Rage Room," he said softly.

A gurgle from her belly made both their eyes drift down to her abdomen.

Mason turned around and headed toward the front door. "Dinner is waiting for us. Figured we could just eat in the dance studio parking lot."

She nodded, then shut off the last remaining light and set the alarm. "Sounds good."

He held the door open for her and she walked out, instantly pulling her hood up over her head, as it had once again started to rain. She locked the door then followed him to his Volvo.

He hit the fob for the SUV, and it beeped open. They both hopped in and were on the road. It was only about seven or so blocks to the dance studio, but he certainly didn't want her walking there in this weather. The wind had picked up as well, and he could feel it hit the side of his vehicle, rocking it to and fro like a ship at sea.

A few minutes later, they pulled up to the strip mall that housed not only Benson School of Dance, but also Mitch Benson Photography, The Lilac and Lavender Bistro and The Rage Room. He turned off the ignition but left the radio on.

Lowenna seemed to have calmed down even more on their short drive. They hadn't said anything, but he was okay with that. The woman beside him confused the hell out of him. How could she continue to allow a horrible person like her sister be a part of her life? Not to mention dictate and demand Lowenna do up a bunch of free chocolate for the wedding. Did Lowenna not have a spine?

No, she did. She'd been very upfront and confident when she told him what she was after with all her interviewing and then making sure he knew that she was nobody's charity case. The woman definitely had a spine.

So then why was she putting up with her sister? Why

wasn't she simply walking away and truly living her best life? After everything Doneen had done to Lowenna, had Mason been in her shoes, he'd consider himself an only child and go to great lengths to avoid the fuck out of a toxic person like Doneen.

"You going to just stare out the window and count the raindrops, or are we going to eat?" she asked, her voice shaking him from his thoughts.

He cracked his neck side to side, then nodded. "Sorry, lots on my mind. Hand me that paper bag down there." He pointed toward her feet.

She grabbed the bag and handed it to him, then unbuckled her seatbelt. "Care to share?" she asked, a glint of amusement in her eyes and a more playful smile now tilting one corner of her lips.

He shook his head. "Naw, it's nothing serious."

"Everything okay with Willow?"

Grunting and nodding his reply, he opened the bag and passed her a cardboard container of Gai Pad Med Ma Muang, or cashew chicken. His heart warmed at her affection for his daughter. She really did love Willow, and Willow lit right up whenever Lowenna held her or played with her.

"This smells amazing," she said, thanking him when he passed her a fork. "I'm absolutely starving. I'm glad you convinced me not to wait until after dance class. I probably would have gnawed my own arm off once I got home, or even worse, run next door from my building and bought a slice of pizza from that horrible convenience store."

"Tim's on Tenth?" he asked, opening up his box of extra spicy drunken noodles. "That place has given everyone I know food poisoning with either their hotdogs, pizza or sub sandwiches."

"For me it was the sushi," she said before shoving a forkful of dinner into her mouth. "I'd just moved into the building and was getting the chocolate shop up and running. I was run off my feet and starving, so I ducked downstairs and grabbed a box of California rolls. Then I was praying to the porcelain gods for the next forty-eight hours."

He winced. "Ouch. Yeah, I avoid that place like it's a leper colony. It's so weird that he's still in business. And that's a decent part of town too."

She nodded, her mouth full.

"Years ago, like I'm talking when I was still in high school, I bought a hotdog from him. I still have nightmares from those two days stuck in the bathroom. Even now, when I drive past, I have flashbacks. Pretty sure I have PTSD."

She chuckled, covering her mouth with the back of her hand so that food didn't fly out. "Yep, I hear you." She swallowed. "So thank you for saving me from a most likely untimely demise by tainted pizza. I really do appreciate it."

He reached back into the paper bag and pulled out a couple of juice boxes. "My pleasure. Grape or fruit punch?"

Her smile was sweet. "Fruit punch, please," she said, taking it from him. "I haven't had a juice box in years."

He shrugged. "Me either, but I found them in my fridge at home so I just grabbed them. I usually try to have some on hand for when some of my buddies come over with their kids."

"That's kind of you. I take it a lot of your friends have kids then?"

He nodded. "Most." A country song came on the radio, and he quickly shoveled a forkful of noodles into his mouth before reaching over and turning the dial so the music flooded the small space.

Lowenna's nose wrinkled. "You like country?"

He grinned and continued chewing. "Love it." Then he quickly swallowed and began to sing the words to Tim McGraw's "I Like It, I Love It" until she was giggling at him.

"Well," she started, her smile nearly touching her ears, "at least you have a nice voice."

He tipped an invisible Stetson at her. "Why, thank you, ma'am. Got a nice horse, nice dog and a nice truck too."

She rolled her eyes.

He offered her his takeout box. "You wanna swap? I got extra spicy drunken noodles, and you said earlier that you like spicy."

Nodding, she went to take the box from him and pass her his, but instead, he twirled a bunch of rice noodles around on his fork and told her to open up.

With curiosity and amusement in her eyes, she obliged, and he slipped the fork past her lips. She closed her mouth around the fork and tugged it off with her teeth. Their eyes locked in a way that made all the blood leave his brain and pool between his legs.

He pulled the fork free and watched as her pink tongue darted out and slid across her plump bottom lip.

"Mmm," she hummed before beginning to chew. "That's delicious."

Swallowing, he nodded. "More?" He could feed her and watch her eat like that all night long.

"Please."

In his mind, this was the absolute best kind of date. Two people hanging out, enjoying good food, great music and getting to know each other.

Too bad it wasn't a date. At least not in her eyes. Not yet.

He fed her again, and this time she closed her eyes as she rolled the flavors around on her tongue. Now this was a woman who knew how to enjoy food properly.

He loved it when he found a woman who knew how to eat. How to take pleasure in the simple things in life.

She opened her eyes and grinned at him. "Sorry, I kind of get caught up in my food sometimes. I love food, and there was a time when I couldn't really eat anything because it made me nauseous or I couldn't even keep it down at all, so now that I can eat again—I eat a lot. And I enjoy every minute of it."

He laughed. "Nothing wrong with loving food. Besides, I could watch you eat all day. It's sexy as hell."

Her cheeks pinked up in a really pretty way, and before he could stop himself, he reached forward and cleaned a speck of sauce from the corner of her mouth with his thumb.

Her lips parted, and he felt the warm puffs of her breath against his knuckles, her chest suddenly lifting and falling in a way that made her breasts strain against the buttons of her shirt.

He brought his thumb to his mouth and licked off the sauce.

Lowenna cleared her throat and averted her gaze from his, her cheeks now an even brighter pink. Fuck, she was sexy when she blushed. She was sexy no matter what, but the flush of color in her cheeks just ramped that sexiness up to eleven. He needed to figure out a way to keep her flushed.

"You want some of mine?" she asked, scooping some of her rice, chicken and cashews onto her bamboo fork.

He bobbed his head. "Please."

Now it was her turn to feed him. She cupped her hand beneath the fork as she brought it to his mouth, and just as she got close to his mouth, she opened her mouth.

"I'm a big boy, you know," he said with a chuckle, "I don't need you to show me what to do. I know I need to open my mouth."

She paused with the full fork in front of him. Her eyebrows lifted. "What did I do?"

"You opened your mouth like a parent or guardian might when trying to feed a child. It's instinct, I know, but it was really cute. You're really cute."

Ah, there we go. Even redder cheeks.

God, he could fucking grab her by the back of the neck and crush his mouth to hers right now. He wanted to, wanted her so badly.

But they weren't there yet. He was playing the long game with Lowenna and needed to keep it cool. This was still a business transaction as far as she was concerned, and he didn't want to scare her off with his true feelings.

So instead, he simply opened his mouth like a good boy and made an "ahhh" sound until she put the fork in his mouth, giggling.

"You have a great laugh," he said, pushing the delicious cashew chicken and rice into the side of his cheek to speak. "I know I've said that before, but you really do."

He resisted the urge to brush the back of his hand against her now absolutely crimson cheeks. How red could he get them? They were probably as hot as the sun.

"This is really good too," he said, chewing and swallowing. "You want to switch for a bit?"

She nodded and passed him her container. "Sure. My mouth will be on fire, but it makes me feel alive. I love a good burn on my tongue." She dove into his drunken noodles with a big smile on her face.

"Not so much fun coming out the other end though," he said before he could stop himself.

Her eyes went wide, her jaw slack, and she pivoted her head to look at him.

"Shit, sorry. That came out of my mouth before I could stop it. I realize our relationship has not yet gotten to the toilet humor level. My apologies."

Though she didn't look too offended or put out. And she certainly wasn't regarding him with the look one might give a person they were itching to get away from.

Her lips lifted into a lopsided smile, her gray eyes

sparkling. "You're right about that," she finally said. "But what's life without a bit of risk? We all need to walk on the wild side once in a while, and when the risk is just so damn good, I think I'll take my *comeuppance* tomorrow."

He snorted, relieved that she appreciated his poop joke. "Is that what you call it?"

"Well, no. I call it the *ring of fire*, but I was trying to be polite."

Mason tossed his head back and laughed. "First thing you need to know about me, sweetheart, you don't need to be polite. Or politically correct. I much prefer honesty and candor. Always have, always will. If you want to sling toilet jokes at me all day long, I will be one happy man. Like a pig in shit, really. In fact, I think it'll just make you sexier."

She sank her top teeth into her bottom lip. "Good to know." She slid her gaze away from him and down to her food, but as Mason sat there, continuing to watch her, her eyes once again slid to his. "The same goes for me. Honesty always, please. And I'm A-OK with the potty humor. Life is too short to not laugh about shit. Literally and figuratively."

They both started to laugh when a knock at Mason's driver's side window had them nearly jumping out of their skin.

"You two coming in?" Adam asked, rain dripping from his nose. "You're fifteen minutes late already. Everything okay?"

They'd managed to fog up the windows pretty good, and suddenly that image from *Titanic* with Rose and Jack in the car and the handprint on the window flashed into Mason's mind. He quickly pushed it away and rolled down his window. "Sorry, man. Lost track of time. Good company and good food will do that. We were just having dinner. We'll be right in."

Adam lifted one eyebrow, his gaze drifting over Mason's shoulder to Lowenna for a moment. The woman simply shrugged and smiled before she began to shovel Thai food into her face like it was her first meal in a week.

Adam's eyes fell back to Mason, his grin was amused and knowing. "Okay. See you in a minute." Then, with a laugh, he ran back toward the door to the dance studio, his blue shirt now dark blue from the heavy falling rain.

"Whoops," Lowenna said, taking a sip of her juice box until it made that slurping sound at the bottom. She began to pack up. "Thank you so much for dinner. That hit the spot."

Mason took an enormous bite of his rice and chicken, nodding with a full mouth. "We should do this every dance lesson night if I don't have Willow."

He scooped up the last bite of rice, then tossed the box into the paper bag she held out for him. Her gorgeous smile and bright eyes made his heart do a cartwheel.

"It's a date," she said, as they both grabbed their coats and prepared to open their doors and run out into the rain.

He grinned back at her before they opened their doors. "It's a date."

Then they opened their doors, slammed them, met at the front of his SUV and, grabbed each other's hands as they ran toward the dance studio, the sound of the rain, wind and Seattle traffic no match for their laughter.

7

IT WAS LATE SATURDAY AFTERNOON, and Lowenna was at the shop, busy working on the latest additions and changes to her sister's chocolate sculpture. She was set to leave for Violet's baby shower in roughly an hour but needed any free time she had to test whether Doneen's absurd request would even work.

Xi and David were busy in the back, organizing the cooler and finishing up the lemon ganache bonbons while Lowenna growled and grumbled at the chocolate heart arc that kept falling.

Swearing under her breath for the umpteenth time, she blew the stubborn tendril of hair off her forehead and tried again with the centerpiece. The only reason she was doing all of this shit in the first place was because her mother had guilted her into it.

Yes, *guilted*. As she'd told Mason, Adeline Chambers was an expert guilt tripper.

Cursing under her breath again, she reached for the razor blade on the table and trimmed off a jagged edge of chocolate, her mind wandering back to that conversation with her mother she wished she'd let go to voicemail.

"You know your sister," Lowenna's mother said with a fatigued sigh. "She wants her wedding to be *spectacular*. And since we paid for your wedding, we have to pay for hers."

Lowenna rolled her eyes, grateful that she was on the phone with her mother and she could do any facial expression she wanted without feeling like a bitch.

"Yeah, but it's a little weird don't you think that the two weddings you're paying for have the same groom?"

"That's irrelevant."

"Is it, Mom?"

"Lowenna, please."

"What can I do for you, Mom?" As much as Lowenna loved her parents, their pacifist nature irked her from time to time, particularly when it came to her sister. Since the girls were children, they just let Doneen railroad them until she got her way. And that train just kept on chugging along, taking out Lowenna and anyone else in its path until Queen Doneen got what she wanted. But she was tired of talking about Queen Doneen, she was busy at work and had no time for small talk.

Her mother's sigh told her that Lowenna was not going to like what she was about to hear. "I was wondering if you'd be willing to help us with the guest favors. Your sister's preferences for the wedding are becoming rather pricey, and any bit of financial help would be greatly appreciated. Your father is worried he may have to postpone retirement because of this wedding."

Lowenna took a deep breath. She wasn't even sure she was going to go to the wedding—not that she'd received a save-the-date yet—but the last thing she wanted to do was supply her sister and ex-husband's nuptials with any of her chocolates.

"Mom, I'm not sure that's such a good idea—"

"Please, honey? It would mean a lot to me and your father. And I'm sure it would mean a great deal to your sister, too."

Yeah, right. The only thing that meant a *great deal* to Doneen, *was* Doneen.

"It could also be a way for the two of you to mend fences. I know your relationship has always been strained, maybe this could be a new leaf. Extend an olive branch by doing this for your sister."

I'd rather hit her in the face with an olive branch.

"She's marrying my *ex*-husband, Mom." Lowenna closed her eyes and shook her head. Her parents had no idea that Doneen and Brody had started sleeping together while Brody and Lowenna were still married. They thought that when they announced their relationship was when it started—HA! Not quite.

"Yes, but—"

"Mom, they're getting married on Val-en-tine's Day. Not only is it my birthday, but it also happens to be like the absolute busiest day of the year for the chocolate industry."

"Lowenna, honey, please."

She could practically see her mother building up the tears, preparing for them to dribble down her cheeks like raindrops on a window.

"Your father and I would love it so much if our girls could become close. She's all you'll have in this world when your dad and I finally go. Don't you want to have a relationship with your big sister? I fear I'd remain in purgatory for eternity if I died and my daughters hadn't reconciled."

Oh, for crying out loud.

"If it's the money you're worried about, we could pay you … a small sum. The family discount maybe?"

Jeez, her mom was really laying it on thick this time. Had

she rehearsed this? Was Lowenna's aunt standing in the background holding up cue cards? Her mother certainly seemed to have an answer for everything.

"Just think about, okay, honey? It would mean a lot to your dad and I if you were able to help us out. And who knows? Maybe by the end of it all, you and your sister will be like best friends. I hear she still hasn't picked a maid of honor."

Lowenna fought the urge to laugh. Yeah, right, like she'd ever be her sister's maid of honor. More like *made* of humiliation.

Growling and throwing a big middle finger up toward the sky—because her sister wasn't around to aim it at—she pinched the bridge of her nose and muttered the one word she would regret until the end of time. "Fine."

She refused to admit to anybody, even herself, that after everything Doneen had done to her, she still held on to the tiniest shred of hope that their relationship could improve. She was, after all, her sister. And Lowenna had idolized Doneen growing up. They didn't have to be *best* friends, but her mother's words held truth to them. When their parents died, Doneen was all she would have left.

"Oh, honey, thank you so much," her mother cheered into the phone. "Your father is going to be so happy. Your sister, too. I can't wait to tell them."

And then, like a snowball that just keeps growing after it'd been kicked down a steep, snowy mountainside, that one gesture of goodwill toward her parents, and in the hopes of reconciliation with her sister, was taken by Doneen and expanded and exploited until Lowenna was ready to explode.

She went from doing the guest favors as a favor to her mother and father, to help their bank balance not dip into the red, to doing a goddamn centerpiece for Doneen's dessert table, and now the chocolate covered strawberries.

It was shortly after she agreed to do the guest favors that a save-the-date turned up in her mailbox, complete with an option for a plus one.

That's when Lowenna decided that if she was going to go to the stupid wedding and provide them with a bunch of free chocolate, she was also going to show up with the twenty-first century's version of Fabio on her arms. Minus the hair though, she didn't really want a man with longer, more magnificent hair than her.

Cue the Craigslist ad, and what soon became an endless stream of dick pics and Nigerian princes offering to be her date in exchange for a five-thousand-dollar cash advance on a multi-million-dollar investment deal. She'd just about given up hope until Mason offered up his services. Now, she had a man a trillion times sexier than Brody as her date to the wedding, and he was a doting single father to boot.

Score!

She couldn't wait to see the look on Doneen and Brody's faces when she and Mason stepped out on to the dance floor and showed those no-rhythm losers just how much better her life was now that she was cancer *and* Brody free.

The door dinged, bringing her back to the present, but she ignored it for a moment, her fingers pressing down gently on the arc while the other hand grabbed the can of freeze spray and hit the melted chocolate with it so the chocolate arc would bind instantly to it. She bit down hard on her tongue, hoping to God it stayed in place this time.

"You're awfully rude not acknowledging a customer that comes in," came a familiar, irritating and snotty voice behind her, making Lowenna jump and release the chocolate, causing it to topple over and smash onto the floor.

Growling, she bit down even harder on her tongue until she tasted blood, then turned to face her sister.

As always, Doneen was dressed for a day at the office—

even though it was her day off—with black trousers, a silk cream blouse with pearl buttons, impeccable makeup and long, dark brown hair perfectly coiffed like a Stepford wife. Something she shoved in Lowenna's face any chance she got —that Doneen's hair was long and luxurious, and Lowenna was just now pulling off her short, chin-length bob.

Fuck Doneen.

It'd taken forever for Lowenna's hair to grow back, and even longer for it to look even remotely attractive. With the back of her wrist, she tucked that stubborn stray strand behind her ear, wishing she had the balls to put Nair hair removal lotion in her sister's shampoo bottle. Give Doneen a taste of the *bald* life. See how she liked it.

"Isn't that why you have a bell on the door, to alert you of customers?" Doneen went on. "What if I'd actually wanted to buy something?" She clucked her tongue. "Really not very professional, Lowly."

Lowenna inhaled deep through her nose, held it in for a moment, then released it through her mouth. She hated Doneen's nickname for her. *Lowly.*

Like seriously, how horrible could you get? She might as well have just called her dirt or shit or flea. It would have had the same affect.

Lowenna lifted her gaze to her sister's light gray eyes. "What can I do for you, Doneen?"

Doneen's smile was anything but genuine as she wandered around the stainless-steel table Lowenna was working on.

She was now in the employees-only section of the shop and had not been invited back.

What gave her the right?

The same "right" she thought she had when she slept with your husband. The Doneen Chambers sense of entitlement.

"I came to see how things are going on the chocolate

feature. I've spent the entire day going around to all the services I've hired for the wedding to check in face-to-face on their progress and make sure we're all on the same page. Just came from the florist." She rolled her eyes. "Rude woman, but she's the best in the city by far. Apparently, white tulips are not in season." She huffed. "Who cares? Make it happen. It's fucking winter, and yet there are still flowers in her shop, yet not in the gardens. Why are tulips any different?"

Lowenna shook her head and shrugged. "I know nothing of flowers, but hasn't that place been in business for years? She probably knows what she's talking about."

Doneen snorted. "Doubt it." She clicked her black ankle boots around the table, her eyes squeezing into thin slits as she inspected the enormous chocolate piece Lowenna was working on. "What happened here?" she asked, pointing to the spot where Lowenna had been trying to adhere the thin arc to the base of the structure. "I don't like how messy that looks."

"You snuck up behind me, startled me, and I let go of the chocolate before it dried," Lowenna said plainly. "I hadn't held it long enough for the chocolate to adhere."

Her sister snorted. "So jumpy. Well, I don't want to see that mess on my wedding day. Remember, we *are* being featured on the *Washington Weddings* blog, and I'll probably mention who did my chocolates. I'm sure you'll see a *huge* boost in sales after that. That blog and online magazine are really big." She puffed up her chest and pushed her nose into the air. "I'm going to be famous."

Lowenna was forced to turn her head, then her whole body away from her sister so that Doneen didn't catch the eye roll or sneer.

"I mean, I'm already *kind* of famous. What with all my Instagram and Facebook followers. I'm still trying to build my brand as an influencer, but working a full-time job in PR for the city *and* planning a wedding—*the* wedding of the year—is so taxing."

Lowenna poked her finger down her throat, pretending to gag. Could her sister be any more pretentious?

Did she want to know the answer to that?

"Anyway, I just came by to check in. I'd like your speech by next week, please. So I have time to go over it, make corrections and all of that. Don't want anything last minute or to get overlooked."

Lowenna turned back to face her sister, flashing an enormous fake smile. "Of course not. I've already started working on it. You will have it by its due date."

"Good. I'd also like to know what you plan to wear to the wedding. It is black tie and upscale. We're expecting everyone in floor-length gowns."

Did Mason have a tuxedo?

She nodded at her sister. "I'll send you a photo of my dress in the coming weeks."

"The same with your dress for the rehearsal dinner."

Why?

More importantly, should she ask Mason to go to that with her? Wouldn't people wonder why he was at the wedding but not the dinner beforehand? She could offer him more money, ask for the extended full boyfriend experience. Would he go for it?

Snap, snap!

"Earth to Lowly," Doneen said, snapping her fingers in front of Lowenna's face.

Lowenna blinked and pushed the corners of her mouth up into a fatally saccharine smile. "Sorry, just mentally going through my closet to figure out what I can wear to the rehearsal dinner."

Doneen squinted, and her brows tightened into a quizzical V shape. "If you say so," she said slowly. "Just make sure you wear something nice. We're going for *classy,* not *trashy.*"

Right. Because a sister who sleeps with her dying sister's husband is the definition of *classy.*

Lowenna's fake smile grew even bigger, and she offered an enthusiastic double thumbs-up to emphasize her agreement. "Right. Got it. Classy, not trashy. I'll see what I can do."

Doneen let her harpy gaze slide around the kitchen. It landed on a tray of key lime white chocolate bonbons that Lowenna needed to add to assorted boxes. She wandered over to the adjacent table and without even asking, picked up a chocolate and popped it into her mouth.

Her eyes widened as she chewed, the first smile of her visit faintly tilting her lips. Then she walked over to the garbage can next to the sink and spat the masticated bonbon into the bin before reaching for a napkin and wiping at her mouth.

What the fuck?

"Calories," she said plainly, clicking her boots back over to stand in front of Lowenna. "Need to make sure I look stellar in my dress. And chocolate is *not* the way to go about it." Her eyes drifted down Lowenna and another smile, this time sinister as could be, curled her mouth. "It's all about self-control and priorities ... you know?"

Lowenna nodded. "Yep. Priorities, got it." She took a deep breath, tucked that infernal stray lock of her hair behind her ear—not that it would stay there—and then showed Doneen her back. "I need to get to work. I have a baby shower to go to tonight, and I want to finish up on your chocolate feature before I go."

"Whose baby? Who do you know that's pregnant?" Doneen's tone was as accusatory as it was curious. As if what she really wanted to say was *"You have friends that I don't know? You have friends? You've been invited somewhere?"*

Lowenna gritted her teeth. "A friend."

"It must be so hard for you," her sister replied, leaving the rest of it hanging, because she knew Lowenna knew exactly what she was referring to. "Aren't you just going to be inflicting unnecessary pain on yourself by going and seeing this glowing pregnant woman, knowing you'll never have that?"

Lowenna squeezed her eyes shut and counted to ten.

One ...

Don't punch your sister in the face.

Two ... three ... four ... five ... six.

"I mean, can't you just *send* a gift and save yourself the inevitable heartache?"

Seven ... eight ... nine ... ten.

Slowly, she opened her eyes and turned to face her sister, using every ounce of restraint she had to not grab the nearest rolling pin and club her sister over the head with it. Instead, she smiled. "I'll be fine, Doneen. Really. I appreciate your concern though. Babies are everywhere. I can't hide from them. The same goes for pregnant women. And just because I can't *carry* my own baby doesn't mean that I couldn't one day still be a mother."

She blew out a long, slow breath from a thin gap between her lips, hoping that steam hadn't started to seep from her ears.

Doneen's eyes turned hard for a brief moment before they narrowed and she tilted her head to the side. "Fair enough, I suppose. I don't know if I'd want to do that personally. Adopt. But to each their own, I guess. I'm looking forward to carrying Brody's baby."

And there was the red-hot poker directly into Lowenna's heart.

"And I'm sure you'll make beautiful babies," she said,

fighting to get each word out past the lump in her throat, the pain in her chest and the sting of tears in her eyes.

Her sister was being cruel for no other reason than to hurt Lowenna.

Why?

Lowenna glanced above the door at the clock. She had just shy of an hour before she needed to get ready for the baby shower.

Her sister needed to go.

Straight to hell.

"I'll send you what you need within the week, Doneen," she said, unable to keep all the bitterness from her tone. "But I really need to get to work. I have a lot to do before we close up shop."

Doneen's face pinched tight, causing her nose to turn up and wrinkle in a way that always made her look like a bit of a shrew. She'd had a rhinoplasty a few years ago, claiming it was for a deviated septum when they all knew it was to eliminate the bump on her nose and narrow it. Only Lowenna had never really cared for the finished product. It was too thin and turned up in a weird way at the front. But unlike her sister, who had no problem telling Lowenna when she couldn't pull something off—like her pixie cut or bob—she kept her mouth shut about her sister's botched nose job.

Her eyes flicked from her sister to the front door. "Don't you have somewhere else to be? Like touching base with the DJ or wedding planner or something?"

Ruling over the demons in the fiery pits of hell?

Finally, it looked like her sister got the hint, and she nodded. "Yes, I do. I have to go and see the DJ and discuss the music. I need to add to the *Do Not Play* list. Even if people request it, he is not allowed to play it."

Well, now, as much as she wanted her sister to get the

fuck out of here, Lowenna was also curious. "Like what songs?" she asked.

"'Who Let the Dogs Out?' 'Foxtrot Uniform Charlie Kilo,' 'The Bad Touch.' Pretty much anything by the Bloodhound Gang. No rap. Very little hip-hop. We're going for classy, remember. Dancing is great, but grinding and getting disgusting on the dance floor is not. No 'Macarena.' No 'Chicken Dance.' Nothing stupid."

So lame, boring and stuffy.

Lowenna simply nodded. "Gotcha."

Doneen tucked her purse beneath her arm and tapped her French manicured nails on the stainless-steel table. "All right, well, I'm off. Send me your speech and make sure that mess on the chocolate feature is tidy by the big day."

Lowenna smiled like she did when she was dealing with a pain-in-the-ass customer—because at least they were paying her—before she spoke. "I'll get right on it." Then she watched her big sister leave her chocolate shop and head down the sidewalk toward her car. Only when she knew Doneen was out of sight and out of earshot did she throw her head back and let out the mother of all screams.

She needed The Rage Room, and she needed it BAD!

8

THE CLOUDS HAD OPENED up and let loose, emptying everything they had into the downtown core of Seattle until the gutters struggled to keep up and water pooled into ankle-deep puddles in the streets.

It was days like these that Lowenna wished she hadn't sold her car to help afford the equipment she needed to start her chocolate shop. Most days she didn't mind. She lived close enough to work that she walked and got her exercise lugging groceries home from the market in Pike Place. If she needed to get anywhere far, she hired an Uber or rented a car using one of those car-share apps.

But on days like today, she wished she had a vehicle to hide in for the eight-block drive to The Rage Room, rather than run in her soaked boots through the puddles, hiding beneath the eaves of closed-up shops when she could.

It was dark out now, but the streetlights and glaring headlights from the ample evening traffic lent enough of a glow to the night that she could see every drop of rain falling in front of her.

The overhead sign for The Rage Room was just a few

yards away. She clutched the gift bag and her purse tighter beneath her arm under her coat and picked up the pace. Not that she could really get any wetter, but she needed to smash things, and she needed to smash them now. After her sister's impromptu and unwelcome visit, she'd hardly been able to concentrate on what she needed to do, let alone keep her hand steady enough for the chocolate to adhere properly. In the end, she simply gave up and finished helping Xi with the pistachio macaroons.

Heaving open the door a couple of moments later, she stepped inside the warm entryway in front of the desk. She shook herself clean of the raindrops from her coat before removing it and hanging it up on one of the coat hooks.

"Hey, stranger!" Luna, the owner, greeted her, coming out from the back room behind the front desk. "How goes it?"

Lowenna wiped the damp hair off her face and glanced up at the pink-haired, tattooed beauty who ran the shop. "It's wet, and I need to smash some shit, that's how it goes. I'm here for the baby shower. Are they here yet?"

Luna's grin made her already stunning face light up even more. "Yeah, they're in the party room in the back. I think you're the last to arrive." She popped out from behind the counter and led Lowenna down the corridor to the party room. "Tough day at the shop?" She craned her neck around to glance at Lowenna, concern in her light blue eyes, while the double hoops in her nostril wiggled when she scrunched her nose.

Lowenna rolled her eyes. "You could say that." Then she remembered the small token for her host and reached into her purse. "Here. For your, uh … exemplary service, as well as your discretion." She handed Luna a small box of mixed bonbons and macaroons. "I appreciate you photocopying that save the date and always having it in a frame for me when I come."

Luna's knowing smile stretched across her face as she stopped in front of an already open door with voices spilling out. "We always want to go above and beyond for our customers. I have files of photos for a lot of people, not just you. And if what you've said about those two is even remotely true, they're getting off easy with you just smashing their photo."

Lowenna's gaze slid to the side and her lips twisted.

Luna chuckled. "I hold grudges, too. Don't worry. The party's in here."

Lowenna stepped through the door to find a few women all smiling and laughing, sitting on couches. All of them—except for Violet—held wineglasses.

"You came!" Violet said from one corner of the couch. "I'd get up to hug you, but I'm a whale and, well, I'm not going to."

Lowenna chuckled as she made her way across the room and bent down to hug Violet where she sat. "I wouldn't dream of making the mama-to-be stand up any more than she has to. You're not a whale, by the way. Nothing more than a basketball beneath your shirt, I swear. How are you feeling?"

"Fat, sore and tired," Violet said bluntly. Lowenna pulled away, still laughing. "It'll all be over soon."

Violet took a sip of what looked and smelled like sparkling apple juice and rolled her eyes.

"And then the *real* work begins," one woman with curly dark hair past her shoulders said with a laugh. She thrust her hand toward Lowenna. "Paige McPherson. Violet's having my ex-husband's baby."

Lowenna shook the woman's hand. "Right. Mason filled me in on this wild dynamic. And you're dating Violet's brother? Is that right?"

Paige took a sip of her wine, her light brown eyes dancing with mirth. "Yep. Mitch. Good memory."

"And you're also catering the wedding," Lowenna went on.

Paige's smile shrank. "I know she's your sister, but I've also heard that your relationship isn't that great. Is she always like this, or is it just the bridezilla mentality?"

Lowenna sighed at the same time she accepted a glass of wine from one of the other women. "She's always like this, I'm afraid. I'm sorry if she's been rude or unkind in any way. She's not a representation of the rest of our family, I swear. The rest of us are actually quite nice."

Paige laughed. "Anytime she pisses me off, I just pull up her invoice, and those zeroes behind the one calm me right down."

Laughter flitted around the baby-themed decorated room.

"And I'm Tori." Another woman squeezed her way onto the couch and held out her hand. She was gorgeous from top to toe with dark brown hair in a demure ponytail behind her and bright blue eyes. "We're all so glad you could come."

Lowenna shook her hand. "You're helping Mitch with the photography?"

Tori nodded. "That's right."

A woman who looked quite similar to Tori but was just a touch shorter and had lighter blue eyes brought over a plate of mini-doughnuts. "I'm Isobel, Tori's sister, and thankfully, I don't have to deal with your sister at all. I just get to hear about her from all these unfortunate souls. Doughnut? Paige made them."

Lowenna took one and thanked her, glancing around at all the other women in the room who had lasered their eyes in on her—the newcomer. "I do want to apologize for any stress or frustration my sister and/or Brody have caused any of you. She really is the worst, and I am not immune to her cruelty. She was in my shop this afternoon making demands and changes. Wants me to submit my speech for approval before-hand and send her pictures of what I plan to wear to the wedding and the rehearsal dinner so she can approve or veto."

Every eye in the room went bigger than the dinner plates they were soon going to smash, and mouths dropped open in shock.

"You're fucking kidding," blurted one woman with long ash-blonde hair and brown eyes. She was sitting closest to the food table and had three mini-doughnuts on her ring finger. "I know Brody, and he's a tool, but just wow!" She shook her head. "I'm Aurora, by the way, and I work with your asshole of an ex-husband." She gave a wave before pulling one mini-doughnut off her finger with her teeth.

"And I'm your sister's florist and not at all immune to her ridiculous requests either," said a woman with a bob just a touch longer than Lowenna's and a sophisticated look about her. "Haven't met one like her in a long while. Makes me want to tack on a couple hundred bucks to her bill just for the emotional torture."

Lowenna winced. "I'm really sorry, guys."

Heads shook.

"Not your fault," the florist said. "It takes all kinds to make the world go 'round. I am spending a significant amount more at the liquor store these days though." She chuckled, and her sapphire-blue eyes glimmered bright with amuse-ment. "I'm Zara."

Lowenna nodded. "Lowenna, nice to meet you"—her eyes darted to each woman—"to meet *all* of you." She frowned and stared down into her wineglass. "I'm going to guess you've all heard about me though?"

She lifted her gaze back up to them.

Heads bobbed.

"Sure have," Tori said. "The guys say they don't talk at

poker night, but they do. And then they come home and talk to us."

Aurora and Zara nodded. Violet went "mhmm" and Paige and Isobel said "yup" in unison.

"We're sorry for all that your sister and ex-husband have put you through," Zara said, her eyes filling with that look Lowenna despised—pity. "Especially when you were ... "

Lowenna quickly shook her head. "It's okay. Thank you." She plastered on the biggest smile she could before taking a sip of her wine. "It's a party. The last thing I want to do is talk about my sister, my ex or cancer. Let's talk about babies and smashing stuff." She reached beneath her arm and pulled out a semi-crumpled but perfectly dry gift bag. "Where are we putting the presents?"

Tori took it from her. "I can put that with others," she said, standing up and walking over to the gift table.

Lowenna thanked her. "I also brought chocolate, if anyone is interested?" She dug into her purse, grateful that she hadn't let her sister's nasty comment a few months ago sway her into ditching the giant messenger bag she loved dearly and going with a sleek clutch as Doneen had suggested. Her messenger bag just held so much. It was so practical.

"Wine, cheese and chocolate," Violet said. "The way to most women's hearts. And in a few weeks, I'm going to be drinking *all* the wine again."

Lowenna retrieved the box of truffles and bonbons she'd brought with her and passed it to the guest of honor first. "Well, I'm not a cheesemonger or a vintner, but I am a chocolatier, so hopefully that's enough to keep me in your good graces."

Violet opened up the box, her green eyes filling with hunger at the same time her tongue darted out and slid across her lips. "Absolutely," she said, grabbing one of the pear, cinnamon and caramel bonbons from the box.

The mama-to-be popped the treat into her mouth, and Lowenna could practically feel the woman's taste buds come alive, her face was so animated and joyful.

It always made Lowenna feel like she was floating when she watched a person eat and enjoy her chocolate or confections.

They were her passion.

Her blood, sweat and tears.

Her babies.

And each and every day she sent those babies out into the world in the hopes that the world would love them. In the hopes that the world would embrace them and make all her struggles, her hard work and sleepless nights not suffered in vain.

Thankfully, the world usually did. The world usually loved her babies, loved her chocolates, her creations just as much as she did. And it always made her float.

Phew.

"These are incredible," Violet said, grabbing two more from the box before she passed them to Paige beside her. "You two should collaborate. Might win a Nobel Prize or a Michelin star or James Beard or something."

Paige grabbed one of the habanero truffles from the box and popped it into her mouth. Her nostrils flared as the heat hit her. "Wow. That's some fire." Nodding, she grabbed a couple more chocolates before letting the box make its round through the other guests. "Yes, we should definitely talk. The business space next to my bistro is for rent. You should move in there. More room, and we could build a door between our shops. Chocolate has never been my forte. Too finicky for my liking."

Lowenna grinned. "I like finicky. Yes, it can be frustrating, but when your vision finally comes to life, it's ... "

"Orgasmic?" the woman who had introduced herself as Isobel piped up, popping one of the goat's milk caramels into her mouth. "I feel the same way when I produce a slam-dunk graphic, particularly if the customer goes ape over it."

Paige pointed at her and then touched her nose. "I definitely went *ape* over the logo you made for me. It was perfect."

Isobel beamed, continuing to chew. Her face lit up, and she pinned her blue-eyed gaze on Lowenna. "Holy fuck, that's good. Is that goat's milk and caramel?"

Lowenna nodded. "It is. It's a fan favorite. One of my favorites too."

Isobel shut her eyes and sat back against the couch, chewing slowly. "Guys, I think I might actually have a mini-climax here. Be warned. Things might get a bit weird in a sec."

The rest of the women in the room lunged forward and grabbed chocolates from the box. All of them then sat back against their seat backs and shut their eyes.

Silence filled the room. Followed by low moans of delight.

It took no time at all for Lowenna to figure out she really liked these women. She already knew and really liked Violet. And the others were just as sweet, sassy and sarcastic.

"Yeah ... " Zara said, finally breaking the quiet. "Orgasmic."

"Everything okay in here?" Luna poked her head around the corner into the room. "It suddenly grew really quiet." A petite blonde woman was behind her, her sky-blue eyes full of curiosity.

Slowly, eyes around the party room opened, serene smiles still glued to all the women's faces. Lowenna loved that her chocolate had that effect on people. She would never grow tired of watching people eat her creations.

"We're doing just great," Violet said with a smile. "Just enjoying some chocolate."

A knowing grin slid across Luna's face. "Ah, gotcha. I get the same way when I eat anything from Wicked Sister."

Lowenna's face grew warm, and her heart fluttered.

"Sarah?" Violet asked, her eyes drifting over Luna's shoulder to the woman behind her. "Is that you?"

The blonde woman stepped out from behind Luna and made her way into the party room. "Hey Violet. Great to see you, and congratulations on the baby. That's fabulous news."

The two women embraced, Violet once again not getting up from her spot on the couch.

"I promise that Adam and I will still have something for Art in the Park this year. We've already been working on our new routine. Might not be as long or as wild, but we'll have something."

Sarah's red-painted lips broke into a big grin. "I never doubted you for a second."

"You here to let out some rage?" Violet asked, confusion bunching her brows.

Sarah shook her head and glanced back at Luna, who still hung by the door. "No, uh ... Luna and I ... "

Understanding quickly dawned on all the women's faces.

Violet's green eyes went wide. "Oh!"

"I like to take all the broken dishes and stuff from here and make mosaic art with them," Luna started. "Had a few of my pieces in an art show in November that Sarah was in charge of and, well ... " She shrugged, love glowing in her eyes as she stepped into the party room and looped her arm around Sarah's waist, pulling the blonde woman into her and kissing the side of her head. "For me it was love at first sight.

Sarah here took a bit of convincing. She still thought she was straight." She rolled her eyes and grinned. "Silly woman."

Sarah's fair complexion pinked up quickly. "I'm bi. But Luna won my heart pretty easily. She's just so ... "

The two women could not have been more different. Luna was tall, almost statuesque with a bright shock of short, pink hair, numerous tattoos and piercings, heavy eye makeup and an almost punk-rock clothing style. While Sarah on the other hand was short and curvy with long blonde hair, no tattoos from what Lowenna could see, only one piercing in each ear and subtle makeup. She also dressed quite chic. At the moment she was sporting tailored dress pants and a matching jacket in a flattering navy and white pinstripe, and she had a soft, sky-blue colored silk blouse beneath it.

But love came in all forms, and given the way the two women were looking at each other, Lowenna could tell there was a lot of love between them.

"I'm so happy for you guys," Violet said, grabbing another chocolate from the box. "This is awesome, and Luna, let us all know when you have your next art exhibit. I know I'd definitely love to attend."

Luna tugged Sarah closer into her embrace and nodded. "For sure. Now, are you ladies ready to smash shit?"

A series of *hell yeahs* and *definitelys* echoed around the room.

Paige and Tori helped Violet to her feet, and within moments, all the women were filtering out the door toward the smash rooms. With walls made of transparent acrylic glass, the smash rooms each housed tables and shelves covered in things you could demolish. Plates, vases, lamps, printers, old photocopiers, toasters, fax machines, mugs and bowls, wooden furniture. Anything that could be destroyed using a crowbar or a baseball bat and Luna probably had it in the room. She also had a series of "weapons" lining the wall.

Lowenna usually preferred the aluminum baseball bat, as it packed a good wallop, but sometimes she mixed it up and reached for the tire iron or putting wedge.

She assumed everyone had their preferred weapon that they felt best "let out the rage."

"Now there are seven of you, and I only have eight rooms, and there are other patrons here smashing shit. So what I've done is designate six rooms to your party. Three of you will smash at the same time, then we'll switch, and you can move over to the other three rooms while the first three rooms get cleaned up. Then we'll have the last person"—she glanced at Violet—"I'm assuming the mama-to-be, will want to go apeshit in the last room?"

Violet shrugged. "Sure. I don't have a lot of rage in me right now—or energy for that matter—so the final smash might be lost on me. Maybe we should let Lowenna go first, and then the rest of us go in two sets of three. I think she's got the most rage right now and understandably so."

Lowenna's chest and cheeks grew hot. But she also didn't correct Violet. By the time Doneen had left, Lowenna was ready to take a baseball bat to the entire chocolate feature. It beat taking the bat to her sister's face, which was what she really wanted to do.

Any hopes she may have harbored for a miraculous reconciliation with her big sister were tossed into the trash, just the chocolate her sister had chewed and then spat out.

It'd taken her a bit longer than it should have to come the realization that Doneen and her would never be besties, but now that she had, she was going to let the anger take over. No more being the doormat to keep her sister or parents happy. She was a goddamn cancer survivor, an entrepreneur and good person. She didn't deserve her sister's shit and abuse —nobody did.

Her hands twitched at her sides as the need to grip a

baseball bat or putting wedge coursed through her veins like an electric pulse.

Words and murmurs of agreement flitted through their small group.

"That sounds like a good idea," Aurora said from the back of the group. "Do we have a big picture of Brody we can put in a frame so she can smash his stupid face?" Her laugh was sharp and hard. "I wouldn't mind one of those myself, actually. Bastard made me pick up his dry cleaning for months. As if my plate as a first-year associate wasn't already full as fuck."

Luna grinned, her smoky-eyed gaze falling on Lowenna. "I actually do happen to have their picture. And I have a *working* photocopier." She glanced at the other women. "Would you all like a photo of Lowenna's fuckface of an ex-husband and his *blushing* bride-to-be?"

"Sure would," Tori said. "A lot of us are involved in their wedding in some way, and not a one of us can stand them."

Sarah rubbed Lowenna's back. "I can do that. I'll be right back." Then she smiled at the group before taking off down the hall toward the office.

"So, how do you guys all know each other?" Luna asked, leaning against the wall. Her eyes fell to Lowenna. "You dating a Single Dad of Seattle?"

Lowenna averted her gaze, her bottom lip getting snagged under her top teeth.

"She's dating Mason," Tori said, waggling her dark, perfectly threaded brows up and down. "Or at least she's kind of dating him."

Luna's mouth formed the perfect *O*. "Ohh, lucky girl. Mason's a hottie."

"Mhmm," Tori said, nodding. "I could watch that man with his baby all day long. Gives me chills and makes my ovaries explode every time I see him wear her in the Ergo."

"You say the same thing about Aaron and Sophie," Isobel said. "Mark's not sure he wants you to be alone with my boyfriend anymore. Thinks you might go into oestrous, your baby fever is so damn strong."

Tori shrugged. "What can I say? We got some hot men in our little makeshift family, and I want a baby."

"You also want to finish grad school and your business class," Isobel replied, her tone just a touch lecture-like

"Like I always say," Paige cut in, "it's not how you get your appetite as long as you go home to eat. Mitch likes how *excited* I get after I see Zak work out at the gym. I usually run home and jump his bones."

"That's *my* boyfriend," Aurora said with a chuckle.

"And he's hot as fuck," Isobel said matter-of-factly, all the other women nodded behind her.

Aurora nodded as well. "That he is."

"All right," Sarah said, coming back down the hall with a slew of photos in her hand, as well as a stack of ugly picture frames. "Let's smash the shit out of this bastard's face."

While Sarah and Luna went to task getting the rooms set up and adding the photo frames with Brody and Doneen's save-the-date, Lowenna got on her gear: protective goggles, work gloves and, because sometimes sharp chunks started to fly, Luna now made her customers wear lab coats to protect their arms. Apparently during the summer, a few people had shown up to The Rage Room wearing shorty-shorts, tank tops and flip-flops, and when the china and glass started to fly, it had scratched up and cut some limbs and feet. Now Luna was covering her ass by making sure everyone wore pants and long-sleeved protective gear, and if they didn't come with close-toed shoes, she had rubber rain boots people could borrow.

"How are things going with you and Mason?" Tori asked, sidling up next to Lowenna as she placed the goggles over her eyes. "Violet says you guys are doing really well in dance lessons, better than your sister and ex-husband."

Lowenna pulled on her gloves. "Things are going well. My sister just informed me of a rehearsal dinner though, and I'm not sure I can ask Mason. I've already asked so much of him."

Tori shook her head dismissively. "Oh, he'll totally go if you ask him. I still can't believe you're paying him. I hope he offered to do it for free."

Lowenna nodded. "He did. But I can't ask that of him."

Isobel, with a wineglass in her hand, came to stand next to Tori. "By the time the wedding rolls around, you won't be paying him, mark my words. I can see it in your eyes when you talk about him or any of us mention his name—you like him. And I bet you he feels the same way."

Lowenna reached for the aluminum baseball bat off the wall, shaking her head as she tightened her grip. "No. I can't let myself get distracted. I have a job to do."

"You mean the chocolate for the wedding?" Tori asked in surprise. "Because I'm sure you can do both. Date Mason, fall in love and get married while still running your chocolate shop."

Lowenna made sure her goggles were secure, then she nodded at the women, who all took a step back out into the viewing area. Tori shut the door.

A tap on the acrylic glass had Lowenna turning her head.

"Beat the living shit out of him," Violet mouthed. The rest of the women nodded and gave their own words of encouragement, not that Lowenna could really hear them, as the glass was pretty thick and intended to be kind of soundproof.

She gave them a thumbs up before lifting the baseball bat behind her. She set her eyes on the tacky porcelain frame in the center of the table in front of her, zeroed in on Doneen's face, and swung the bat with all her might.

The photo frame took instant liftoff and sailed across the

small room into the white concrete wall on the far side, where it smashed into half a dozen large chunks before it slid down to the wall and shattered further.

Did that ever feel good.

Cheers nearly as loud as the fans at CenturyLink Field during the playoffs erupted beyond the glass. She turned her head, the corners of her mouth nearly reaching her ears. All the women were cheering and clapping. Tori and Isobel were banging on the glass, encouraging her to do more.

It had only been one swing—a good swing—but she already felt better. Maybe it was the wonderful company and how welcome they all made her feel. But whatever it was, company or catharsis or a bit of both, Lowenna had a hard time setting her mouth back into a thin line of concentration. She wanted to smile. She wanted to laugh.

You have a great laugh.

Mason's words came back to her, and then his face and his dashing smile flitted behind her eyes.

How was she supposed to harness the rage now when all she wanted to do was smile? When all she wanted to do was hear his voice, hold his baby, dance with him until her feet fell off.

"Hit stuff!" came a loud voice from beyond the glass.

She turned to see all the women giving her various perplexed looks.

"Go crazy!" Tori said, having been the one to call out to her before. The wine in her glass sloshed nearly to the rim as she rapped on the glass again.

Then Zara opened the door. "Everything okay?"

Lowenna nodded. "Just building the rage, that's all."

Zara's blue eyes said she understood there was more to it than that, that she was able to read between the lines. But she didn't say anything else and just nodded, smiled and shut the door again.

Taking a deep breath and lifting the bat up into the air once again, Lowenna pushed thoughts and images of Mason and Willow clear out of her head and let Doneen and Brody's faces replace them.

Her sister called her Lowly.

Her sister called her wicked.

Her sister blamed her for bringing cancer into their family and for exaggerating her condition.

Her sister started sleeping with Lowenna's husband while she was struggling to get through her chemo treatments. While her hair was falling out in her hands, her lips grew chapped and mouth became filled with sores, her sister was betraying her.

Droplets of sweat beaded on her brow as the heat of rage flowed through her.

Then she thought of Brody.

Stupid, selfish, *traditional*, status-climbing Brody.

While she was vomiting in the toilet after treatments, covered in a chemo rash and damn near wishing for death from the extreme headaches, Brody was sneaking out to go and have sex with Doneen.

While she was saying goodbye to any chance she might have of carrying her own baby, Brody was plotting and planning their divorce, dreaming of having a baby *the traditional way* with Lowenna's sister and her intact, cancer-free uterus. Brody was betraying her.

She gripped the bat tighter, lifted it behind her head, shut her eyes, screamed like a banshee and swung the bat down hard into the tacky seventies-style vase on the table.

She did it again to the lamp on the desk and then the printer and the fax machine. The ugly mishmash of plates and bowls all stacked up against the wall on a shelf. Then she took down the shelf. Splinters flew in every direction.

With each swing, with each smash, with each shard that flew past her, the rage inside her grew stronger. Grew hotter. Showing Brody and Doneen up at the wedding with a hot date on her arm wasn't enough anymore.

She needed to get revenge.

She needed to find a way to get even.

After everything Doneen and Brody had done to her, and continued to do to her, they deserved humiliation. Pure, no-holds-barred humiliation.

Now, she just had to figure out how to make it happen.

By the time she was done, by the time the room was successfully destroyed, Lowenna was soaked in sweat and hotter than a summer forest fire. With each swing, she had envisioned a new way to exact her revenge. With each swing, that revenge grew more and more severe. She'd entered a dark place she hadn't gone before, and even though she knew it shouldn't, it made her feel good.

Her chest heaved as she put the baseball bat back into its resting place and opened the door, pulling her goggles off her face and handing them to Luna.

Eight sets of eyes, because Sarah was still there too, all stared back at her. Disbelief and perhaps even a touch of fear twisted their faces.

"Holy shit," Aurora murmured. "That was intense."

"Yeah," Tori said, her throat bobbing on a swallow.

Zara held out her wineglass to Lowenna and she took it gratefully, draining it and wiping the back of her wrist over her mouth.

"Feel better?" Luna asked.

Lowenna nodded. "Yeah. I do. Things seem clearer than ever now."

Slowly, each woman seemed to relax and smile. Tori, Aurora and Paige all began to suit up.

Isobel stepped toward Lowenna and brought her voice

down a touch. "Be careful. I know they hurt you, and I know you're angry, but whatever you're planning, just ... " She brought her voice down even lower. "Just be careful. Rage is a powerful thing, but it can also be blinding and dangerous when left to its own devices."

Lowenna lifted her gaze to the young woman's face. She would probably put Isobel around twenty-six or twenty-seven. Not much younger than Lowenna, but she *looked* young. Her eyes, however, were the eyes of an old soul. Wise and knowing. Isobel studied Lowenna's face just as intently as Lowenna studied Isobel's.

The sound of the women chatting and laughing around them seemed to fade into the background.

Then Isobel grabbed her hand and placed two of her fingers on Lowenna's wrist, her grip firm but gentle.

Lowenna's instinct was to pull away, but she couldn't, and after a second, she didn't want to. Her curiosity got the better of her, as it almost always did. Her pulse, however, picked up, as did her temperature.

"I can feel your pain," Isobel said, her voice now a faint whisper. "It's so strong." She blinked, and suddenly tears formed in her light blue eyes. "Your anger is stronger though because they keep hurting you. They keep taking from you. They keep demanding of you. They won't just let you be."

Lowenna went to pull her hand away again. Now Isobel was just starting to freak her out. It was like the woman had managed to crawl inside Lowenna's head, inside her heart and feel everything she was feeling. Despite how hot she was, an icy chill dripped down the length of her spine, and she took a step back, disengaging her hand from Isobel's. This time Isobel let her.

"Don't let them take anymore," Isobel said, seeming unaffected by Lowenna's discomfort. "You can be the bigger, the *better* person and *not* do what it is you're planning to do."

What the hell was she planning to do? She hadn't even thought that far yet. All she'd realized in that rage room was that she needed to plan something. Her ideas while she swung the bat had been outrageous and completely insane. Anonymous tip to the police that Brody was the Tacoma Strangler, or spill nail polish on Doneen's dress right before the ceremony. You know, ridiculous things that she'd actually never do, but made her feel better as she fantasized about getting even.

But one thing she'd come out of that room knowing was that one way or another, she needed to exact some kind of revenge on her sister and Brody. They couldn't be allowed to get away with how they treated her.

"You can say no. You can walk away," Isobel said softly. "Revenge is not the answer."

All the moisture left Lowenna's mouth at the same time the oxygen fled her lungs. She drew in a big breath through her nose and reached for Isobel's wineglass. She allowed her to take it. "Are you some kind of freaky witch or something?" she murmured into the wineglass as she took a big sip.

Isobel's eyes glowed before she tossed her head back and laughed, her dark ponytail swishing gently behind her. "No. I just feel things really strongly, feel *people* and their emotions as if they're my own. I can read people. And I can read you."

Lowenna hadn't even been paying attention to what was going on around them, but the muffled sounds of smashing and crashing drifted behind them. It looked like the next round of demolition had started.

"Talk to Mason," Isobel said. "I bet he can help you overcome all this pent-up rage and hate. He's never really opened up to me about it, but I know that the man has some demons of his own that he conquered. He might be able to help you." Then she wandered away toward one of the other rooms to observe the destruction, leaving Lowenna standing there, still with a heaving chest, sweaty brow and complete and utter confusion clogging up her brain.

It wasn't until her phone in her pocket began to buzz that she shook herself clean of the last few moments and pulled it out to see who was messaging her.

If it was Doneen, Lowenna feared she might become homicidal.

Thankfully, though, it was Mason.

At poker with the guys. How is the baby shower? Let's chat tonight. Let me know when you're home, and I'll give you a call.

Instantly, her heart rate went down and her pulse no longer thundered wildly in her ears. Her temperature also began to cool.

She took a few deep, grounding breaths before she texted him back.

Baby shower is going great. All the women are so lovely. A chat sounds good. Good luck and I hope you win all their money.

She was about to shove her phone back in her pocket when it buzzed again. She didn't think he would message back that quickly. After all, he was at guys' night.

Can't wait. Xoxo ;)

Did he just winky-face emoji her?

He did. And he put kisses and hugs at the end of his message too.

Now she was pleasantly tingly all over, and every ounce of rage that had been crawling around inside her like a cluster of venomous spiders was replaced with an almost immediate sense of calm and joy. Because she was thinking of Mason. Because tonight she was going to talk to Mason.

"You okay?" Isobel approached her again, her eyes flicking to Lowenna's phone.

Lowenna nodded before she stowed her phone into her back pocket. "Everything's great. That was just Mason checking in."

Isobel's smile said it all. "You should see yourself right now. You're glowing. I don't feel any pain or rage coming off you anymore. And all that from just a couple of text messages."

Lowenna rolled her eyes.

"Roll your eyes all you want," Isobel said with a chuckle, looping her arm around Lowenna's shoulder and steering them both in the direction of one of the rage rooms so they could go and observe the havoc. "But you've got it bad, and it's because he makes you feel so good."

Lowenna rolled her eyes again but didn't say anything. She knew by her reflection in the acrylic glass that Isobel's words and the truth they held were written all over her face.

9

MASON SHUT the door to Willow's room behind him after checking on her and making sure she was still breathing. Even though he had one of those high-tech video baby monitors and kept the volume on high, he still went in a few times a night and checked on her.

She was his life. His everything. And also, he just liked to go and watch her sleep because she was just that freaking cute.

Poker night had been fun. They'd gone to Aaron's place instead of Liam's as they usually did, because Isobel was out at the baby shower, so Aaron needed to stay home for Sophie.

Even though Mason didn't head home with a wallet lined with the other men's money, he'd still enjoyed himself and their fatherly griping and banter.

He'd been looking forward to calling Lowenna all night though. He also didn't feel bad about texting her, because even though Liam told the guys to *not* call or text their women during poker night because it was "guy time," none of the men listened. And now Mason had someone he could miss, someone he could think about and text.

Well, kind of.

He was still technically her gigolo.

But that's why he was calling her tonight. He was working on making her more than just his ... what was the female equivalent for a *John*?

Johanna?

Jane?

Either way, he needed show her that there was more to him than just a pretty face and two left feet, though one was working on righting itself (thanks to Vi and Adam).

Grabbing a beer from the fridge, he wandered into his living room and slid onto the couch, propping his feet up and cracking open the bottle, taking a long swig before he brought her number up on his phone.

It started to ring.

And ring.

And ring.

Shit, was she not home yet? Isobel had arrived home just as they were all packing up their poker stuff at Aaron's, so that meant the baby shower was over, right? Had one of the other women given Lowenna a ride, or had she walked home in the dark and rain all by herself?

Oh God.

Was she okay? Had she been mugged? Or worse?

Panic ratcheted up through his body as her phone continued to ring in his ear.

"Pick up, woman," he growled. "Damn it, pick up."

More ringing.

Did she not have voicemail?

He was about to hang up, call his mother and ask her to come over and watch Willow again so he could go our searching the streets for Lowenna when a frantic *hello* interrupted his racing thoughts.

Oh, thank God.

"Lowenna?"

He let out a deep exhale, running his fingers through his hair at the same time he tipped his beer back and took another long guzzle.

She must have felt his panic through the phone. "Sorry, I was in the shower. I wasn't sure when you would call and I was all gross from the day, so I hopped in the shower when I got home. Violet gave me a ride so I didn't have to walk in the rain."

Well, now he had images of her in the shower, and something very different from panic began to flood his veins, pooling between his legs.

He adjusted his jeans to relieve the sudden strain at the front of them. "It's okay. I should have had you text me when you were available to talk. I'm glad Vi gave you a ride. I didn't like the idea of you walking home."

Her warm chuckle on the other end of the phone made his heart rate ramp up. "No?" she asked, humor in her tone. "Afraid I might get mugged?"

"Uh, yeah. Just because it's not the wrong side of the tracks doesn't mean where you live and work isn't without its degenerates who would love nothing more than to shank you for your purse."

A mixture of emotions tangled inside of him. If anything had happened to her, he'd never be able to live with himself, but at the same time, he had no real claim to her either. She'd probably been walking home alone for months, if not years, and was perfectly fine.

"If you can't get a ride next time, call me, okay?"

He could practically hear her roll her eyes on the other end of the phone. "Yes, sir. I will call you, so you can leave your baby and come drive me three blocks."

He resisted the urge to growl. "Well, at least call an Uber then."

He wished they were Skyping because he really needed to see her facial expressions. He could just imagine her fighting to keep a straight face through his mini-lecture.

"Let's hang up and video chat. I want to see you," he said. "You're probably rolling those gray eyes of yours at me, and I'd rather see it than just think it."

Fuck, he loved her laugh.

"Okay," she finally said, still laughing. "Gimme a minute to put on more than a towel."

"No need to get all dressed up for me," he said, suddenly picturing her wearing nothing *but* a towel and then it magically slipping off. "I'm totally cool with a towel. Or no towel at all. Easy breezy, that's me."

"I'm rolling my eyes again," she said with another laugh. "Hang on."

A few noises that made his cock twitch and grow came across from her end. She'd probably put the phone down and was now naked and getting into her pajamas.

"Okay. There. I'm in my pj's. Let's hang up and Skype."

"Okay."

Moments later, her gorgeous face appeared before him, rosy from the shower, with her dark hair wet and slicked back against her head, making her cheekbones pop. Her bright eyes glittered over the rim of her wineglass as she took a sip, the corners of her mouth turning up into a small, demure smile.

"So, how was poker?" she asked, setting her wineglass down.

He lifted one shoulder. "I didn't get fleeced. Liam is the resident card shark though. On average, he wins the most out of any of us."

"This Liam guy sounds like quite the character. The ladies mentioned him a few times at the baby shower, too. I'm looking forward to finally meeting him."

A frisson of something Mason could only attribute to jealousy licked up his spine, then sat and niggled at the back of his neck like an annoying tickle. He straightened up where he sat and cleared his throat, shrugging again. "He's a cool guy ... I guess. I mean, if you like the older type with lots of money, a fancy car, fancy house and a black heart. Guy has sworn off love. He has a friend with benefits, and that's all he says he ever needs or wants."

Mason didn't like speaking ill of his friend and their club founder, but he also didn't want her developing any kind of interest in the guy. For all he knew, she was slowly turning anti-love too, and Liam was just the kind of guy she was looking for.

He needed to help her see that love wasn't the enemy and that Liam certainly wasn't the man for her.

"So, tell me about The Rage Room," he said, leaning back against the arm of his plush, brick-colored leather couch. "How'd it go?"

A heat of some sort flashed behind her eyes before she smiled, though it wasn't a smile he was used to. This smile held an almost sinister tilt to it.

"It was good," she said, sipping her wine again. "Really got some clarity. Let the fury fuel me."

"That's how you get the best bang for your buck."

"Yeah, *bang*, along with crash, smash and *destroy*." Her nose wrinkled. "But I'd rather not talk about that right now. Let's talk about something else." She scraped her top teeth over her bottom lip, a look that made her instantly look all sexy and innocent. "Isobel mentioned something, and she told me to ask you about it ... "

All he did was lift his eyebrows up a fraction, encouraging her to continue.

"She said you have some demons in your past that you've conquered and that maybe you could help me fight my own."

Her sexy throat bobbed as she swallowed down another sip of her wine. "What did she mean by that?"

Who told Isobel? That's what Mason wanted to know.

Had Mitch told Paige and Paige told Isobel? Did Isobel know the details of Mason's past?

It wasn't like he was a murderer or wanted for tax evasion or anything, but he wasn't necessarily proud of who he used to be either. A shark, a wolf, an apex predator of the most ruthless kind. Out for blood, or in his case—money.

Willing to do whatever it took to make his company as much money as it possibly could, no matter who got hurt, no matter who lost their job because of it.

The bottom line was money, and the more the better.

Until his conscience got the better of him and he was forced to quit, take off traveling and find out what life was really about, find a greater purpose and meaning to his existence on the blue and green marble spinning around in space.

"Still there?" Lowenna's voice brought him back to the moment. She was looking at him curiously, her head tilted slightly, her lips twisted.

Shaking his thoughts free, Mason smiled and nodded. "Yeah, sorry. Just ... " He chuckled awkwardly. "Just figuring out how to best explain my *demons*, as Isobel called them."

Lowenna nodded. "You don't have to. I ... " She began to stumble over her words, her eyes no longer glittering and instead appearing unsure, almost timid. "I just thought we could get to know each other. Go deeper than the superficial ... you know? You know so much about me and my *demons*, it's only fair, isn't it? I need to know about you just as much as you need to know about me if we're going to pull this off and dupe everyone at the wedding into believing we're in love."

Right. The business arrangement.

"Fair enough." Exhaling and suddenly feeling defeated,

though he couldn't quite say why, he set down his now empty beer bottle on the coffee table, propped his phone on his knees, then leaned back against the couch once again, tucking his hands behind his head. "I grew up here in Seattle. I wrestled for my high school and was awarded a few scholarships. I went to college in Oregon on a wrestling scholarship, where I earned a degree in business and finance. Then I got my MBA at Stanford. I worked for a pretty successful hedge fund company while in California and was headhunted by Boon Investments here in Seattle. They brought me back, set me up with a fancy corner office, and from the get-go, I was the man they sent all their *dirty work*. I was their top closer. Apparently, I have a way of convincing people to do things."

Her face remained stoic, but her brows lifted just enough to tell him the video hadn't frozen. He couldn't get a read on her though.

Finally, she spoke. "I can believe that. You convinced me to hire you. Could probably convince me to do a lot of things."

Wait, what?

Whoa!

He cleared his throat. "You sure that wasn't the kiss?" He had to say it. She'd practically set him up for it. They hadn't spoken about that kiss since that night, but he'd sure as hell thought about it. Thought about it a lot. Particularly in the shower ...

"You kiss all the people you're trying to convince like that?"

His smile grew bigger. "Only the pretty ones."

She rolled her eyes. "Okay, so they hired you to do their dirty work. And then?"

"And so I did. For many years. I convinced companies to sell to us for a fraction of what they were worth, then I facilitated in the firing, laying off and dismantling of those companies and their employees. I bought up mom and pop shops or independent, local companies and sold them to franchises. I did whatever I was asked, whatever it took to get owners to sell."

"You manipulated, lied and ruined lives," she finished for him.

He nodded. Even though his ulcer was long healed, something akin to phantom pain stabbed hard in his gut at the memory of all the lives he'd had a hand in ruining. Making sure she couldn't see him, he held his hand against the side of his stomach and fought back a wince.

"Yes, I did."

"And what made you give that life up?"

He snorted a laugh. "You mean besides my conscience attacking me, a life-threatening ulcer and an addiction to sleeping pills?" He shrugged. "It came on slow, the change. I knew all along that what we were doing—what *I* was doing was wrong. Even though it was legal, morally it was wrong. But the money blinded me from seeing the true picture, from seeing how many people and lives I truly hurt. Then the ulcer came and the inability to sleep. And finally, after being called out by a man who had built his company from the ground up, only to watch his son sell it off to us as if it were no more than a tacky lamp at a rummage sale, I started to realize that much like Dr. Frankenstein, Raymond and Ulysses Boon had created a monster out of me."

Angus Nordman had slammed his empty glass down on the bar and glared at Mason, his jowls still trembling with the rage that burned hot in his yellowing hazel eyes. The man's health was not good. "You'll regret your actions, Mr. Whitfield. Mark my words, things have a way of coming back around. I don't know how the fuck you sleep at night, tearing apart innocent lives. Laying off good, hard-working people. And for what? The bottom dollar?" Angus scoffed. "Rot in hell, you motherfucker." Then he stalked off out of the bar, the steam from his ears lifting up into the rafters of the Sandpiper Pub.

Mason would remember that afternoon, that moment and those words every day for the rest of his life. Angus Nordman was one of the most honorable, hardworking men in the city. And he'd trusted Mason, only for Mason to do a deal behind his back with Angus's son Gus and sell the man's business—his legacy—out from under him. A furniture-making company that had started out in Angus's woodshop forty years ago was now a multi-million-dollar business with a warehouse and over thirty master carpenters that Gus wanted to franchise and outsource to China. And Mason helped make it happen.

Angus died six months later of a heart attack, and Gus was now living with a trophy wife on Bainbridge Island, spending his days on the golf course while a factory in China produced all his father's old furniture designs.

Mason still felt sick to his stomach every time he thought about Angus Nordman and what he'd done to his company, what he'd done to the man's life. Perhaps he'd still be alive if Mason hadn't helped Gus sell out.

Or would Gus have just found someone else to close the deal?

"So then you what? Gave all your money away to the poor?" Lowenna's brittle voice brought him back to the present, and he shook himself mentally to clear his head and the haunting of Angus Nordman. He couldn't tell if she was being sarcastic or not. Either way, the look she was giving him made the bottom of his stomach feel extra heavy.

He shook his head. "Shortly after, I quit my job. I kept my condo, and a friend of mine managed it for me, rented it out —mostly to celebrities in town for movie shoots—and I went off traveling. I spent a lot of time in India and Thailand, did some yoga and meditation retreats, spent some time on Bali with the monks. I took a monthlong vow of silence while there, learning a lot about myself."

"I don't think I could handle a vow of silence. I'd maybe make an hour. Even at home, at the shop, I talk to myself." She laughed at herself, smiling and shaking her head. "I don't know how the monks do it."

Mason joined in her laughter. "Yeah, it was tough at first, not being able to speak to anybody, to get my point across without words. But it didn't take long until I welcomed the calm and the quiet. Welcomed the thoughts in my own head and the sound of the birds and the rustle of the breeze through the trees. I've never slept better in my life than I did in that month."

She frowned in thought. He loved how rosy her cheeks were after her shower, all fresh-faced without any makeup. Just Lowenna, pure, beautiful Lowenna. "Makes sense, I guess. Still not sure I could do it."

Still chuckling, he continued. "But even with the vow of silence and all the volunteering and giving back, it was a friend I met along the way who put it all into perspective for me."

Her brows lifted before she stifled a yawn. "Must have been some friend."

"Oh, he was." He smiled and glanced off toward the corner of the room, where a picture of him and Paul sat on his bookcase. "I was in Thailand at a bar one night, minding my own business, taking in the craziness that is the tourist scene. There was a band on stage, and people were dancing, but there were also people sitting in the booths and at tables just enjoying the music and atmosphere. Everybody was having a great time until a white man in his late sixties with a thick accent yelled across the bar at the bartender. He used the N-word and demanded the guy bring him another beer."

Lowenna's mouth form a surprised *O*. "He didn't?"

Mason nodded. "He did. The bartender was a big, black guy. And by big, I mean tall as fuck and built like a brick shithouse. He stalked his way out from behind the bar." Mason paused and tapped his lip with one finger. "I'm going to say *ambled* is a better word. Took his time. Smooth gait, calm demeanor. The whole bar turned dead quiet though, watching to see what happened. The music even stopped as he walked straight up to the drunk guy ... "

She lurched forward where she sat. "Did he punch him?" Her gray eyes were huge, her face full of anticipation, almost giddy. "He punched him, right? Please tell me the bartender punched that racist jackass."

He chuckled. He loved how invested she'd suddenly become in his story. "Not quite. The man did get a black eye though."

Her brows pinched. "Wh-what? How?"

"Paul, that's the name of the bartender, he walked right up to the racist jackass customer, pulled down his zipper, pulled out his cock and bopped the man right in the eye. Prince Albert penis piercing and all."

He hadn't timed that quite right, because just as he told her about the penis ring, she'd taken a sip of her wine, and now that wine was all over her screen. Red droplets dripped down over the image of her face.

He loved how reactive she was to things. Her face, her body language, all of it.

It made him wonder if she was this easily stimulated, this responsive in the bedroom as well.

"He had a penis ring?" Her voice was a high-pitched squeak as she used the sleeve of her housecoat to wipe the screen of her phone, giving Mason a view up her nose but also of her breasts. The sides of her robe had slipped open to reveal a low-cut tank top and definitely NO BRA.

Once she finished wiping the screen of her phone and corrected the angle, Mason continued. "Yes, he had a penis ring."

"And then what happened?"

"He told the guy to get out of his bar and said if he saw him back in there again, he'd hit him in the other eye."

"He didn't!"

Mason chuckled. "He did. And that's how I met my friend Paul, one of the greatest human beings on this earth."

Shaking her head, she was all smiles. "And he's the one who helped rid you of your demons?"

"He did. Paul was just like me back in the UK. He worked for a big investment firm, made a lot of money, ruined a lot of lives doing it. Then he got sick, had an aneurysm in his brain and had to go to the hospital, nearly died. He fell in love with his doctor, a Thai woman doing a surgery fellowship in London. They got married, and he followed her back to Thailand, where she works as the chief of surgery at a big hospital in Bangkok and he runs the bar and takes care of their two kids."

"Wow. What a story. What a life."

Mason nodded.

"Why'd he have a penis ring?"

It was hilarious that that was where her mind still was. It had taken Mason a bit of time to come to terms with it too and then finally work up the nerve to ask Paul about it.

He lifted one shoulder and adjusted his position on the couch. "He wanted it. Said it was a whim back in his college years but that he'd never had a complaint from a woman, so he kept it."

Lowenna's face got all scrunched up. "Did ... he ... did he ... "

"Did he what?"

"Did he convince you to get one?" She chomped down

hard on her bottom lip, her face going an even rosier red in embarrassment.

Mason tossed his head back and began to laugh. "Uh, no," he finally said. "He did not. Not that he tried to convince me. I would never dream of putting a steel rod through my favorite body part. It's big and beautiful enough as it is without bling."

There it was. Just the reaction he was hoping for.

Her eyes went wide, her gasp loud, her cheeks practically scarlet.

Now, he needed to just drive it all home.

"He did, however, convince me to get these ... " He reached behind him and pulled his shirt off over his head. Another gasp from Lowenna made him smile beneath his shirt.

"Your nipples are pierced?" Her voice once again went high-pitched.

"They are."

Her fingers touched the screen as if she were trying to reach out and touch him, touch his chest, touch his nipples and the barbells that went through them. Her tongue slid across her bottom lip as her fingers slid across the screen. "And your tattoos?"

"One for each country I visited. Twenty-six in total. Lucky number thirteen on each arm." He lifted up his left arm and twisted it around to reveal the big tattoo on his forearm that said *Willow*. "Except this makes number twenty-seven. I got it the week after Willow was born."

"It's beautiful," she whispered. "They all are."

Their eyes locked, and her tongue once again darted out and coated her lips in a shine he wanted to lick off himself.

"Thank you," he replied, his heart rate suddenly picking up. "Do you want me to put my shirt back on?"

She didn't say anything, but that was undoubtedly a head shake.

He grinned. "Okay then. It's a bit chilly in here though. My nipples are a bit ... "

She exhaled through her mouth. "Hard."

Man, she was cute when she was flustered and obviously turned on.

This was going just as he'd planned. Better, in fact.

"Continue with your story," she said, reaching for her wine. "How did Paul help you with your demons?"

He thought she might have forgotten what they were talking about. Wouldn't be the first time his nipples, tats and abs made a woman forget what she was talking about.

Snickering at the same time he made his pecs bounce, he continued with his story. "After that night with the racist bastard, I went back to Paul's bar every day, got to know him, his wife and kids. It was Paul who showed me what I was missing in my life, what I was missing in my heart. And that was a family, that was Willow. Paul had an aneurysm, high cholesterol and blood pressure as well as a debilitating ulcer in his gut before he quit his job and moved to Thailand with Boonsri. When I met him, the man couldn't stop smiling, said he was in the best shape and health of his life. He was happy. He was content. He was fulfilled.

"Paul hired me as a bartender for a few months and taught me the ropes of mixing drinks and running a bar, and that's when I realized that I wanted his life. I wanted to run a business, be around people and have a family."

"I traveled the world for a little bit longer, met some more incredible people, and then I returned home to Seattle, sold my condo, bought the bar and a townhouse in a great school district. I thought about waiting for the perfect woman to come along and doing the whole family thing the traditional way, but fuck traditional. Traditions are just peer pressure from dead people. We make our own traditions. We blaze our own trails."

"I love that," she whispered. "Fuck tradition. Fuck Brody and wanting to have a family the *traditional* way."

"Right!" He lifted his hand and pointed at her. "You get it. Fuck tradition. Totally. And fuck Brody."

Her smile and the relief and freeing look that came over her made Mason want to reach into the phone, grab her and haul her into his lap so they could say *fuck tradition* together.

But instead, he simply continued with his story. "I wasn't willing to wait, to go through all the dating BS and shit. I'm a thirty-eight-year-old man. I don't have all the time in the world anymore if I don't want to be a geriatric dad. So I approached my friends with the egg and womb, and ten months later, Willow came along, chasing away the last of my demons, and now I couldn't be happier. I'm demon-free."

"Demon-free," she breathed. "That sounds amazing."

"You could be too, you know. You don't *have* to go to the wedding. You don't *have* to make the chocolate centerpiece or give a speech. Sometimes being the bigger person isn't the best route. Sometimes you have to be the *absent* person. Sometimes you have to walk away. To save your sanity, to save *yourself,* you have to walk away completely. It's called self-care."

She snorted, the expression on her face saying she wasn't at all convinced.

"It doesn't make you the weak person or the selfish person, Lowenna. It makes you the person who loves herself enough to know when she needs to get out, when she needs to take care of herself *first.* We don't do that enough. We're always worried about others, often forsaking ourselves in the process. It comes back to the airplane oxygen mask. Yours first. You can't help anybody else if you're dead. Whether it be literally or simply on the inside."

She blinked a few times, her expression becoming almost blank. "It's easier said than done," she whispered.

"Maybe. But you have to start somewhere. You're continuing to let them take from you. Take your energy, take your happiness. And I know you hate them for what they've done, yet for some reason, you just keep going back. Hate is poison. A poison we take ourselves, hoping the other person dies from it." Whoa, that was deep. Did a monk tell him that? He couldn't remember. Probably, though. "The only real person who suffers from hate is the person *who* hates."

Her bottom lip trembled, and the cords in her throat grew tight.

"Look, I know you won't be able to have any babies of your own, but there is always adoption or—"

"I can have babies of my own," she said, cutting him off. "I just can't carry them."

"What do you mean?"

"I froze my eggs."

He much preferred this vein of conversation. It sparked an unmistakable glimmer of hope into her beautiful gray eyes.

"I didn't think I was going to be able to afford it," she went on, "but then one day I showed up to work and there was a cashier's check waiting for me. Waiting for *The woman with cancer who needs to freeze her eggs*. It was the most bizarre thing in the world."

What?

It couldn't be her, could it? What were the odds?

Mason's chest began to rise and fall erratically at the same time his brain went fuzzy and an icy chill sprinted down the length of his back. "Where ... where did you work?"

Oblivious to his change in body temperature, irregular breathing or rapidly beating heart, she shrugged. "The Sandpiper Pub."

Holy shit.

A ringing started in his ears, and her face on the screen

went all blurry. She was still talking, but all the words seem garbled together. He blinked and squeezed his eyes shut to try and focus, but he couldn't.

Was this some kind of joke?

Once again, he was transported back to that afternoon at the pub. Angus had just left, and Mason was drowning himself and his ulcer in scotch and pity.

A conversation between two of the waitresses behind him piqued his interest, and he strained his ears to listen.

"Did you hear about ... " The name was muffled so he hadn't been able to hear it.

"No, what, is she okay?"

"No, came in crying the other day. It's stage three," the first waitress said, sympathy in her tone.

"Shit," the second waitress said. "Is she getting it removed?"

"Yeah. But first she wants to freeze her eggs. Asked anybody and everybody to let her know if they need a shift covered. The procedure isn't cheap. Add on top of that all her medical bills for surgery and chemo, poor girl is going to be broke. And all to simply be able to survive. I tell you this country's medical system is so fucked up. Only those who can pay survive."

"Yeah, but doesn't her hubby have a decent job with medical insurance?"

"His plan doesn't cover it. Hardly covers her medical expenses."

"How much does it cost?"

"I think she said the egg freezing alone was like eighteen grand or something after everything was said and done. You have to pay each year to rent space in the facility freezer. And what with the surgery and chemo, she won't be wanting to have kids for the next few years. Not until she's at least in remission."

If she survived at all.

They didn't need to say it out loud for it to be said.

"I wouldn't want kids with her husband anyway. Even if he is good-looking, he's a jerk."

"Agreed."

The softer-spoken waitress whimpered. "The poor thing. Why do shitty things have to happen to good people?"

"I know, right? Working her ass off at that fancy bakery all day, then coming here at night, and now cancer. Life is not fucking fair."

"No kidding."

Not only was life not fucking fair, life was fucking weird as shit.

Of all the bars in the entire city ... first the Sandpiper and then Mason's bar. What were the fucking odds?

The ringing in his ears had finally ebbed and his vision cleared, though the sweat on his brow was new, as was the whirling vortex of dread he felt in his gut.

Lowenna was still chatting away, oblivious to his weird epiphany.

"Yeah, it was crazy," she went on, her words drawing him out of his spiraling thoughts. "I only told a few people at work that I had cancer. Told even fewer that I wanted to freeze my eggs. And I certainly didn't tell *any* customers, but one day I show up to work and there is a two-hundred-thousand-dollar cashier's check waiting for me."

Oh, he knew how much it was for.

"Did you ever find out who gave it to you?"

She shook her head, her bright silver-gray eyes hitting him so hard, he felt that to his very toes.

He shook off their effect. He needed to keep his head on straight.

Had his executive assistant done what he'd asked and kept everything a secret? Nobody was supposed to know about his anonymous gesture. He wasn't doing it for the gratitude or the warm fuzzy feelings that came from doing something bigger than himself—he did it because his life was coming up roses compared with hers and she needed to catch a break. She needed the opportunity to have a family of her own if she wanted one, money be damned. He did it because it was the right thing to do. Those with less should be helped by those with more. It was a simple concept that not enough people in the world understood.

Who would have thought that five years later, he would meet that same woman in his bar, she'd hire him to be her date and he would fall hard for her?

"Believe me, I tried to find my benefactor. I wanted to thank my mysterious fairy godmother or godfather. They ... whoever they are, saved me. Brody's benefits covered a bit of my medical bills but not everything. And because of my mystery benefactor, I was able to have sixteen eggs harvested, and they are currently sitting in a freezer facility at the fertility clinic across town." Her eyes glittered once again. "Maybe I knew that things with Brody and I were headed south, because I never told him I froze my eggs. Something in me, something in the back of my mind told me not to tell him, so I didn't. I kept it a secret. Took the hormones in secret, and now I'm glad I did."

Should he tell her?

Should he come clean?

He didn't want her to look at him differently, to feel like she owed him anything. Or to think that he gave her the money out of pity or something. She made it very clear that she didn't want to be a charity case. In her mind, this was still a business transaction, an exchange of service for cash. He was her boyfriend for hire because he fit the bill for what she was looking for to show up her sister and ex-husband.

He wanted to be more.

He needed to be more.

He still had time to woo her and make her give up the guise of fake boyfriend and let him really be her boyfriend. But her walls, despite how many windows she had in them allowing him glimpses into her world, were still up, topped with razor wire. She was gun-shy of love. Possibly of men.

Understandable.

But he needed to change that.

"Come for dinner tomorrow night," he said, blurting it out before he had time to second-guess himself.

She'd been busy chatting about the egg freezing procedure, and he'd cut her off. Her quick inhale of breath and surprised eyes told him he'd caught her off guard.

"For dinner?" she asked. "Tomorrow?"

He loved how flustered she got. Loved the way it made her eyes glitter and her cheeks flush.

"Yes, tomorrow. For dinner. I have a bunch of suits in my closet. You can go through them and pick out which one you want me to wear."

The palm of her hand smacked her forehead. "Shit. I forgot to tell you."

He lifted his brows.

She shook her head. "Bridezilla informed me the other day that it is a black-tie affair. I need to be in a gown, apparently, and you need to be in a tux." She grimaced. "Do you have a tux?"

He flashed her his flirtiest smile and waggled his eyebrows. "You'll have to come over for dinner and find out."

10

LOWENNA THANKED her Uber driver and opened the car door, a bottle of wine, her purse and a box of chocolates under her arm. Mason's townhouse was just up the cobblestone path, surrounded by shrubbery and trees. A small patch of grass out front guarded by a white picket fence made the whole house homey and inviting. The perfect place for a family.

And that's exactly who lived there.

A family.

A family of two.

Two perfect people she was getting to know and beginning to fall for.

Blowing out a breath and watching it disappear up toward the stars, she flipped the latch on the fence gate and made her way toward the red front door with the porch light on.

What was she doing there?

Having dinner, that's what.

Was she taking the business arrangement too far? Was he going to charge her for this? The lines were becoming so blurry between her and Mason, they were becoming friends, and he was so flirty and so handsome, and she liked him. She really, really liked him. Wanted him.

But she couldn't allow herself to get distracted. She had revenge to plot.

As she lifted her hand to knock on the door, the image of him shirtless with his nipple piercings and tattoos flitted back into her mind. Would he open the door that way?

What would she do if he did?

Drool and fall to her knees, probably.

She was about to knock when the door beneath her hand swung open and a beautiful man—with a shirt on—holding a beautiful baby stood there smiling at her.

"You made it," he said, all sexy eyes and hidden nipple rings. "You caught an Uber?"

She nodded and stepped over the threshold as he moved back and welcomed her inside.

Damn, he looked delicious. A tight black T-shirt hugged his muscles and showed off his tattoos, and a pair of dark wash jeans showcased thick thighs and that gorgeous ass.

She was in trouble. Big trouble.

"Welcome, welcome," Mason said, setting Willow down in a bouncy chair just inside the living room before he helped Lowenna with her coat and purse.

She blew out a long, slow breath. "Thank you. Um, here." She thrust the box of chocolates and the bottle of wine into his arms. "These are for you."

He leaned forward and pecked her on the cheek, taking the wine and chocolate from her at the same time. "Thank you."

The feel of his lips on her cheek left a lasting tingle that sprinted right down the center of her body and landed directly between her legs. Her clit pulsed. Her nipples tightened, and her entire core clenched.

And he smelled so damn good too.

Tonight was going to be pure torture.

She regathered her wits, swallowed and nodded. "You're welcome. Thank you for the dinner invitation. It's been a while since I've had a nice home-cooked meal."

He cocked one brow. "Really? You're a chef."

"Chocolatier. But I also work a ton, so it's usually takeout because I'm too tired to cook."

"Fair enough." He hoisted Willow back up into his arms and carried her, the box of chocolates and the bottle of wine into the rest of the house. "Just this way. Let's walk and talk. I've got a cheesecake in the oven, and the timer is about to go."

A *cheesecake!*

"You baked?" she squeaked, following him down the hallway toward the kitchen, which smelled *amazing*.

She loved his house. Very masculine but also warm and cozy, with dark wood accents and rich toasted-marshmallow-colored walls. The art represented his travels with tapestries and carvings, paintings and masks. It was stunning.

Mason set the chocolates and wine down on the granite countertop. "Can you take Willow for me? I just need to check on the cake."

He passed her the baby and opened the oven. "And yes, to answer your question, I baked. I actually bake quite a bit. Prefer bread, but I've been known to bust out the odd cake or cookies when the person is special enough."

When the person is special enough.

"Am I special enough?"

He hit the timer for the oven and added another three minutes before turning around to face her, a big smile on his face. "You are *definitely* someone special enough."

Heat tingled in her belly and breasts at his words and the way his sapphire eyes glittered when he looked at her. She bounced a fist-gnawing Willow in her arms, then held the baby out to look at her. "You hear that, Willow-baby? I'm someone special. Well, I think you're someone special, too." She kissed Willow on the cheek, her baby-soft skin like warm silk beneath her lips. "Oh bunny, I could just smooch you all day."

"That's what I call her," Mason said, stirring a pot on the stove. "Have you heard me call her that?"

Lowenna shook her head. "I don't think so. She just feels like a sweet, soft little baby bunny."

He grinned. "I agree. So, I hope you like roast chicken with veggies and quinoa."

Lowenna's stomach rumbled. "I do, very much." She kissed Willow again, then turned her around so she could look out and watch her daddy cook.

"She really likes you," he said, turning the temperature down on the stove element.

"Well, the feeling is mutual." She pecked the top of Willow's head, causing the little girl's arms and legs to kick and flail around. "So, are you going to model all your tuxedos for me tonight? Do I get a fashion show?"

"Do you want a fashion show? Start with the evening wear and then move on to the underwear and swimsuits? I could peel one layer off at a time, turn it into a striptease-fashion show." He grabbed the bottle of wine off the counter and waggled it at her. She nodded, and he began to pour her the deep, rich pinot noir she'd brought into a stemless glass. She tried her damnedest to focus on the baby in her arms and the wine being poured into the glass, but she couldn't stop envisioning Mason shirtless with his tattoos and piercings walking up and down the hallway in nothing but a pair of tight black boxer briefs.

Yes, please.

He handed her the glass of wine, taking the baby from her arms. She instantly took a long sip, letting the fruity vino slide across her tongue and take the edge off her wicked and oh so dirty thoughts. "We'll have dinner first though. Then I'll bathe Willow, put her down and then show you what I *have*."

Show you what I have.

Was there an innuendo hidden in that statement? It certainly made her begin to think about what he *had*.

She already knew he had rippling muscles, sexy as hell tattoos, nipple piercings, stunning blue eyes. What else did he have?

She was particularly curious about what was beneath those perfect-fitting jeans.

Damn, it'd been a long time since she'd had sex. Not since before her diagnosis. Because once she was told she had the big C, Brody refused to touch her. She was Cancer Girl, gaunt and bald and constantly nauseous. And by the time she went into remission, Brody was in her sister's bed and she was focusing on starting her business. She had no time for men or sex.

But now ... with Mason strutting his fine self in front of her several times a week, suddenly sex was all she could think about.

Well, sex and showing up her stupid sister and stupid ex-husband. Proving to them and everyone else once and for all that she was better off without Brody, without a uterus and that they and all the other people who pitied her could take a flying leap off the nearest building.

"I think I have two tuxes for you to choose from." His voice, although not loud, was deep and booming enough to rattle her brain like a rock in a tin can, drawing her from her gutter-brained thoughts. "And would you prefer a bowtie or a traditional black necktie? My tie collection is a bit extreme, so if you'd like to go wild and have me wear a pop of color, we have that option too." Comfortable doing things one-handed, he bounced a once again fist-munching and super slobbery Willow on his shoulder at the same time he grabbed a couple of plates out of the cupboard and walked them over to the table against the window. "I hope you don't mind if Willow eats with us."

She shook her head, her body warm and not just from the wine. "Not at all. That sounds absolutely lovely."

"It's just, when I'm home at dinnertime, I sit her in her highchair—now that she can sit up on her own—and she watches me eat. I'm trying to get the routine of a sit-down family dinner instilled in her."

How sweet.

"When can she start eating real people food?" Lowenna asked, desperate to keep the topic PG-rated and drag her mind from the filthy gutter.

"Doctor said any time after four months, if she's interested. She's kind of interested, but any time I offer her anything, she just plays with it, then spits it out or chucks it onto the floor."

She was tempted to take the baby from him once again so he had the freedom to use both his hands as he set the table, but she also enjoyed watching him in domestic dad mode. So instead, she leaned against the wall and sipped her wine, her nipples pebbling beneath the silk of her bra as he reached up into the top cupboard to grab a couple of napkin rings and his midriff became exposed—or should she say, his abs and a light dusting of hair disappearing beneath the waistband of his jeans peeked out at her, tempted her.

Annnnd right back into the gutter she went.

She took another sip of her wine and averted her eyes,

letting them roam around his kitchen. But the pull to watch him, to study him was too strong, and before long, she was once again focused on the tightness of his shirt and the way the muscles of the arm that was cradling Willow bunched and flexed.

The timer for the oven began to beep, and he quickly handed her Willow, muttering that he needed two hands. He tossed on a pair of matching oven mitts, then pulled out the cheesecake, placing it on a hot pad on the counter.

The scent that percolated around the warm, homey kitchen with its dark wood cabinets and black marbled granite counters, made her stomach rumble again. She pressed her mouth against Willow's ear. "You smell that, little bunny? Daddy knows a way to a woman's heart, and it's definitely cheesecake."

He smiled at both of them as he pulled off the oven mitts. "Raspberry cheesecake, to be more precise."

"Mmm, I love raspberries."

He went to take Willow back from her, but she turned away from him. "Nuh-uh. Don't take my baby from me yet. I'm not done with my snuggles." She squeezed Willow tighter against her and inhaled that perfect, delicious, unique baby smell, closing her eyes as it hit her square in the solar plexus. "One day I'll have a baby of my own," she murmured. "One day I'll hold a baby of my own." She opened her eyes. "You think your friend is open to doing more surrogacy?" she asked, simply trying to make conversation now. She'd revealed to him that she had frozen her eggs, and he'd gone a little weird. His eyes had gone all twitchy and his cheeks flushed.

She wasn't sure what his issue had been, but then he'd shaken it off and seemed normal again. And when she showed up on his doorstep, he was once again fine. Maybe it had all been in her head. Either way, she felt comfortable enough with him now to discuss more of her fertility woes and hopes.

But given the way he was looking at her now, once again with that twitchy eye and flushed cheeks, she wasn't so sure bringing up his surrogate was such a good idea.

Her brows knitted together. "Everything okay? Did I say something wrong?"

He blinked slowly and shook his head. "No ... nothing's wrong. It's just ... "

What was going on with him?

She dug her teeth into her bottom lip, waiting for him to reveal ... *something*.

His throat bobbed on a swallow. "It's just I'm really happy that you haven't given up hope on having a baby of your own. I can talk to my friend if you're really interested. Her pregnancy with Willow went so smoothly, she has offered to carry for me again."

Oh. Phew.

He stepped forward, bringing his scent into her space once again. Her knees wobbled slightly, but she quickly locked them into place. She was holding a baby, after all. His knuckle slid down Willow's cheek, but his eyes remained on Lowenna. "You have a way with babies. At least my baby. Look at how calm she is, how relaxed."

Heat raced into her cheeks, and she turned her face away to hide the blush, not to mention the fact that she had to squeeze her thighs tight when everything inside her pulsed. Forcing out a raspy chuckle, she adjusted Willow in her arms. "Are you saying babies are like animals? They can smell fear?"

He tucked a knuckle beneath her chin. The slight pressure forced her to turn and face him. "They can sense when someone is genuine, when someone is trustworthy and kind. And that puts them at ease. Willow is a pretty easygoing baby, for sure, but that's not to say she hasn't lost her shit when the wrong person has held her. But not you. She's been nothing but content with you, and that says a lot."

All the oxygen fled her lungs as his expression grew more intense by the second. A shiver dripped down her spine at the same moment a warm simmer grew in her belly. She licked her lips.

Was he going to kiss her?

She kind of hoped he would.

She more than *kind of* hoped. She wished. She needed. She wanted.

She wanted him to kiss her.

So badly.

So badly, the need for his lips on hers again made an ache form inside her chest that was nearly unbearable.

"Mason ... " she whispered.

"Let me feed you," he said, his voice a rough and gravelly timbre, nothing but a baby between them now. "Then we can have some wine and talk."

Her sudden dry mouth made it tough to swallow. "Right, wine. *Talk*."

A cocky grin slid across his lips, and he released her chin. "And don't forget the striptease." He planted a kiss to the side of Willow's head, then his head lifted and he placed a feather-light kiss to Lowenna's cheek. She squeezed her eyes shut and held her breath, hoping for more.

There was no more, though. He lifted his mouth from her and stepped back toward the stove just as she opened her eyes, lightheaded and disoriented as she leaned back against the wall.

"Um ... you mean fashion show."

"Sure, whatever. Fashion show, striptease, let's just see where the night takes us." His brows jiggled salaciously as he pinned her with a hungry look, like she was a tasty-looking impala on the Serengeti and he a handsome, ravenous lion ready to chase her down and consume her.

A ripple of lust made her tremble at the idea of letting her thoughts and fantasies become real. Of letting him *consume* her.

But first she'd have to let him catch her.

She pushed down the lump in her throat and swallowed. She'd had to set her wine down on the counter to hold Willow. Now she desperately wished she could grab it for a big, long sip. She stared longingly at her wine, and her tongue slid out and grazed along her lip.

His gaze flicked up to hers from where he was shaking what looked like salad dressing in a dressing bottle.

"What?" she asked, wondering if he could read every thought that was parading through her mind at the moment. Every dangerous, complicated, dirty thought.

He set the shaker down and grabbed her wine, bringing the rim of the glass to her lips. "Drink. Your arms are holding precious cargo, but your eyes say you're thirsty."

She took a sip, her eyes locking on his.

"Is it good?" he asked, pulling the glass from her mouth.

She nodded and licked her lips. "Delicious."

His brow twitched, then he put the wineglass to his own kissably soft lips and took a sip, smiling with not only those lips, but also with his eyes. Eyes as blue and deep as the Pacific Ocean. And the man behind those eyes was just as powerful and just as complex and strong as the sea—probably equally mysterious too.

His Adam's apple jogged in his neck as he swallowed the wine. "You're right," he said, putting the glass down on the counter. "It was delicious."

Lowenna raked her teeth over her lip again.

Now she not only wanted him to catch her, she wanted to slow down, stumble and let him fall clear on top of her.

Pinning her to the ground and scraping his teeth over her neck.

Consuming her. Devouring her.

"Dinner's just about ready," he said, pulling the aluminum foil off the beautifully roasted chicken. "You hungry?"

She nodded and rubbed Willow's back. "Starved."

11

FUCK, she looked good with his baby.

Natural.

Motherly.

And Willow just adored her.

Even though Willow couldn't talk yet, both she and Lowenna had protested when he went to put his daughter to bed. Willow wanted to spend more time with Lowenna and Lowenna with her.

And who was Mason to argue with the gorgeous women in his life?

So now, there Lowenna sat on his bed, holding his baby and making her giggle, while Mason modeled his two tuxedos for them.

He owned two because, well, why not?

Back when he had piles of money and a job that required him to wear suits all day long, he found a kickass tailor named Simon down in Pike Place, and the man made Mason look good.

He'd bought his tux for his sister's wedding, and he'd needed one with tails for a fancy black tie fundraiser many moons ago. He'd had Simon nix the tails afterward though. They just weren't him.

He did up the final button on his vest, then stepped out of his walk-in closet, the tux jacket in his hand. "So, what do you think?"

Lowenna's pupils dilated and her nostrils flared as her eyes raked him from head to toe. A sexy pink bloomed on her cheeks at the same time her jaw went slack and her lips parted.

He grinned, reaching over to grab the wineglass they shared and taking a long sip. "I'm going to take your silence as a *yes*."

As if she belonged there, Lowenna nodded and reclined back onto his bed, turning on her side and propping her head on her hand. Willow was wriggling and kicking on her back, all smiles. "You can take my silence as a *hell* yes."

She looked good on his bed.

She looked good on his bed with his baby.

Like she belonged there.

With them.

"So you like this tux then?" he asked, unbuttoning the vest and sliding out of it, taking care to drape it over a chair in the corner of the bedroom.

She picked up one of Willow's bare feet and kissed the bottom of it. "I do. And I think you should wear a silver tie if you have one. My dress is silver."

"To go with your eyes?"

She lifted those gorgeous gray eyes to his face. "You know what color my eyes are?"

Loosening the sleeves and collar of his crisp white dress shirt, he slipped onto the bed so that Willow was now between them. He mimicked how Lowenna was positioned, his head in his hand, elbow propping him up. "It's hard not to miss those eyes," he said quietly, tickling Willow's belly and making her smile.

"I doubt my ex-husband can remember what color my eyes are. So yeah, they *can* be hard to miss."

"Your ex-husband was a fool."

"Correction, he *is* a fool." She pouted. "He's not dead."

He snickered. "Right."

She covered her mouth to hide her yawn, at the same time flopping onto her back and throwing her arms above her head.

Now, he was having visions of her in his bed without any clothes on, Willow in her own room, and Mason sliding between Lowenna's thighs, showing her just how alive they could both feel. Just how much he wanted her.

But now it wasn't just Willow that lay between them. It was the secret he'd been struggling all night to find a way to tell her.

That he, of all people, was her mysterious benefactor. Her fairy godfather, as she put it.

If he told her, would that change things between them? Would she look at him differently? And if so, would that tighten their bond or loosen it completely?

He knew that the last thing she wanted was to be looked at with pity-eyes. To be considered a charity case or some-body's good deed.

She yawned again. "I don't know how you do it. Raise a baby *and* run a bar. I'm exhausted after a day of work and just a few hours with this little bunny." She glanced over at Willow. "But she's a very sweet, exhausting little bunny. Makes it easier to forgive her for my heavy eyelids."

He watched closely as Lowenna's chest rose and fell with each breath, her breasts round and full, and her nipples tight and pointing straight up to the ceiling.

He wanted to suck one of them into his mouth until she

bowed her back and slammed her eyes shut, moaning his name and digging her nails into his ass as he pumped furiously into her.

"You okay?"

Fuck, his eyes had been glued to her chest, and his mind had soared directly into X-rated movie territory. Her words had him blinking and shifting his focus to the now snoozing baby between them.

"Yeah, uh, just ... "

Her lips twisted. "Staring at my boobs?"

Shit.

She chuckled softly. "I think your baby's out. Oh, to be able to fall asleep so quick and easily."

Phew. Saved by the baby.

Though Lowenna also didn't seem to mind that he'd been staring at her chest. Did that mean she was interested in him as well? So far the signals she'd been throwing him were confusing as fuck. One minute she was flirting, the next minute she was all "this is a business transaction." And he certainly couldn't get a read on her now.

"I'm going to go take Willow to her own bed," he said, sitting up and scooping his snuggly little baby into his arms. "Then I'll come back here and stare at your boobs some more." Even though he was all grins, inside he was worried she wouldn't take it for the joke it was.

Well, it was *kind of* a joke.

She yawned again and shut her eyes. "Sounds good. They are pretty great boobs. I'm glad they didn't disappear when I lost all that weight during my chemo." Her mouth settled into a slight, curved smile, and she wriggled her bottom on his bed to get more comfortable.

His cock twitched as he walked around the bed to the door, his eyes on the incredible woman peacefully resting right where he normally slept. "Be right back," he whispered, Willow cradled against his chest.

"Mhmm."

His body warmed as he took one final glance at Lowenna before he left his bedroom and wandered down the hallway toward Willow's room. "Do you like our new friend?" he whispered to his now snoring infant. "Daddy likes her."

Daddy REALLY likes her.

He laid his daughter down onto her back, rested his hand gently on her chest and closed his eyes, counting her breaths.

He stood like that for a full minute. Sixty seconds. Counting each rise and fall of her tiny chest. He opened his eyes, taking in the vision that was his infant daughter. His flesh and blood. His reason for getting up each and every day. His joy. His heart. His life. His everything.

With one last glance at Willow sleeping soundly in her crib, he headed back toward his bedroom and the sleeping beauty on his bed.

He turned the corner, and there she was.

"Lo?" He approached her.

No response.

"Lowenna?" he said, his voice just a fraction louder.

Her killer tits rose and fell in slow, even breaths, practically heaving out of her light gray V-neck sweater. Her cleavage was rocking tonight too. As was her ass in those tight black pants she'd shown up wearing. They played up those hips and curves until he was forced to grab an apron and tie it around his waist to hide the boner that had sprung up in his jeans when he opened the door and took her coat. Fuck, he was popping chubbies around this woman like he was a goddamn fifteen-year-old and not a thirty-eight-year-old man who knew how to control his erections.

Yet, when it came to Lowenna, he had a hard time controlling anything.

And now there she was, lying on his bed.

A true sleeping beauty.

With a great rack. And it was even better when she lay down and they spilled out of her top toward her chin.

Should he kiss her? Could he?

Would that wreck everything?

Don't deviate from the plan. You still have two weeks until the wedding to woo her. Once the wedding is over, you'll tell her how you feel and then go from there. Don't fuck up this wedding and her plan by deviating from your own plan because you can't keep your inner fifteen-year-old in check.

Right.

But since meeting Lowenna, hell, since *seeing* Lowenna across the bar all those weeks ago, he'd become smitten with her. Enamored with her beauty and the mystery that surrounded her like a halo. He'd gone and kissed Emmett at midnight on New Year's Eve even though he had a gaggle of gorgeous women around him because he hadn't been able to get Lowenna out of his head. She was all he'd been thinking about at that party, and when the countdown began, he knew there was nobody else he wanted to kiss.

Even though he didn't know her yet, hadn't officially met her, she was the only one he wanted to ring in the new year with.

Emmett had been in the middle of relationship drama with Mason's florist, so to ward off the hopeful lips of one of his stiletto-clad fans, Mason had grabbed Emmett and planted a big kiss on his lips when the clock struck midnight.

It'd certainly done the trick with the women. They'd all moaned and grumbled, saying that the best ones were always gay.

And then Mason had gone home and played his own New Year's Eve fantasy in his head in the shower. One where he finally walked up to Lowenna at the bar, pulled her to her feet and kissed her like she'd never been kissed before, and all to the sound of the ball dropping in Times Square and people cheering for the new year. Followed, of course, by white-hot sex in his office at the bar. Of course.

Maybe next year?

For now, he had a new fantasy to fuel his nights. Her, sleeping on his bed peacefully.

What he did to her in his mind was all his and would definitely be played out this evening as he took himself in his fist to relieve the tension. But for now, he was going to remain the gentleman his mother had raised and let Lowenna be, as much as it pained him. As much as his cock standing at full attention in his dress pants protested, he was going to leave her be.

He sat down on the edge of the bed next to her waist and took her hand. It was soft, and the fingernails were trimmed neatly. A bit of black was under her left pinky nail. Probably chocolate. It seemed she always had chocolate somewhere on her when they met. Either her neck, chest, wrist, the side of her face. She brought her work home with her.

Gently, he turned her hand face up and began to trace the lines of her palm with his index finger. His mother had gone to a palm reader once, then she came home and insisted she was now an expert and wanted to read Mason's palm. She was relieved he had a long life line but got all pouty when his heart line was broken beneath his pinky finger

"What does that mean?" he'd asked, not really believing in all that voodoo hocus pocus crap but also hoping that a broken heart line didn't mean he was going to die young of a heart attack or something.

His mother pursed her lips. "It means what I've been telling you all along, that you put too much stress on money and the material things in life. That true love will be a struggle, if not impossible, because you're too busy. Too consumed with money."

Mason had rolled his eyes at his mother and then tugged his hand away. But that didn't mean that over the next few weeks he didn't catch himself staring at his hand, at that broken heart line.

He'd gone to a palm reader while in China, hoping that his mother had been wrong and that he wasn't a lost cause. That he could find love. Could palms change over time? Could the lines grow?

He traced his finger over Lowenna's heart line. It was perfect. Curved beautifully, intact, landing beneath her index finger and extending all the way to the edge of her hand.

"That tickles," she murmured, her voice groggy as she began to stir. Thick, dark lashes blinked open a few times before revealing sleepy gray orbs he wanted to wake up to every morning.

"Want me to stop?" he asked, tracing his finger over her life line. It was short.

Hmm. He pursed his lips together.

He still didn't completely agree or believe all that voodoo stuff about palms, but the woman in China he'd gone to see had been awfully convincing, and she seemed to know her shit.

"What did you make that face for?" she asked, cocking one brow at him playfully, an expression that made her look downright irresistible.

"This is your life line, and it's short." He traced his finger over it again, happy to be holding her hand, touching her. He'd rather be hammering her body into his mattress as their naked bodies, slick with sweat, slid against each other over and over again. But at least this was something.

"What does that mean?" she asked, panic filling her eyes. "Does that mean I have a short life?"

He shook his head. "No. It doesn't. It means you are prone to illness."

"Which I am. Cancer girl, remember. I was also a preemie baby and had to stay in the hospital for three months after I was born. Had a big hole in my heart they had to fix, then I contracted some infection. I nearly died."

Jesus Christ, this woman had really been through the wringer. She needed to catch a break. She needed her win.

"Yeah, well, that explains the short life line. But it also means that you are a person of integrity. You're down to earth, kind but also a little timid." He linked their fingers together. "You're not timid, are you? You beat cancer. You kicked its ass. That doesn't say timid to me. That says warrior."

He grinned when she rolled her eyes. "It nearly killed me, and it cost me my uterus, one ovary, my cervix and let's not forget ... my marriage. But sure, I kicked its ass."

Now it was his turn to roll his eyes. He pulled her up to sitting, much against her groans of protest.

"But I was comfy," she whined. "Your bed is really comfy."

Their fingers were still linked together. She hadn't pulled away. He took that as a good sign. "It is really comfy," was all he said. If she wanted more, she had to take the next step.

Her eyes slid down to their intertwined hands. "Maybe I should go. Order an Uber and head home. I have to be at the shop for six o'clock tomorrow."

Damn it. So close.

She didn't release his hand.

Her gaze drifted back up to his face. "Thank you so much for dinner tonight. It was wonderful. I really needed to get out of the house, get out of my head and spend some time with a friend."

A friend.

Was he being thrown into the friend zone?

Was there any coming out of it if he was?

He'd never been in the friend zone before. Well, he had, but she came out of the closet like a month later, so it made sense. Otherwise, he'd always gotten the girl. He'd always been the boyfriend. He'd never really had girls that were his friends. He had girlfriends and fuck buddies but never any girls that were his platonic friends—besides his lesbian friends who were Willow's aunts.

And he certainly didn't want to start having girls who were simply friends if Lowenna wanted to be the first one.

No. This couldn't happen.

She sank her teeth into her bottom lip and averted her gaze over to the nightstand on the opposite side of the bed, where a nearly empty glass of wine sat. "I know it's a lot to ask, and I will pay you extra ... "

Fuck, he hated when she brought up the fact that she was paying him. Hated it.

"But the night before the wedding ... it's the rehearsal dinner and ... "

"I work."

Christ, why had he just blurted that out? He was the boss. He could work or not work. There were always students willing to pick up a shift either on the bar or as a server. His staff was amazing.

Because you're frustrated. You're being thrown into the friend zone, and she just reminded you that you're her gigolo.

She slipped her hand from his and glanced down between them. "Right. Okay. I just thought I'd ask." She turned to go. "Thanks again for dinner, the fashion show and the palm reading." Her laugh came out forced. She showed him her back and headed out the bedroom door and down the hall. "Here's hoping all my *illnesses* are behind me. Maybe my life line will grow. They can still grow at thirty, right?"

Without glancing behind her, she made her way to the front door, pulled out her phone and tapped it a dozen times.

Finally, she lifted her gaze to his. "Uber is just around the block. Should be here in a minute."

With an ache in his gut and a rock in his throat, he grabbed her jacket from the coat closet. She allowed him to hold it out for her, and she slid her arms into the holes.

"Thank you," she whispered, turning to face him. "I had a nice time." Then she leaned in, bringing her scent of chocolate and spice with her, and pecked him on the cheek.

Pecked him on the fucking cheek. Like he was her geriatric great uncle or something.

It was dry and quick, almost more of a hover with a kissy noise than anything else. At least when he'd kissed her on the cheek earlier, he'd lingered, made real contact and did it seductively. This kiss was none of those things.

He swallowed down the razor blades in his throat and forced the corners of his mouth to lift up into a smile. "I had a nice time too."

Headlights flashed through the living room window, indicating the Uber had pulled up to the curb.

"Well, I should get home. That catnap on your bed wasn't enough. Though, if you hadn't woken me up, I would have probably slept straight through the night."

He reached for her hand again, his other hand opening the door for her. "Next time I won't wake you. Next time I'll just crawl into bed next to you. Let you sleep and cook you breakfast in the morning."

Something wild and needy flashed behind her eyes. A response that made him no longer need to force his smile. "Goodnight, Mason," she said, her chest lifting and falling quicker than a moment ago.

He brought her knuckles to his mouth and planted a kiss before turning her hand around in his and pressing his lips to her life line. "Goodnight, Lowenna." Then he released her, watching her stumble just slightly out into the dark, her eyes saucer-size, an expression of surprise on her beautiful face before she finally turned around and opened the gate.

That's right, baby. You wanted the boyfriend experience? You're going to get it. No way are you tossing me into the friend zone.

Then he waited until she was safely in the Uber and it had pulled away before he closed the door, gripped his cock and went to go take a long, cold shower.

12

IT WAS one week until the wedding, and Mason was busy at the bar, slinging drinks and managing the rowdies. Not that he ever really let the place get out of control. He ran a tight ship, and not only did his staff keep the patrons from getting belligerent but most of the patrons knew he didn't tolerate that shit. A simple eyebrow lift from him at the bar had people falling into line.

"You excited for next weekend?" Scott asked.

Mason's fellow Single Dad of Seattle usually spent every other Friday night at the bar. Scott and his ex-wife alternated weeks with their son Freddie. And this week Freddie was with his mother until Monday night when Scott picked him up from school.

Mason finished filling up Scott's pint of San Camanez orange wheat ale and slid the glass across the bar. "Kind of. I'm looking forward to Lowenna finally getting to show up her sister. She deserves a win. Woman's been through hell these last few years."

"You going to the rehearsal dinner?" Scott asked, dipping his thick-cut wedge fry into ketchup and taking a bite. Even though Mason was friends with all of the single dads in their little group, besides Mitch, who he'd known for twenty years, he and Scott had bonded more than he and any of the rest of the guys. They had a similar sense of humor, and Scott had quickly become a regular at Mason's bar. He showed up around eight o'clock, sat at the bar and watched whatever hockey game was on the television, keeping Mason company until he closed. Usually Friday nights were busy, but on the off-chance the place was quiet and Mason sent the servers home, it was nice to have someone to chat with.

Wiping down the bar in front of him, Mason gave his friend a look. "How do you know there's a rehearsal dinner? Is Liam going to it?"

Scott shook his head. "No. Liam hates that fucker. I just assumed there was one. I thought most big-ass weddings had a rehearsal dinner the night before. You know, just another opportunity to spend money, fawn over the happy couple and give stupid speeches. For the groomsmen to scope out the bridesmaids. Figure out which ones will be easier to bang on the wedding night."

Gross.

"So I'm guessing you and your ex *didn't* have a rehearsal dinner, then?"

Scott shoved another fry into his mouth before he took a sip of his beer. "No, we did. It was dumb. Dumb speeches, expensive restaurant, lots of wine. And I think one of my groomsmen gave my ex's sister crabs." He lifted his shoulder. "She's a crab herself, so I don't care, but it was still a dumb party."

Chuckling, Mason watched as a new drink order came up on the screen. He began to mix it. "Well, she invited me to the rehearsal dinner, but I said I had to work."

"But you like this chick. You want to date this chick, right? Can't you get someone else to cover your shift?"

Yes to all of those things.

"Yeah."

Scott's brown brows furrowed. "So then wouldn't the rehearsal dinner be another *date?*"

"She offered to pay me extra. And every time she brings up that she's paying me, it makes me see red. I hate that our relationship is starting off on this foot, with me as her boyfriend for hire. Her gigolo." He poured the vermouth into the martini shaker, then leaned over the bar, bringing his voice down. "I've never told a soul this, so keep it between us."

Scott leaned in over the bar, his face pure curiosity and excitement, like the church biddy eager to hear the latest pew gossip. "Okay. It's in the vault."

Mason rolled his eyes. "Five years ago, I was at the Sandpiper Pub, where I overheard a few waitresses talking about a co-worker and her battle with cancer."

"Lowenna?"

He nodded. "Yeah, but I didn't know it at the time. Anyway, they started talking about how her medical bills were through the roof and that she wanted to freeze her eggs too but couldn't afford it. So I ... "

"You paid for her medical bills and fertility expenses? Does Lowenna know this?"

Mason shook his head. "No, and I have no idea how to tell her. When she told me that a cashier's check from an anonymous donor ended up at the restaurant for her, I was blown away. I never intended for anybody to find out. That wasn't why I did it."

"You have to tell her. It could change everything."

That was exactly what he was afraid of.

"Yeah, but what if it makes her hate me?"

"She can't hate the guy who pretty much saved her life."

"She's so independent though. Hates being looked at like

Cancer Girl or with pity eyes. She might not hate me, but I bet I could kiss any possibility of going from gigolo to boyfriend goodbye."

"Yeah, but you guys have gotten to know each other now. She wouldn't just pull the pin on everything now, would she?"

Mason stirred the drink he was mixing before placing the strainer over the top. "I thought I could tell her the other night when she came over for dinner, but I chickened out. We were having such a nice time. I didn't want to ruin it. And then she went and called me her *friend* and brought up the fact that she's paying me, and the whole night kind of just went to rat shit after that."

"You have to tell her. If you want a future with her beyond this wedding, you need to tell her. You can't build your relationship on a lie. Particularly not one this massive."

Yeah, he knew that. He just didn't know how to tell her.

Scott leaned back over the bar and handed Mason his phone. "You should send her this video. She should make *those* for the party favors."

Mason squinted at the screen. He watched in fascinated horror, listening intently to the man and woman on the screen being interviewed.

His gaze flew up to Scott, who was now silently dying with laughter. "Can you imagine opening up your guest favor and seeing *that*? Talk about *where fudge is made*." He continued to laugh, which morphed into more of a cackle. "Send it to her."

Could he? It was so crass. But also fucking hilarious, and she did say she liked toilet humor. He handed the phone back to Scott, then went about pouring the martinis into their wide-mouth glasses. He grabbed two skewers, shoved three olives on each, then placed the glasses on the bar for the waitress.

Mason's phone on the back of the bar made a little chirp. "There, I sent it to you. Do with it as you will. But I think it's hilarious, and if she doesn't actually do it, she'll at least get a chuckle out of it. And if she doesn't, if she gets offended and calls you disgusting, then she's not the woman for you anyway." Scott lifted his beer into the air in a solo cheers before slamming back half of it. He wiped the back of his wrist across his mouth and made a satisfying *ah* sound. "I know that if I opened up a chocolate asshole when I got home from a wedding, I'd be wondering if it was the bride or the groom's. Just saying." Then he dug into his fries and let his eyes drift up to the hockey game above their heads on the enormous television.

ONE WEEK TO GO.

One week until V-day.

More like *D*-day.

Judgment day.

And of course, Doneen had called and texted Lowenna three times that day, adding on more specifications for the guest favors, the chocolate-covered strawberries and the centerpiece. She wanted gold ribbons for all the boxes. But no glitter on the ribbon because glitter was tacky, and the bows had to be off center, not in the middle, because off center was classier. She wanted two chocolates in each box, but two *different* chocolates. Because how would it look if guest A and B each received chocolates and guest A got a salted caramel chocolate bonbon and pistachio cream bonbon, while poor little guest B only got two strawberry and basil cream bonbons.

Oh, the horror.

The humanity!

Surely, guest B would be beside themselves and write Doneen and Brody a scathing letter, going into detail about just how slighted they felt, how completely and utterly devastated only one flavor of chocolate made them feel.

For fuck's sake.

She could not wait until all this shit was over. Until she was done with her sister and Brody and their ostentatious, pompous-ass wedding once and for all.

Busy assembling guest favor boxes, she cracked her neck side to side a few times to relieve the ache from standing in one spot for several hours with her head bent just so. It was after hours, and the shop was closed, but she had so much to do, she couldn't just head home like her staff.

Sometimes she listened to podcasts when she was forced to work late, other times music, but tonight she was enjoying the silence. Enjoying the quiet.

Doing a quick count of how many boxes she had assembled, she was thrown off her counting when her phone on the counter made a little *whoop, whoop.*

If it was Doneen with more changes, she was going to rip out her hair. Then she was going to go find her sister and rip out her hair too.

She peeled off her latex gloves, grabbed the bottle of wine she was using to help her get through the evening and picked up her phone, tipping the bottle up into her mouth at the same time she brought up the text message.

It was from Mason.

He'd gone a little weird Sunday night at his place after dinner, first being all flirty and sweet and then cold and withdrawn, only to end the night with a kiss to her knuckles and a smoldering look she'd deposited directly into her spank bank.

Tuesday and Thursday's dance lessons had been fine,

though. He was his old, charming self, twirling her around the dance floor and only stepping on her toes twice.

He really was improving while at the same time confusing the crap out of her.

She brought up his message.

It was a link to a video along with a message.

In case you haven't started preparing the guest favors yet, you might want to check this out.

She clicked the video link and took a sip from the wine bottle at the same time.

Bad idea.

When the image of a chocolate butthole came on to the screen, followed by the sweet little old English man who made the personalized asshole molds, Lowenna spat her wine clear across the kitchen.

The video went on to interview the man about his process. Then an American woman went to him, and the whole video followed her journey into getting her asshole cast so she could get it bronzed.

She watched that video three times and finished her bottle of wine before she worked up the courage to text Mason back. Only now she was tipsy and giggly.

That was quite interesting. Are you offering to be my model?

He texted back almost immediately.

I'm ready and willing. Just give me a minute to run home and shower first.

She snorted and shook her head.

You're terrible. I needed that though. Bridezilla has been terrorizing Tokyo again today. The bows on the boxes of chocolates must be off center, otherwise the world will implode.

She leaned against the stainless-steel counter that ran the whole length of the back kitchen, staring at her phone, waiting for his reply.

Well, duh. Of course it would. I thought you were smarter than that, Lowenna. Centered bows are for philistines. Get with the program.

She giggled. Another text message popped up.

I'm heading home to go and clean my butthole. See you in 10?

She tossed her head back and laughed.

Sounds good. I'm still at the chocolate shop. Bring your butt-hole, and we'll make magic.

Best offer I've ever received from a woman.

Now her sides and face hurt from laughing so much.

I'm actually at work, but if you want me and my butthole to come by, we can.

She knew he was joking, but a little part of her was also disappointed that she wasn't going to get to see him. It was probably for the best; she still had a lot of work to do. And Mason was a distraction—in the best way possible, of course. But she'd have to stay even later tomorrow night if he came by and they spent the rest of the evening goofing off. Casting his asshole or not.

She texted back.

It's probably for the best. I still have a shit-ton of work to do. No rest for the wicked sister.

She tipped the already empty wine bottle up and shook it over her mouth, hoping there were a few more drops clinging to the sides.

No such luck.

He texted her back.

Don't work too hard.

She set the wine bottle down and glanced at her assembly line of chocolates and gift boxes. She still had a long way to go.

I'll try not to. I can't wait until this nightmare is over.

Sweet dreams, Lowenna.

That last text was accompanied by a photo of his smiling

face and his bare chest, nipple piercings and all, and his rocking eight-pack of abs.

Her gasp echoed around the empty shop.

Zoom! Slam! Boy, did that ever get tossed into the spank bank fast. She nearly lost a finger, the vault door shut so hard and quick.

Another text message dinged.

Just a little something to tide you over. ;) Sleep tight.

She swallowed and fanned herself, still staring at his picture.

Yeah, she wasn't going to be getting much sleep tonight. Not after that picture.

Nope.

She scrolled up in her messages to the video link again and clicked it. The man who made the asshole molds had an email address.

Hmmm.

Well, if she wasn't going to be getting much sleep tonight, she might as well work.

Work and plot.

She brought up a blank compose page in her emails and pasted the man's email address into it.

Then, giddily, with shaky fingers and laughter bubbling in her chest, she began to compile her query.

Revenge came in all forms.

Even in the shape of a butthole.

13

IT WAS the last day of dance lessons and two days to the wedding. Lowenna had been a frazzled, beautiful, wild-haired mess when she burst through the dance studio doors ten minutes late.

"I'm sorry, I'm sorry," she said, kicking off her boots as she made her way across the dance studio floor toward Mason, Violet and Adam. "I know I'm late. I just had to finish the centerpiece, and much like the bride, it was being a pain in the neck."

She ripped her off socks, tossed them into the corner with her haphazardly discarded coat and boots and then sidled up next to Mason, her chest heaving and her hair stuck to her forehead and cheeks. But her eyes were bright and her cheeks a sexy pink.

Despite the chaos that seemed to spiral in with her, she was gorgeous.

"Did you run here?" Mason asked with a chuckle, bouncing a whimpering Willow in the carrier on his front. His daughter had been miserable all night and all day, most likely because she was working on popping a couple of teeth and they were giving her—and him—some serious grief.

Lowenna nodded and pushed the damp hair off her face. "It only started to downpour for the last half a block." Her pretty gray eyes lifted to him, and she batted her damp, spiked lashes. "I was hoping I could flirt my way into a ride home if the weather doesn't let up."

Adam snorted.

Violet giggled.

Mason grinned down at her. "I think something can probably be arranged, though you're going to have to flirt pretty damn hard. I live in the opposite direction, so I'll really be going out of my way." Out of his way four blocks, but whatever.

Heat flickered in her eyes, and her smile went a mile wide. Then she leaned in and pecked Willow on the cheek. "Hey, sweet girl. I've missed you something fierce. How's my baby?"

"Teething up a storm," Mason said, fighting back a yawn, but also loving that Lowenna called Willow *my baby*. He'd taken the whole day off work to be with his daughter—and also get some sleep. The poor thing had been up most of the night crying, only content when she was on him. So that's how they went through the darkest, loneliest hours of the day —the wee hours of the morning. He sat up with Willow on his chest, reclining in his La-Z-Boy making soft *shushing* sounds as she sucked furiously on her thumb.

He'd tried a few times to put her down in a crib, but he never even made it past the rocking horse in her room before she started to wail. And he just couldn't handle the sound of her crying. Particularly when he knew it was because she was in pain.

He'd even gone so far as to call Emmett, who not only was a single dad to a little girl as well but was also a doctor.

Unfortunately, Mason hadn't looked at the time when he called his friend, and poor Emmett was roused out of a deep sleep thinking that the city was on fire or there was a rocket headed for the Space Needle.

"Give her some Tylenol. The amount for her age and weight should be on the bottle. See if she'll suck on a cold, wet washcloth, and then just give her what she needs otherwise: comfort and patience. This is a hard time for parents," Emmett had said, exhaustion clear in his voice.

Mason paced up and down his dark hallway, bouncing a mewling Willow against his chest. "Should I take her to the hospital?"

"Why? All babies teethe. Besides, the hospital is no place for an infant unless they're seriously ill. That place is a cesspool of germs. She's likely to catch something if you take her there."

Oh God.

Now he was beginning to panic. If Willow spiked a fever or began to vomit, he wouldn't be able to take her to the hospital in fear she might contract pneumonia or Ebola or something.

"You're a good dad," Emmett said, the sound of a yawn coming through the phone. "You're worrying just as much as the rest of us did at this stage of the game. But I assure you, she's just teething. She's okay."

Holding Willow against his chest with one hand, his fingers splayed over her back, he ran his other hand through his hair. "Thanks, man. I'm sorry I called you so late."

"It's okay. Kiss Willow for me and try to get some rest."

"Thanks."

But he hadn't gotten much rest. Maybe a few hours collectively in the recliner but nothing significant enough to chase away the yawns or the feeling of concrete in his shoes as he slogged around the house with Willow in the carrier.

She even lost her mind when he put her in the car seat to drive to the dance studio. Which was why she was now, once again, in the carrier on his chest, barely keeping it together.

"You going to dance with the baby on you?" Adam asked, his arm around Violet as she rubbed her very plump belly.

Mason nodded. "I think I might have to. Little bunny won't let me out of her sight or put her down."

Adam rolled his eyes. "I remember that stage. Though Mira preferred Paige at this age because she had the working nipples."

"Did you guys bring your dancing shoes?" Violet asked, wincing a little as she cocked one hip and shifted her weight to her other foot.

Mason nodded, as did Lowenna.

On Tuesday, he'd only stepped on her toes once, and she said she barely felt it because she was in her fancy stilettos with the closed pointed toe and the *extremely* high heel. He still wasn't a foot guy, but if he was, Lowenna's feet in those black, sparkly things would be what he was into.

"Okay then," Violet said, waddling over to the stereo in the corner. "Put on your dancing shoes and let's get going."

"I can hold her if you want," Adam offered as Mason grabbed his black dress shoes from his bag and sat down on a chair against the wall to put them on. Willow began to warble in protest when he was forced to bend over and tie his laces. Her warble quickly turned into a shriek, and he bolted right up. "Sorry, baby. Sorry." He glanced at Adam. "I'm not sure she's going to let you hold her, dude. Kid is losing her mind these days if she's not with me. My mom can get away with watching her and holding her, but not even my dad can settle her anymore."

Adam's face was that of understanding and pity. "I get it. We're going to be there ourselves pretty soon." He glanced back at Violet, who was hunched over just a touch, her hands on the mirror, her head hanging down between her arms.

"She okay?"

"Braxton-Hicks are killing her."

"You sure she's not in labor?"

Adam shrugged. "She might be. But that stubborn woman of mine wouldn't tell us until the dance lesson was over even if she was."

Mason snickered, then leaned over to try and tie up his laces again.

Willow squawked.

"Here, let me." Lowenna *clickety-clacked* her sexy shoes over toward them. She was wearing a pair of tight black leggings or yoga pants or whatever the chicks called them, and they showed off her curves, her ass, her thighs and her calves like she was wearing fucking black body paint.

You cannot get a boner while wearing a baby. You cannot get a boner while wearing a baby.

She sank to her knees and leaned over.

She sank to her fucking knees.

Oh, God help him.

She was in a tight light blue tank top thing with thin straps and a low cut, with just an inch of lace along the neckline. And of course when she leaned over to tie his shoes for him, the front of her top billowed and he could see right down her shirt, into her cleavage to see that she was wearing a black lace bra.

You cannot get a boner while wearing a baby. You cannot get a boner while wearing a baby. You CANNOT get a boner while wearing a baby.

"There," she said, standing back up. "All tied. You're good to go."

He swallowed and stood, thanking her and adjusting his daughter in the carrier while also inconspicuously double-checking that he didn't have a half-chub. He would never forgive himself if he did.

Phew.

Thankfully, his *other* head had been smart enough to stay hidden, and he was good to go.

The music started, and Violet slowly made her way toward them all in the center of the room. His friend looked so uncomfortable, so exhausted.

"We're only going to dance for a minute or two," she said, nearly out of breath as she took Adam's hand. "I'm doing more *dictating* these days than I am *demonstrating.* My hips can't take much longer than a few minutes of standing."

Lowenna's lips dipped into a frown. "You should just go sit down now. We know the steps." She glanced up at Mason. "Right?"

He nodded. "Right. Go sit down, Vi. We got this."

He fucking hoped they had it.

Even though he had improved over the last several weeks, he still felt like a bumbling idiot on the dance floor. Big and awkward and more suited for being the bouncer than the dancer.

But he needed to do this for Lowenna. He had committed to doing this for her.

He took her hand and rested the other one on her waist, both of them adjusting themselves to accommodate the now sleeping infant between them.

Adam helped Violet over to the chairs along the wall, and the two of them sat down. The relief that crossed Violet's face was instantaneous.

"Ready?" Lowenna asked, squeezing his hand, her eyes hopeful and bright. "You can do this. *We* can do this."

We.

Was there a *we*? A *them*?

He didn't have time to think much more on that before

Violet called from the sidelines, "And five, six, seven, eight ... "

Lowenna and Mason locked eyes, gray to blue, hopeful to nervous.

And then they began to dance.

"You guys were amazing!" Violet clapped, beaming from her seat. "I'd get up and hug you, but I don't want to."

Lowenna's breath was coming just as quickly as his. They'd done a quicker step and tempo on that last dance, but thankfully, by grace and by God, he hadn't stepped on her toes once.

Willow was also still asleep.

Babies were crazy.

Or maybe she was just absolutely exhausted from being up all last night and barely napping that day. Mason was tired too.

Lowenna's gray-silver eyes glowed beneath the overhead lights, and her smile was bright enough to power the entire city. All he wanted to do at that moment was scoop her up into his arms, twirl her around the room and kiss her. Celebrate that their dance had been flawless, that they'd actually done it. Together. Let her know that they were better together, that *he* was better when they were together.

"I'd tell you to bow, but you don't want to piss off the baby," Adam said, clapping along with Violet. "You guys looked great. Didn't need us beside you at all."

"They also look good together," Violet added. "And with that baby between them." She shook her head, grinning. "Mhmm, mhmm, it's like you're the picture-perfect family. Mom, dad and baby. Who cares about the fundamentals when you all look that good?"

Mason was hot, and not just from their rigorous dancing.

Heat raced through him at Violet's words. But he also wanted to see Lowenna's reaction and slid his gaze to the side. The corners of her lips had turned down.

"Jumping the gun a bit there, Vi," Lowenna finally said, her chuckle so forced it sounded more like a dry heave.

Violet shrugged. "I don't know. I mean you guys have been spending a lot of time together. Even though I know this started out as a business arrangement, who says it can't be more? You're *practically* dating. Why not make it official?"

What the hell was Violet doing?

Mason cleared his throat and was about to say something, anything, to change the subject, but Lowenna beat him to it.

"We're just trying to get through the nightmare that is Saturday. One step at a time."

Mason hadn't realized it, but he and Lowenna were still holding hands. He certainly realized it now when she pulled her hand free and took a step away from him.

Oh, fuck, had Violet just made things worse?

He glanced at his very pregnant friend, but she didn't appear to be the least bit remorseful for her words. If anything, she seemed convinced that what she'd said was brilliant. The woman's smile was huge, and her green eyes danced.

He'd have to have words with his best friend's little sister later.

"I should probably get going," Lowenna said, ditching her shoes and padding barefoot over to the corner, where her boots had been kicked off.

"I'm driving you," he said, following behind her. "If you want to try one more dance, I'm sure Vi and Adam wouldn't mind."

She shook her head but didn't look at him. She balanced on one foot and tugged on her hot pink socks. "I'll just call an

Uber. Probably faster than you weaving through the dark, rainy night to get me home. Besides, you look tired." She lifted her head. She looked a million miles away. "I'll see you Saturday for the wedding."

Right. Saturday.

Not tomorrow.

Not Friday, the rehearsal dinner. Because he'd gone and rudely refused her request when she called him a *friend* and offered to pay him more. Once again reminding him that this was all a transaction. The exchange of money for a service. And his service was to convince everyone that the two of them were madly in love.

She dipped her head again and zipped up her boots. "I have a busy day tomorrow. I should get home." Then before he could protest or convince her to stay, she threw a wave over her shoulder at Adam and Vi and was off toward the front door, her coat and purse tucked haphazardly under her arm.

Moments later, the bell chimed, and he saw her stalking off down the sidewalk in front of the studio, her phone out, the backlight illuminating her face.

"What was that about?" Vi's voice brought his wandering thoughts back to the moment. "Everything okay between you? I didn't overstep, did I? I was just kidding around." She'd heaved herself up from her chair and was now standing beside him, her hand on his shoulder.

Mason shook his head and blinked before turning to face his friend. Adam had come to stand next to Vi. "I love her."

Violet's mouth opened to form a little *O,* and her eyebrows shot up her forehead. "Oh, wow. I didn't know it'd gotten that serious."

He swallowed. "She'd been coming into the bar for weeks before I finally spoke to her. And even then, before I even knew her name, I'd fallen for her. But she looks at me as just a friend ... " He dipped his head and kissed the top of Willow's head. "Oh, and her gigolo. I'm a friend and a boyfriend for hire."

"How can you change that?" Violet asked, squeezing his shoulder.

He shook his head. "I have no idea. Every time I think we're getting somewhere, she pulls back. She flirts and jokes and then all of a sudden she reins it all back and brings up that I'm her date for hire." And every time it gutted him. Made him see red that he'd agreed to such a stupid arrangement. He should have just been his charming, charismatic self and convinced her to date him for real, and then he would just accompany her to the wedding. But she'd been so adamant that it be a business deal, he hadn't argued hard enough.

She threw him off his game.

He'd been known as one of the best closers in the city. He could convince almost anybody to take the deal his company was offering. He just had a way with words. And that way with words also worked with the ladies.

But for some reason, he struggled to find those words when he was around Lowenna. He couldn't close the deal with her.

"You need to go above and beyond the job description, bro," Adam said quietly. "Knock her socks off. Surprise her. Show her that it's not a business arrangement anymore, that it's personal. Make her see what the rest of us already see."

How could he do that?

He blinked a few times and took a deep, grounding breath before he raked his fingers through his hair and chuckled. "Holy fuck, having baby girls makes you get in touch with your emotions." He forced out a breathy laugh. "My five-years-ago self would be asking my now self if I need to go change my tampon."

Violet rolled her eyes. "Emotions aren't a bad thing."

Adam slapped Mason on the back. "Don't I know it, bro. I'm going to be living in a house with *three* women."

Mason's gaze flew down to Vi's belly, then back up to his friends' faces. "It's a girl?"

Violet and Adam exchanged loving glances. "We tried to wait, but patience is neither of our strong suits." Violet rubbed her belly. "We're having a girl."

"That's awesome, guys."

Adam looped his arm around Violet and tugged her into his side. She leaned against him, her eyelids getting heavy. "Let us know how the wedding goes. We're very interested to hear how the bride and groom dance."

"Oh, I'm sure we'll be able to find it on YouTube," Violet said with an eye roll. "She has a blog and Instagram followers. *Many,* apparently. That video will be viral before the weekend is over. She's going to make sure of it."

Mason cringed. He was both dreading and interested in finally meeting the infamous Doneen and her douche-canoe of a fiancé, Brody. Having a wedding on Valentine's Day was one thing, but also on Lowenna's birthday ...

And then it hit him.

It was tough to make a circle with only three of them, but he did the best he could. Both Adam and Violet looked at him with curious expressions.

"I think I know how to surprise her," he said. "But I'm going to need the help of all the single dads ... and their women."

Violet and Adam's faces split into big grins.

Violet waddled over to the mirror, grabbed a chair and set it down where she'd just been standing. She sat down with a satisfied *ah.* "Okay, let's get planning."

14

LOWENNA CRACKED her neck side to side and tried to massage away the knots of painful tension glued to her shoulders. It was Friday night, the night before the wedding, and of course, she was still at the chocolate shop. She'd sent her staff home at closing time after calling everyone in early that day to help with Valentine's stock as well as the chocolate-covered strawberries for the wedding.

Doneen had called around four o'clock with a *quality check,* as she called it, wanting to know how things were going. She also made sure Lowenna knew she wouldn't be missed at the rehearsal dinner if she had to cancel to finish up perfecting the chocolate centerpiece.

The bitch.

Was she micromanaging all of the vendors or just Lowenna?

She wasn't sure which would be worse.

Knowing she was probably going to be working late, she brought her dress and makeup to the shop with her that morning. It would be a rush getting out of there on time. She had to put the final touches on the centerpiece, get dressed, put on makeup and fluff her hair. Not to mention call for a cab or Uber, which most likely was going to be impossible. It was Friday night, the restaurant was out past Lynnwood, and it was pouring rain. Any form of hired transportation was going to be unavailable.

Doneen and Brody wanted an elaborate four-foot-high chocolate centerpiece made of milk, dark and white chocolate. It had 3D busts of a man and woman locked in a passionate kiss, sitting atop a bed of shaved white and milk chocolate roses, while a paper-thin chocolate heart framed their kiss. Then, in white chocolate lettering on the heart, it said *Doneen and Brody Forever.*

Gag!

Her sister had come up with an absolutely impossible design and then expected Lowenna to execute it—for free.

At first, Lowenna wasn't sure she would be able to pull it off, but then the more she thought about it all, the more she knew she had to. People would be in awe of her raw talent. And then once she gave her speech, they'd not only think her a chocolate visionary but also a woman with a backbone who refused to lie down and let two cheating bastards walk all over her.

She grabbed the bottle of liquid freeze and gave the white lettering a few shots. Doneen wanted block letters, poured by hand, but Lowenna had a steady hand, and her freehand cursive was gorgeous. So she took the liberty of changing the plans and piping out *Doneen and Brody Forever* in white chocolate. Even though in her mind she was writing, *Bitchface and Micropenis Forever.*

Once she knew the chocolate had set, she carefully rolled the entire centerpiece back into the cooler. Pablo was a genius for suggesting they assemble the piece on a rolling trolley. It made way more sense than lifting it back and forth from the cooler to the kitchen.

Now it was time to get dressed. But not without a bit of a celebration of her own first.

After their first successful week of being open, she and her small staff of four had a little party after closing. Pablo brought tequila. That was when they came up with their tequila lime bonbons. They'd become a huge crowd pleaser when they finally debuted them, and Pablo—the chocolate painting wizard—made them look so decadent in neon green, they were almost too pretty to eat ... almost.

She grabbed the half-full bottle of tequila from the pantry, then slipped into the cooler and placed four tequila bonbons on a plate before making her way over to the table that housed the nearly three hundred wrapped and ribboned wedding guest favors.

She didn't bother with a shot glass, but before she took a sip, she held the bottle up to the stack of boxes. "Here's to you, *sister dear.* May you get your *just* desserts." She tipped the bottle up until her mouth was full, cringed and then swallowed.

Fuck, that shit was foul.

They used way better tequila in their bonbons than the turpentine that Pablo had shown up with.

She chased her shot with a chocolate, then did it three more times, loving the way her decadent creations banished the taste of sewage from her tongue and how her toes tingled and her limbs loosened with each drink.

Once she'd had her four shots and four bonbons, she tucked the tequila away and headed off toward the bathroom to get ready.

Hopefully, the booze in her system lasted until the cab got to the restaurant and she could get some wine into her system. No way in hell was she going through tonight sober.

Roughly twenty minutes later, Lowenna stepped out of the bathroom, makeup on, hair fluffed and dress mostly on.

She'd stupidly gone with a dress that had a zipper at the back, but she had no date to help her do it up.

Maybe the cab driver would take pity on her and help her out?

She slid into her black and white zebra striped faux fur pumps, checked her makeup in the mirror, grabbed her purse and coat and then began to close down the shop.

Might as well get this nightmare over with.

She flicked off the lights, set the alarm and headed to the door only to scream bloody murder when she lifted her head and came face-to-face with a man.

THAT HAD NOT AT ALL BEEN the reaction Mason was anticipating when Lowenna saw him standing on the other side of her shop door. The woman was terrified.

He knocked on the door. "Lowenna, it's me, Mason."

She'd already grabbed a rolling pin from somewhere and had lifted it above her head. What the hell was she planning to do with that? But then recognition dawned on her, and she set the rolling pin down on a counter and made her way closer to the door.

She unlocked it and stepped out, stumbling just a touch but regaining her footing a second later. She quickly locked the door behind her.

"Alarm's on," she murmured. It was dark out and raining, but the small amount of light from inside the shop let him see enough of her. Her cheeks held color, her eyes a sparkly glow. She looked more beautiful than he'd ever seen her.

So you like the look of women who are scared out of their skin? Maybe you should discuss that with your therapist ...

"What are you doing here?" she asked, lifting her gaze to his. They were standing beneath the eaves, dry enough but not for long. The wind had picked up and was now pushing the rain sideways.

"I came to take you to the rehearsal dinner," he said, shoving his hands into the pockets of his heavy black wool coat.

She blinked a few times, confusion darting behind her eyes. "But you said ... "

"I know. But this is important to you. I moved some stuff at work around. My mom took Willow. If we're supposed to be madly in love with each other, people are going to wonder tomorrow why I wasn't at dinner tonight." He reached for her coat to help her put it on, holding it out for her. She spun around, showing him her back, and that's when he noticed that her dress was undone.

Who was she going to ask to help her with her dress? A stranger?

Frustration at someone else getting to see so much of her bubbled like lava in his veins.

The zipper ran all the way from between her shoulder blades to just above her ... oh, fuck, was that a G-string?

Yes, yes it was.

He didn't say a word but simply pulled up the zipper, making sure he went slow as fuck and allowing his knuckles to graze her silky-soft skin.

He felt the gooseflesh ripple along her back, and the woman actually shivered when he reached the top, a deep breath fleeing her lungs, causing her slender shoulders to slouch and a sigh to escape from the depths of her chest. He encouraged her to put her arms through the sleeves of her coat. It was, after all, still winter.

She spun around to face him, her cheeks an even darker shade than before. "Thank you for coming," she said, blinking back tears. She swallowed hard and sniffed, running the back of her wrist beneath her nose. "I'm so glad that I don't have to go through tonight alone. I was dreading it."

She shouldn't have to be doing any of it alone. She shouldn't *be* alone.

She should be with me.

But he obviously didn't say that. Instead, he apologized. "I'm sorry I was such an ass earlier, dismissing coming tonight the way I did."

She shook her head and hiccupped a small sob. "You could not be further from an ass in every way possible. You are amazing. You are a ... a godsend and *exactly* who I want to be with ... " She took a couple of deep breaths and released them through her mouth, past the bright red lipstick he now envisioned seeing rimming the base of his cock. "Tonight."

He'd held his breath, only to release it forlornly when she ended that statement with *tonight*.

Stowing his disappointment, he chuckled. "Well, I'm not sure I was sent by God ... but I am glad I was able to make it. Help you out."

With teary eyes, she grinned up at him. "Well, you're certainly a tremendous friend and a knight in shining armor, *my* knight in shining armor. Or in your case"—she stepped forward and opened up the sides of his coat, which he hadn't bothered to button—"a knight in a very handsome suit. You look hot." Her teeth scraped over her bottom lip. "Like seriously hot. Doneen is going to hate me." She wrinkled her nose. "Well, she's going to hate me even more than she already does. I can't wait to see the look on her face when I walk in with you."

All he wanted to do at that moment was move into her, encourage her to slide her hands across his abdomen and wrap them around his back beneath his coat as he pinned her up against the door to her shop and took her mouth. Showed her just how crazy she made him, just how in love with her he already was, just how amazing a *real* boyfriend he could be.

But instead she said the one thing broke the spell. Severed the moment of enchantment completely.

"Of course, I'll pay you more for tonight. I really appreciate you helping me keep up appearances."

Keep up appearances.

Fuck him.

It was like he was on the losing end in one of Luna's rage rooms. A sledgehammer landed hard on his chest, causing his heart to shatter like a tacky crystal goblet. He shuttered his eyes for a moment, took a couple of his own deep breaths, then opened his eyes once more, flashing her the biggest, fakest, happiest smile he could muster. "Of course. We have to keep up *appearances*. Wouldn't want anybody to think that I'm not ass-over-teakettle in love with you."

"Isn't the saying *head over heels?*"

Yeah, he was that too.

But all he did was grunt, smile another fake smile and loop his arm over her shoulders, reaching for his umbrella that was leaning against the display window of the shop. He opened it up over them and escorted her down the sidewalk toward his warm, waiting truck.

MASON HELPED Lowenna down from her seat in his truck. The woman was dressed to fucking perfection in a dark purple—though chicks would probably call it *plum*—dress with a deep V-neck and long sleeves. It hugged her like a second skin and came just above her knees. And those shoes —maybe he did have a foot fetish—because they were sexy as fuck. He hadn't noticed them outside her chocolate shop, but he sure as fuck noticed them when she swung her legs out over the side of his truck and reached for his hand so he could help her down. They were wild—literally. Black and white zebra striped faux fur with a crazy-high heel. Fuck. Then all he could picture was her wearing those—and nothing else. Legs in the air, soles to the ceiling, nails raking down his back as she cried out his name and came undone, her pussy rippling around his cock as he hammered her hard into his mattress. Maybe he could hammer her hard enough, one of those shoes would fly off and conk him in the head.

Life goals!

When said shoes hit the ground, he didn't let go of her hand. "You ready?" he asked, slamming the truck door, then hitting lock on the fob.

She glanced up at him beneath her lashes. "No."

He released her hand and tugged her into his embrace. She fit just perfectly beneath his arm. "Well, neither am I. But let's get it over with anyway."

After speaking with Adam and Violet at length after their final dance lesson yesterday, he decided that he needed to step up his game with Lowenna. Be honest about his feelings and see how she responded. He was tired of pretending, tired of *giving her the boyfriend experience* when he could simply *be* her boyfriend.

As her boyfriend, as someone who loved her for her, he could help her learn how to get rid of the demons. The self-doubt, the hate and the anger. And he planned to show her that tonight, to show her what a life and a love with him could bring her—could bring both of them.

After he handed his keys to the valet, a BMW, a Mercedes and a McLaren waiting in the queue behind him, he and Lowenna made their way toward the front doors. Yeah, this hotel definitely catered to the upper echelon of society. He blew out a breath. *Show time!* Then he did what he'd been longing to do since that first night. He stopped them where they stood just outside the hotel lobby, leaned down and kissed her.

It was light. It was quick and more chaste than he would have liked. But they were not in a place to be sucking face and grinding like horny teenagers against a concrete column out front.

Chaste kiss or not, she was shocked to say the least because she definitely wasn't kissing him back.

She also tasted like tequila.

He pulled away and bit back his grin when color rushed into her cheeks. "Just keeping up appearances," he murmured against her mouth, loving the surprise in the silver flecks of her eyes. "You never know who could be watching." Then he pecked her one more time, only making her eyes grow wider, and ushered them toward the doors to the hotel.

Mason rolled his eyes. Of course Doneen and Brody would pick a place like this to hold their rehearsal dinner. It was posh, it was pretentious, and it was overpriced.

"They footing the bill for tonight?" he asked, holding the door open for her.

She tossed her head back and laughed as they stepped inside. "Such a silly man."

"Is it Brody's parents? Because that's tradition."

She shrugged. "Well, the bride and groom sure as hell aren't footing the bill, I'll tell you that."

Hmmm ...

Le Petit Amour was on the top floor of a *very* swanky hotel just north of Seattle between Lynwood and Mukilteo. It overlooked the Puget Sound on one side and had an award-winning golf course and country club on the other.

"This isn't where the wedding is tomorrow, is it?" he asked as they made their way toward the elevator.

She nodded, stepping inside, but not so much that she

dislodged from beneath his arm. "Yep. They reserved the grand ballroom. But they refused to use the onsite catering service because Doneen didn't like the head chef of the catering division. Said she was making flirty eyes at Brody."

He hit the elevator button for the restaurant, and the doors closed. "Of course she did."

"I think it was all in her head. Now that she knows he's capable of cheating, she's going to always be suspicious of him."

Mason snorted to himself and tugged Lowenna closer. "Sounds like those two deserve each other."

"Mhmm hmm, oh boy, do they ever."

It was a slow ride up, as their car was forced to stop for every monkey in a suit or gown that was also headed to dinner on the top floor. By the time they reached the top, there were well over a dozen people in the elevator, and Lowenna was now plastered against his side.

Just the way he liked her.

How could he get more people into the car on the way down? Maybe he'd have to carry her if it got too full.

As they stood there watching the floors climb, he glanced down at her and made sure to keep his voice just above a hush. "Not that I mind, but have you been drinking?"

She nodded and grinned. "Yep. Had four shots of tequila before I left. No way in hell am I going into this night sober. Should have grabbed the bottle and took a few shots before we handed the keys over to the valet. I think it's starting to wear off."

Mason shook his head and chuckled, continuing to whisper. "Don't worry, I won't let the big, bad sister from hell hurt you tonight. You have your protector here." He furrowed his brows in a serious way and nodded, which only made her giggle and tuck in closer to him.

Eventually they made it to the top, and the bronze

mirrored doors slid open to reveal swank and pretension dripping from every inch of the crown molding, the velvet valances and the crystal chandeliers. The only reason he knew what any of that shit was in the first place was because the first interior decorator he'd hired for the bar after he bought it had tried to get him to implement such ridiculous things. Needless to say, she hadn't lasted long.

The people in front of them filed out first, leaving him and Lowenna at the back, her tight beneath his arm, right where she belonged.

"Well," he started, giving her a gentle squeeze, "shall we ... "

"Get this over with?" she grumbled, stepping forward. "I guess we shall."

They checked with the maître d' before they were led through the restaurant toward the back and beyond some dark red velvet curtains, where the sounds of laughter and voices called them like a banshee on a cliff—to their doom.

The maître d' held the curtain open, allowing Mason and Lowenna to step forward into the large private party room. Instantly, voices hushed and all heads turned toward them. He still had his arm casually looped over her shoulder, so he felt her entire body tense up beneath his. She also squeezed in tighter to him, if that were at all possible, and rested her free hand on his chest.

"Lowenna," a woman in her mid-fifties said, standing up from her spot at the table to approach them. "Doneen told us all you had to cancel."

What the fuck?

Lowenna embraced the woman and pecked her on the cheek. "Well, I managed to get all my work done on time, so I decided to come. Helps that I had a ride." She glanced up at Mason, fear and anger duking it out for top spot in her stormy gray eyes. "Mom, this is Mason."

"Oh!"

"Mason, this is my mother, Adeline Chambers, and my father, Conrad, is at the end there with the blue and silver tie." Her father gave a wave and a smile.

Mason took Adeline's hand, giving it a firm but gentle squeeze. Women deserved a handshake with confidence behind it just as much as a man did. It frustrated his mother to no end when she'd meet a man and he would give her a limp-fish handshake as if he figured his *true* handshake would crush her delicate feminine fingers. She'd raised Mason to give women proper handshakes because it meant you saw them as equals.

Which they were.

If anything, women were the stronger, fiercer sex. He'd learned that very early on in life. Women were meant to be revered and respected. And he revered and respected the shit out of the woman in his arms right now.

"Nice to finally meet you, Mrs. Chambers."

She was a lovely woman, with the same coloring as Lowenna, same expressive eyes too. But her hair held strands of silver throughout and was longer and styled into a fashionable updo at the back of her head.

Adeline's smile was enormous as she took Mason's hand. "So lovely to meet you, Mason. We had no idea Lowenna was seeing anybody. Is this new?"

He glanced down at Lowenna and squeezed her against him again before bending down and pecking her on the top of the head—a move he planned to do a lot tonight. "A few months, I'd say. But I fell hard and fast. When you know, you know."

Adeline's eyes glittered. "Well, welcome. We're so happy you were able to join us. We can certainly make room at the table for two more." She began shuffling chairs and asking people to scoot over. But the maître d' was on top of things and had two penguin-suited waiters bringing in a couple more chairs and a two-top square table. In no time, Mason and Lowenna were seated at one end of the table, close to Lowenna's parents.

And he didn't even have to be introduced to them to know that they were also across from the bride and groom. The steam rising up from bridezilla's ears could have powered a locomotive, and the dark red stain on the cheating groom's cheeks rivaled a candy apple.

"I wish you'd told me you were bringing a guest," Doneen said through gritted teeth once they were all situated. "Is he coming to the wedding too?"

Lowenna nodded. "My apologies. And yes, he is. I *did* tick plus one on my invitation."

"Then you must have received the wrong invitation card."

Lowenna shrugged and patted Mason's thigh beneath the table, which immediately made his cock jerk. This was the first bit of affection she'd initiated. It must be show time. "Well, there's nothing I can do about that. Mason is my boyfriend, it's serious, and I would like to have him with me at your wedding."

Doneen's pale gray eyes shifted to Mason. "Well, this just means that someone I invited who I *wanted* to have a plus didn't get to have one."

Lowenna shrugged again. "Sorry, sis. Not my problem. I didn't send out your invitations."

Mason loved that Lowenna wasn't cowering or letting her sister bully her. He'd never taken Lowenna for a doormat, but he certainly thought she put up with too much from her bitch of a sister. It was nice to see that she was able to stand up for herself.

"Wine?" A waiter behind them held two bottles, one of red, one of white.

Lowenna nodded. "Red, please."

"Certainly."

Mason spied the liquor menu in front of him and snatched it quickly, flicking to the back. He pointed to the scotch—the expensive shit. "I'll have this, please."

The waiter's eyes were the only thing that betrayed him, and even then, just barely. They flared slightly before he masked his reaction and nodded. "Certainly, sir." Then he was gone.

Mason stowed the liquor menu back on the table and let his gaze slowly drift up to Brody's face. Still red as a fucking tomato.

This was going to be fun.

"Tell me, *Mason,* is it, what do you do for work?" Brody cleared his throat and took a sip of his white wine, his brow lifting just a touch. What a smug fucker.

Mason leaned back in his chair and looped his arm around the back of Lowenna's seat. "Used to be the top closer for Boon Investments here in town. You heard of 'em?"

Brody scoffed. "Heard of them? Of course I've *heard* of them. My firm represents them."

His firm. But not Brody.

Interesting.

Mason shrugged and thanked the waiter for his scotch, taking a sip before he spoke. "Anyway, yeah. I was their closer for a number of years. They recruited me out of grad school. But then I grew a conscience, ditched the suit, took off traveling for a bit, and now I own Prime Sports Bar and Grill."

"You own it?" asked an attractive younger woman down toward the end of the table. "I *love* that place. Your blackberry mojitos are to *die* for."

Mason grinned. "Why, thank you. Came up with that little gem myself. The trick is to use three different kinds of mint. We like to use spearmint, peppermint and chocolate mint. Feel it gives the drink more depth."

The woman batted long eyelashes and nodded eagerly. "Well, I just love it."

Heads around the table bobbed, and other people chimed in on their adoration and love for Mason's bar. Not that he needed it, because he knew he'd built a successful establishment, but it was always nice to hear how much people liked his place. Made it all worthwhile.

"So you're a *bartender* now?" Brody asked, his nostrils flaring as he squinted hazel eyes at Mason. "From a Fortune 500 company to slinging beer behind a bar?" He snorted. "Seems like a stupid choice to me."

Mason was unfazed by the pompous prick. Liam and Atlas had given him the rundown on Brody. He knew where to hit him where it hurt. He shrugged and took another sip of his scotch. "Yep. I sleep better at night and hire people from all walks of life. Immigrants and refugees, people looking to get back on their feet after a hard time, whether it be addiction, illness or a bad relationship. I don't judge as long as their work ethic is good. Even have a couple of guys on work release in the kitchen, have kids they want to provide for and show that they can make something of themselves."

The sound of women crooning and gushing around the table made the corner of Mason's lip twitch up. He hadn't told Lowenna any of that, so when he finally brought his gaze down to her, she was looking up at him with such fascination, he knew he'd done the right thing waiting to tell her until now.

"You look shocked to know all of this, *Lowly,*" Doneen asked. "The first you've heard of who your boyfriend keeps company with. Derelicts and convicts. People coming here to steal the jobs of hardworking Americans." This woman was a true piece of work. And her beauty didn't hold a candle to that of her baby sister. Though that may have just been because he knew how ugly a person she was on the inside.

Her red painted lips curled up into a bitchy smile as she waited for Lowenna to respond.

And she did so perfectly. "I knew, and I couldn't be prouder. Every time I hear it, it's like hearing it for the first time, and I just fall harder for him. He's making a difference in the world just like he wanted to."

Mason smiled down at her before pulling her close so he could peck her on the cheek. Her face grew warm beneath his lips. Now it was time to bring out the big guns.

"Thanks, babe," he said. "But you know that I do it to show Willow how the future should be. Everyone taking care of everyone." He fixed Doneen with a look he hoped made her insides turn ice-cold—well, *colder* than the frigid bitch already was. "And that nickname—*Lowly*— it stops tonight. You know it's mean. I don't want to ever hear it again."

Doneen went even redder than her fuckface fiancé's, if that was possible.

A hush had fallen over the table as everyone waited for the bride to retaliate.

She didn't. She did look as though she was not only constipated as fuck but had also just bit into a lemon.

"Who's Willow?" Lowenna's mother asked.

Mason turned his attention to Adeline. "My daughter."

Brody and Doneen exchanged glances, each of their eyes sharpening into thin slits and their mouths turning up into evil smiles.

"So you're divorced, then?" Doneen asked. "That must be really hard on your daughter." The bitch's tone said exactly what she intended to say but left unsaid.

Mason shook his head. "Nope. Not divorced."

"A widower, then?" the same woman down the table from earlier asked.

"Oh, how tragic," another woman said, her eyes sad.

"Nope. Not a widower."

Brows furrowed and lips curled in confusion.

"So then ... "

"I'm a single dad by choice," he said plainly. "Realized I wanted to be a dad, hadn't found the right woman yet, so I went at it alone. Found an egg, found a surrogate, and nine months later, I became the proud father to Willow Olivia Whitfield." He brought up his phone and the picture of her he kept as his wallpaper, then passed it down the table.

Woman after woman oohed and ahhed over his sweet, little angel.

He grabbed Brody's attention. "I'm actually buddies with a couple of guys, other single dads, who work at your firm. Play poker with Liam Dixon and Atlas Stark. You know 'em?"

Brody's pallor went the color of pea soup.

And BOOM goes the dynamite!

"You know Liam and Atlas?"

Mason nodded. "Yeah, for sure. I'm good friends with Zak Eastwood too. I think he's dating Aurora Stratford, who also works with you."

Brody's skin pigment paled even more.

Mason just continued, enjoying the way the man began to squirm in his seat. "They brought me into their single dad fold. We play poker on Saturdays, have playdates with our kids. We're talking about a big camping trip with everybody this summer. Atlas has given me a shit-ton of Aria's hand-me-downs for Willow. They're like my brothers."

At their last poker night, Liam and Atlas had debriefed Mason on Brody so that he would be fully prepared for anything this douche had to throw at him. But they knew that the one thing that would stick in the man's craw more than anything was how tight Mason was with the two lawyers—Brody's bosses.

For the past two years, Brody had tried his damnedest to befriend Liam and Atlas, get into their inner circle: go to lunch with them, work on cases with them, handle clients with them. And at every turn, Liam and Atlas had resisted because they hated Brody and how he treated lower-level lawyers and support staff at the firm. They also just thought he was a Class-A status-climbing tool, and neither of them wanted to befriend him, let alone even breathe the same air as him.

He watched as color traveled up from the collar of Brody's white dress shirt into his neck and cheeks. His Adam's apple jogged in his throat before he finally spoke. "Well, it's nice that they're willing to slum it with a bartender," he finally said.

"Shut it, Brody." Lowenna's voice beside him made his body go still, and his head snapped down to look at her. She was glaring at her ex-husband, her arms crossed in front of her chest, pushing up her breasts and making her cleavage look so damn fuckable.

Brody settled his gaze on Lowenna. "What? I'm just saying, *we're* lawyers, and Mason is a … "

"Watch it," Lowenna said, cutting him off.

Yes! There was the fire he'd fallen for on that first night. The woman who looked him in the eye and told him that under no uncertain terms was she going to be anybody's pity project or charity case. He was beginning to wonder where that little firecracker had disappeared to.

Mason rested his hand on Lowenna's shoulder. "It's okay, babe. I love my job, I'm good at it, and I make a fuck-ton of money doing it. I don't have to justify my choices to anyone, and neither do you. It's an honest career, and I help a lot of people."

Lowenna didn't bother turning to face him. She just continued to throw dagger-eyes at her sister across the table.

Doneen cleared her throat. "I think that's enough interviewing of our *uninvited* guest for now. I'm just glad that they were able to accommodate us with an extra table and chairs on such short notice." Her fake smile had to hurt her face. He hoped it did.

He set his lips against Lowenna's temple. "I love it when you get all protective of me, babe. It's hot. You do know I can defend myself though, right?"

She turned her head until they were eye to eye, their lips just inches from each other. He breathed her in. She smelled of wine, chocolate and Lowenna. A scent that had imprinted on him weeks ago and he'd never been able to get enough of. If he could bottle it, he would.

"I know you can," she whispered. "But when someone cuts down *my man*, I am going to fight for him. I am going to fight for *us*."

Us.

Was this her acting?

He sure as fuck hoped not. Things had become so muddled, so fucked up with this whole charade, that he couldn't tell what was real, what was put on and what he was simply misinterpreting as more, but it was no more than wishful thinking. Hopeless dreams.

He wasn't acting at all. Everything he did, he did because it was how he felt, how he wanted to be with her. She just needed convincing, and if he had to tell her it was him "keeping up appearances," then he would.

For now.

She pressed her lips against his and closed her eyes.

He was in fucking heaven.

He closed his eyes too and let her lead their kiss.

Audience be damned, he was ready and willing to pry her lips open and explore every contour of her mouth with his tongue. But he had to pace himself. They hadn't even had appetizers yet.

It was a light kiss, but it wasn't short. And when she

finally pulled away and opened her eyes, he saw something flash behind the bright silver that he hadn't seen since that first night when he kissed her—hope.

That hoped fueled his own.

Goosebumps broke out over her skin. An uncontrollable reaction he liked to see.

He'd like to make her lose more control.

He knew they were being watched—by everyone—so he kept his reaction cool, cupping her cheek and running the pad of his thumb over her bottom lip. "If I haven't told you already, you look incredible tonight. I love this dress ... and those shoes." His eyes flared. "How come I haven't seen these babies before?"

Her nose wrinkled, and her lips parted. Warm puffs of air hit his knuckles. That's when he noticed her chest was now rising and falling as if she'd just sprinted up all those floors rather than riding the elevator.

"I want you to keep them on *tonight*."

Her throat undulated.

"But take everything else off." He made sure to keep his voice down low enough that only Doneen and Brody would be able to hear them and not Lowenna's parents a few feet away.

He kept his eyes glued to his woman, watching as her cheeks pinked up real pretty and her eyes gained that sparkle he'd come to love.

A cleared throat across the table drew them away from each other. It was bridezilla, and she was shooting laser beams out of her eyes and puffing smoke from her nose and ears.

"Sorry," Mason said in the most unapologetic tone he could muster. "But I just can't keep my hands ... or lips off this woman. You remember what it was like when you first fell in love, right? Where you were just obsessed with each other? Constantly sneaking kisses whenever you could."

The bride and groom squirmed in their seats, and he felt Lowenna chuckle softly beside him.

"I promise, the rest of the night is going to be about you two," Mason said, holding up his hands. "Not another word about us and how much I freaking love this woman." He signaled the waiter who was standing near the door should anybody need anything. "A round of champagne, please," he said, "and just add it to my bill."

The waiter nodded. "Right away, sir." Then he was gone.

Mason turned back to face Brody and Doneen, all smiles. He couldn't say the same for the two sourpusses across from him. That only made him smile wider.

Lowenna scooted her chair closer to him and looped her arm through his, her other hand landing on his thigh and squeezing it.

This was going to be a *fun* night!

15

THEY WERE WELL into their main course, Mason having opted for the fifty-two-dollar rack of lamb with truffle butter risotto and a winter vegetable medley, and Lowenna preferring something light, ordered the maple-glazed sockeye salmon with wild rice pilaf and sautéed green beans.

"How's your meal?" Mason asked, taking a sip of what appeared to be his third scotch.

She dabbed at her mouth with her cloth napkin and turned to face him, sipping her wine. "It's amazing. How's yours?"

He lifted a fork with a piece of decadent-looking lamb on it and brought it to her lips. "Try it for yourself. I can guarantee you've never had anything that melts in your mouth so easily."

Another innuendo?

She kind of hoped so.

With heat in her cheeks, she opened her mouth and let him slide the fork inside. She tugged off the delicious piece of lamb with her lips and slowly chewed it, savoring the incredible spices and flavors. She shut her eyes to get the full experience.

"Told you," he murmured.

Her eyes were still closed, but she couldn't mistake the press of his lips against hers. It was gentle, soft and quick, but no less invigorating or heart-pounding. When he pulled away, she opened her eyes and blinked at him, praying that the warmth in her cheeks and chest wasn't visible to the rest of the world. "You had a bit of sauce there," he said, wiping the corner of her mouth with the pad of his thumb and then popping it into his mouth. "It's good lamb, but it tasted even better on you."

Holy Jesus, was the man trying to make her spontaneously orgasm at the dinner table? Because that was what was going to happen if he kept traveling down the road they were on. Mason was doing a bang-up, above-and-beyond job of convincing everyone that they were madly in love. Hell, even she was beginning to believe it.

But wasn't that the point?

He was just being a great actor. Giving her the boyfriend experience and then some. It was all an act. A believable act, an Oscar-worthy performance, but a performance nonetheless.

Sigh.

She wasn't so sure she wanted it to be an act anymore.

But she had to wonder if they were too far down the rabbit hole of make-believe, of him being her boyfriend for hire, for them to take a step back and try to make this something real.

It sure felt real. Her body was having a hard time discerning fact from fiction, as was evident by her hard, achy nipples and the dampness between her legs.

Lowenna was on her fifth glass of wine, having decided that if she was going to sit through an entire seven (yes,

SEVEN!) course meal with her sister glaring at her and her ex-husband just existing, she was going to do so drunk. The tequila had worn off by the time they got their appetizer, so she needed to double down if she intended to make it through to dessert without stabbing someone in the back of the hand with her salad fork.

Thankfully, the wine was good and potent, and she was well on her way to a loopy buzz by the time the sixth course came around. She was no longer hungry, but she was tipsy and horny and growing increasingly curious about those nipple rings beneath Mason's shirt and whether he liked them to be tugged on during sex. If she stared at his chest long and hard enough, she could make out the slight pucker of the barbells when he shifted and his dress shirt pulled tight over his pecs.

Her mouth watered at the thought of taking one of those nipples into her mouth, tugging until he groaned, shoved his hands into her hair and ...

She reached for her water glass and chewed on a few ice cubes. She needed to cool down.

Throughout the remainder of the meal, she and Mason continued to shoot each other sly side-eye glances. Followed by little smirks. She'd giggle and dip her head bashfully, and he'd bob his eyebrows.

It was all for show, but that didn't make it any less fun. That didn't make the butterflies in her belly any less frenetic. They didn't know that Mason's attentions were all an act, and if she didn't know any better, she'd believe he was genuine too. It made her realize how much she missed flirting, how much she missed the newness and excitement of a budding relationship, of the courtship. When you spent every moment away from the person thinking about them and every moment with them just completely infatuated, exploring their body, their heart and their mind.

And to anyone at that table besides the two of them, that was exactly how they looked.

Infatuated.

Obsessed.

Head over heels.

In love.

With an amuse-bouche, appetizer, bread, salad, soup, entrée and still a dessert to come, she wasn't sure she had any more room left once she pushed her nearly empty dinner plate away, sitting back and resting her hand on her belly.

"Food baby?" Mason asked, wiping his mouth with his cloth napkin.

She reached for her water. "Yep. A big one. And the dessert is cheesecake, I can't *not* eat it. But I'm not sure I have any more room."

"So we get it to go." He lifted one shoulder. "And then I eat it out of your belly button later."

Once again, heat crawled into her cheeks, and it most definitely wasn't from the wine. He caressed her with his sapphire gaze, making every muscle inside her clench tight. The warmth from her cheeks traveled downward, swirling through her abdomen and settling between her legs. Her toes curled in her heels. The heels he wanted her to keep on while taking off everything else.

A look from him was enough to get her going.

"Well, that'll be the only baby she'll ever have in her belly," came Doneen's shrill, venom-infused voice, breaking the spell between Mason and Lowenna. "You know she's barren?"

A lead weight slammed into the bottom of Lowenna's *barren*, forever childless stomach, and she hid her face, picking at her food.

"Don't hide," he whispered, his finger coming up beneath her chin, forcing her to lift her head. "Be strong."

She clenched her teeth tight and nodded, watching as his eyes shuttered and his expression grew blank before he slowly pivoted his head to face Lowenna's sister. "Is she barren? Huh. Because what *I* know, the Lowenna that *I* know, is a warrior who fought and vanquished cancer. But what warrior doesn't arrive home from battle without scars? Without losing a piece of themselves in the process?" His gaze narrowed on her sister. "She's not barren. She's alive, she's thriving, and if she wants to be a mother one day, she will be, and she will excel at it. Willow fucking loves her."

"Still can't carry a child though. Can't have a baby of her own," Doneen countered, not backing down, her back straight, her eyes mere slivers of pure judgement that stared right into him.

Mason lifted his scotch and drained it. "I can't carry a child either. Doesn't make me any less of a parent."

Lowenna could have kissed him, torn off his clothes and ravished him right on the table. He said all the right things. Who cared that they were all for show? At that moment, she believed every word that came out of his mouth—including the thing about the cheesecake and her belly button.

Doneen rolled her eyes and opened her mouth to say something, but Mason cut her off. "This topic of conversation is over. Yes, I know Lowenna can no longer carry a child. Yes, I know that she had cancer. But none of that changes how I feel about her or the fact that I want to have a future with her and raise a family. My surrogate has already agreed to another pregnancy if I want another child." He glanced down at Lowenna, reached for her hand and brought the back of it to his mouth. She simply stared at him in awe. "You've got frozen eggs too, right, baby? We can have our own little miracle when we're ready."

Gasps around the table echoed, and Lowenna fought the urge to move her eyes from Mason's handsome face to her sister or Brody. Nobody knew that she'd frozen her eggs—nobody. And she hadn't been sure she wanted anybody to know. But what she did know was that the way Mason was speaking, defending her and looking at her made her want the whole world to suddenly know she had eggs frozen and that she was going to be a mother to her own children one day—and an amazing mother to boot.

Mason's presence, his touch and support helped her find a confidence and strength inside herself that she didn't know she had. Made her see herself in a light that she thought had long been snuffed out.

"You froze your eggs?" her mother asked, her voice breathy.

Lowenna finally removed her gaze from Mason's face—albeit reluctantly—and faced her mother. "I did, yes."

Brody made a dismissive noise. "I would have remembered that."

Lowenna went to speak, but Mason got there first, his ire for Doneen and Brody a tangible entity she needed to keep caged. "Would you have, man?" He still held Lowenna's hand, his grip tightening.

He needed to rein in that anger. She had no intention of letting anybody at that table know she knew that Brody and Doneen were sleeping together while she was battling cancer and they were still married. That was for tomorrow, and she couldn't let him ruin her grand reveal.

She tugged on his hand until he faced her. His tight jaw relaxed and his eyes softened.

"I kept it a secret from everyone, babe," she said. "I wasn't sure if they were going to find any viable eggs, so I didn't want to get anybody's hopes up."

She was deliberately avoiding looking at Brody or Doneen, but she managed to see their reactions out of the corner of her eye, and it was pretty epic. Both of them were wide-eyed and slack-jawed.

"How'd you pay for that?" Brody asked, shaking his dumb bobblehead.

Mason didn't bother turning his head. "Doesn't matter, man. Not your problem." He pushed his plate away, pulled his hand from Lowenna's and stood up. "Please excuse me. I'll be right back." Then without telling anyone where he was headed or even glancing at Lowenna, he left the party room.

All eyes fell on Lowenna. She swallowed hard, digging down deep for the strength she knew she still possessed but that Mason so easily helped her uncover. She didn't need him, but she sure as heck liked having him around.

"Real prize you've brought to dinner," Doneen said blandly, poking at a cherry tomato on her plate with a fork and nibbling on it like a hamster.

"I dunno," Lowenna's father said. "I like him. Seems real down-to-earth, genuine, kind." He smiled at Lowenna. "And he seems to make you happy, sweetheart."

Lowenna's heart swelled in her chest, and she smiled at her father, a very gentle and docile man by nature. "Thanks, Dad. He makes me very happy."

"I still want to know how you were able to afford freezing your eggs," Brody piped up. "We were struggling to keep up with your medical bills, and we never discussed freezing your eggs. Why didn't you tell me?"

What, was he having a change of heart all of a sudden? Now that Lowenna had the ability to have children of her own, he was suddenly seeing her in a more motherly light? He'd been the one to call their whole marriage quits because he wanted to have a family the *traditional* way. Or had that just been an excuse to end things so he could take his affair with her sister public?

Mason returned but didn't sit down. Instead he placed

both of his hands on Lowenna's shoulders and squeezed. "We're leaving, babe. We've got a big day tomorrow. They're boxing up our dessert."

She craned her neck around to stare at him, her eyes taking a moment to adjust and un-blur themselves from the quick movement. That wine was hitting her hard. "We're leaving?"

He nodded and pulled her chair out for her. "Yep. Need to get you home and into bed." His low voice rumbling and the way he said *bed* made everything inside her tighten. Her nipples throbbed, her core clenched and her toes curled for probably the umpteenth time that night. He began to massage the base of her neck with his thumbs, and without even realizing it, she'd shut her eyes.

"Well, it was so nice to meet you," Lowenna's mother said, "and we look forward to getting to know you even more tomorrow. The wedding is sure to be a wonderful occasion."

Oh, it was going to be an *occasion* all right. He released her neck and shoulders and made to help her rise from her seat. He never stopped touching her. Whether it be holding her elbow, her hand or her neck, his hands were always on her. And she was grateful for it, because once she stood, the wine hit her like a freight train and she swayed.

"Goodnight, sweetheart," her mother said, standing up from her seat. Both of Lowenna's parents were soft-spoken, shy people. Since as long as she could remember, they'd allowed Doneen to bully them—and Lowenna. Which explained why they hadn't stood up for Lowenna at all over dinner. But Mason had.

Mason had been her hero.

Lowenna's mother embraced her, and then her dad, though through it all, Mason still never let go of her.

He wrapped his arm around her waist, and she leaned into him. He turned them so they faced the long table of dinner companions. "So nice to meet everyone. I look forward to cutting a rug on the dance floor with you all tomorrow night." Then he pecked Lowenna on the side of the head. He was doing that a lot. "But now I've got to get this gorgeous creature to bed."

It wasn't until they reached the elevator that Lowenna released the breath she'd been holding. Her brain was mush, her heart confused, her legs a bit noodly, but boy, was she happy.

She hadn't been that happy in a long, *long* time.

The look on her sister's face and Brody's face too. She should have hired a photographer to capture the moment so she could put their reactions on her fridge.

Mason hit the button for the elevator, his arm still wrapped around her tight.

"That was a fun night," he said, staring straight ahead. "You weren't kidding about those two. Wow! Liam and Atlas debriefed me on him, but her ... " He blew out a whistle. "She's a real piece of work." He held a small bag in his free hand that housed the two boxes of the amaretto pistachio cheesecake they'd ordered. Her mouth flooded with moisture at the thought of the dessert.

And then her core warmed when she thought of him eating it out of her belly button. She knew it was said in jest, but that didn't mean it hadn't stuck in her head since he mentioned it. The elevator door slid open, and with slight pressure at her back, he encouraged her to step inside.

Nobody else went in with them, but the moment the door closed, the small space was stifling. She became acutely aware of how close they were, the heat of his palm on her hip, the scent of him and way he made her feel like she'd not just had a few glasses of wine but a few bottles.

"What's this?" He bent down, unwilling to release his arm around her and instead juggling the dessert bag among his fingers, to pick up what looked like a room key card off the elevator floor.

"Looks like a key card," she whispered.

"Hmm, it does."

He handed it to her, and she turned it around in her hand.

The number 503 was clear as day in gold lettering on one side, while the hotel name was inscribed on the other. It was no ordinary key card, because this was no ordinary hotel.

Lowenna swallowed. "Someone must have dropped it."

A deep groan filled her ear. "Someone must have."

Her gaze flicked up to the lit floor numbers above their heads. They were currently on the twelfth floor.

Was this a sign?

They'd pretty much been handed a room key. Were they meant to go use it? At least check it out? Raid the minibar.

Wouldn't it be poetic if that key card somehow belonged to her sister and Brody and they went and raided the minibar? Racked up a couple hundred dollars' worth on their bill.

She knew that her sister and Brody were staying here in a normal suite tonight and then the honeymoon suite tomorrow night.

She bounced on her toes with glee as the most diabolical plan for tomorrow began to take shape in her mind.

Mason glanced down at her and grinned.

She grinned right back, so hard and so wide, her cheeks hurt.

She was happy, giddy in fact with how well the night had gone, that she wanted to continue to ride her high for as long as she could. And by ride her high, she meant ride Mason.

All his talk about *getting her to bed* had made her thoughts leap headfirst into the gutter, and they'd stayed there ever since.

She glanced again at the lit floor numbers overhead.

Floor nine.

Floor eight.

Floor seven.

It was now or never.

She twitched and was about to hit the button for number five when the car settled to a stop.

On. The. Fifth. Floor.

The doors slid open to reveal a man and woman roughly the same age as Mason and Lowenna sucking face as if they were both desperate for the other's air. His hand was on her butt, her arms wrapped tight around his neck, and there wasn't an inch of air or space between them.

Mason had to clear his throat twice before the couple untangled themselves, stepping onto the elevator all glassy-eyed and puffy-lipped.

"Sorry," the man said. "Just can't keep my hands off this woman."

His companion giggled.

Mason glanced down at Lowenna and she up at him.

The door began to close, but before it did completely, they both lunged forward at the same time and stopped it with their free hands.

After that it was all a bit of a beautiful, wine-infused blur.

They raced down the hall, laughing until they located suite 503, and then with eyes locked and a racing heart, she slid the key card through the panel and held her breath.

The light flashed green, and a click on the other side told them it was unlocked.

Mason reached forward and took the card from her, his hand engulfing hers and stilling the slight tremble that had sprinted up from her toes and into her fingers.

He turned the latch on the door and held it open for her.

It was dark and quiet inside.

She stepped over the threshold and flicked on the light,

the sound of the door clicking behind them making her jump.

Timidly, she turned the corner into the suite.

It was empty. It was clean. By the looks of the swan-shaped towels on the bed, housekeeping had just been in. Perhaps it was they who had dropped the key card. Either way, they suddenly found themselves in a room.

With a bed. A big bed.

And he had said to everyone at the table—several times—that he wanted, no, *needed* to get her to bed.

She stared at the enormous king-size bed and its plush comforter and down pillows, but she didn't feel a lick of tired. She felt anything but.

She was energized and excited, happy, drunk and gloriously confused.

His hands on her shoulders was only one way she knew that he was behind her. But even if he had refrained from touching her, she would have known he was near. His warmth and overwhelming presence made the hair on the back of her neck and arms tingle and stand up.

"You are a warrior, Lowenna," he whispered, his mouth right next to her ear. His lips fell to that extra-sensitive spot just below her ear. She tilted her neck to the side to give him better access. "You are a gorgeous, warrior princess with a heart of gold and a rocking ass." He moved his hands from her shoulders down her back and squeezed said ass, making her laugh. "And amazing fucking tits."

Still laughing, she spun around in his arms and looped her arms over his shoulders, clasping them behind his neck. "Thank you for tonight. I'm so glad I didn't have to go it alone."

His grin stole every last molecule of oxygen clean from her lungs. "They're really going to shit themselves when they find out I paid for the entire table."

She took a step back and released her hands from around his neck, but his fingers tightened in the flesh of her ass and he wouldn't let her flee.

"You did *what?*"

"Figured it would really stick in ol' Brody's craw that I footed the bill for the whole table.. You know, me being a *lowly* bartender and all and you slumming it with me."

"Holy shit, but there were like sixteen people there. That bill is going to be ... " She tried to do a bit of math in her head, but it was too full of wine to do anything more complex than her six times tables.

"It'll be pricey, probably." He shrugged. "But whatever."

"Did you find out who was *going* to pay the bill?"

He nodded. "Brody's parents."

She shook her head. She couldn't pay for everyone's meals. But she was paying Mason. It didn't make sense. She suddenly began to feel ill.

"I ... I think I need to sit down."

He released her butt and guided her down to the bed, shoving the swans out of the way. Once she was sitting, he sprang back up, raided the minibar for a bottle of water and opened the cap before he handed it to her.

She thanked him and took a big sip.

"I can't afford everyone's meals," she said, wiping the back of her wrist over her mouth. "I can't pay you back for—"

But she wasn't allowed to finish that statement before his lips crashed against hers.

"Don't mention money again to me, got it?" he said against her mouth. "I hate it when you bring up the fact that I'm your *date for hire*." Without breaking the kiss, he took the water bottle from her and set it on the nightstand, then he eased them both back on the bed, one hand cupping her face, the other one threading his fingers through hers.

He'd never mentioned before that he hated being her

hired boyfriend. Why hadn't he told her? Why was he still going along with it all if he hated it?

But his tongue massaging hers and his exploratory hands quickly pushed those thoughts from her mind, and her hands did their own bit of meandering and exploring.

She slid his suit jacket over and off his broad shoulders, then loosened his tie. Deftly, because she was now focused on what she wanted, on what she *needed*. She opened up a few of the buttons on his shirt, then pushed her hand inside, feeling his warm, smooth skin beneath her fingers. He was smooth, but damn, was he ever hard.

She found what she'd been searching for and tugged gently on the nipple barbell.

A groan filled her mouth at the same time his fingers pushed the hem of her dress up and skimmed along her inner thigh, tickling and chasing the shiver that raced up from her toes. They nudged aside her damp panties.

She pulled again on his nipple, and he spread her swollen lips and pressed against her clit with his thumb. Her hips leaped off the mattress.

They still hadn't stopped kissing, and as she knew from the night they first met, the man could sure as hell kiss.

He rocked against her, and she could feel the iron-hard length of him on her thigh. She wanted to feel that length of him in her hand, in her mouth, inside her. She wanted all of Mason and not just once.

He broke the kiss, and the tip of his tongue laved at her bottom lip before he tugged on it between his teeth, drawing a whimper from the back of her throat. He'd gone and shaved —unfortunately, but his whiskers were coming back, and they were rough and wonderful against her cheek. His warm, wet kisses peppered her jaw before he nipped at her earlobe and that tender spot where her neck met her shoulder. The warmth of his breath drifted over, causing a shiver to take hold of her body and all the hairs on her arms to prickle. He tucked his mouth into her neck, and his tongue did figure eights over the hollow of her throat, no doubt feeling her thundering pulse.

Lowenna shoved her fingers into his hair and tugged on the ends, gently nudging his head down.

His chuckle was deep and dark. "So bossy."

She threw her head back against the bed and exhaled, his lips traveled down her neck and chest until they reached the V of her dress. Her breasts swelled and ached at the thought of finally being touched. Her nipples pearled to painful points. With his free hand, he pulled the neck down and fished out a breast, swiping his tongue over the hard, crimson bud, making it peak even tighter, aching for more and making her dream of what that mouth might feel like lower down on her body, between her legs.

He blew cool air lightly across the tip before raking the rough stubble on his chin over the taut nub.

She trembled beneath him, and her pussy pulsed. Her eyelids grew heavy, her senses drugged by the sexual hunger emanating off him, by her own starvation and need for release. She bowed her back as he slipped two fingers into her slick channel and began to pump, his thumb strumming back and forth over her clit like the strings of a guitar. She churned her hips just a touch, and he pressed up hard inside her, hitting that sweet spot just right.

He sucked hard on her nipple, and a whimper escaped her when the pleasure sprinted straight to her clit.

"You taste incredible," he purred against her heated flesh, pushing the other breast out of her dress as well and capturing the tight bud in his mouth. Every word he spoke, every move he made, every look he gave her was designed to seduce her. And it was working like a charm.

She was putty in his hands. A slave to his ministrations

and the magic his body, his mouth, his tongue and fingers wielded.

With his free hand, he scrunched up the hem of her dress until her midriff was exposed, his fingers still fucking her, still hitting that spot, still grazing her walls, bringing her climax closer and closer.

He swirled his tongue over her nipple one more time, tugged hard enough to pull a gasp from her and then continued his journey down her abdomen. He nuzzled her belly button, swirled his tongue around and around, tickling her.

"Cheesecake," she panted.

He lifted his head, his fingers inside her stilling. "Huh?"

"Cheesecake. You ... you said you were going to eat cheesecake out of my belly button."

The corners of his mouth curled up into a devious smile, and his fingers slipped from inside her as his weight left the bed and he stood up. "So I did. And we can't make me into a liar, can we?"

Lowenna's bottom lip snagged beneath her top teeth and she shook her head, her eyes devouring him like *he* was a giant piece of amaretto pistachio cheesecake she couldn't wait to sink her teeth into.

She heard the plastic bag rustling and watched as he pulled a white cardboard box free and opened it. With a plastic fork from the bag, he scooped out a piece of cake.

She waited for the cool sensation of the cake to land on her exposed skin, but it never happened.

Instead, he brought the fork up to her mouth. "Open up, baby."

Smiling, she did as she was told and accepted the fork. At the same time she closed her lips over it, Mason slid two fingers back inside her.

Her eyes fluttered shut.

The flavors and pleasure were too much. Too intense. Her back bowed again, and her hips shot up high off the bed. That's when she felt the cool dampness land in her navel.

It was the shock to her system that she needed, the jolt required to drag her back from the edge.

His warm tongue twirled around her belly button, scooping out the cheesecake. Each swipe of his tongue sent a new wave of ecstasy down to where his fingers joined her, to where he pumped and coaxed the orgasm back to the cliff edge.

She pulled in a ragged breath, then breathed out.

"Let go, baby," he whispered, his lips landing on the lower part of her stomach, just above her panty line.

She shook her head, her hair splaying across the duvet. "No, I can't."

Not yet.

His eyes drifted up her body. "You *can't* or you *won't?*"

She swallowed. "I ... I won't. Not yet. I ... I want *you* ... "

Why was she suddenly nervous to tell him she wanted all of him? That she wanted to feel more of him inside her, all of him inside her. When Mason made her come, she wanted it to be because they were connected, because he was about to come too. Maybe they could come together.

His fingers hooked into the sides of her silky black G-string, and he pulled it down over her thighs. "Not tonight," he whispered, tossing her underwear to the floor, then rising back up and pressing his nose to the trimmed and shaped dark hair at the apex of her legs. He inhaled deeply. "Tonight, you are drunk. And that is *not* how we are going to do this. Not the first time, at least."

She shut her eyes and shoved the heels of her palms into her sockets, twisting. When she removed her hands, her brain swirled and colors flashed.

Yep, she was drunk.

He nuzzled his nose above her pussy, his breath a hot beat against her slippery folds. His fingers still moved inside her. With his shoulders, he spread her thighs, then sank down to the floor on his knees.

"Tonight is about you, my warrior." He hummed, his lips just hovering over her clit, the buzz of his words the only thing touching her.

She shimmied her bottom on the bed and jerked her hips up.

He pulled his face away completely and, with his free hand, turned her over onto one butt cheek. Then he spanked her.

She yelped from the surprise and sting of pain. She hadn't been expecting that at all.

But one thing she knew for sure—she liked it.

Where his hand had been was now a blooming warmth that spread through her like a wildfire, settling where his fingers were still connected to her, where his thumb flicked and fiddled with her clit.

"How badly do you want to come, Lowenna?" he asked, settling her back down on the bed, both cheeks to the duvet. His thumb fell away from her clit and his tongue replaced it.

"So bad," she breathed. She wanted to churn her hips again, press her mound against his mouth, but she knew better. His spank from earlier had been a warning. *He* was in charge of her pleasure tonight.

"How bad, baby?" His fingers slipped out of her, and both his hands palmed her bare thighs, spreading her legs wider. He lifted his head and removed his tongue.

Her chest rose and fell erratically.

He wasn't even touching her now, and yet she could probably come. She was so charged, so turned on and swollen.

"Mason," she whispered. "I'm so close. I want to come so, so bad. I want *you* to make me come ... please."

With both hands on her thighs, he pushed them even farther apart, bent his head low and swept his tongue up through her folds. From perineum to clit and back. Over and over again, he licked her like she was a melting ice cream cone and he wanted every single drip on his tongue.

The man definitely made her melt.

Unable to stop herself, she bucked up into him, gripped the bedspread until her knuckles cramped and let go.

He sucked hard on her clit as the climax picked her up, spun her around and then sent her sailing headfirst off the cliff and out into the abyss. His tongue twiddled and flicked on her hood as it swelled and pulsated with each delicious wave of her release.

With a final hard suck to her clit as the climax began to wane, he plunged his tongue into her pussy and drank her down, lapped up her juices, fucked her just like his fingers had. Like his life depended on it. Another, bigger, more intense orgasm than the first rocked her soul. She hadn't even come down from the first climax, and already the next one was overhauling her senses, wracking her body until she was afraid she couldn't take any more pleasure.

Her thighs shook uncontrollably. Her head thrashed on the bed. Her breasts ached.

And Mason did all of this to her.

She'd grown tired of her trusty vibrator and had pretty much become celibate over the last few months. Too tired in the evening to even think about sex and too lonely to continuously do it by herself. So she just didn't bother.

But these last few moments, Mason had done a damn good job reminding her what she'd been missing, what she'd been *lacking* in her life.

And that was Mason ... and orgasms ... and orgasms from Mason.

Spent from his attention, she released her vice grip on the

bedspread and tossed her forearm over her eyes, her whole body on fire and feeling like she'd just done sprints at the track. She was on an adrenaline high, full of endorphins and dopamine and all those other feel-good chemicals that people chased. She wanted to ride her high for as long as she could.

He released her thighs, and she heard him stand up and head to the bathroom. The faucet ran, and then a few seconds later he was back, his weight causing the bed to dip.

Gently, his fingers wrapped around her wrist, and he pulled her arm free from over her eyes. He was sitting up on the bed, grinning that crazy-sexy smile on that crazy-talented mouth and staring at her.

She bit her lip.

With his other hand, he pulled it free from her teeth and shook his head. "No shyness. Not with me."

She swallowed and nodded.

"You want to sit up?"

She nodded again, and he helped her up. Though that might have been a bad idea because spots clouded her vision and her head spun when she was once again vertical.

Maybe she shouldn't have had those last couple of glasses of wine ... or that cheap tequila.

She shut her eyes for a moment to keep her dinner down.

The last thing she wanted was for Mason to see her get sick from having had too much to drink. She was thirty goddamn years old. She should know how to hold her booze.

He handed her the water bottle, and she took a sip, pulling her dress down over her knees and tucking her breasts back into the top of her dress at the same time. Even though he told her she wasn't allowed to be shy, she was having a hard time looking at him.

She located her G-string, but it was too far away on the floor, and for some reason she didn't think he'd be too pleased with her if she stood up and retrieved it. So instead, she simply sat there, staring at her knitted hands, her stomach churning, her pulse thundering in her ears and her thighs slick.

"Lowenna." His deep, calm voice drew her to look at him. How could she not? His gaze was kind but avid, almost concerned. Heat still flickered behind the intense blue, but there was also a wariness there now too. "You okay?"

She nodded for what she felt like was the millionth time. "Yeah." She exhaled. "I'm more than okay."

That earned her a big smile.

"Good. Me too." He reached over and tucked a strand of hair behind her ear, his hand lingering and then cupping her cheek, his pinky finger resting along her neck, undoubtedly feeling her rapid pulse. "I've wanted this for so long, Lowenna. Wanted you. Since the moment you came into my bar and sat there with your little notebook and pen, interviewing man after man ... " He shook his head and huffed a laugh, glancing down at his lap. "Even if you weren't interviewing gigolos or, I dunno ... if you were a madam of some kind, I wanted you. Wanted to get to know you, everything about you."

She blew out a breath and leaned into his hand, closing her eyes. "Mason ... I ... " She blinked rapidly a few times as she took a moment to process everything he'd just said. When she lifted her head to his meet his gaze once again, the look that greeted her was no longer worrisome or wary. It was intense and heated, and it made her entire body tremble instantly.

He ran his free hand through his hair, exhaling another shaky laugh. "Hell, I didn't even know you yet, had the opportunity to kiss half a dozen women on New Year's Eve, and I didn't, because all I could think about was you. I'm falling for you." His lips twisted. "Or maybe I've already fallen, I don't know. But I don't want this to be a business arrangement anymore. I want us to be real. I want us to be together. I don't want to just give you the boyfriend experience, I want to *be* your boyfriend."

Holy shit.

Desire ... and something else rolled through her in big, lazy waves, touching every inch of her until her entire body burned like the surface of the sun for the man whose soulful blue eyes were at that moment looking at her like no man had ever looked at her before.

She went to open her mouth to say something, anything, when her stomach lurched.

Her eyes went wide as panic replaced every other feeling inside her. Her hands flew over her mouth, sending the water bottle to the floor as she stood up and raced to the bathroom. She fell to her knees and managed to get the lid to the toilet up just in time before ...

Oh God!

She alternated between vomiting and groaning.

How embarrassing.

How utterly embarrassing.

Here Mason had just poured his heart out to her and she'd gone and responded by barfing.

Romantic.

She gripped the bowl as wave after wave of nausea ripped through her.

A warm hand landed on her back and began to rub while another one gathered her hair off her face.

"Baby," he cooed, clicking his tongue. "Oh, honey." The tone of his voice didn't sound the least bit upset. If anything, he sounded amused. But perhaps that was just the wine talking, and she couldn't really discern tone or tenor from the most definite death of many of her brain cells. "I've gotcha," he said, tucking her hair up into what felt like a hotel bathroom shower cap. "Can't find a hair elastic, so this will have to do." He resumed rubbing her back and making deep, low, comforting noises that she assumed would cause even the most skittish of horses to relax.

"I can't in good conscience drop you off at your house tonight, not like this."

"Just leave me here to die," she murmured, shutting her eyes.

She felt his warm chuckle through his hand on her back. "Uh, not going to happen. You can come stay at my place. I'll sleep in the guest room, and you can have my room with the master bathroom. You can live on the tile floor if you need to."

She opened her eyes, sat up, flushed the toilet and accepted the towel he handed her. "I'm so sorry," she said, her words muffled by the plush white towel she was wiping across her mouth. "You just ... you did *that*, and then you poured your heart out, and I ... I ruin everything by puking. I was going to ... " She twisted her lips and rolled her eyes.

"You were going to what?" he asked, his grin so devilish, if her mouth didn't taste like a port-o-potty at Coachella, she might consider kissing him.

Her eyes drifted down to his lap. "I was going to *return the favor*." Heat bloomed in her cheeks.

He smiled even wider. "No, you weren't, but I appreciate the offer."

She went to open her mouth in protest, but he cut her off with his finger against her lips.

"I told you, you're drunk. It won't be like that for us ... not the first time. When we"—his lips twisted—"when we finally do what grownups do best, we'll both be sober."

She couldn't believe guys like him still existed. The decent, respectful kind.

She glanced down at her lap, her stomach doing a

painful, alarming somersault. "I like you, too, Mason. Like *really, really* like you. It hasn't been an *arrangement* with me for a while either. I've just been so caught up in this wedding and work that I refused to let myself think that you might not be pretending anymore. I didn't want to get my hopes up."

She went to look at him, but the wine in her stomach had other ideas, and instead she found herself once again hovering over the bowl, his hand on her back as every grape from that batch of wine came back up.

"I'm sorry you have to see me like this," she wailed in between bouts.

His lips fell to her sweaty temple. "A *real* boyfriend, not just the kind you hire, stays even when his woman is puking." Then he continued to rub her back at the same time she began to fall in love with him.

16

THE WEDDING WASN'T until three o'clock, with the reception to follow at six, so Mason figured they had the better part of the morning to discuss last night and see where they stood. See if Lowenna remembered anything.

Another reason why he didn't fuck drunk chicks. He wanted them to remember him taking them, pleasuring them, making them lose their mind. The only reason a woman shouldn't be able to remember having sex with him was when she blacked out mid-orgasm because it was so intense, her brain short-circuited. Not because she'd consumed half the Napa Valley's supply of merlot.

Only when he went to knock on his bedroom door, with a steaming cup of coffee and two Advil for his impromptu houseguest, the door swung open to reveal an empty room.

He checked the en suite bathroom, but that was empty too. The bed had been remade, the towels folded. The only trace that Lowenna had even been there was the scent of chocolate in the air—and even that was slightly masked by the smell of vomit.

He hadn't bothered to check his phone yet, as Willow had

been a demanding little thing when she woke up at five o'clock, only to promptly pass out around seven thirty with Mason in the guest bed. He'd woken up again around eight thirty, moved Willow back to her crib and went to check on Lowenna.

But when he realized she'd gone AWOL, he ran to his phone in the guest room, pulled it from the charger and checked his messages.

Sure enough, there was one from her.

Sorry to leave without saying anything this morning. I didn't want to wake you as I heard Willow up early and figured the two of you had fallen back to sleep. I have so much to do before the wedding so I need to get an early start. I'll see you at the hotel at 2:30, okay? Thanks so much for last night. Holding my hair, letting me crash at your house, defending my honor in front of the big sister from hell, and ... the other thing too. Xoxoxo

Mason smiled at her coy mention of *the other thing.* If he wanted to get specific, it was actually *two* other things, because he'd made her come twice.

But who was counting?

He was, that's who.

He'd planned to make her come a few more times too, but apparently her stomach had other ideas.

He texted her back, grinning as he made his way into the kitchen, sipping the coffee he'd intended for her.

Happy Birthday, gorgeous! I was hoping to sing to you this morning. Willow says I have the absolute BEST singing voice.

He hit send, but not before taking a shirtless selfie with a big smile. Then he sent her another one.

In all seriousness though, I hope you're feeling better. I'd hoped we could travel to the wedding together, but I understand if you have work to do first.

Should he send her a winky face or hugs and kisses? She'd sent him a slew of *x*'s and *o*'s, but it was always okay coming from a woman. Women got away with being openly affectionate and cute. Would it be weird coming from him?

Fuck it.

He added *xo* to the end of his text, then hit send.

He hadn't even had time to push the bread in the toaster down before she texted back.

Dear God you're fucking sexy! More of those pictures, please!! Also, thank you! And I'm sure Willow is right. You can sing to me during the wedding ceremony, how about that?

He laughed out loud. Wouldn't that just be perfect? Just as the bride and groom began to recite their vows, Mason could stand up and start singing "Happy Birthday" to Lowenna.

He kept reading.

It is Valentine's Day after all so we all got to the shop crazy-early to open up. Needed to make sure the shop was ready for the last-minute shoppers. There was a line around the block when we opened.

Wow! Why wouldn't there be a line though? Lowenna's talent with chocolate was unsurpassed. She could do anything and do it exceptionally well. And all of Seattle was figuring that out pretty darn quickly.

And oh shit, right! Not only was it her birthday, but it was also Valentine's Day. He needed to get her some flowers and ... ?

Well, he couldn't very well buy her chocolates. Lingerie? Wine?

He'd think of something before he saw her, something awesome.

Another text message from her popped up.

Shop's been slammed since we opened. CHA-CHING! And I need to get the centerpiece, guest favors and chocolate strawberries to the hotel. Not that I don't trust my staff, but I'll never hear the end of it if one of those bows on one of the boxes suddenly slips from off center to center. The world will surely implode, didn't you know that? Xoxo

There she went with more *x*'s and *o*'s. Did she mean them?

He'd come clean with her last night about his feelings, and thank fucking God, she'd admitted she liked him too.

He loved her, but he would take her *liking* him for now.

He texted her back.

Can't wait to see you, birthday girl. Happy Valentine's Day!

Then he added a winky face, a bunch of celebration and birthday emojis *and* another *x* and *o*. He rolled his eyes and stowed his phone in his flannel pajama pants. The woman was rendering him into a lovesick fifteen-year-old. Even worse, a lovesick fifteen-year-old *girl*. Because he'd certainly never acted like this when he was fifteen, but he remembered his sister Nova overthinking everything when it came to boys.

But he wasn't a boy.

He was a man, and he'd shown Lowenna such last night when he spread her thighs wide and buried his face in her sweetness. She'd wanted to take it further—and holy fuck, so did he—but he'd never fucked a woman the first time while she was drunk. Never. That was just not how he rolled.

He also didn't have any condoms on him.

She can't get pregnant, numbnuts.

Right.

But still. He'd been checked since his last partner, which had been quite some time ago. He scrubbed his hand over his face and sipped his coffee. Had it been since June since he'd gotten laid?

A wine rep from Oregon had come by the bar peddling her vino and flaunting her cleavage, and she'd all but lifted her skirt and bent over in the wine cooler. How could he say no?

Well, he had. In the wine cooler. He would never, ever

fuck at work. But he did take her up on her offer to stop by her hotel room later that night and let her show him *all* that Portland had to offer.

He shook his head, releasing the memory of … fuck, he couldn't even remember that wine rep's name. Gina? Gia? Mona? He knew it ended in an *A*. Either way, Gina, Gia or Mona wanted nothing more from him than orgasms, and he was content with the same from her. He'd had too many other things on his plate to think about. Like getting the bar up and running and his baby on the way.

But now … now he had his baby. She was happy, healthy and freaking perfect, and his bar was raking in the money hand over fist. Now he wanted more than just a woman in a hotel room and a handful of orgasms. Now he wanted a future. He wanted a woman whose name he'd never forget because it was so unique and so her. He wanted a woman who made him laugh and smile and look forward to waking up each morning cupping her boob, kissing her neck and smelling her morning breath.

Because that's what a real life with a real love was all about. Gross morning breath and all. He just had to find the time tonight to convey all of that to Lowenna because he couldn't bank on her remembering it all from last night.

The toast popped up in the toaster, and he pulled it out, tossing it onto a plate.

He snapped his fingers.

"Faye! That was her name." He blew out a breath. He'd never forgotten the name of a woman he'd slept with in all his life, and he wasn't about to start now. "Where the hell did I get Gina or Mona from?"

He was about to slather on the peanut butter when Willow down the hall let him know she was awake and she was hungry.

"Coming, baby," he said, taking a final sip of his coffee

and heading off toward the nursery. Oh, how nice it would be to share the parenting and domestic duties with someone. While he saw to the baby, she could be preparing breakfast or vice versa. Then when Willow got a bit older, he and Willow could prepare breakfast in bed for *her*.

He opened the door to Willow's room and turned on the light. She was on her belly because she'd now figured out how to roll and was giving him her best stink eye.

He bent down to pick her up, and that's when it hit him.

He reared back and coughed.

Damn, his baby was a shit machine.

"Yeah, it would be nice to have someone to share *this* responsibility with too. I need latex gloves and a surgical mask." Then he gingerly picked up his child and carried her like she was made of sewage-covered crystal over to the change table.

THE WEDDING CEREMONY went off without a hitch.

It was also long and boring as hell.

The bride and groom had written their own vows—because of course they had—and by the sounds of things, they'd each written a goddamn novel.

Lowenna found herself not only nodding off, her cheek repeatedly hitting Mason's shoulder, but as she zoned in and out, listening to the vows, she came to the hilarious realization that Brody most definitely hadn't written his own.

He was not a wordy or overly articulate person.

Yes, he could speak English and do it well enough. But he spoke basic language with little to no descriptive verbiage, and the vows he was spewing at Lowenna's sister were so fluffed up and bedazzled, the man himself was struggling to read it all, let alone pronounce all the words.

Who in their right mind writes this garbage? *For so much of my life I was in eternal darkness, destined to traverse the land blindly, only hoping for a single spark to guide my way, and then I found you. Not just a spark or a solitary flicker, but a woman as bright as the sun itself. Your smile alone illuminates the world like the glow of a billion stars. I revolve around you, my sun. You are my world, my universe, my everything.*

Gag!

Barf!

Was he fucking serious?

She hadn't felt hungover at all until that word vomit, but when Brody stumbled over the big words like *illuminate* and *traverse,* and then he called Doneen his sun, Lowenna had to cover her mouth for fear of losing her cookies in her seat.

Like seriously? Brody didn't have a sentimental or romantic bone in his goddamn body and he wrote that? *Puh-lease.*

Doneen wrote it and then told him to read it, one hundred percent.

By the time the wedding ceremony was over, all the guests were passing yawns back and forth as they filed out and cheered for the happy couple, who made their way back up the aisle. Doneen's smile was huge, her makeup and hair flawless, of course. Brody looked happy but also a touch scared.

Lowenna knew him well. She knew when the man finally realized he was in over his head with something, and he had that look the moment the reverend pronounced them husband and wife. Doneen threw herself at him, led the kiss, then led him down the aisle like a trained puppy.

He'd never had a spine when he was married to Lowenna either.

Only unlike Doneen, Lowenna had never bullied Brody, but maybe that's what he needed?

A hand on her thigh had her turning her attention from the commotion in the aisle to the incredible man beside her. "You okay?" he asked, linking his fingers through hers.

She nodded and smiled at him, squeezing his hand. "I am, actually. Bored out of my tree and glad that shit is over, but I'm okay."

His blue eyes went wide. "I know, right, like what the fuck?"

A hand landed on Mason's shoulder between them, and they turned to see who was behind them. Lowenna recognized Aurora, who waved, and she was sitting with three incredibly handsome men.

"What the fuck was up with those vows?" the man with the dark brown eyes and mischievous smile asked, shaking his head. "Like seriously, I think I might need to go puke somewhere."

Mason turned in his seat to better see the people behind them but didn't release Lowenna's hand. "I know, right? *You are my sun.*" He stuck his finger down his throat. "Gonna wolf my breakfast at that disgusting display."

The other three men chuckled.

"So is this the infamous *wicked sister?*" the man with the dark eyes asked. He extended his hand toward Lowenna. "Liam Dixon. Nice to finally meet you."

She took his hand. "I am that sister. Wicked as they come. Don't stand too close, otherwise when the house finally falls on me, you might get trapped too."

The redheaded man who was sitting next and awfully close to Aurora peered over the row. "I don't see any ruby slippers. You can't be *that* wicked."

Lowenna chuckled and snapped her fingers. "Oh, I knew I was missing something. Damn flying monkeys—must have left them on my other broom."

He laughed and patted Mason on the back. "I like her. Funny and cute."

There was a third man sitting next to Liam who had remained quiet. His dark gray eyes held a sadness that hit Lowenna hard in the chest. When he caught her looking at him, he smiled grimly and offered her his hand. "Atlas Stark. Liam and I work with Brody, and we hate him."

Direct and to the point. She liked this guy.

She took his hand and shook it. It was warm and firm. "Nice to meet you. I hate Brody too, so we have at least one thing in common besides the gray eyes."

His small smile faltered, and something flashed behind those gray eyes, but then his grip on her hand tightened, his smile widened just a touch and the gray in his eyes lightened. "Observant. I like that." He released her hand and reached into his coat pocket, pulling out his phone. "This is the nanny. I've got to take this." Then he stood up and pushed past everyone else still in the row until he found an alternate exit and disappeared outside.

Liam linked his fingers together and stretched his hands out far in front of him. "Well, shall we go find this open bar? Put these narcissistic motherfuckers in the poorhouse one scotch at a time?"

Zak nodded. "Sounds good to me."

She was about to ask the guys to go easy on the bar as her parents were actually the ones footing the bill until she noticed that Zak was in a kilt instead of trousers.

Then she forgot her words.

Damn. Kilts were so freaking hot.

Aurora touched Lowenna's arm. "You coming, Lowenna?"

She hummed, her head bobbing slowly. "Yeah, but uh, first I have to go do a few things."

Zak, Aurora and Liam all flicked their gazes to Mason as if

something wasn't going quite according to plan. She recognized that look well. She hadn't been aware of it at the time, but that was the same look Doneen and Brody gave each other all the time when they were sneaking around behind Lowenna's back. Like they had a secret, a plan, and Lowenna's sheer existence, her continued survival, threw a giant wrench into that plan.

Unease wormed its way into her belly, and she glanced up at Mason, slowly tugging her hand from his. "What's going on?"

He shook his head, his eyes big, bright and innocent. "Nothing. What do you have to do?"

Her eyes squinted. "A few things."

He flashed her a grin she knew was meant to disarm her, but it didn't work. He reached for her hand again. "Well, whatever you have planned, it can wait. Let's go upstairs for a sec, okay?"

She reared back. "Upstairs? As in a hotel room?"

He nodded. "Yeah, but I guarantee you, it's not what you think." He stood up and pulled her with him, tugging on her arm until she was forced to stand as well. "Come on."

"I ... I have to go to my work van and grab something first though." He couldn't derail her plans now. He just couldn't. She only had a small window while the *happy* couple were off getting their photo taken by Mitch and Tori and the rest of the guests were making their way to the reception hall for drinks and appetizers. She had to make the most of this window. She had to start her revenge.

"Can it wait?" Mason asked, helping her meander through the last remaining guests who were filing out and heading to the other side of the hotel for the reception.

She shook her head. "I'll be five minutes. My van is just out front in preferred parking. I swear." She didn't dare bring what she had into the reception with her or even into the kitchen. In the wrong hands, it could be bad news. So she made sure to get good parking out front and kept the bag in the van. She shook herself free of his grasp, readjusted her shawl and then took off toward the exit.

She couldn't let whatever plan Mason and his friends had derail her plan. And boy, did she have a plan. A multilevel, hit them where it hurts, hit them where it counts plan.

By the end of the night, Brody and Doneen wouldn't know what hit them—in more ways than one.

17

THEY RODE the elevator in silence.

Lowenna was champing at the bit to get her plan under way, only Mason appeared to have other ideas and was hauling her up ten floors to a hotel room. For what?

So they could finally finish what they started last night, only this time he could do so with a clear conscience because she wasn't drunk—yet?

She glanced at him out of the corner of her eye. He seemed nervous. Staring straight ahead, fists bunched at his sides, shoulders nearly touching his ears.

If anybody needed a drink to loosen the hell up, it was him.

When the elevator doors finally slid open, he let her go ahead of him. She had no idea where they were headed, so she waited for him to step off the car, and then she followed him.

They didn't have to go far. He stopped in front of room 1009, which was just three doors from the elevator. Then he pulled a key card from his pocket.

Her brain raced back to last night and their fun, reckless

decision to go and utilize the hotel room the fates had gifted them. Too bad her need to numb the effects of the night had reared its ugly, wine- and tequila-flavored head and she found herself on the tile floor of the bathroom praying to the porcelain gods for salvation.

"It won't be like last night," he said, reading her mind.

So this was about sex then.

She would have taken him for more of a romantic than just whisking her upstairs in the middle of the wedding and *getting it over with*. Because that's certainly how it felt.

He slid the key card into the door, and it flashed green and then clicked, but before she could step away in protest, he opened the door and practically shoved her inside.

All of Lowenna's hackles instantly jolted up, and she braced herself for God only knows what, but instead she was nearly knocked clear on her ass by the lights flashing on and over a dozen people cheering *Happy birthday!* at her.

Blinking again and again and again because if she rubbed her eyes she'd look like a raccoon in no time, her gaze slid around the hotel suite, taking in everyone, all the women from Violet's baby shower as well as more faces she didn't recognize. All of them smiling at her with bright eyes and party hats.

There were balloons, a banner, champagne in a bucket and what appeared to be a beautiful cake sitting on the table.

Emotion choked her throat as she turned around to face Mason. His smile was small and almost sheepish, and when he shoved his hands into his pockets and rocked back on his heels, it only added to his whole cavalier appeal. "Just because Dumb and Dumbass are getting married and it's Valentine's Day doesn't mean it's also not your birthday. It should be celebrated, with a party." He reached for a stunning bouquet of flowers off the table and handed it to her, along with a gift-wrapped box and a beautiful bottle of wine.

"It's also Valentine's Day, so you get double the celebration—at least from me." He kissed her on the cheek, followed by a deeper, more intimate one on the lips.

"Get a room," Zak called before Mason lifted his head, grinning.

Heat flew into her cheeks.

Luna from The Rage Room wandered over from the crowd and gently placed a party hat on Lowenna's head. "Welcome, birthday girl!" She hugged Lowenna, then whispered, "Next session at The Rage Room is on the house."

One by one, all the guests came up and hugged her, including people she didn't recognize, like Liam's brother Scott; Tori's boyfriend, Mark; Zara's boyfriend, Emmett; and Isobel's boyfriend, Aaron. She recognized Mitch as he'd been busy flitting around all morning and afternoon taking pictures with Tori.

"We can't stay long," Mitch said, pulling away after hugging her. "Mr. and Mrs. Asshole are just touching up makeup and hair before we're allowed to go and make them look good." He rolled his eyes and glanced at Tori. "Not even Photoshop can take care of their kind of ugly. That shit is inside."

Tori nodded. "Agreed."

"Shall we pop some bubbly and get this party started?" Liam asked. He grabbed the champagne from the ice bucket, then went to an empty corner of the suite. "Thought for a second we might have to kidnap you," he said, deploying the cork. "You women and your independence and own agendas." He clucked his tongue, grinning as he wandered back over to the table and began filling champagne flutes.

"Mark my words, Liam, one of these days you're going to get knocked flat on your ass by an *independent* woman with her *own agenda,* and you will fall in love and never look back," Isobel said, thanking him for her champagne.

Liam shook his head as he handed Lowenna her champagne. "Not freaking likely, Miss Jones. I'm a born-again bachelor, didn't you hear? Love doesn't exist. It's a fabricated no—"

"Can it!" Atlas snapped.

Liam frowned but then shook it off and raised his glass into the air. "To Lowenna—"

"I'll give the toast, if you don't mind," Mason cut in, sidling up next to Lowenna as they all gathered into a circle, their glasses raised toward her, her heart beating wildly as tears threatened to ruin her makeup.

Liam frowned again but nodded. "What the hell is with everybody cutting me off?"

"It's because a lot of what you say is annoying," Atlas added.

Chuckles drifted around the room, but Liam seemed to shake off the insult.

Mason cleared his throat before lifting his glass higher into the air. "To Lowenna, the most incredible, strong, smart, creative, beautiful woman I've ever met. You are a warrior through and through, and you deserve only good things to come to you from here on out. Take today as a rebirth, as a new beginning. Don't look back, only forward—to the future. May it be as bright as the sun itself. Like the glow of a billion stars. Not just a spark or a solitary flicker. Be the universe, Lowenna."

She glanced at him, and her lip twitched.

His twitched too.

She knew he was mocking Doneen and Brody's vows.

Snorts around the room said everyone else knew it too.

"Good one," Zak guffawed.

"I don't get it," Mark said, glancing at Tori.

"I'll explain later," she whispered.

"To Lowenna," Zara repeated. "Happy birthday!"

"Happy birthday, Lowenna!" everyone cheered, clinking their glasses. Then the sound of those irritating noisemakers people usually blow for New Year's Eve started going off.

Lowenna grabbed a tissue from a nearby box and blotted at her eyes, unable to keep the smile from her face.

Nobody had ever thrown her a surprise party before. Never. She found Mason standing off to the side, champagne flute in his hand. He was waiting for her.

She approached him, pushed up onto her tiptoes and pressed her lips to his. It was difficult to wrap her arms around his neck because she was still holding her champagne, but she managed, and he deepened the kiss, wedging his tongue into her mouth, reminding her just how damn talented it was.

Her knees threatened to buckle, but his lone arm around her waist held her in place, kept her safe, kept her standing.

Hoots and hollers from the people behind them had them finally pulling apart, grinning as she sank back down onto her heels and stepped into his side. He looped his arm around her.

"That's what I'm talking about," Scott whooped. "It's like *Pretty Woman. Princess Vivian! Princess Vivian!*" He came up and elbowed Mason. "That the first time you've kissed on the lips? Hookers don't normally kiss on the lips, right?"

Mason glared at Scott, and Lowenna's cheeks burned.

"I'm kidding," Scott said with a laugh, backing up a bit and holding his hands up in surrender. "I'm kidding. I saw you guys kiss a minute ago. Was *that* your first kiss?"

Mason growled.

Lowenna swallowed down her embarrassment and leaned into Mason for strength. "Thank you all so much for coming. I don't even know some of you, and yet you still came to wish me a happy birthday. It just ... " She was starting to get choked up again. "It just means a lot to know that I now have friends, because I hope that even if we only met today that now, tomorrow and every day after, I can call you a friend."

"Do friends get to taste-test new chocolates?" Scott asked.

Mason elbowed him.

Lowenna burst out laughing, using her tissue to once again dab at her eyes. "They do, Scott. They sure do."

His smile was boyish and cheeky as he leveled his twinkling eyes at Mason. "I like her. You should marry her, or else I might."

Mason tightened his hold on her, squeezing a chuckle from the back of her throat. She glanced up at her man, her savior. "Was this your idea?"

He set his champagne down on the dresser and hooked his knuckle beneath her chin, tilting her face up. "With a little help from some friends, yes. Although corny and a mock of something far worse said downstairs, I meant what I said in my toast. You only deserve good things. You only deserve wins. And you should look at today as a new beginning. Don't look back, only forward. Don't let your demons win." With his knuckle still beneath her chin, he brought his mouth down to hers and brushed a light kiss against her lips. "Be the sun," he whispered against her mouth.

She sank into his body instantly, the hard planes of his muscles enfolding her.

"Get a room!" Zak called out again.

Oh! What an excellent idea.

As she continued to kiss Mason, once again wrapping her arm around his neck, she began to hatch a new plot, an even better plot than before. She'd been unsure at the idea of Mason procuring a hotel room for them simply to *get it over with*, but now, after this party, after his toast and the way he was looking at her, she didn't want to get anything *over with*. She wanted to start something.

She wanted to start a relationship with him. She wanted to start a future, a forever, a happily ever after with Mason.

Holy shit.

She loved him.

She loved Mason.

Beyond a shadow of a doubt, she was in love with this man. She knew she'd been developing feelings for him, that it'd gone beyond the date-for-hire relationship they'd started out with, but it was like a baseball bat to the back of the head with the overwhelming force of how much she loved him.

She broke their kiss and opened her eyes. Heat flicked in the dark blue of his irises.

She was about to profess that love, overflowing hotel room be damned, when she was cut off by the chorused "Happy Birthday" song and Paige coming forward carrying the cake.

Two candles, a three and a zero, sat burning in the middle of a gorgeous, delicious-looking round cake with gum paste flowers, white icing and beautiful, delicate detailing and piping. It had to be a Paige McPherson original. Lowenna followed Paige's bistro on Instagram, and the woman was a dessert legend.

They came to the end of the birthday song, the candles burning in front of her, everyone watching, waiting.

I wish for Mason. I wish for Willow. I wish for happiness and love.

She took a deep breath and blew out the candles. Everyone cheered and clapped, then Paige whisked the cake away to begin slicing it.

Lowenna turned back to Mason. "Thank you again, for everything. I—"

"Here's the first slice for the birthday girl," Liam said, interrupting them and handing Lowenna a plate with cake.

Smiling, she thanked him.

Looked like her proclamation of her epiphany would have to wait just a little longer.

Mason pecked her on the side of the head. "This is just the beginning, babe," he murmured. "Tonight, we're going to dance our hearts out, and then I'm going to take you home and make good on where last night went wrong."

"Or"—she batted her lashes at him—"we could make good on last night sooner than tonight. Tonight could just be an encore." She put a forkful of cake into her mouth, pulling the spongy deliciousness off with her teeth. Oh, God, was that ever good. Rich and moist and perfectly wonderful. Paige had outdone herself creating such a whirlwind of flavors in a pastry. It was vanilla cake, no doubt about it, but the rich aroma and flecks of purple said it also had lavender in it.

How fitting for the Lilac and Lavender Bistro, but also uniquely incredible. She'd have to consider incorporating lavender into her chocolates in the future.

"Like now?" Mason asked.

Oh shit, she'd been so caught up in the food, she'd completely forgotten that she just propositioned him for sex.

She swallowed her cake and nodded. "Yes."

His eyes danced around the room at all the smiling, happy people before he glanced back down at her, panic in his eyes. "This isn't my hotel room, though. It's Mitch and Paige's. They're staying here tonight, as they're both working the wedding. They just offered it up for your party. I can't really kick everybody out."

She grinned at him. "Don't worry, I have the *perfect* room for us." Then she took another bite of her cake, closed her eyes and let the flavors take her away.

18

A DEEP, masculine groan filled her ear as they once again rode the elevator in complete silence. Only this time, the silence wasn't awkward in the least. It was filled with the promise of what was to come. Pheromones and desires bounced around the small space as Mason stood behind Lowenna and buried his nose in her neck, growling and nipping at that ultra-sensitive spot right below her ear.

She shut her eyes and leaned back into him, feeling his need for her against her butt.

"Have I told you how fucking sexy you look in this dress?" he asked, tracing his tongue over her bare shoulder. "Though I bet you'll look even better out of it." His hands looped around her waist, and he moved them up to cup her breasts over her dress. Her nipples instantly pebbled, and her core tightened.

The wedding was black tie and formal, so Lowenna had hunted high and low for the absolute perfect dress. A few years back while sifting through magazines during a round of chemo, she came upon this ultra-chic gown being worn by none other than the stunning Jennifer Lawrence.

She'd ripped the page out of the magazine and ever since carried it around in her purse on the off chance she might one day stumble upon a knockoff in a store window.

And she had. She'd found it. A near replica for a fraction of the price, just days after Mason had offered to be her date. Just like J-Law's dress, Lowenna's was silver and shimmery, low-cut in the back, a deep V in the front and with a high slit up her thigh. The straps were skimpy, but she covered her shoulders with a white faux fur shawl. Best of all, though, the dress fit her like a freaking glove. It hugged her curves, showing off everything she'd worked so hard to regain after having wasted away to a skeleton because of the chemo. Now, she had her shape back, her toned muscles and womanly figure. And this dress—although still a bit out of her price range—was worth every penny. She felt like a million dollars, and standing next to the incredibly sexy Mason in his black tux, she knew she'd made the right choice bringing him as her date.

"You should open your gift," he said, taking the small box from her hand and pulling on the satin bow until it released. With his hands still in front of her, he lifted the lid of the box to reveal a stunning pendant.

She gasped, then craned her neck around to gape at him. "You shouldn't have. Mason, it's way too much."

He dismissed her protestations with a simple headshake before he pulled the necklace free, undid the clasp and looped it around her neck. "Chocolate diamonds on the outside, for the most incredible chocolatier, and an amethyst in the middle because that's your birthstone. And the heart shape is because your birthday is on Valentine's Day and"— he spun her around in his arms—"because I love you."

Holy shit.

She was about to say something, anything, really. Even a lame *thank you,* but the elevator stopped, dinged, and the doors slid open. He turned her around in his arms again, and with his hand on her lower back, he encouraged her forward, taking her hand once they were in the hallway.

"This way," she said, finally finding some words and pulling him along, the key card for the honeymoon suite burning a hole in her sweaty palm.

She had a small fabric bag with her necessities in it, and Mason was kind enough to carry her shawl, because right now she didn't need it. She was burning up.

They came to the double doors of the suite, and she waved the key card until the light flashed green and the lock clicked open.

Taking a deep breath, she turned the latch, pushed the door open and stepped inside.

Mason let out a low whistle behind her. "This is some room you got."

With her lip between her teeth she surveyed the space.

The bed was a big, beautiful four-poster with a red satin canopy, more throw pillows than there were snowflakes in the North Pole and a cream bedspread with red flowers embroidered all over it. It was a lush place.

Doneen and Brody would be very happy spending their first night as husband and wife in this room, in that bed.

But Lowenna was going to spend some time with Mason there first.

She didn't need the vanity mirror to tell her he was behind her. She felt him. Felt his heat, felt his strength and the safety and security he embodied like an intrinsic part of him. He pushed her head forward and began planting warm, wet kisses along the back of her neck, sliding his tongue over her shoulder blades and the shell of her ear.

"Do you like the necklace?" His voice was like a zephyr in her ear.

She squeezed her eyes shut, hoping that when she

opened them, this wasn't all some incredible dream. She stroked the pendant that hung perfectly at the top of her cleavage. "I love it, Mason. I absolutely love it. Thank you."

"I want to see you wearing it ... and nothing else." His hands roamed her body, exploring her curves. His fingers tried to tug at her nipples beneath her dress, but she wasn't wearing an ordinary bra, and his grunt of frustration had her laughing.

He spun her around, his hands sliding beneath the straps of her dress and sending them over her arms so the whole dress dropped to the floor like a pool of silver at her feet.

His eyes crinkled at the corners, his mouth turning up in confusion. "What the hell kind of bra is that?"

She smiled. "It's a backless, strapless bra. See ... " She pulled one silicone side piece free from around her ribcage, and the rest of the bra popped off her chest easily and painlessly. "The things us women must do to look good." She tossed the bra to the floor and stepped into his arms.

"Baby, you'd look good in a paper bag. *The Paper Bag Princess*. I read that book to Willow all the time. Need to teach her young that a man who can't appreciate you when you have nothing isn't a man you want when you have something."

She looped her arms around his neck and pressed her breasts against his chest. "I couldn't agree more." Up on her tiptoes, she went in for a kiss, letting him take the lead as he most often did, prying her lips open and twirling his tongue around hers like it was a lollipop he just couldn't get enough of.

Now there was only one layer of fabric between them—his, and she needed to rectify that immediately.

Not breaking the kiss, she pulled her hands down from around his neck and began to unbutton his coat, then his vest, then his shirt, pulling his tie loose and unfastening his pants.

"You got a plane to catch or something?" he murmured against her mouth, guiding them over to the big bed, his lips still on hers, his hands chasing tingles all up and down her back and the cheeks of her butt.

She nipped his bottom lip and tugged before releasing it and replying, "No plane, just six weeks of fantasies fueling me."

His deep groan and the way he dipped his head and raked his teeth over her collarbone said he felt exactly the same way. That he'd been holding back for the sake of what she now realized was a stupid arrangement.

"Me too, baby. Though, as I told you last night, it's been longer than six weeks. Since that first night you came into the bar and sat down with your notebook and pen, I've wanted you. Dreamt of you. Fantasized about you."

She pulled away, her eyes hooded, her whole body on fire. "Did you think of me when you touched yourself?"

Not an ounce of hesitation flickered in his eyes. "Every time."

Oh God.

The way he said it, so unapologetic, so confident, it just made everything inside her want him more, need him more.

The back of her legs hit the edge of the bed, and he pushed her down until she sat in nothing but a bright red G-string.

"I want to take this slow, Lowenna," he said, his voice hoarse and gravelly as he finished unbuttoning his shirt to reveal those abs that looked better than chocolate and ink she wanted to run her tongue over.

He relieved himself of his coat, draping it over a chair, followed by his vest and shirt. His pants were open but hung low on his hips, that decadent line, the perfect V dipping beneath the waist, taunting her.

He caught where she was looking and chuckled. "What would you like to do?" he asked, stepping before her, pushing her knees wide to accommodate his breadth.

With a slight shake to her hands, she lifted them from the bedspread and rested them on his hips, holding his pants in place. Her thumbs traced along the sexy line, feeling his warm, silken skin beneath the pads.

"I want to lick this line," she said, angling her head forward and doing just that. Running her tongue over the ridges, tasting him. He tasted incredible. "Then I want to kiss this line." She moved over to the other side of his abdomen and slowly peppered kisses up and down the line.

His fingers threaded in her hair, but he didn't apply any pressure, just pulled slightly until a warmth and slight ache on her scalp sent prickles racing down her naked back.

She ran her thumbs back over the lines once again, then pushed his pants down, sending his black boxer briefs with them.

His cock sprang up and slapped his belly with an audible *thwack*, the crown a deep, dark purple and glistening with precum. She gripped him by the base and angled him into her mouth. Her lips closed around his cock and she sucked, her eyes drifting shut for just a moment, a groan coming up from deep within her chest at just how satisfying it was to finally have Mason in her mouth, to finally taste him.

To finally have him.

HOLY FUCK, could this woman give head.

She was like a Dyson or a Hoover or something. The

woman had some serious suction. The term *chrome off a bumper* came to mind. Jesus fucking Christ.

Mason was close to blowing his load already, and it'd only been a minute or two with Lowenna's plump, luscious lips wrapped around his dick.

All his midnight fantasies were coming to life. All his endless showers turned cold as he spanked the monkey thinking of this moment. Lowenna, gloriously naked in front of him, her hand pumping him, her mouth sucking him as he prepared to finally sink inside her and claim her as his.

Because she was his.

There was no going back from this now. No going back to a simple business arrangement where he was her gigolo and she was the angry and jaded sister out for a revenge date.

No, this went so much deeper than that.

Oh fuck, and Lowenna just went deeper too. She took him to the very back of her throat, let him bottom out, knock her tonsils, and the woman didn't even gag.

Jesus Christ.

He wasn't a small guy either. He'd had enough mouths on his dick in his thirty-eight years to know that he was a hard one to take all the way.

But fuck if his Lowenna didn't give it her best shot. As far as he would go, she took him, no complaints, no balking. She sucked and she sucked, swirling her tongue up and down his shaft, scraping her teeth, nipping the base, only to pull him all the way back out and wedge the tip of her tongue into the hole at his crown.

Best. Fucking. Head. Of. His. Life.

Despite that she was currently blowing his mind along with his cock, he didn't want to come just yet. Even though he wanted to take it slow, savor this moment, savor her, they were on a schedule. Besides, what they didn't do now, they could do tonight or tomorrow or every day after that. Because for him, Lowenna was it. Lowenna was the one.

He felt his need to come growing and reluctantly, almost painfully pulled from her hot, talented little mouth. Her whimper of protest hit him in the gut, and he almost gave in to his baser instincts and grabbed her by the neck and blew his load down her throat—but he didn't. He was a gentleman —kind of.

When she glanced up at him with confusion in her eyes and swollen lips, his insides twisted. "Was I not doing it right?" she asked, her puffy lips dipping into a small, very fuckable pout.

Kicking out of his pants and boxers, he leaned over her, planted his hands on the bed and guided her down beneath him. "You did abso-fucking-lutely everything right, baby. That was incredible." He caged her in, planting his hands on either side of her head, his thighs pressing down on her hips as he gave her some of his weight.

He dipped his head and brought one of her cherry-red nipples into his mouth, sucking until he heard her gasp. "But I want to be inside you and, well … " He kissed a path over her chest to the other breast, loving how her back arched and her puckered peaks pointed skyward, calling to him. "I'm not exactly a young man anymore, and sometimes I can be a bit of a one-trick pony." He took the other nipple into his mouth and sucked just as hard as before.

Her nails raked a deep track down his back until they couldn't go any farther, and she dug her fingers into his hips. "But I bet it's a really, really good *one* trick," she breathed, the sexy line of her throat bobbing as she swallowed.

He laughed, nuzzling the valley between her breasts. "That it is."

"I'm okay with that."

Slowly, because he really did want to treasure his first

time with this spectacular woman, he alternated between licks and kisses down her body, spending an extra-long time along her ribs where the skin is thin and most people are ticklish.

Lowenna certainly was.

She giggled and squirmed on the bed as his tongue danced over her. It was beautiful the way her satin-soft skin blushed from ivory to rose as heat and arousal flooded her. With his tongue, he chased the flush of color across her flesh until he finally reached her mound, practically salivating; her wild, feminine scent drove him mad. She was in another one of those G-strings like last night, only this one was bright red and had a small triangle of lace keeping her modest.

Her fingers pushed into his hair, and she tugged on his scalp. "I'm already wet. You don't need to prep me." He glanced up from where he was flicking her clit through the lace. Her eyes held a need that mirrored his own.

Being with Lowenna, being inside her, watching her body react as they came together was all he'd dreamt of for weeks, and now that they finally had the chance, he struggled not to rush it.

Hooking his fingers into the flimsy string on her hips, he pulled her G-string down, over her cleft, her legs, and then finally tossed it to the floor. He wouldn't go down on her long, but he needed to taste her. After last night, she was a delicacy he now craved incessantly. The feel of her sweet honey pouring across his tongue last night would be a memory he would carry with him forever. He needed more. She was an addiction, and he needed his fix.

"Mason," she breathed, her eyes following his every move. She reached for him. "Don't make me wait any longer, please ... "

The look of need in her eyes made his cock twitch and his balls tighten up painfully. He groaned. "Just a quick taste, love." He flopped down onto his stomach, roughly grabbed her thighs, tossed them over his shoulders, making her squeak in surprise, then dove into her slick heat with his tongue.

"Oh God!"

She bucked up as best she could into his face, but her legs over his shoulders made it tough for her to move. He was in control, which was exactly how he liked it.

For too long in their little dance, he'd been letting her take the lead, following her cues. Playing the dutiful pretend boyfriend hoping that she'd eventually come around.

No more.

Whether she was ready for it or not, he was her *actual* boyfriend now. And he was in control. Her orgasms, every last one of them, were now his.

With one hand, he spread her lips and began flicking at her shiny, swollen clit, relishing the way her thighs squeezed his head and shook as he spent a considerable amount of time on that one spot right near the tip that seemed to be her *extra* happy button. When he flicked it, she went nuts. Her head thrashed, her legs vibrated and her whole body clenched.

She was a joy to watch unravel. And he didn't waste a second of his time between her legs with his eyes closed. No, he watched her.

Head thrown back, eyes shut, fingers twisting in the bed, puffy lips parted, she was the most exquisite thing he'd ever seen, and the way she gave herself over to him, to the pleasure, was mesmerizing. He could watch her teeter on the edge of ecstasy forever.

Apparently Lowenna wasn't so keen on that idea. She released the duvet and tapped him on the head, her eyes out of focus as she glanced down her naked body at him. "You gotta stop," she panted. "I'll come and I ... I don't want to ... yet."

With a final sweep up between her slippery cleft, gathering as much of her sweetness on his tongue as he could, he reared up onto his knees.

Fuck, she was beautiful. Every goddamn inch of her was pure perfection, and the way she looked at him, like he was tastier than chocolate, made him nearly come on the spot.

"I have condoms in my bag on the table," she whispered. Her breath was coming as quickly as his. They were both panting, and they hadn't even gotten started yet.

His eyes fell to the table across the big hotel suite. That was a long way to go to leave this stunning creature alone on the bed.

He grinned down at her. "I have a couple of condoms in my pants pocket too," he said, sliding off the bed and reaching for his pants.

She lifted a brow at him, her mouth twisting into a sexy smirk. "Do you now?'

He grabbed a condom out of his pocket and nodded, grinning at her as he tore open the foil and rolled it on. "Sure do, sweetheart."

He knelt back on the bed, pinning her body beneath his once again.

She hummed and hooked her arms around his neck, arching her hips up to notch him at her center. "So prepared."

"For you, absolutely. I've thought of nothing else since you first stepped foot in my bar."

"Really? A *wicked* woman like me?"

He smiled down at her. "Definitely a wicked woman like you?"

The beauty of her grin winded him. "Corruption is my middle name."

His head dipped, and he drew a diamond-hard nipple into his mouth and tugged. "I like bad girls. You're exactly my type."

Her inhale was quick, surprised, followed by a low moan deep in her throat. "I've never been called a bad girl before. Careful, or it might go to my head. I might handcuff you to the bed and steal your wallet."

His teeth scissored over her bud at the same time his hands, one by one, reached behind him and grabbed hers from around his neck. He intertwined their fingers and pushed the backs of her hands into the bed.

"I love you, Lowenna," he said, lifting his head from her breast and staring down into her eyes at the same moment he eased himself inside her. Slowly, so that he felt every inch of her and she felt every inch of him. Her body stretched around him, accepting him. Squeezing him.

Her eyes fluttered closed, and her lips parted.

"No, baby, eyes open. Look at me. Watch me."

Silver-flecked eyes blinked open, darkening to a stormy gray as he seated himself fully to the hilt. She was tight and slick and oh so soft. She fit him like a glove. And the way she squeezed him, tightened her perfect little body around his, pulled him deeper, it was magical. She was made for him and he for her. They were meant to be.

"Mason," she whispered, "I ... I love you too."

A low and pleasant hum warmed his blood.

She loved him.

She. Loved. Him.

His fingers flexed against hers. She tightened her grip on his.

Then he kissed her like that kiss had always been inside of him, waiting to come out. It was unlike their kisses from before, when he knew he loved her but was unsure of how she felt about him. This kiss was a kiss of two people in love. Because *she* loved *him.*

He began to move, sliding in and out of her, feeling her lift to meet him and squeeze around him, doing her best to match his cadence.

He started out slow with long, luxurious glides, in to the base, then out to the tip and back, coasting across her channel, hitting every nerve ending he could only to finish with a hip tilt that made sure the bottom of his stomach rubbed her clit.

He knew the exact moment it did because she would shudder beneath him and her eyes would slide out of focus for a second.

Her low moans and feminine whimpers encouraged him, along with her sweet scent—so feminine and so uniquely Lowenna. Chocolate and spice.

It fit her to a T. She was sweet like chocolate but hot and full of fire like spice.

She arched her back and rocked her hips, lifting her legs to wrap and lock them around his waist, her heel digging into the cleft of his ass. It changed the angle and tightened her around him. He wasn't going to last much longer.

With every pump, her perfect, round tits jiggled, those sensitive nipples tight and hard and just begging for his mouth.

He bent his head one more time and swiped his tongue across one of the buds, moaning at just how good she tasted. He moved his mouth to the other one and tugged hard with his teeth until she inhaled sharply. He smiled against the generous swell of her breast when her gasp turned into a groan.

"You like the teeth?" he asked, scissoring his teeth over the nub again.

"So much," she breathed. "So, *so* much."

"Baby ... " he groaned, scraping his teeth one more time over her nipple before lifting his head and pressing his forehead to hers. "You feel so fucking good. You're so damn tight."

She slid her tongue along his bottom lip. "Yeah," she exhaled on a harsh whisper, her breath hitting his lips in warm puffs. "Harder, Mason. Faster. More."

More.

She could have it all.

His eyes locked with hers, even though their faces were too close to focus, and he began to move, grunting hard with each powered thrust.

Her fingers tightened in his. Her back bowed, causing her breasts to brush his chest, her nipples hard points he felt against his skin. Her eyes closed again, but he kissed her quick.

"Eyes on me, baby."

Her gray eyes hit his, and an ache swelled in his chest at the total love and devotion he saw in them. This was what he'd been missing in his life. This was *who* had been missing in life.

She blinked. "Mason ... I-I'm not going to last. It all feels too good. Too damn good." She made to twist her head away, but he pressed his forehead tighter against hers. He wanted to watch her come undone, watch her lose herself to him as he lost himself inside her. She was it for him, so they had the rest of their lives to close their eyes during sex, to look away or do it in the dark, but this time, their first time, he wanted to see it all.

"Me too," he breathed, pumping hard, deeper and faster. "Gonna come, baby."

"Oh God!" She arched her back even more, stilled, stiffened, tightened around him, shut her eyes and let go.

Fucking heaven.

Every ripple, every contraction of her pussy around his

cock was pure bliss. She milked him, pulled him deep.

He was lost in her. Lost in Lowenna.

"Open your eyes, Lowenna!"

She did as he commanded. Still caught up in the throes of her own release, she stared up at him, her eyes focused solely on him.

Yes.

His balls cinched up, his body stiffened, he stilled and came hard inside her.

She squeezed her muscles around him as he powered up hard, going as deep as he could go, his cum filling the condom, his mind wishing there was no barrier between them.

He wanted to shut his eyes, to ride out the waves of pleasure in darkness, letting his other senses become heightened, but he'd ordered her to keep her eyes open, so he had to do the same. She watched him come undone, it was mesmerizing. Her gaze softened, became almost hooded as he reached his crescendo and then made his way down the other side. She pulled her forehead away from his and planted a kiss over his eye, then his cheek, finally burying her face in his neck and kissing and nuzzling him there.

That kind of softness was exactly what he needed after coming like that, after finally getting what he'd wanted, what he'd *needed* for so long.

She was his and he was hers, fully and completely.

"My fingers are cramping," she whispered, tugging on his hand.

He lifted his head up and disentangled his fingers from hers, placing them on either side of her shoulders. She smiled up at him in thanks and wriggled her fingers a few times before lifting her arms and trailing her nails lightly down his back.

Gooseflesh broke out on his skin and he shuddered above

her, making both of them laugh, the corners of her eyes crinkling in a way he loved.

He assumed he was probably getting heavy for her, so he rocked them side to side a few times before rolling over on the bed. She was now on top, her body shifting forward and pushing her breasts into his face.

"Mmm," he hummed, laving at a nipple. "My new favorite place."

She chuckled as she pushed herself up to sitting, his cock still nestled inside her—though a fair bit softer than before. "I think this is my new favorite place too." She traced her fingers over the ink on his chest and upper arms. Her fingers found his nipple rings, and she strummed them with her thumbs. The light touch sent a small sizzle down to his balls. But they were to empty to react.

"I forgot about these," she said bending forward and flicking one with her tongue.

"Next time, sweetheart. Because trust me, there will *be* a next time."

"And a *next,* next time?" she asked, her words sending warm puffs of air over his chest.

He chuckled. "And a *next, next,* next time."

Taking the barbell between her teeth she tugged.

He inhaled sharply. "As much as I'm loving this, babe, I'm gonna slip out in a sec." He ran his hands down her arms.

Releasing his nipple, she nodded in acknowledgment before pouting. "I know." With a sigh of acceptance and reluctance in her eyes, she swung her leg over his torso and climbed off him and then the bed. Then she swayed that perfect body, that luscious ass and those rocking curves off to the bathroom.

Mason's head collapsed back to the bed. His cock twitched and he shut his eyes and grinned. "Don't take too

long, baby. I can definitely go again in a few minutes."
Thank God.

"Roger that," she called from the bathroom, the sound of the faucet running. "Glad you're not a one-trick pony."

His smile widened, and he tucked his hands behind his head. It'd been torture, these last couple of months, but boy, had it been worth it. *She* was worth it.

19

"Don't touch! Don't touch!" Lowenna exclaimed, swatting Mason's hand away as she climbed onto the bed and stood up.

"What are you doing?" he asked, buttoning up the last button of his coat.

She jostled her eyebrows as she pulled on a pair of latex gloves.

Operation Revenge was currently underway.

She made to open the bag, but he rushed over and, not even needing to get on the bed, stopped her before she could pull anything out. "What are you doing, Lowenna?" he enunciated, his eyes narrowing and the intense blue in his irises turning dark.

Letting out an exasperated huff, she took his offered hand and stepped off the bed. "They're rose petals."

"For who? It's a little late if they're for us."

"Ummm ... " Her gaze slid sideways. "The newlyweds."

His mouth dropped open, and his eyes grew saucer-size. "This is *their* suite?"

She shrugged. "Might be."

His head began to shake, as if she were no more than a petulant tween who had just come home late from curfew and her father was about to scold her. "What *else* is in the bag, Lowenna?"

Rolling her eyes and resisting the urge to stomp her foot, she finally shrugged. "Itching powder."

He stepped away and buried his face in his hand. "Fuck."

"What?" She didn't understand his reaction. She thought he hated her sister and Brody as much as she did. And people said women were confusing.

Ignoring the look he gave her, his head still hung and shaking, she made to stand back up on the bed and finish what she hadn't even had a chance to start.

His hand around her wrist stopped her though. "You can't," he said, his voice low and full of warning. "You. Can't."

She attempted to jerk free of his grasp, but he simply pulled her into his chest. "Don't, Lowenna. Don't stoop to their level. You are better than this. Look forward, not back. Don't trip over what is behind you. Don't let the toxic hate consume you."

She gritted her teeth, finally bringing her gaze to his. What met her was so much love and unbridled hope that the armor around her heart began to crack, and the frustration she'd been feeling toward him and his insistence she halt her revenge efforts dissolved.

"Choose love, not hate," he whispered, dipping his head and sliding his mouth over hers so effortlessly, it was if they'd been kissing for years.

She let him lead her in another hot, passionate kiss, her hands drawn to the back of his neck as if by magnets, her breasts pressing hard against his titanium chest. She moaned deep in her throat and opened for him as he explored every contour of her mouth with his wickedly talented tongue.

When they finally parted, she had jelly for limbs, a full heart and a pulsing body, aching for more orgasms.

His grin stole the breath she'd been struggling to catch clear from her lungs. It was dazzling.

"Ready to go?" he asked, taking her hand in his and tugging her toward the door. "I think the reception is about ready to start. Bridezilla and the Groom from the Black Lagoon should be done with their photo shoot by now."

Still stunned by his kisses, she allowed him to lead her out of the hotel room, her bag from earlier with the box of condoms and itching powder in his free hand.

"How'd you get the key card to their room?" he asked as they made their way to the elevator.

It felt like the hotel hallway was a thousand degrees, based on how hot she was at that moment. Mason just had a way of cranking up her temperature. He also had a way of making her want to take off all her clothes. Sheepishly, she glanced up at him. "I asked the front desk. I told them that I'm the bride's sister and that I wanted to go and leave a surprise in the honeymoon suite for the happy couple."

Ever since all those orgasms just a short while ago, she felt invincible. Like she could do anything. Take on the world. Take on the villains.

And she really needed those superpowers if she was going to stand up in front of everyone and hit them with the truth.

She needed the courage to do what needed to be done.

The elevator doors slid open, and they stepped inside.

"Why were you going to do that?" he asked after they stood there in silence for nearly a full minute, watching the numbers drop over the door.

"Do what?"

"The itching powder. The sex in their bed. Why?"

Cocking an eyebrow, she glanced up at him like he'd

sprouted another head. "For revenge. You know them now. You know what kind of crap-face people they are. They deserve all of that and more."

And they'd be getting more. Much, much more.

His eyes slid away from her, and he glanced ahead at the brass mirrored doors. "I thought bringing me, being your sexy confident self with a man a million times better than Brody, was your revenge. You wanted to show them that you're better off without them. Isn't a full life and success the best revenge of all?"

She shook her head, giving him another bewildered look before scoffing, "No."

His brows pinched for a moment, then he exhaled and slumped his shoulders. "Okay, then."

As if they were a real part of her, all those superpowers from all those orgasms began to fade away. They left her like a choppy breath after a sprint into the wind. The loss of her superpowers tasted metallic and choked her throat tight until she was forced to swallow and breathe in deep through her nose.

He hadn't let go of her hand, he hadn't stepped away, but she felt him *pull* away from her.

The elevator doors slid open, and they stepped out into the lobby, still hand in hand. He glanced down at her. "Ready?" The sparkle in his eyes had faded, and the look he gave her held a vacancy that alarmed her.

But she pushed it all away and nodded. "Yeah."

He nodded too, faced forward and tugged her toward the grand ballroom. "All right, then, let's get this over with."

By the time they entered the ballroom, arm in arm, the bride and groom were already inside, greeting guests.

No thanks.

They beelined it for the bar, where some friendly faces greeted them.

"Scotch?" Liam asked, nodding at him as they approached.

"You know it." He squeezed Lowenna's hip. "Drink?"

"Red wine, please."

Liam's head dipped to acknowledge both of them, then he turned to the bartender to order the drinks.

"We've been here for a while now," Zak said, his arm around Aurora. "Gotta drink these motherfuckers into the poorhouse." He clinked his beer bottle against Aurora's wineglass. "Right, babe?"

Aurora simply grinned and lifted her eyebrows. "This is already my third. Gotta pace myself, though, if I want to make it through dessert."

Liam handed Mason and Lowenna their drinks. "Speaking of food, when the fuck do we get to eat?"

"You just had cake upstairs, and I see a table full of appetizers," Mason said, immediately taking a sip of his scotch.

"Yeah, but it's Paige's food. I've gorged myself on her appetizers, but now I want the main course. I *always* have room for Paige's food. And I need to make sure I get one of everything. I swear to God, if they pull table numbers out of a hat and my table is last, I'm going to fire Brody's ass on Monday."

"God, can we?" Atlas grunted, sidling up next to them all, stowing his phone in his pocket, then sipping his drink.

"Are we all at least sitting together?" Mason asked. His hand flexed on Lowenna's hip, and he pulled her closer to his side. He hadn't looked at her in a while, and it was throwing her off.

Liam shook his head. "Afraid not, man. You and Lowenna are sitting with a bunch of their family. We're all together, though."

His fingers kneaded her hip once again.

She was about to say something along the lines of *I'm sorry, I can see if we can switch seats*, when Brody's brother,

Brady (yes, Brody and Brady—yeesh!) began tapping a micro-phone on the stage.

"Hello, everyone," Brady began. He was the spitting image of his older brother and equally douchey. "We're going to ask that everyone find their seats, please, then we'll start pulling table numbers from a hat for the buffet."

"Motherfucker," Liam grumbled, ordering another drink. "Gonna drink my dinner then, I guess."

Mason steered her toward the table where Lowenna's parents, grandparents, aunts and uncles were sitting.

"Is this the handsome Mason we've heard so much about?" Lowenna's Aunt Margery asked, pecking Lowenna on the cheek as they approached their table.

Lowenna embraced her father's sister. "This is." She parted with her aunt and looked up at Mason. He was all smiles, completely in boyfriend mode.

One by one, all of Lowenna's family members came up and hugged her and either shook hands with Mason or hugged him. Praising her new choice of partner, how hand-some he was, how tall, how blue his eyes were. You name it, her aunts or grandmothers mentioned it. Particularly her Aunt Nellie, who held on awfully tight to Mason's bicep for a solid thirty seconds, her eyes sparkly as she gazed up at him.

Lowenna was so caught up in introducing her new boyfriend to everyone, answering questions about how they met, how long they've been together and how the chocolate shop was doing, that by the time she lifted her head toward the stage, Doneen and Brody had their food, but neither of them were eating.

Her sister's face was a mottled red, her eyes narrowed, brows pinched, and she was glaring at Lowenna. Brody was staring too, but his focus was on Mason, and although he wasn't happy either, she doubted he was trying to shoot laser beams from his eyes like his wife.

Lowenna cleared her throat and rested her hand on Mason's hip. "We should sit down. They're calling tables."

He grunted and bid her Uncle Ron adieu, pulling her chair out for her before he pulled out his own.

"Such a gentleman," Aunt Nellie said across the table. "I can tell he really loves you. See it in his eyes. You two are just beautiful together."

Heat raced into her cheeks. "Thanks, Aunt Nellie."

Mason leaned over and pecked her on the temple. "It was love at first sight ... at least for me. This one took a bit more convincing." He threaded his fingers through hers beneath the table, then lifted the back of her hand to his lips. "But now, we're all about the future. Looking forward to happiness and new beginnings. Right, babe? No need to dwell on the past and all that negativity, all that pain and hurt." The glint in the dark blue of his eyes said more than his words ever could.

Lowenna took a long sip of her wine before answering. "Yep, forward. Happiness. New beginnings. Sounds great."

She avoided his eyes when she set her wineglass down because she knew what stared back at her—pure disappointment.

20

WITH DINNER over and done with, it was time to dance.

And oh, what a dance it was.

Violet and Adam weren't kidding when they said Brody and Doneen were terrible. After months and months of lessons, they still botched countless moves, couldn't get in sync, and Doneen, the control freak, kept trying to lead. It was painful to watch, and unfortunately, it was nearly seven minutes long, so they had to watch for a while.

Lowenna exchanged glances with Tori and Mitch across the room a few times as they circled the uncoordinated couple on the dance floor, taking pictures of them but also hoping they didn't get kicked in the skull.

It would be safe to guess every person in the ballroom was worried about possibly getting kicked in the skull or, at the very least, Doneen's shoe flying off into the crowd.

Thankfully, though, no one was maimed.

By the time the rhythmless couple vacated the dance floor, panting and smiling to the thunderous applause, Mason, Lowenna, Liam, Atlas, Zak and Aurora could hardly contain themselves. They were all standing off in one corner, hiding their mouths behind their drinks out of fear someone might see them smirking or, worse yet, crying from laughter —because Lowenna wasn't far off.

Then the DJ began to pump the beats, and anyone who was interested was welcomed onto the dance floor.

"They don't have to ask me twice," Zak said, draining his beer and offering Aurora his hand. "Shall we, my love?"

Aurora set her wineglass down on a nearby table. "Lead the way, handsome."

"Where'd Zak get a kilt?" Mason asked, tipping up his scotch.

"Guy's half Scot. He and Adam have them. Grandparents took them to Scotland when they were kids," Liam replied, surveying the now full dance floor.

Mason frowned in understanding before he finished his drink. "Shall we show them how we do it?" he asked, offering Lowenna his hand. "You paid for lessons. We might as well get your money's worth."

She'd love nothing more than to be in Mason's arms in front of everyone, because now, they weren't putting on airs. It wasn't fake. She wasn't just getting the *boyfriend experience*. After that brief bit of weirdness in the hotel room and elevator, he had been nothing but sweet, sexy, perfect and attentive.

She finished her wine and set it down on the table before she took his hand, giggling as she jogged after him in her heels. "Careful. I don't want to trip."

They entered the dance floor, where they found Zak and Aurora. Zak was smiling and spinning his laughing woman out, but the man had very little rhythm. He also didn't seem to care.

"Looks like your brother got all the dance talent," Mason

said, taking Lowenna in his arms and setting them off to an easy step.

Zak's eyes lit up. "He sure did." He pulled Aurora back into his chest, and they started to sway—not to the beat.

It was a beautiful, magical night. One Lowenna wouldn't soon forget.

Everyone loved Mason.

Everyone loved her and Mason together.

And their dancing was infinitely superior to the debacle that had played out just moments ago in front of everyone. Honestly, why did Doneen and Brody put themselves through that? Did they not know they sucked?

The music turned to a slow ballad, and a few people left the dance floor. Zak and Aurora were now glued to each other, barely moving as they kissed and smiled and laughed.

"Let's get out of here," Mason whispered, tightening the hold he had on Lowenna's waist. "You're better than this, and what we have now is real, isn't it? We have nothing to prove ... *you* have nothing to prove." He jerked his head behind him. "Let's head back to my place, spend the rest of the night in bed."

Oh God, yes, please.

She opened her mouth, though she wasn't sure what to say, but he made that decision for her by crashing his mouth into hers. It was no sweet peck either. It was hot, it was dirty, and it was full of tongue.

Right there on the dance floor, in front of her family, their friends and everyone else, Mason and Lowenna sucked face. And it was awesome.

She didn't care one bit, because she was in love.

She was getting the full boyfriend experience because he *was* her boyfriend. She knew that now. No question. He was hers.

She wrapped her arms around his neck and played with

the short hair that tickled the nape, her eyes closed as they continued to effortlessly glide around the dance floor.

His lips were like velvet, his tongue strong and in control. The way it twirled and twisted around hers, mated with hers, danced with hers. Then he'd pull back and nip her lip or suck on her tongue, sending a deep quake down to her toes.

The song was still slow, and their steps were too, but Mason had managed to maneuver his thigh between her legs, and every once in a while, when he'd step her back, the top of his leg would brush against the apex of her thighs, sending a rush of pleasure racing through her.

She'd shudder in his arms, their lips still together, arms still wrapped around each other.

She was close to coming, just from the dance. From the kiss, from Mason.

He knew exactly what he was doing. When her knees threatened to buckle, he'd pull her tighter against him, catch her before she fell.

He broke the kiss, and she opened her eyes. His mouth moved across her face in a path of kisses. "Come home with me," he whispered into her ear at the same time he stepped her back one more time, this time an even bigger step than before. His thigh and the lace of her G-string grazed her clit. "*Come*, Lowenna."

And she did.

It was small, it was secret, but it was no less amazing. No less exhilarating.

In his arms, on the dance floor, in a room with over three hundred people, guests, staff and the like, Lowenna came.

She squeezed her eyes shut again and rested her cheek against his, holding on to his neck as the climax took hold of her.

"That's it, baby. Just let go." His grip around her waist was firm, holding her up, holding her steady, shielding the majority of her reaction with his body.

She trembled as the orgasm began to dissipate, the after-effects leaving her boneless and tired.

"Want to sit down?" he asked, keeping them dancing. Thank God the song was still slow. She wasn't sure she could do a foxtrot to save her life.

She exhaled and nodded. "Yeah, I think so."

He wrapped his arm around her waist and led them off the floor and out of the ballroom into sort of a wide, high-ceilinged atrium. Various doors lined the walls, which formed a circle. A round bench with plants in the middle sat in the bullseye of the floor.

He encouraged her to sit down, which she did, gladly. Then he took her feet in his lap, removed her heels and began to massage her aching feet.

Could this man get any more perfect?

"I meant it," he said after they sat there for a moment in companionable, pleasant silence, her brain and toes slowly turning to mush. "Come home with me. Let's spend the night —and the morning—in bed. My mom can keep Willow if I need her to. Let's blow this popsicle stand and go be together."

Her eyes were closed and she was leaning back, relishing the way the pads of his big, strong thumbs kneaded the balls of her feet. She couldn't remember the last time a man had massaged her feet—if ever. Finally, she opened her eyes, though they remained a touch unfocused, and she nodded. "I ... I will. I want to, but only after the speeches, okay? I promised Doneen I would give a speech."

A flicker in his eyes burned behind the intense blue, and he released her feet, grabbed her heels from the floor and helped her back into her shoes. "What's going on, Lowenna? I get the feeling you're not telling me something."

She shrugged. "Doneen asked me to give a speech. And I intend to do just that."

"That's not *just* it. I know you better than that. Tell me the truth. What's going on? What are you planning to do?"

Fine. He asked. She'd tell him. She wasn't ashamed or embarrassed. All those emotions had disappeared long ago, leaving nothing but rage in their wake.

"I'm going to let everyone at this wedding know *exactly* what kind of people the bride and groom are. How they got together, *when* they got together. Who they really are. I want revenge. I want to not only show them up with a spectacularly hot date, have sex in their bed, put itching powder in their sheets—though you nixed that." She rolled her eyes. "I want to *humiliate* them. Just like they've humiliated me by making me come to this godforsaken wedding. By making me create that centerpiece for them, the guest favors, the chocolate-covered strawberries. All they do is take, take, take."

She wiped a tear from her eye as she struggled to take back control of the emotions inside her.

"I hate them, Mason. Hate them. They deserve to pay for what they did to me. The constant humiliation and torment. Doneen has been torturing me since we were kids, and then she went and stole my husband. Said I brought cancer into the family, that I was wicked. You heard her last night, rubbing it in that I'm *barren*. She's evil." The words tasted bitter in her mouth. Their immediate heat burned her tongue, and she worked her jaw side to side, swallowing slowly to savor their rough, jagged edges.

The anger was what had fueled her for so long. She couldn't stop now. Not before the grand finale. Not before the rest of the world learned the truth about Doneen and Brody Hawthorne. Not before she got her revenge.

She'd been staring down at her lap for some time, so

when she finally lifted her head to face him, what stared back at her was terrifying.

The man was looking at her like he had no idea who she was but what he did see disgusted him.

"You can't do that, Lowenna," he said slowly, shaking his head. "You can't."

The hell she couldn't.

She stood from the bench, wobbling just a touch on her heels before she steadied herself, glaring down at him, the rage inside her redirecting itself, taking new aim. She planted her hands firmly on her hips. "Who the hell are you to tell me what I can and can't do? You've seen what horrible people they are, how they treated me, how they treated *you*. They deserve to be humiliated. The world deserves to know the truth."

He stood up to his full height, which was a hell of a lot taller than her. She was forced to crane her neck to glare at him. He was glaring back. His hands shot out, and he bracketed her arms, gripping her biceps tight, and he shook her gently, his eyes beseeching, almost fearful.

"Listen to me," he said, emphasizing each word. "Listen to me. They are not worth the energy. They are not worth all the time spent thinking and planning this revenge. You are letting your past trip up your future. Trip up your present. You could be putting all of this, *them* behind you, focusing on the good, on the future, on being happy, and yet you just keep letting the past, letting *them* win and pull you back into the darkness. If you go up on that stage and humiliate them, it won't be them who the world, who the guests look at with disdain, it will be you. The bitter little sister who couldn't move on."

"Bitter. Little. Sister?" She spat out each word and shook herself free from his grasp, taking a step back. Fury pumped hot through her veins; the feeling of flames licked up her cheeks. "You wouldn't even be at this wedding if it wasn't for me. *I* invited *you*. And now you think you can tell me what to do? The world deserves to know just who the real *wicked* sister is."

"I wouldn't be here?" He enunciated the words through gritted teeth. Frustration and disdain wrapped up in his tone. "*I* wouldn't be here?"

She shook her head stiffly, eyes laser-focused on his face. "No. You wouldn't."

"Fuck, *you* wouldn't be here if it wasn't for *me!* You wouldn't fucking be alive. Wouldn't be here to *exact* your *ultimate* revenge. You're wasting your life, your *gift*, *my* gift by being angry and vengeful." He shook his head and looked away, raking his fingers through his hair. "Such a fucking waste of your life."

"Excuse me?" She reared back. "What the hell are you talking about?"

He was still shaking his head. A twinge of anger laced his voice. "Who the hell do you think was your *mystery benefactor?*"

Her body went ice-cold.

No.

She took a step back and then another, her head shaking side to side, eyes struggling to focus, hands trembling.

"No," she breathed out. "No. I-it can't ... you're lying."

"Why would I lie?"

Why would he lie?

But it was also impossible. Wasn't it? He would have said something sooner if he was telling her the truth. Before the declarations of love, before the sex. Before everything.

"I was at the Sandpiper Pub five years ago when I overheard a couple of the waitresses talking about their co-worker who had cancer and was struggling to pay her medical bills, wasn't sure she would have enough to freeze her eggs. So I had a cashier's check drawn up, keeping me anonymous, and my secretary dropped it off. I never thought I'd ever meet you. I just knew that it was the right thing to do. It was after that, that I quit my job and went off to find a greater purpose in life. *Your* story helped me change mine."

She sat down on the bench again, her head hurting from the information overload. This just didn't make any sense. She lifted her eyes to his. "Why didn't you tell me sooner? Why am I only finding this out *now?*"

"I wanted to tell you since the moment you told me about the anonymous benefactor, since I put all the pieces together. I just couldn't find the right time."

Couldn't find the right time? How about when he cooked her dinner and she was lying on his bed, playing with his baby? How about before the rehearsal dinner? How about before they had sex?

Their voices had returned to normal, and Lowenna's heart no longer thundered in her chest. "I ... " She hung her head for a moment before lifting it once again. "Thank you ... for saving me ... for ... "

Anything else she could have said would have sounded hollow. How do you thank someone for giving you such a large sum of money? Money that not only saved your life but gave you the opportunity to have a family, start a business, start a new life? You just couldn't. Even though she was furious with him for keeping it a secret, her overwhelming gratitude bulldozed any of her last remaining ire. She couldn't stay mad at a man who had given her a second chance at life.

His smile was small and grim as he lifted one shoulder in a tight shrug. "You're welcome. I'm glad you're alive. I'm glad you were able to freeze your eggs." Gone was the love from his eyes, the fascination and obsession with which he'd looked at her upstairs. He'd looked at her like she held all the answers to his questions about the future. Now ... now he looked at her like she was nothing but a pile of more questions.

Unanswerable questions.

As her stomach twisted into a tight knot, she asked her own question. "So where does this put us?"

"All right, ladies and gents, it's time we hear from the best man, the maid of honor and anybody else who would like to give a toast to the happy couple. Get ready to hear some embarrassing stories, because as I already told my big bro, nothing is off-limits tonight," Brady's voice in the microphone boomed out of the ballroom into the atrium.

"I have to go give my speech," she whispered, her fingers twisting in the fabric of her dress.

Again, a slight shrug and an expression of sadness. "I don't think I can be with you if you're going to give the speech you plan to give," he said, every word sounding like it was a jagged shard he had to painfully pull from the back of his throat. "I gave up that life a long time ago. I'm not a ruthless, angry person anymore. I'm not out to best somebody else, show them up or get my revenge. I'm a happy person now, content with living my best life for me and my daughter and nobody else. And I want to instill that kind of life into my daughter."

Her bottom lip dropped open, and a small piece of her heart chipped away from his words.

"Don't stoop to their level, Lowenna. You're better than that. You're better than them. *Be* better. Don't let your demons win. Don't let them rule your future because they tormented your past."

The sound of the best man, Brody's college roommate Chet, giving a horribly sexist speech grated through the hotel. She glanced toward the doors back into the ballroom, her feet growing itchy wanting to move, wanting to get in there.

"I love you, Lowenna, I do. But I'm not sure we're in the same place in our lives. I'm not sure you're ready to be happy." Then he stood up and walked back into the ballroom, leaving her sitting there with tears sliding down her cheeks and her heart breaking in her chest.

21

"Now let's hear from the bride's sister," Brady said, still guffawing from his last stupid joke, his nose and cheeks red from having imbibed one too many vodka Redbulls. Would the man ever grow up? Probably not. Neither of the Hawthorne brothers were particularly mature or smart or kind or—according to Brady's drunk girlfriend at Lowenna and Brody's wedding—very good in bed. Though it appeared that Mindy was now an *ex*-girlfriend, because Brady had shown up with a new piece of arm candy who was shamelessly flirting with a very uninterested-looking Atlas.

As Lowenna made her way toward the stage, she felt the heat of over three hundred pairs of eyes on her. Though she *really* only felt the sear of one.

He was sitting at their table, with her parents, aunts, uncles and grandparents, watching her climb the stairs, waiting for her to seal their fate.

But she couldn't back down now. She couldn't throw it all away.

The world deserved to know the kind of people Brody and Doneen really were. They deserved to know that Brody was a cheating bastard and Doneen was the wicked sister who had slept with her dying sister's husband.

"Here she is," Brady said, teetering on his feet as he leaned forward and planted a sloppy drunk kiss to Lowenna's cheek. "Care to make it a family affair?" he whispered into her ear. "You should come to my hotel room later."

Her mouth turned down into a frown of disgust, and she pulled away from him. "You have a girlfriend."

And she had Mason. Emphasis on the past tense. What remained of her broken heart tightened painfully in the hollow of her chest.

Brady shrugged and sipped his drink. "We're not exclusive."

God, he was a tool.

Lowenna rolled her eyes and accepted the microphone from him, resisting the urge to push him off the stage. One tiny shove and he'd be over the edge and flat on his ass.

She bit down on the inside of her cheek. Another time. She needed to focus on her mission.

Operation Revenge.

Licking her lips, she took a sip of the champagne she'd snagged from a passing waiter on her way up to the stage. Why the hell did they only fill them halfway? Cheap bastards.

Her eyes scanned the crowd, then they moved to Doneen and Brody. Doneen's eyes narrowed on her, her cheeks flushing a deep red beneath her perfect bridal makeup. She lifted one eyebrow just enough for Lowenna to see it.

It was a warning.

"*Stick to the script,*" her sister mouthed, her eyes gray flames of fury.

Lowenna's nostrils flared and her lip curled up. Fuck Doneen and her *script*.

This was why that bitch deserved to be taken down a peg. This was why she deserved humiliation.

Lowenna swallowed, took a deep breath and then went for it. "Most of you know me as Doneen's little sister, but some of you also know me as Brody's ex-wife." She shrugged and laughed. "I know, right? Cue the banjos."

The crowd laughed awkwardly.

Doneen and Brody didn't.

"But what a lot of you don't know are the true Brody and Doneen. What they're *really* like. Who they *really* are. How and when they *really* got together. Well, I'm here to shed a little light. I'm here to offer you the truth about our blushing bride and the handsome groom."

Doneen's face turned the color of pea soup, and Brody began to choke on his water.

Her gaze swung to Mason, but all that she found was an empty chair.

His coat was gone.

He was gone.

Her bottom lip wobbled, and she took another sip of her champagne, her palms now sweaty and struggling to maintain a grip on her flute.

She swallowed again. "Brody and Doneen are two of the most ... "

The crowd was absolutely silent. You could hear a pin drop, it was so dead quiet. Liam was leaning forward on his seat, his eyes eager. Atlas appeared bored, and Zak and Aurora were busy whispering and giggling.

"Brody and Doneen first got together ... "

The click of a camera to her left drew her attention. It was Tori. She was just below Lowenna on the stage, her camera pointed directly at her, clicking away.

Tori pulled the camera away from her face and smiled up

at Lowenna. "You got this," she whispered. "Picture everyone in their underwear."

Oh God.

Her family was in that crowd.

A throat at the head table cleared, and she pivoted her gaze once again back to the bride and groom. They both looked like they were ready to barf.

Lowenna shut her eyes, exhaled a deep breath through her mouth, tightened her grip on the microphone and began. "Sorry about that. The champagne got all bubbly in my head. Let me start over. Brody and Doneen are the perfect match. They are two sides of the same coin, each other's better half. Both have ambition and passion, are career-driven and determined to reach the top. Never have I ever met two people more *meant* for each other than Brody and my big sister." She swallowed again, the lump at the back of her throat a painful knot she struggled to speak over. "Now, their relationship might be a bit unorthodox to some, given that Brody used to be married to me, but I assure you, we're all good. Not all relationships must end poorly, and I am truly happy that my sister has found her true love." She lifted her champagne toward Brody and Doneen. "Take care of her, Brody. Treat her like a queen because otherwise, I'll help her bury the body."

Laughter drifted through the crowd.

Shrugging, she turned back to the crowd. "After all, what are sisters for?" She raised her glass. "To the happy couple. May their love be everlasting."

"To the happy couple," the crowd replied. Glasses clinked and people cheered as Lowenna took the final sip of her champagne, set her flute down and then dutifully made her way over to the head table.

Brody was the first to stand and embrace her. "Thank you," he murmured as he hugged her stiffly.

She barely touched him and then retreated as quickly as

she could, giving him a small, tight smile in return. "No sweat."

Doneen was next. She leaned her slight frame toward Lowenna and gave her a superficial hug. "You didn't stick to the script," she gritted out.

"And you didn't wait until my husband and I were divorced before you started sleeping with him."

Doneen gasped and her body went rigid, the bones of her shoulder blades sticking out as her back went ramrod straight. She went to pull away, but Lowenna held her for just a moment longer, just to instill a bit more fear.

After counting to five in her head, she finally pulled away, making sure to plaster on a big, cheesy grin before she faced her sister and then the crowd. She'd even managed to squeeze a tear out for good measure.

Doneen looked like she was going to barf. Lowenna simply smiled wider, turned back to the audience, waved and then took her leave.

She needed to find Mason. She needed to let him know she chose him, she chose *them* over getting her revenge.

She descended the stairs of the stage and took off in the direction of the doors toward the atrium. Hopefully he had just stepped out for some air because he didn't want to hear her speech.

Her pace picked up until before she knew it, she was running. She burst through the doors into the atrium, out of breath as she spun around, searching for Mason.

Tears stung her eyes, and the lump in her throat had tripled in size.

"He left," came a voice behind her.

She spun around to find Atlas leaning against the doorjamb, studying the ice in his glass. She'd hardly spoken a work to the blond, stoic, gray-eyed single dad who seemed to hate every minute of being at the wedding besides the free booze. The man just seemed like a grump.

"What do you mean *he left?*" she asked, the achy hollow in her chest growing.

Atlas took a sip of his drink and shrugged. "Said he needed to get home to Willow, so he left."

On Valentine's Day! On her birthday! He just ... bailed?

She struggled to get the words out. "Did he say *why?*" How could he just leave her without even saying goodbye?

He warned you, remember? And Mason is most definitely a man of his word.

Disappointment crashed into her and her throat grew tight at the same time tears burned the back of her eyes.

Atlas pushed off from the doorjamb and approached her. He was a tall, lean man with broad shoulders, a square jaw and handsome features. The air around him seemed to almost sizzle with a sense of danger ... but also immense sadness.

It was so weird that she picked up the sadness part, but she really felt it the closer he came to her.

"That wasn't the speech you intended to give, was it?" he asked, looking down at her and cocking one eyebrow.

She felt like a child being chastised, the way he was looking at her, and she immediately dropped her gaze to the floor. "No."

"You had plans to embarrass them." It wasn't a question.

"Yes."

"And Mason wasn't on board."

She lifted her eyes to his face. "No."

His mouth dipped into a frown. He shoved one hand into his pocket and rocked back on his heels. "Makes sense why he left then. Guy's all sunshine, rainbows, unicorns and shit."

"I need to talk to him."

Atlas grunted. "Yeah. Lemme know if you want to split a

cab or something. I'm fucking done with this place." Then he drained his drink and took off back into the ballroom, leaving Lowenna standing there alone—as the universe clearly intended her to be.

SHE NEEDED to get out of there. She needed to go find Mason. God, what a terrible day this was shaping up to be.

A terrible Valentine's.

A terrible birthday.

She hardly had anything to drink; she was fine to drive. So after a round of quick goodbyes to her grandparents, aunts, uncles and parents, Lowenna ducked into the bathroom to check her makeup before she hit the road in the company van.

She was just touching up her lipstick when the toilet in the larger handicapped stall flushed and the door opened to reveal none other than Doneen, the blushing—more like fuming—bride. Her sister's eyes turned lethal, and she glowered at Lowenna in the mirror as she came up behind her. She moved over to the adjacent sink and washed her hands, her lips pursed tight, her nostrils flaring.

Was Lowenna going to get out of there unscathed?

Lowenna grabbed a tissue and blotted her forehead and beneath her eyes, grateful that her waterproof makeup had held up and she didn't have raccoon eyes.

Doneen dried her hands, her eyes locking with Lowenna's in the mirror. She hesitated, opened her mouth. Lowenna froze. But then her sister closed her mouth again and turned to go.

Holy crap. Wow. Maybe she really was going to get out of there without having to endure the wrath of Bridezilla herself.

She watched as her sister made to leave.

Phew.

The sound of the door locking made Lowenna jump. At first, she thought her sister had locked her *in* the bathroom—alone—but when Doneen turned around and stalked back toward her, Lowenna was beginning to wish she was in there alone.

"How dare you?" Doneen's voice cut an angry swath through the air.

Lowenna's brows rose. "How dare *I*? How dare *you*. You honestly didn't think I knew you were sleeping with Brody while we were still married. While I was fighting for my life, going through chemo, losing my uterus and cervix ... my ability to carry a child."

Doneen's cheeks burned bright, but her eyes formed thin slits which were only accentuated by her thick, sculpted brows that sharpened into a deep V. "Get off your high horse, Lowenna. It wasn't *that* bad. You're alive, aren't you? God, you're such a fucking drama queen. It's *always* about Lowenna. Lowenna, Lowenna, Lowenna."

Lowenna made to take a step back, but the sink was right behind her, so she couldn't.

"Ever since you were born, it's been the fucking *Lowenna Show*. Allll about you."

"Excuse me? It most certainly fucking has not. What family did you grow up in? You've been a bully my whole life, always pushing me out of the way so you could take center stage."

Doneen rolled her eyes. "Only way to get attention in the Chambers house was to demand it. Otherwise, all eyes were on you, all the time. First, you were a preemie in the NICU with a hole in your heart, so I was left with family daily while Mom and Dad went to visit you, tend to you, see you. Then you were a newborn, home and *so* fucking demanding. We couldn't go out to playdates or playgroups because Lowenna's immune system couldn't be compromised by all the germs. Because of *you*, I did absolutely nothing as a child."

"I was a baby, you psycho!"

"And obviously a cuter one than me, because all I ever heard growing up was *Lowenna is such a cutie. You should put Lowenna into modeling. Oh, Conrad, you're going to have to keep the boys away from Lowenna.* As if I were a fucking troll with a lazy eye and hunchback, destined for the nunnery."

This crazy bitch was not serious. She was blaming Lowenna for all the crap *other* people said.

"So that gave you permission to treat me like shit my entire childhood?"

Doneen shrugged. "Only way I got attention."

Lowenna shook her head. "That's bullshit. You locked me under your bed when you babysat me. Told me you'd hurt me if I told Mom and Dad."

The corner of Doneen's mouth dipped slightly, and her eyes slid to the side. "You're alive, aren't you?"

Lowenna squeezed her eyes shut for a moment, then flared them open in disbelief. "You're messed up, you know that? Seriously messed up."

"And then you had to bring *him* to my rehearsal dinner and wedding." Doneen pointed to the door, making Lowenna's eyes follow.

"Who? Mason?"

"All I've heard all fucking night is, *That Mason is such a charmer. He and Lowenna are such a striking couple. You can tell he really loves her. She deserves this after everything she's gone through.*"

She sure fucking did deserve Mason, his love and their happiness, after everything she'd been through.

"Now it's not just the *Lowenna Show*, it's the *Lowenna Show* featuring Mason the bartender."

Lowenna lifted a shoulder. "So? You're *alive*, aren't you? You're married, aren't you? To *my* fucking husband no less."

Doneen's nostrils flared and her jaw clenched. "So it's MY day! And all I've heard is how great *you* are. How great your boyfriend is. You know Aunt Nellie slipped up and actually said that Mason was a real improvement from your ex-husband until she saw my face and realized who she was talking about."

Okay, well, that was downright hilarious.

Lowenna snorted, then hid her smile and laugh behind her hand.

Doneen's eyes flashed fire.

She needed to get to Mason. She needed to clear the air with him. This was not where she wanted to be right now, locked in a bathroom with her psycho big sister, who clearly had a major ax to grind.

All the fight inside her, all the need for revenge and getting even, fell away the moment she realized Mason had left. Because when he left, he took her hope for the future with him. And she desperately wanted that back. She wanted a life and future with Mason, Willow and her frozen eggs more than she wanted anything else in the world.

Her shoulders dropped with a sigh, and she brought her voice right down. "Doneen, you slept with my husband. Then he divorced me because I couldn't give him children. You asked me to be your maid of honor. Then, when I agreed to do the guest favors as a favor to Mom and Dad, you took advantage of my generosity and piled on an enormous chocolate centerpiece *and* chocolate covered strawberries—all for free. And at the busiest time of year for people in the chocolate business. Come on, admit it, you've been a bitch to me my whole life, but all this was a new low, even for you. Everything you've done to me, everything you've asked of me … I haven't deserved any of it. And yet, I still did what you asked, all of it."

Doneen's jaw tightened, and she exhaled deep through her nose.

Don't let the anger consume you.

Don't let the demons win.

Choose love, not hate.

Mason's words came back to her, his blue eyes, so bright and full of hope and happiness. Willow giggling as he blew raspberries on her belly while the three of them lay on his bed.

That was what she wanted.

That picture, right there.

Mason.

Willow.

Hope.

A future.

A family.

Before she could think twice about what she was doing, Lowenna lunged forward and wrapped her arms around her sister. But unlike their hug on stage, where both women had been faking it, Lowenna wasn't faking it now. She squeezed her sister tight.

At first, Doneen resisted, even tried to push Lowenna away, but as Lowenna held on tight, refusing to let go, Doneen's body eventually relaxed and her hands fell to Lowenna's back.

"I'm sorry for my part in the demise of our relationship. I'm sorry that Mom and Dad were so consumed with my needs while neglecting yours. If I was the firstborn and you had been a preemie and demanding newborn, I'm sure I would have felt similar." She squeezed Doneen tighter. A tear slipped down her cheek, falling down her sister's back.

"You're my sister, Doneen. The only one I have. I hate our relationship, hate it."

Doneen shuddered in her arms, then exhaled, her entire body slumping against Lowenna's. "I'm sorry for sleeping with Brody while the two of you were still married."

Lowenna's eyes practically popped out of her head.

"And thank you for not telling all the guests that. I could tell you were thinking about it."

"I'd planned on it," Lowenna said, finally pulling away.

"I could tell."

"I'm also sorry I asked so much of you for the wedding. You really did an amazing job on everything. People have been raving about the centerpiece and strawberries."

"Which I'm sure irritated you to no end."

"It did."

Lowenna chuckled. "Sorry for being *so* damn good at my job."

Doneen took a step back. "I don't like you."

Well, fuck.

Love, not hate.

"I don't like you either, if we're being completely honest."

Doneen nodded. "Fair enough. I've never been kind to you, so I would think you were crazy if you did."

"Well, most of the time I think *you're* crazy, sooo ... "

Doneen huffed. "We'll never be friends."

"You're right. I don't see that happening. Doesn't help that I can't stand your husband."

Her sister's smile was tight. "Thank you again for not telling all the guests about our affair."

"You can thank Mason for that. He's the one who convinced me to put my anger behind me."

"And have you?" Fear glimmered behind her eyes, and for the first time ever, Lowenna's big sister looked incredibly small.

"You don't have to worry about me telling anybody. I promise. It's in the past."

Doneen's shoulders dropped down from her ears, and she exhaled. "Thank you."

They would never be like Tori and Isobel—best friends. Hell, they would probably never even be acquaintances. But Lowenna was going to take this bathroom tête-à-tête as a win and move on—move forward. She made to step around Doneen. "I should go find my date."

"You're happy with him?" Doneen asked.

Lowenna paused and faced her sister again. A lump formed in her throat. She was beyond happy with Mason. She was in bliss with Mason, in heaven with Mason.

Mason was her happily ever after.

But now she might have gone and mucked it all up. All because she let her anger, her lust for revenge, her hate consume her. Cloud her vision to what was really in front of her—happiness.

But instead of getting into that, she simply nodded. "Mason makes me very happy."

Doneen's smile was small, almost grim. "I hate that your new boyfriend is hotter than my husband. Like *way* hotter."

Lowenna tossed her head back and laughed. "I don't."

Still chuckling, she unlocked the door. "Congratulations, Doneen. You make an absolutely stunning bride."

Doneen's smile was small but undeniably the most genuine Lowenna had ever seen. "Happy birthday, sis."

22

MASON HELD his breath and squeezed his eyes shut as he gently shut Willow's bedroom door, praying that she didn't wake up the moment the latch went *click*. He really needed to get that damn creak in the floor fixed. Or at the very least spray-paint a big *X* over where the squeak was. Every time he set the sleeping baby down in her bed, turned to go, he'd step on that fucking spot and Willow would start to wail again.

They'd been at this since they got home from his mother's over an hour ago.

Willow just did not want to go down.

It was times like these he wished he had functioning nipples. As easy as Willow was, he was jealous of the breastfed babies out there that just passed out on the boob so easily. Drunk on milk with noodle limbs, easily transferable to their crib.

Not his baby. It took forever with the formula and the rocking to get Willow to sleep, then when he thought she was asleep and would try to put her down, she'd freak out and the whole thing would start over again.

But it looked like he was about to catch a break ... finally.

The door clicked ever so softly. His lungs burned from how long he was holding in his breath.

And ... nothing.

Phew.

"Thank you, baby," he whispered, exhaling that long-held breath and opening his eyes.

The moment he got home, he'd ditched his tuxedo jacket and loosened the collar and cuffs of his white dress shirt. His tie was somewhere on the kitchen counter next to his beer, which was now probably piss-warm.

Running his fingers through his hair and breathing out another long breath, he made his way into the kitchen and grabbed his beer bottle. Yep, warm.

He took a swig anyway and blanched when the disgusting shit hit his tongue.

One sip was all he could take, and he dumped the rest down the sink. He probably shouldn't be drinking anyway. He should be sleeping.

In his bed.

Alone.

Just like he did every night.

That hadn't been the plan tonight, though.

Lowenna was supposed to be in his bed. Lowenna was supposed to be with him.

He hung his head and shook it, staring at his black socks on the tile floor of his kitchen, his heart aching as he thought about her.

How could he have been so wrong? He'd fallen hard for her. He'd fallen in love with her. But she loved revenge more. She wasn't ready to let go of the past, to stop looking behind her at everything she'd lost, and he knew he had to let her go.

He wasn't there anymore, wasn't consumed with anger, and he couldn't be with someone who was. It was toxic. Anger and hate over things that had already happened, over things we had no control over, were poison to the mind and heart, and if he could do one thing for Willow it would be to raise her in an environment as toxic- and poison-free as he could.

He knew he couldn't bubble-wrap his daughter, that the world was full of shitheads and shitty things, but what he could control—to some degree—was the kind of environment and people he raised his daughter around. And a person as hell-bent on revenge as Lowenna was not someone he wanted in Willow's life—or his.

He turned off all the lights in the kitchen, living room and dining room, then headed to the front door to double-check that it was locked.

Bright headlights turning into his driveway blinded him and made him pause.

He didn't recognize the vehicle.

A car door slammed, and the sound of heels on the walkway drew near. He peered out the side window once again and flicked on the porch light.

The silver of her dress sparkled along with her eyes. Although they were certainly sad, they also held a strong glint of confidence and conviction. She glanced at the doorbell.

Please, PLEASE don't ring it.

But she didn't move to ring it. Her fist lifted in the air and moved toward the door, preparing to knock, but then it dropped, and her shoulders slumped. She grabbed her phone from her purse, the backlight on the screen illuminating her face.

His phone beeped and buzzed on the kitchen counter, but he didn't bother running to get it. Instead he opened the door.

"I didn't want to ring the bell or knock in case Willow was sleeping," she whispered, lifting her head to look at him, her eyes beseeching. Deep fathomless pools of quicksilver.

It didn't matter that he'd left the wedding, that he'd given up on them. When he saw her, when he looked into her eyes, his reaction was visceral. Primal.

Every hair on his scalp stood to attention, every skin cell tingled, every neuron fired. She was magnificent.

But she wasn't his.

Not anymore.

"What are you doing here?" he asked, wanting nothing more than to grab her by the face, crush his mouth to hers and whisk her upstairs to his bed.

But he couldn't.

She wasn't his.

She went to open her mouth, but a shiver wracked her body, and she wrapped her shawl tighter around her shoulders.

Fuck, he was an idiot.

"Come inside," he offered, holding the door open for her and encouraging her to step forward. "It's freezing out here, and you're wearing"—he pointed at her slinky dress—"*that.*"

Her lip jiggled as she stepped over the threshold into his home. He shut the door behind her and followed her into the living room, turning on a light so they weren't standing there in the dark.

When he walked out of that wedding, she was getting ready to roast and humiliate the bride and groom. She was about to show over three hundred people her ugliest side, how low she could stoop, how much she was unwilling to let go of the past, of the hate and anger.

He couldn't watch. It was bound to be a train wreck. A train wreck in a forest fire with barrels of gunpowder on every train car. Cataclysmic.

He hated having to ask again, but he really did need an

explanation for why she was there. "Lowenna," he exhaled, shoving his hands into his pockets and leaning against the load-bearing beam that stood fixed between the living room and dining room. "What are you—"

"I didn't do the speech," she blurted out, cutting him off.

"But ... but you were up there. I saw you. I heard you."

She shook her head, stepping toward him, the faux fur shawl on her shoulders slipping over her arms.

"You left before my conscience got the better of me. Before *you* and your love and your hope and your optimism got the better of me. You should have stayed. I gave a speech, yes," she went on, nodding. "But I didn't give *the* speech. I didn't go through with it. I didn't humiliate them. I congratulated them, gave them my best wishes and that was it. I couldn't do it, not after I saw you walk away and what going through with it would mean to us ... what it would *do* to us. You're more important than revenge, than hate. My love for you is stronger than all the anger that I've held onto for much too long. I'm so sorry for the things I said earlier, for what I put you through, for how I behaved. I'm ashamed of how I allowed the anger to consume me. To be the driving force behind so many of my actions. I wasted a lot of time hating when I could have been loving."

Mason shut his eyes and shook his head. "Lowenna, I can't be—"

"Doneen and I talked."

He opened his eyes again.

Her head bobbed, and she smiled. "Yeah, like *really* talked. She locked us in the bathroom, and we kind of had it out. Then we had a heart-to-heart, and we hugged."

"You hugged?" Did she put a *kick me* sign on Doneen's back?

"Yeah, we hugged. She apologized for sleeping with Brody

while I was still married to him and for all the grief and shit she's put me through."

"Wow!"

"And I feel so much better." Tears welled up in her eyes, but her smile was big and beautiful. Not an ounce of tension remained in her jaw. "It was closure for me. For us. I'm not angry anymore. I don't want to get even or get revenge. I don't hate my sister. She and I will never be friends. But at least we're no longer enemies." Her throat jogged on a swallow as she stepped toward him. "I want love, not hate. I want the future ruling my choices, not the past. I want joy, not anger." She pressed her hand against his chest, over his heart.

His heart pounded hard as she pushed up onto her tiptoes, her lips hovering just inches from his.

"I want you, Mason."

He brushed a strand of hair off her face, cupping her head in both his hands. "You've really given up this whole revenge *thing?*"

She slid her tongue along his bottom lip. "I'd give up everything for you. For Willow. For us. For our future. You want to look to the future with me? Plan for forever. Build a life and a family?"

He squeezed his eyes shut for just a moment, imagining a life with Lowenna and Willow and possibly other children. Her, walking down the aisle wearing white. The two of them welcoming another child. Playing at the beach with their kids. Witnessing their children graduate high school and then college. Sitting on a porch, gray and wrinkly, holding hands as they watched their grandchildren arrive for Thanksgiving.

He saw it all. And in it all, he saw Lowenna by his side.

He opened his eyes, and there she was, blinking up at him, patiently waiting.

"So, stud? What you do say? Wanna plan a forever with me?" Her grin made everything in his body grow warm.

He pressed his forehead to hers. "Absolutely." Then he took her mouth, and quickly a simple kiss became so much more as he sealed their lips together, as his tongue, sweeping through her mouth, teased hers.

She whimpered and melted against him, moaning and humming as he slipped his hands down from her face to around her waist.

"Take me to bed," she murmured, breaking their kiss just long enough to slide her hand between them and cup him. "Let's celebrate Valentine's properly."

Groaning, Mason scooped her up into his arms, making her squeal, and in less than ten long strides, he was down the hall and into his bedroom.

They collapsed onto the bed in a fit of laughter, their lips roaming, hands exploring. Slowly, gently he peeled her dress over her shoulders and down her body. As he were unwrapping a fragile, precious gift.

Because she was a gift.

Even though they'd been together earlier that day, it was still a sight to behold, seeing her in nothing more than that weird bra and that sexy G-string. His mouth watered at the thought of tasting her again, at the thought of getting to taste and take her any day and every day for the rest of their lives.

Lowenna was a flavor he would never tire of.

———

Mason's long, strong fingers worked the pearly buttons of his shirt through the holes, revealing sexy tattooed skin inch by luscious inch. And with each button released, Lowenna's nipples hardened, her pussy throbbed and her taste buds tingled.

The man was pure perfection.

An inked, pierced and muscled god ... and he loved her.

He. Loved. Her.

"What's that look for?" he asked, unfastening his trousers and letting them drop to the floor, the tent in his black boxer briefs enough to house an entire circus.

"What look?"

His mouth slid into a wily grin. "You're smiling, but your eyes are saying I'm a porterhouse steak you can't wait to sink your teeth into." He crawled onto the bed, hovering over her and nipping at her chin.

She arched her back beneath him, wrapping her legs around his waist. "Because you are. And I'd love nothing more than to *sink my teeth into you*." She opened her mouth wide and bit his shoulder, giggling when he sucked in a sharp breath.

Growling, he reared back up. "Panties off, woman. I shouldn't have to ask. It should just be a given. When you're in my bed ... *our* bed, you need to be naked." Gruffly, with a need and ferocity that aroused her to no end, he hooked his fingers beneath the strings of her G-string and pulled it over her mound and down her legs. But he didn't toss it to the floor; no, he put it to his nose.

She gasped. "You did not just ... "

He took a big inhale, grinning, before he finally tossed the underwear to the ground. "Damn straight, I did, woman. No better scent, no better flavor than yours."

That was dirty but oh so hot.

He continued to smile. "Admit it, you're turned on by that."

Raking her top teeth over her bottom lip, she looked away, unable to keep the eye contact he was giving her. It was too revealing, too intense. He saw right through her, saw all of her.

"Do I have to smell *your* underwear? Is this a reciprocal thing? Is this something that really gets you going?" she asked, finally sliding her eyes back to his, one eyebrow lifting on her forehead in query.

Mason tossed his head back and laughed a big, hearty, manly laugh. Still laughing, his chest and shoulders shaking above her, he shoved his hands beneath her back, rocked them and then rolled until she was on top. With his hands he encouraged her to sit up until she was straddling his torso, her hands on his chiseled chest, fingers tracing his tattoos.

With his hands now free, he reached up and relieved her of her bra, tossing it to the side, off the bed. "No, you do not have to smell my underwear ... unless you want to. But even then, I would think that to be a bit weird. Some things do not work both ways."

He cupped her breasts and swiped his thumbs over her nipples until they peaked hard and tight. A shiver raced down to her clit, and she trembled over him.

"I mean it," she said once the ripple of pleasure had dissipated, "no more anger. No more hate. No more revenge. I'm moving on."

He lifted an eyebrow. "Promise? No more pranks. No more itching powder?"

Uh-oh!

His eyebrow dropped to join the other one, then they both narrowed. "What did you do, Lowenna?"

She bit her lip, her eyes sliding to the side. "Um ... "

His head began to shake. "Oh no, Lowenna, what did you do?"

Grumbling, she fixed her gaze back on him. "It's your fault, really. You gave me the idea ... I just took it a step further."

"Me! What did I do?"

"You're the one who sent me the link to that old English guy."

"You didn't!"

"I didn't what?"

"Make a mold of your asshole and then give it to them?" At this point she wasn't sure his eyes could get any wider or his voice any higher. It was a pretty hilarious look for him, particularly because he was also naked.

She squeezed her eyes shut for a moment and shook her head. "No. I did not make a mold of *my* asshole. But I did have the English guy send me a mold of his. With which I made a bunch of chocolates and a few with chocolate laxative. And I may or may not have left those laxative buttholes in their honeymoon suite." She bit her lip again.

"May or may not?"

"May."

"Oh God, Lowenna ... "

"What? I was still hell-bent on revenge. And then when Doneen and I talked, I was so shocked and then determined to get to you that I completely forgot."

Once again, his body started to shake with laughter beneath her. His eyes were closed, his mouth open in a big smile as a sound she'd come to love rumbled from his chest. "Oh, my love," he finally said, opening his eyes, "they are in for a pretty interesting night and morning, aren't they?"

"She *did* have her wedding on my birthday," Lowenna said sheepishly.

"And she *did* sleep with your husband," he added.

"True enough."

He rolled his eyes, still laughing. "Okay, but no more revenge plots. That was it."

She held up her pinky finger. "I promise."

He linked his finger through hers, and they shook. Then

he pulled her forward, using just their pinkies until their lips locked.

They were both breathless, and Lowenna was incredibly wet, by the time they broke the kiss. Her heart full and her brain gloriously fuzzy.

She lifted her head and gazed down at him.

"You're it for me, Lowenna," he whispered, reaching up and cupping her cheek, bringing her face down to him once again, his lips brushing over her eyes, her cheek and along her jaw. "You've been like a song in my head for months. Over and over you've played until I went to sleep thinking about you and then woke with you on my mind again."

Tears stung the back of her eyes at his words.

He was the same for her. A love song, a ballad she kept putting on repeat. Only it took her a bit longer to learn the words of the song than it should have, but now, it was her favorite tune and one she wanted to hum and whistle forever. It was the song she wanted to dance her life to.

"You, me, Willow, we're going to be a family." He buried his face in her neck.

"And maybe some frozen-egg babies too?" she asked, unable to stop that persistent tear from slipping down her cheek, a small sob choking her from just how happy she was. Truly. Finally.

He lifted his head from the crook of her neck and cupped her face again, his eyes so full of love, she thought her heart might burst. With the pad of his thumb, he wiped away her tear. "And all the frozen-egg babies we can make."

She laughed through the tears, through the sob. "No condom, okay? I'm clean."

"Me too." His voice was rough and deep like a well-aged whiskey. It made everything inside her clench and pulse.

"Just us." She shifted until he was notched at her center, the tip of him bobbing at her slick entrance.

Mason bucked up and sheathed himself to the hilt inside her, both of them letting out a moan of satisfaction when he seated himself fully. When they became one.

"Just us," he repeated, then took her completely, and she gave him everything.

Her present, her future, her forever.

EPILOGUE

2 years later ...

MASON YAWNED his millionth yawn for the night as he wandered up and down his hallway, bouncing and swaying his six-week-old son in the stretchy wrap he wore on his chest.

Wyatt Oscar Whitfield had been up off and on since midnight, and it was now four thirty in the morning. Mason could count on one elbow just how many hours of sleep he'd gotten.

Finally, though, it looked like Wyatt had settled a bit and was dozing. Mason didn't dare try to get the little guy out of the carrier. Oh no! That would not work. Wyatt—much like his big sister when she was this age—much preferred to sleep vertical and attached to someone. God forbid Mason extract him from his cozy cotton cocoon and try to get some sleep himself.

He stood in front of the living room window, gazing out at the dark street, wondering just how many other parents were currently up with their newborns.

316 | WHITLEY COX

Probably more than he realized.

A creak on the floor behind him had him wincing. Even the slightest sound could wake Wyatt, and then he'd be back to square one. Slowly, he spun around, hoping that Willow hadn't gotten up needing help with the potty.

Thankfully, his daughter was still happily asleep in her room. Lowenna blinked tired eyes at him as she cradled Wyatt's twin brother, Warren Oliver Whitfield, in her arms. She yawned. "This one's fed and has a full belly. Finally. How about that one?" Her hoarse whisper indicated just how exhausted and depleted she was.

Lowennna, the selfless, amazing mother of his children. She had decided that she wanted to try to breastfeed their twins. So she took a drug with some crazy possible side effects that encouraged lactation. It worked like a hot damn, and his wife was a milk machine.

Which was great, because their sons were hungry little beasts, so Lowenna spent nearly every waking minute feeding one baby or the other. Although they did top the boys up with formula, Lowenna was determined to breastfeed as much as she could—and it was taking its toll on her.

"Come sit down," he whispered, extending an arm out, which she stepped into immediately. Her body went lax against his as he led her over to the couch, his other hand gently patting Wyatt's butt.

She plopped down on the couch, Warren still in her arms, fast asleep. He was the easier baby of the two. Poor Wyatt was a touch colicky and not so easily soothed as his fraternal counterpart. He also very much preferred Lowenna to Mason, so it was a bit surprising he was as asleep and content in Mason's arms as he was.

He didn't think about that too long, though, in case he jinxed himself.

His gorgeous woman closed her eyes and leaned her head

back on the couch, the baby cradled safely in her arms. "Can you imagine if more of those embryos had implanted? I'm exhausted with two babies and a toddler. I couldn't imagine if we had triplets or"—her eyes flew open—"or quadruplets." She shut her eyes again and shook her head. "I don't know how some parents do it. This is exhausting."

Bravely, Mason eased himself down on the couch next to her, still patting Wyatt's butt. "Yeah, me either. Though I must say, I am happy to have someone in this chaos with me this time. Those first few months with Willow where it was just me ... I don't know how many times I thought I'd made a mistake becoming a single dad—going it alone. Lay awake at night a lot wondering how I was going to get through the next day and the next and not inevitably screw her up for life."

Lowenna chuckled softly beside him, her head falling to the side to rest on his shoulder. "There's nobody else I'd rather weather this diaper storm with."

Mason snickered. "Me either, baby."

Too good to be true, because most things in life are, Wyatt began to stir and fuss in the carrier. His head bopped vigorously on Mason's bare chest in search of sustenance. "Looks like twin B is hungry," he said, hastily pulling his squirming newborn out of the stretchy wrap before he woke up his brother.

Every one of Lowenna's movements was slow and precise, fatigue in her weary muscles and joints. Once Mason had Wyatt out of the wrap, they did the baby shuffle. Mason took Warren, plopping him in the wrap, where he snuggled right down and promptly began to snore, while Lowenna put Wyatt to her breast. The baby immediately began to guzzle.

"Hungry beast," she whispered, running her knuckle over his cheek.

"Voracious." Mason pecked her on the temple. "You're Super Mom, you know that?"

She shut her eyes and leaned her head back on his shoulder. "I don't feel like Super Mom. I feel like *Tired Mom*."

"You can be both." He grabbed a blanket off the corner of the couch and draped it over their legs. She nestled right in next to him, her arm cradling Wyatt, whose eyes were glued shut, his hands holding his mother's breast like it was a bottle. "Thank you for this life," he said, resting his hand on her thigh beneath the blanket. "For our sons, for being the most incredible mother to Willow. The most amazing partner to me."

She opened her eyes and lifted her head from his shoulder. "I should be thanking you. Without you, I'd still be on the train of vengeance. Plotting Operation Revenge 2.0. You gave me something bigger, something greater to hope for, to love."

"I love you."

Her smile was small and serene. She was so tired. "I love you, too." Another yawn claimed her smile. "What time is it? All the days and hours seem to be blending together."

He glanced behind him at the clock on the mantle. "Closing in on 5 a.m."

She blinked a few times before her eyelids drooped, then finally closed. "I feel like just a minute ago I was sweeping up the mess Willow made on the floor after dinner."

He snorted. "That was last night. We were at my parents' for dinner tonight." His gaze fell to the still-nursing Wyatt. "You really are tired."

She yawned again. "Just a little." Then she perked up. "Wait! Is today Monday?"

Mason squeezed his eyes shut and tried to envision his work calendar in his head. "Yes, I think it is." His eyes flew open. "Oh shit!"

"It's okay." She shook her head. "We both forgot."

Damn it.

"I'm so sorry, baby. I knew it was coming up. I just thought I had more time. I could have sworn it was next week." How could he forget his wife's birthday? It was on the calendar with a holiday marker and everything.

"I forgot, too." She kissed him on the shoulder. "Happy Valentine's Day, Mase. There isn't anybody else I'd rather spend it with than you, be it in bed naked with chocolate body paint or sitting on the couch in the middle of the night, covered in spit-up with our starving newborns. As long as you're my Valentine every year, I'm happy no matter where we celebrate."

And this was why he loved this woman so goddamn much.

"Mase?" she said, her head back against the couch, eyes closed.

"Hmm?"

"Marry me?"

Mason sat up straight and pivoted to stare at her, jostling Warren slightly but not enough to wake him up. "Lo?"

She opened her eyes and smiled serenely at him. "Marry me."

Fuck, she really was perfect.

Without saying a word, but careful not to disturb his kid, he pried himself off the couch and took off down the hall toward their bedroom. He was back in a flash, box in hand. He handed it to her.

With confusion in her tired gray eyes, she opened the box, a slow gasp stealing her breath. "Mase ... "

He shrugged. "I was planning to do it tonight, but you beat me to it, you *wicked* woman."

Her eyes no longer held an ounce of fatigue. They were wide and so full of love. "It matches my necklace."

He grinned. "Chocolate diamonds. But instead of another amethyst, I went with a big honking diamond for the middle. And no heart—princess cut all the way for my queen."

She breathed a quiet laugh, shaking her head. "This is gorgeous."

"So, my answer," he started, taking the box from her, removing the ring and gingerly getting down onto one knee on the floor in front of her, "is, yes, Lowenna. I will absolutely marry you." Then he slid the ring onto her finger, kissing each fingertip and the inside of her wrist, before he placed her hand on his cheek and cupped his own hand over it.

Tears welled up in her eyes, her smile a mile wide. He couldn't remember her ever looking so beautiful. Feeding their sons, wearing his ring—she was stunning.

Wyatt popped off Lowenna's breast and nestled his face into the crook of her arm, his eyes shut, lips pursed in a tight, milk-dribbly pout. She gently cradled him in the other arm and encouraged Mason to stand up and sit next to her.

"I can't wait to be your wife," she said, hiccupping a small sob.

"You're already my wife." He picked up her hand, linked their fingers and kissed her ring. "This will just make it *official*." His mouth turned down into a frown. "Now I have nothing to give you tonight, though."

She shook her head. "I want for nothing. I have everything my heart could possibly desire."

"I'll make it up to you, I promise," he said, running the back of his knuckles over her cheek. "Candlelit dinner, flowers, ambience, wine ... " He wiggled his eyebrows up and down. "Kinky sex."

The corners of her mouth lifted up just a touch. "How about us, in bed ... "

"I like where you're going with this."

"And four hours of uninterrupted sleep."

He kissed her hard on the lips. "Damn, woman. I like the

way you think. I'll call my mom, see if she and my dad can take the kids for a few hours."

She chuckled softly. "I like to walk on the wild side." Her face sobered. "But seriously. I'm okay not doing anything today. Home with my family is my happy place. It's the perfect Valentine's, the perfect birthday. You, the kids, this is exactly where I want to be. I haven't made a wish on a birthday cake or star since that party you threw me in the hotel because what I wished for came true. There isn't anything else I want or need." The last few words were choked out, and a small tear beaded at the corner of her eye. "Just you, Willow, Wyatt and Warren and my heart is full. My life is full."

He felt the exact same way.

With his thumb and knuckle, he tilted her chin up. "You, the kids, my heart is full too. My life is full."

"Thank you for being my gigolo and turning into so much more. Who'd have thought a boyfriend for hire would turn into the husband of a lifetime?"

He rolled his eyes and squeezed her chin. "Ha ha."

She grinned up at him with a closed-mouth smile, her eyes crinkling at the sides. "I love you. Forever."

He leaned in until they were nose to nose. "And I love you for always." Then he kissed her because he could, every day for the rest of his life. And that was just perfect.

NEIGHBORS WITH THE SINGLE DAD - SNEAK PEEK

SINGLE DADS OF SEATTLE BOOK 8

Chapter 1

Rain poured and the wind pounded the city of Seattle on a cold and miserable March night. Luckily though, for all the patrons inside the very happening Ludo Lounge where ladies drank for half price until eleven, it could be a zombie apocalypse or the rapture and nobody would be the wiser.

The outside world ceased to exist.

Over the last hour, the music in the lounge had picked up. Going from smooth, club jazz, to full-on dance music with a bass that Scott Dixon could feel in the very deepest parts of his chest. It was no longer cocktail hour—it was time to dance.

Which for many, also meant it was time to start looking for a hookup.

Not Scott though. He wasn't there for that, at least not tonight.

He hardly ever saw Donovan Smythe anymore, now that Scott had switched companies. But when he called Scott up a couple of weeks ago excited about his upcoming wedding and insisting Scott come to the bachelor party, the people-pleasing middle child that he was, Scott agreed.

Now he was regretting it.

There was a reason he and Donovan weren't that close anymore.

Donovan was a bit of a tool, and so were his friends. The group had been obnoxious assholes, hitting on and offending waitresses and talking about heading to a strip club to go and throw quarters at the entertainers.

Scott ordered himself a drink at the bar, turned and leaned back against it, watching the embarrassing theatrics back at the bachelor party table. He cringed inwardly when one of the guys let out a thunderous belch and the rest cheered.

The bartender could take his sweet time making Scott's drink, he had no intention of heading back to those buffoons anytime soon.

"Drink's up, man," the bartender said behind him, only when Scott went to turn back around, a freight train, or something very akin to such, slammed into his side.

"Hey, watch—"His gripe was cut short by the unbeliev-able woman teetering precariously on mile-high heels as she hooked it around the corner toward the bathrooms.

"Sorry," she called back, waiving a hand, her long red hair flipping behind her as she disappeared.

He thanked the bartender for his drink, but didn't budge. They'd ordered Donovan a muff diver and the man of the hour's face had just been shoved into a heaping pile of whipped cream.

Philistines.

He took a sip of his whiskey and leaned his elbow on the bar. There was also another reason why he hadn't moved yet. He wanted to catch another glimpse of the whirling dervish with hair of fire before he rejoined his group.

It didn't take long—maybe thirty seconds—before the redhead in the heels returned, her face scrunched up in what looked like pain, her green eyes darting frantically around the bar.

He approached her. "Is everything okay?"

Her eyes stilled, pinning on him. Her lips dipped into a deep frown as she shook her head. "I have to pee and the lineup for the women's bathroom is ten miles long. I'll never make it."

Scott placed a hand on her shoulder and gently moved her out of the way, glancing down the corridor for the bathrooms with its black painted walls. Sure enough, the lineup for the women's bathroom stretched at least fifteen women deep. The men's room on the other hand was without a lineup at all.

He grabbed her hand. "Follow me." At a quick clip he hauled her down the hallway and turned into the men's room, heaving the heavy door open with one hand while encouraging her to step inside with the other.

Her emerald eyes went wide. "This is the men's room!" Her voice was low, almost a hiss.

Scott shrugged. "So?"

But her desperation won out and with a quick eye shift down the hall toward the long line of women doing the bathroom dance, she nodded, then stepped inside.

"Hello?" Scott called out into the bathroom. "Anybody in here?"

Luckily, there was no answer.

His beautiful companion let out a sigh of relief, her slender shoulders slumping just a touch as she pushed past him.

"You go do what you need to do, and I'll stand watch outside, give you some privacy." Before she could come up with anymore ridiculous protestations, he headed back out.

He still had his drink, so with one hand in his pocket, his shoulder against the doorjamb and a very bored look on his face, he sipped his whiskey and waited for her to emerge.

Not four minutes later, a throat clearing behind him and a gentle tap on his shoulder let him know she was finished. He unblocked the door and held his hand out for her to go ahead of him, not just because he was a gentleman, but also because he wanted to check out her ass.

This woman was hot!

Tall and slim with nice curves, long legs and ... yes! A rocking ass. And it was only played up by the sexy black pants she wore, and those gold strappy fuck-me heels. He gained ground, so he was right behind her. Not to be weird or anything, he just wanted to double-check if she was taller than him in those heels.

Phew.

Not quite.

Scott was a nice six-foot-two, and this beautiful creature didn't quite come up to his forehead. Not that he was an anti-heightest (was that a thing?) he just *preferred* to be taller than the women he dated.

Whoa, now you're dating her? You don't even know her name, slow down there, Sparky. Just because you haven't gotten laid in ... a while, let's just leave it at that. Doesn't mean you need to start picking out China patterns with the first pretty face to cross your path.

He shook himself mentally and stepped back, letting the woman get ahead of him a bit. They exited the corridor, remerging into the lounge. In those few minutes they'd been gone the place had filled up. It was wall-to-wall people, loud voices, laughing and some kind of hip-hop music he couldn't make heads or tails of the lyrics.

Man, he felt old.

He could still hear his party over in the corner booth

laughing it up like obnoxious drunkards though, they were hard to miss.

He was busy glancing in the direction of his party when he was once again slammed, only this time it was in his chest, and it wasn't by a freight train, but a voluptuous, green-eyed wall of beauty.

"Thank you," she said, tucking a strand of hair behind her ear. "You're a lifesaver."

He grinned at her. "All in a day's work. Glad you're okay."

She thrust her hand out. "Eva."

He wrapped his fingers around hers, loving the way her hand felt in his. "Scott." Her shake was firm, but her hand soft and feminine. Her nails were painted a subtle French manicure, and she wore no wedding ring.

"Can I buy you a drink for your gallantry, Scott?" She released his hand and pulled her clutch purse out from beneath her arm, her eye twinkling as her mouth slid up into a mischievous smile. "It's the least I can do." Her eyes drifted to the right and she cringed when a group of women decked out in pink sashes and horrendous wigs let out a loud, shrill cheer. "I'm also not eager to rejoin the bachelorette party I'm here with, so any opportunity to stay away I'm all for."

Without waiting for him to respond, she pushed her way through the crowd hovering in front of the bar, rested her breasts on the bar and leaned forward.

Like a dog with a bone, the muscly bartender lasered in on her in seconds, ignoring patrons who had been waiting far longer. "What can I getcha?" he asked, leaning onto the bar, his gaze drifting down from Eva's face to where her gold heart pendant was wedged between the swell of her chest.

Scott would have done the exact same thing if he'd been that bartender—it would have been impossible not to.

Did she know what she was doing?

She had to. She didn't strike him as a bimbo, just a

woman who knew how to get what she wanted, how to work it.

And there was nothing wrong with working what the good lord gave you. Scott worked his mega-watt smile more times than he could count, to charm a waitress or barista into giving him extra fries with his burger or an extra shot of espresso in his coffee.

"I'll have a tequila, please. Añjeo or extra añjeo on the rocks, if you have it." The bartender nodded. Scott had quietly followed her to the bar and was now beside her. "What are you drinking?" she asked.

"Whiskey."

She nodded. "And a whiskey for my hero, here." She glanced back at Scott, her smile wide, sexy and her eyes teasing.

What was she up to?

Moments later they had their drinks and with Eva leading Scott like another dog with a bone, they managed to find a small section on a cushioned bench away from the crowd.

"You didn't have to buy me a drink," he said, taking a sip of his new whiskey.

She sipped her tequila and shrugged. "Like I said, I'm avoiding going back to those drunk-ass, marriage-loving women and their stupid crowns, leis and sashes." She rolled her eyes. "Thank God I'm not in the wedding party."

"How do you know the bride?"

She shrugged again. "Friend since beauty school."

"Beauty school?"

She nodded. "Yeah, I'm a hairdresser and esthetician."

Well, that explained why she was walking, talking perfection. The woman knew how to take care of herself. Though, Scott would put money on her looking gorgeous without an ounce of makeup on too.

"What do you do?"

"I'm in advertising."

She nodded again, then began to bob her head in time with the beat of the music.

Then the conversation ended.

The air between them began to grow awkward.

He didn't know this woman enough to *like* her, but he certainly found her hot, and what he'd met so far, he liked. Now he just had to figure out a way to charm her into wanting to ditch her party completely and maybe go grab a slice of pizza with him down the block or something. His stomach rumbled at the thought of Guy's Pies. Best pizza by the slice in the entire city.

He took another sip of his drink and cleared his throat. "So uh ... what do you think of my hair? You being a hairdresser and all. Am I an abomination?" Instantly, he cringed.

Seriously? Wasn't that like asking a stranger who'd just revealed they were a doctor to take a look at a mysterious mole on your back? He even had doctor friends and he never asked them for medical advice. He asked his brother for legal advice, but when there's a lawyer in the family why wouldn't you milk that cow?

Her smile was slow, but sexy as hell. She lifted her hand from her lap and ran her fingers through his hair over and over again until he closed his eyes from just how good it felt.

If she brought out those nails and scraped his scalp he was not to blame if his leg started to kick and shake uncontrollably.

"You have great hair," she finally said, causing him to open his eyes again. Her gaze was soft and appraising, her smile sweet. "It's nice and thick, soft. You've got a great hairline too." She tugged at the sides.

"Yeah, what would you do to it if I gave you carte blanche?"

Her eyebrows twitched up a bit. "Carte blanche?"

He nodded. "Yeah."

She raked her top teeth over her bottom lip, continuing to run her fingers through his hair. She added the fingers from her other hand and turned her body so they were now face to face. She tilted his head down so he was forced to stare directly down her blouse into her cleavage. He knew he should shut his eyes, but he just couldn't. It was like staring at an eclipse—so damn beautiful, but it may very well get him in some major trouble too.

"Honestly, I don't think I'd do much," she finally said. "Maybe go a bit shorter on the sides, tidy up the back of your neck a little, but whoever you see does a pretty good job."

"I see an eighty-three-year old barber down by Beechers Cheese. The guy takes nearly an hour to cut my hair, but he does a good job."

She chuckled, and oh what a laugh. It was deep and throaty and sexy as fuck. She still hadn't stopped running her fingers through his hair. "A bit of silver on the sides here, huh?"

He nodded. "Yeah, starting to get some."

Her touch was strong, but gentle. Confident but curious. "But not too much. I'm guessing the men in your family all have their hair, but they went gray early?"

His head bobbed again, in awe of this woman and the pure magic her hands wielded. He was putty. She could pet him like that all night long and he'd lay like a chocolate lab at her feet. "Uh, yeah. My dad, started going gray by the time he was forty, my grandpa's too. My dad's more salt than pepper now, but both gramps' are combing tinsel."

She chuckled that raspy laugh again. "I like that term. You're cute." She still hadn't released his hair.

He hoped she never did.

"You're beautiful."

Finally, unfortunately, she pulled her hands from his hair

and batted long, dark lashes at him as she ducked her head, her smile coy and slightly hidden. "Thank you." She lifted her head again, her gaze settling on him. "Full disclosure?"

You're a hooker and this is all an elaborate ruse?

"Sure."

She took a deep breath which only amplified her killer rack. The buttons on her emerald green silk sleeveless blouse strained against her inhale. Scott did everything in his power not to stare.

He was weak. It was impossible.

"It's my first night away from my kids in ..." she shook her head and blew out a breath in exasperation, "God, I don't know how long. So it's been a while. I just signed the papers last month finalizing a very ugly, very messy, very painful divorce and my kids are with my sister and her very responsible fourteen-year-old daughter. It's the first night where my children have been okay being away from me overnight. We've tried a few times, but my little guy—Kellen, he's five—gets upset when I leave. But I needed a night out ... desperately. We're moving out of my sister's place in a few weeks as I finally bought my own house now that the divorce has gone through." Her eyes turned sad. "It's been really tough on my boys." A wary glint invaded the sadness in the dark flecks of yellow around her irises as she waited for Scott to reply.

He simply nodded, hoping that his small smile and eyes conveyed his understanding and sympathy. She had no reason to be wary of him or his reaction to her honesty, to her plight. He'd been there himself and knew how hard a divorce could be on everyone involved—especially the kids. He took a leap of faith and rested his hand on her arm. "Been through a messy divorce myself. I have a son, and I totally get where you're coming from right now. It's really hard on the kids. It's hard on everyone."

If she thought that her declaration was going to turn him

off, she couldn't be further from wrong. If anything, her honesty, her openness just made her more intriguing. She had wounds and scars just like him. She was human.

Heat flared in her eyes and she shifted closer to him and brought her voice down. "I have a room at the hotel next door," she said, the first sign of real, genuine nervousness entering her eyes. Her voice quavered slightly and her throat bobbed in trepidation. "Would you ... like to join me there?"

IF YOU'VE ENJOYED THIS BOOK

If you've enjoyed this book, please consider leaving a review.
It really does make a difference.
Thank you again.
Xoxo
Whitley Cox

ACKNOWLEDGMENTS

There are so many people to thank who help along the way. Publishing a book is definitely not a solo mission, that's for sure. First and foremost, my friend and editor Chris Kridler, you are a blessing, a gem and an all-around terrific person. Thank you for your honesty and hard work.

Thank you, to my critique groups gals, Danielle and Jillian. I love our meetups where we give honest feedback and just bitch about life. You two are my bitch-sisters and I wouldn't give you up for anything.

Andi Babcock for her beta-read, I always appreciate your attention to detail and comments.

Author Jeanne St. James, my alpha reader and sister from another mister, what would I do without you?

Megan J. Parker-Squiers from EmCat Designs, your covers are awesome. Thank you.

Ana Rita Clemente, one of the first "fans" I've ever met, and now an amazing friend. Thank you for loving my books and proofreading this one. You are a wonderful human.

My Naughty Room Readers Crew, authors Jeanne St. James, Erica Lynn and Cailin Briste. I love being part of such a tremendous set of inspiring, talented and supportive women. Thank you for letting me learn, lean on and join the team.

My street team, Whitley Cox's Curiously Kinky Reviewers, you are all awesome and I feel so blessed to have found such wonderful fans.

The ladies of Vancouver Island Romance Authors, your support and insight have been incredibly helpful, and I'm so honored to be a part of a group of such talented writers.

Author Cora Seton for your help, tweaks and suggestions for my blurbs, as always, they come back from you so sparkly. I also love our walks, talks and heart-to-hearts, they mean so much to me.

Authors Kathleen Lawless, Nancy Warren and Jane Wallace, I love our writing meetups. Wine, good food and friendship always make the words flow.

Author Ember Leigh, my newest author bestie, I love our bitch-fests—they keep me sane.

My parents, in-laws and brother, thank you for your unwavering support.

The Small Human and the Tiny Human, you are the beats and beasts of my heart, the reason I breathe and the reason I drink. I love you both to infinity and beyond.

And lastly, of course, the husband. You are my forever. I love you.

ALSO BY WHITLEY COX

Love, Passion and Power: Part 1

The Dark and Damaged Hearts Series Book 1

Love, Passion and Power: Part 2

The Dark and Damaged Hearts Series Book 2

Sex, Heat and Hunger: Part 1

The Dark and Damaged Hearts Book 3

Sex, Heat and Hunger: Part 2

The Dark and Damaged Hearts Book 4

Hot and Filthy: The Honeymoon

The Dark and Damaged Hearts Book 4.5

True, Deep and Forever: Part 1

The Dark and Damaged Hearts Book 5

True, Deep and Forever: Part 2

The Dark and Damaged Hearts Book 6

Hard, Fast and Madly: Part 1

The Dark and Damaged Hearts Series Book 7

Hard, Fast and Madly: Part 2

The Dark and Damaged Hearts Series Book 8

Quick & Dirty

Book 1, A Quick Billionaires Novel

Quick & Easy

Book 2, A Quick Billionaires Novella

Quick & Reckless

Book 3, A Quick Billionaires Novel

Hot Dad

Lust Abroad

Snowed In & Set Up

Quick & Dangerous

Book 4, A Quick Billionaires Novel

Hired by the Single Dad

The Single Dads of Seattle, Book 1

Dancing with the Single Dad

The Single Dads of Seattle, Book 2

Saved by the Single Dad

The Single Dads of Seattle, Book 3

Living with the Single Dad

The Single Dads of Seattle, Book 4

Christmas with the Single Dad

The Single Dads of Seattle, Book 5

New Years with the Single Dad

The Single Dads of Seattle, Book 6

Valentine's with the Single Dad

The Single Dads of Seattle, Book 7

Upcoming

Neighbors with the Single Dad

The Single Dads of Seattle, Book 8

Flirting with the Single Dad

The Single Dads of Seattle, Book 9

Falling for the Single Dad

The Single Dads of Seattle, Book 10

Lost Hart

The Harty Boys Book 2

ABOUT THE AUTHOR

A Canadian West Coast baby born and raised, Whitley is married to her high school sweetheart, and together they have two beautiful daughters and a fluffy dog. She spends her days making food that gets thrown on the floor, vacuuming Cheerios out from under the couch and making sure that the dog food doesn't end up in the air conditioner. But when nap time comes, and it's not quite wine o'clock, Whitley sits down, avoids the pile of laundry on the couch, and writes.

A lover of all things decadent; wine, cheese, chocolate and spicy erotic romance, Whitley brings the humorous side of sex, the ridiculous side of relationships and the suspense of everyday life into her stories. With mommy wars, body issues, threesomes, bondage and role playing, these books have everything we need to satisfy the curious kink in all of us.

YOU CAN ALSO FIND ME HERE

Website: WhitleyCox.com
Twitter: @WhitleyCoxBooks
Instagram: @CoxWhitley
Facebook Page: https://www.facebook.com/CoxWhitley/
Blog: https://whitleycox.blogspot.ca/
Multi-Author Blog: https://romancewritersbehavingbadly.
blogspot.com
Exclusive Facebook Reader Group: https://www.facebook.
com/groups/234716323653592/
Booksprout: https://booksprout.co/author/994/whitley-cox
Bookbub: https://www.bookbub.com/authors/whitley-cox

JOIN MY STREET TEAM

WHITLEY COX'S CURIOUSLY KINKY REVIEWERS
Hear about giveaways, games, ARC opportunities, new releases, teasers, author news, character and plot development and more!

Facebook Street Team
Join NOW!

DON'T FORGET TO SUBSCRIBE TO MY NEWSLETTER

Be the first to hear about pre-orders, new releases, giveaways, 99 cent deals, and freebies!

Click here to Subscribe
http://eepurl.com/ckh5yT

Made in the USA
Las Vegas, NV
02 February 2022

42829296R00204